Praise for the Nauti Boys series

"The Nauti series is one that absolutely no one should miss. The characters are brilliant, sexy, and real, while the high-octane action and soul-gripping plots have you on the edge of your seat. I loved it!" —Fresh Fiction

"Completely blown away by this surprising story. I could not put [it] down . . . and before I knew it, I had read this entire novel in one sitting. Lora Leigh has spun a smoldering hot tale of secret passion and erotic deceptions." —Romance Junkies

"Wild and thrilling." —The Romance Studio

"The sex scenes are, as always with Leigh's books, absolutely sizzling." —Errant Dreams Reviews

"Heated romantic suspense." —Midwest Book Review

continued. . .

More praise for

Lora Leigh

and her novels

"Leigh draws readers into her stories and takes them on a sensual roller coaster."   —Love Romances & More

"Will have you glued to the edge of your seat."
                                              —Fallen Angel Reviews

"Blistering sexuality and eroticism . . . Bursting with passion and drama . . . Enthralls and excites from beginning to end."
                                              —Romance Reviews Today

"A scorcher with sex scenes that blister the pages."
                                              —A Romance Review

"A perfect blend of sexual tension and suspense."
                                              —Sensual Romance Reviews

"Hot sex, snappy dialogue, and kick-butt action add up to outstanding entertainment."   —RT Book Reviews (Top Pick)

"The writing of Lora Leigh continues to amaze me . . . Electrically charged, erotic, and just a sinfully good read!"
                                              —Joyfully Reviewed

"Wow! . . . The lovemaking is scorching."
                                              —Just Erotic Romance Reviews

Nauti

Seductress

Lora Leigh

BERKLEY BOOKS, NEW YORK

BERKLEY
An imprint of Penguin Random House LLC
375 Hudson Street, New York, New York 10014

NAUTI SEDUCTRESS

An application to register this book for cataloging has been
submitted to the Library of Congress.

ISBN: 978-0-425-25600-8

PUBLISHING HISTORY
Berkley trade paperback edition / November 2015

PRINTED IN THE UNITED STATES OF AMERICA

10   9   8   7   6   5   4   3   2   1

Cover design by Lesley Worrell.
Cover photo by Radius / Superstock.

This is a work of fiction. Names, characters, places, and incidents either are the product of
the author's imagination or are used fictitiously, and any resemblance to actual persons,
living or dead, business establishments, events, or locales is entirely coincidental.

Penguin
Random
House

Nauti Seductress

PROLOGUE

Something was wrong. It oozed through her senses like an oily presence, determined to overwhelm her, to overtake her. Dark, invisible chains held her in that place between sleep and conscious awareness. And no matter how hard she tried, she couldn't push past the restraints tightening around her.

Panic raced through her. She knew she had to fight, knew she had to find a way to open her eyes, to force herself to fight. She had to. If she didn't, then she could die there.

She had to open her eyes. She had to see who was doing this, had to remember. . . . But she couldn't force them open, she couldn't move or fight. With each second the sense of danger grew, wrapping around her with razor-tipped bonds.

Hurting her.

Her blood began heating, almost boiling through her veins with so much pain, such agony. It began in her arm, and inch by inch worked along her body until even her brain was on fire.

She couldn't scream. Her voice didn't work, the screams and the pleas couldn't find a path to emit the tortured sounds reverberating through her head.

Icy terror ricocheted through her.

All I have to do is accept it's real. Just accept it isn't a dream and the pain will go away. I just have to accept it. It's not a dream. Accept it, and the pain will stop.

Just accept it.

Accept it and I won't hurt anymore.

That wasn't her voice. It wasn't her thoughts.

What else could it be? If it wasn't hers, then what could it be?

Oh God, the pain!

It was real. It was really happening. It was real.

The pain eased marginally. Boiling, lava-hot agony no longer ripped at her senses but the pain was still intense, excruciating.

She just wanted it to go away.

The whispers moved around her, voices in her head, or were they in the room with her? Demands that she accept it was real.

She was accepting. God, yeah, it was real. Every agonizing second of it was real.

She just couldn't figure out how it was real. No one should be able to get to her here, at her mother's inn. Her suite was the safest place she could be. Her mother's lover, Timothy, was a retired federal agent and revered security gadgets. He would never allow anyone to hurt her like this. She had to wake up. She had to make it stop.

Pain exploded through Zoey's head with the force of a blow

connecting with it, sending shards of white-hot agony tearing through it.

This wasn't a dream.

"Fight, Zoey . . ." It was a hiss of sound more than an actual order. "You have to fight. Harley will kill you . . ."

Harley?

Why would Harley hurt her?

"Look at him, Zoey." That hissing demand was like static at her ear. "Look at him. See Harley. See who's hurting you, Zoey."

Struggling to force her eyes open, she tried to cry out and couldn't. Tried to deny it was happening.

Harley was on the bed with her, smiling, his gentle green eyes filled with laughter like they always were. Except he was naked. Naked and aroused and he was pulling at the elastic waistband of her pajama shorts, ripping the side of them, determined to remove them.

Dizzy, sick to her stomach with pain and confusion, she tried to fight, struggling against the harsh hands tearing at her clothes, ripping them from her and leaving her naked.

The air surrounding her was icy, sinking through her skin to her bones as she bucked against the hands holding her down.

Twisting beneath him, she managed to roll from the bed, scrambling to get to her feet, to get to the door of her suite and rush from the room. She had to get away. If she could just get Timothy's attention, then he'd make Harley stop. He'd find out why her friend was trying to hurt her like this.

Before she could get to her feet, he tripped her, throwing her to the floor. He flipped her to her back and came over her again. Smiling, always smiling at her.

A flash of a darker expression, a darker face flickered across

Harley's features. A jagged scar across his eye, a mean, malicious gaze, and eyes that weren't Harley's.

Terror raced through her mind. What was happening to her?

She kicked, trying to cry, trying to scream . . .

Oh God, what was happening to her? Why couldn't she scream? Cry?

It was like a dream where all sound becomes blocked, unable to struggle free. But it wasn't a dream.

Terror resounded in her mind, darkened her vision, and stole consciousness. A deep, black void yawned around her, threatening to pull her into it, to smother her. She was going to die here. If she didn't fight, then she would die in the darkness.

Awareness returned seconds later, voices whispering around her, evil, ugly voices.

"Fight me, Zoey," Harley demanded, his voice harder, rougher, unrecognizable as he stared down at her with a gentle green gaze despite the hate-filled sound of his voice. "Mackay bitch. Come on, fight me. Maybe I won't make it hurt so bad. Come on, Zoey, if you don't fight me I'm going to kill you. I'll fuck you so deep, so hard, it will kill you."

She fought, hoarse, terrified sobs trapped inside her, given no voice but echoing through her head with such terror she felt strangled by it.

"Come back here, you silly bitch . . ." She managed to kick out at him, struggling to get away from him.

Why was he doing this? What was happening to him? To her? Why would he hurt her?

What had she done? Why was he so angry?

"Bitch. Humiliate me again," he snarled in that voice so unlike his. "You humiliated me, Zoey."

She shook her head desperately, fighting the hands grabbing at her breasts, bruising her nipples as he pulled at them.

"Bitch. You don't question me," he snarled.

Fury exploded in her head. Fury, terror, and a determination to fight, to defy him. She was a Mackay. He might kill her, but she refused to make it easy for him.

"No," she wheezed, so desperate to scream, fighting for enough air to scream until her lungs burned with it. Curling her fingers, enraged growls left her throat as she fought to claw him, to dig her nails into his flesh and rip it open.

He laughed at her.

"You going to fight me, little whore? Mackay whore. I'll make you my whore. You'll beg me to hurt you, to show you who's boss."

The hell he would. She would die first.

She would kill him before she let him do something so vile to her.

Hard hands snagged her ankles, jerking her legs apart again as Harley tried to slide between them.

He was going to rape her just as he threatened, and no matter how hard she tried, how hard she fought, she couldn't escape him.

Harley . . . ?

His features twisted, flashed from Harley's face to something else. From Harley's deep green eyes to cold, pale ice-blue eyes. From Harley's youthful features, to a flash, so fast it made no sense, to harder, more mature features.

She fought him, trying to slap him, hit him, fighting to find something, anything to protect herself. As she kicked out at him, her foot caught him high on the thigh, his hold loosening, allowing her to scramble away from him.

"Fight, bitch," he growled with such black malevolence it was terrifying. "Fight me. If you don't fight I'll just hurt you worse. Go ahead. Kick."

Oh God, why was he doing this to her? Harley wouldn't do this.

Pain exploded against the side of her head. He hit her. His fist slamming against her skull, scattering her senses.

Oh God, it hurt so bad.

He struck her again. An open-handed slap to her face.

Enraged, furious growls were all she could push past her throat as tears spilled from her eyes.

"Fight, bitch."

She was fighting. Kicking, twisting beneath him, her nails digging furrows into his face, his shoulders.

"Fight me or I'm going to fuck you, Zoey. Where's your weapon? Find it, bitch."

Find her weapon? What weapon?

A scream tore from her as he came over her again, moving between her legs, one hand gripping his penis, lining it up between her thighs.

No, Harley, please. Please no. Sobbing, reaching behind her, she fought to find a weapon.

"Did you find the knife, Zoey?" Insidious, malicious, that ugly voice whispered through her mind. "It's right there. It's right by your hand."

Her fingers closed over the hilt of the knife.

"I'm going to kill you," Harley snarled. "I'll rape you until you die, Zoey, and then I'll kill that fucking Dawg. And his prissy baby girl, Laken? I'll rape her next. I'll fuck her until she begs me . . ." His eyes jerked open wide.

Rage beat at her head, hysteria lashed at her senses. Her fists were beating out at him, slamming against him. He made a gurgling sound, his eyes dimming, turning dull before he fell over to the floor.

Then she saw the blood.

So much blood.

All over her. The knife in her hand, over her naked body, the floor and Harley's body. It stained the wall, the furniture in her bedroom.

"Ahh, ahh God . . ." she sobbed, the knife clattering to the floor, terror gouging at her, tearing through her mind, slamming into it with such force that agony resonated through her head and stole her consciousness.

"You killed me, Zoey," Harley whispered in that rough, unfamiliar voice, his green eyes lifeless, dull as he stared up at her. "You killed me with that knife. Don't you ever forget you killed me, Zoey."

She stared at him, blood flowing around her like a stream, sticky and hot, washing over her feet, then her ankles as she watched it in horror.

"Don't you ever forget, Zoey. Don't you forget, you killed me . . ."

Run.

Run. You have to escape here. Run to Lyrica. Run now. She'll make sure you're safe. Find Lyrica . . . Tell her to find Sam. Lyrica has to find Sam. Confess to Sam. Only Lyrica and Sam can save you . . .

She had to find Lyrica.

She was so cold and dizzy, her senses rocking, pitching her back and forth until she was throwing up, fighting to remain conscious.

She couldn't black out again.

Not again.

"*You killed me, Zoey.*" She felt something wet wiping over her face, the smell of vomit no longer assaulting her senses. "*Why did you kill me, Zoey?*"

"*You can't tell Dawg, Zoey. You can't tell him you killed me. You know he'll tell Natches. Remember? Natches said he loved me like a son. I was his protégé. Remember how much Natches loves me, Zoey?*"

Natches did love Harley. They were always hunting and shooting, and Natches said Harley was his heir to . . . To what? She couldn't remember now. What was he Natches's heir to?

The blackout came again, a vicious, agonizing explosion of pain that brought merciful blackness.

"*I'm Natches's heir,*" dark and grating, the voice reminded her again. "*Natches will kill you, Zoey. Like he killed his cousin Johnny all those years ago. Natches will kill you. He'll pop your little head like a grape . . .*"

"No," she whispered, fighting to drag herself back to awareness. "No. Please . . ."

"*Natches will kill you. Like he killed Johnny when Johnny tried to hurt Christa and Dawg. Remember, Zoey? You heard about it. Cousin Johnny tried to hurt Dawg and Christa and Natches popped his little head with a bullet. You killed me. You killed me, Zoey. Natches will enjoy killing you.*"

Zoey forced her eyes open, blinking, pain raging through her head. She wasn't in the suite she'd moved into at her mother's Bed-and-Breakfast Inn any longer. The bedroom where she had killed Harley was gone. Instead, she was propped against the sliding patio door of her sister's apartment just outside Somerset.

Lyrica.

Lyrica would help her. Her sister would help her, and maybe

Natches wouldn't kill her like he killed Johnny. She would find Sam, and she would tell Sam what happened. Sam would make sure Natches didn't kill her.

"Lyrie." She tried to knock at the door her head rested against.

The glass was cool against her temple but did nothing to help the pain. Her head felt scrambled, as if pieces had been rearranged inside it, leaving her with a feeling of disassociation and complete terror.

"Lyrie, please help me . . ." She tried to knock again, her voice hoarse, weak as she lay at her sister's doorstep.

How had she gotten there?

Her breath hitched as sobs tried to escape yet still lay trapped inside her. She couldn't scream or cry. Her voice was so raw and she was so weak. She wanted a drink of water so bad, but her stomach was still pitching, threatening to be sick again.

"Lyrie, please . . ." Where was her sister?

It was so cold. The cement of her sister's small patio was like ice.

Oh God, was she dressed? Was she still naked?

She couldn't tell. But she was so cold, so cold she was shuddering, icy from the inside out. Where was Lyrica? She was so scared. And she was so cold.

She needed to be warm again. Just for a minute. Just so she could think.

"Zoey?" It wasn't her sister.

The voice was soft, gentle, as were the hands that pushed the hair back from her face with tender concern.

She forced her eyes open, staring into the confused, concerned gaze of her sister Lyrica's neighbor, Samantha Bryce. The police detective, Samantha Bryce.

Sam. She had to tell Sam. Sam would keep her from dying.

Sam would take her away. She would lock her up and Zoey would never be free again.

"I'm so sorry," she whispered. "Tell Momma I'm so sorry, Sam."

"Come on, Zoey. Let's get you inside before someone sees you."

Long brown curls flowed around Zoey as Sam's hair slipped over her shoulder and spilled against her own.

It was longer than Zoey thought. Spiral curls like her own. The long, loose, springy curls and deep waves were warm against her neck and shoulders.

Sam lifted her, cradling her in her arms and quickly moving from Lyrica's patio door to the one next to it.

Icy air surrounded her, but she didn't feel naked. She was in her shorts and tank she slept in. When had she dressed?

"Sam, I'm so scared," she sobbed against the other woman's neck. "I'm so scared."

Sam's heart was pounding hard and fast against Zoey's arm beneath the tank she wore. And though Zoey knew the other woman should be warm, still, that icy freeze encased her.

She would never be warm again. Not ever.

"It's okay, Zoey." Sam whispered the promise, her voice deep, sounding thick, clogged. "I promise, we'll make it okay."

Sam laid her on a bed, easing her back and sitting down beside her.

"Zoey," she whispered, her voice rough and worried. "Look at me, sweetie. Open your eyes."

Zoey fought to open them, but it hurt so bad.

Her head hurt so bad.

"Tell Momma I'm so sorry," Zoey begged, lifting her arm, trying to catch Sam's arm, to make her understand.

Darkness washed over her again.

She thought she heard voices, not in her head but around her.

Sam was cussing at someone. "Fix it!" she demanded. "He's a fucking nutcase," she cried out. "Just do it. Hurry. If she dies we'll all die . . ."

"He'll pop my little head like a grape," Zoey whispered. "Like Johnny. Just like Johnny." She shuddered at the image and grew colder.

So cold. So icy. She had to tell Sam what she had done. She had to.

"I'm so sorry, Momma," Zoey whispered, knowing her mother wasn't there. So glad her momma couldn't see her with so much blood on her.

Someone gripped her hand, holding it firmly as blankets were quickly pulled over her.

I'm here.

We'll get you warm, little one.

. . . heated blankets. Electric blankets. Electric blankets would be so warm, wouldn't they? Wrapped around you like the warmest skin. Holding you close . . .

That voice. She remembered that voice.

At a party. Dancing with him. He'd been just a little bit drunk that night. He'd strolled to her. Striding across the large room where everyone danced, his eyes on her, connecting with hers, heavy lidded, his gaze dark and hungry.

He'd held his hand out and though she'd laughed at him, she'd still accepted the silent demand to dance. To step into his arms. His warmth.

"Dance with me . . ." she sighed. "Hold me."

All my warmth in the blankets around you. Feel it, little one. Feel how warm I'll keep you.

Delicious warmth surrounded her, a cocoon of gentle heat sinking into her skin as the warmth of his hand wrapped around hers, easing her, easing the pain just a little bit.

He was her fantasy.

After that night, his image followed her into dreams and into masturbation. And she'd never seen him again.

She would be gone now if he came back. Taken away and locked up for killing Harley.

"I'm so sorry . . ." She had to force the words past her lips.

"Why? Why are you sorry, little one?" Her eyelid was lifted, light piercing her skull like a sword and causing her stomach to pitch and churn as she cried out with the pain.

The next eyelid was lifted, the lancing white light stabbing into her brain again. She was too weak to fight. She couldn't fight anymore.

"Please don't hurt me," she whimpered, the blissful darkness finally returning. "Don't hurt me more."

"God. Zoey, honey, tell me what happened? Who hurt you, Zoey?" he demanded. "Tell me who hurt you."

Tears slipped from her closed eyes, the horror of the nightmare images racing across her brain filling her with such a desperate, overwhelming need to hide.

"Where's Sam?" She had to tell Sam.

"I'm here, Zoey." Soft, gentle, and so sad. Sam was always so sad.

"Harley." She shuddered in fear. "I killed Harley, Sam. I killed him. I have to tell you. I killed Harley." She kept her eyes closed; she couldn't bear to see the condemnation in Sam's eyes. "I killed Harley, Sam . . ." Her breathing hitched with a cry. "I'm so sorry I killed him. I'm so sorry, but he was hurting me so bad . . ." Panic began welling inside her, racing through her veins, tearing through her mind. "He was hurting me so bad. . . . Please don't let Natches kill me. Don't let him . . ."

Detonations of pain ruptured her mind, sending waves of deep, black nothingness to surround her once again.

Just nothingness where she could hide.

It wasn't cold here, though. The warmth that was wrapped around her stayed, like a pocket of soul-deep comfort amid the terror and icy chill.

"It was just a dream. This is all a dream, Zoey," her fantasy whispered, his voice soothing, filled with the latent hunger she'd heard in it the night they danced. "It was a terrible, horrible nightmare, Zoey . . . It's all okay. Remember, it's all okay. You just had a terrible dream."

The pain in her skull slowly eased. It wasn't gone, but it eased. It wasn't so deep or so agonizing. But she didn't want to think yet. She didn't want to remember yet.

"Zoey, Harley didn't hurt you. You didn't kill Harley. He's fine."

No, it wasn't just a nightmare.

"Don't let Natches kill me. I'm so scared. It was real. I know it was real."

"It was a dream." This time, her fantasy lover's voice was so powerful and filled with demand, surrounding her, even on the inside, with a heat that began to melt the ice trying to overtake her. "This is just a nightmare. Nothing more."

The sound of his voice pulled at her, drew her as it always did in her dreams, making her want to wrap it around her and hold him to her forever.

She could barely hear him, actually had to strain to make the words out, but the throb of power and the determined male force behind it was clearly apparent.

"*You're safe, Zoey. You're safe. Harley's safe. This is just a terrible, terrible nightmare.*"

She couldn't deny him. She didn't want to deny him.

A nightmare.

A terrible dream.

It was more than that and she knew it. There had to be more to it. But she couldn't make the voice understand . . .

"*Zoey, do you hear me?*" *The dark, intently male voice pulled at her senses now as it always did. But only in her dreams. He was only in her dreams, because he'd left and he hadn't come back after dancing with her.*

She only knew this voice in her fantasies, and it soothed her, protected her without smothering her.

"*Answer me, Zoey. Do you hear me?*"

His voice was so strong. It wrapped around her and reminded her of the fantasies that filled her dreams. Fantasies of him. The knight who rescued the maiden, the tough warrior who fought side by side with the sorceress. The dream image of the lover who hadn't yet become a lover.

"I'm scared . . ." She couldn't wake up, she didn't want to wake up, not yet. Not until something made sense. Nothing made any sense. "I'm so scared . . ."

"*Don't be scared anymore, Zoey.*" *Warm, callused fingertips eased from her temple to her jaw.* "*Listen to me, and everything will be okay. Do you understand me?*"

The voice touched her with pure, raw power. It was so strong. Strong enough to hurt . . .

She whimpered at the thought. She didn't want to hurt anymore. But she had to fight. And fighting it just made the pain worse. She had to remember everything. The strange voice and

Harley's face flickering with a darker, crueler face. Sam whispering something, then yelling at someone. And now her dream lover.

She had to remember.

Pain lanced at her head, ripping through it with such agony she wanted to scream. Oh God, it hurt so bad.

"Zoey?" he whispered again, his voice so low she had to strain to hear him. "You have to listen to me so the pain will go away. I can make it all go away, but you have to listen to me."

He was holding her hand, palm turned up as he stroked the skin of her inner arm to the crook of her elbow. There, he massaged the skin, eased the joint. She felt something tighten, and then finally, blessedly, the agony in her head eased a little more.

"See, I'm going to make it better. Trust me, Zoey. Trust me to make it better," he told her in that deep, rasping whisper she could barely hear. "To always take the pain away. I'll take it all away."

Just trust him. That was all she had to do was trust him.

The nightmare would go away then.

Slipping deeper into sleep, into the fantasy she sometimes created for herself, Zoey watched as the shadowy figure moved to her. Strong and tall, pulling her against his warm body. His arms holding her, his voice at her ear.

A sigh slipped from her.

Okay, this was better. The fantasy she had created for herself, the lover who came to her in her dreams and whose touch awakened a sexuality inside her that she didn't possess while she was awake, he would protect her from the pain.

He was there with her now. His gaze was dark, filled with secrets and with hunger. His expression implacable, aristocratic, and filled with arrogance. And her fascination with him never waned.

"You came back . . . I kept watching for you . . . you're only in my dreams now . . ." She fought to speak to him, to hold him in this place where everything was so out of control and filled with pain. "Hold me. Just hold me . . ."

If he would just hold her, take it all away . . .

"I have you, Zoey. I won't let you go. Isn't this part of the dream so much nicer?" There was a hint of sadness in his voice, in his dark eyes. "I always like this part of the dream better than I do the part that rips open my skull and leaves me wanting to scream, but I can't find my voice to do so."

They hurt him too?

No. He was warmth, protection without being smothered. How did she know that? Why did the nightmares come to him too? She fought to tighten her fingers around the hand holding hers. Struggled to find the strength but only succeeded for a moment.

"I hate that part of the nightmare," he agreed, as though that faint pressure was all he needed. "See how much better this part is? See, that's how you know it's just a nightmare. I'll be here with you and if I'm here, then the pain will go away. And if I'm here with you, nothing and no one can hurt you."

Of course. It had to be a nightmare. A horrible, horrifying nightmare. Otherwise, she wouldn't be dreaming of the shadowy lover who usually filled her dreams and kept her waiting for him.

"Just a nightmare . . . When you feel the pain, when it tries to come back, I'll be here with you. The pain can't touch you, Zoey. I'll keep the pain away . . ."

"Don't leave me." She struggled to force the words past her lips, to convince him to stay this time. "Hold me."

"Just for a little while." His lips eased over her fingers. "But I'll be back. If you promise me you'll know it was just a nightmare."

She would promise him anything. "Just a nightmare."

But she knew something wasn't right about that either. Something bad had happened. Something so terrible it was terrifying too, but she didn't know how. She didn't know what it was, or how it happened.

If it wasn't real, then Harley was alive, she reminded herself as the voice stroked the pain from her head, kept her warm and tried to convince her that grass was blue and the sky was green . . . That it was all a nightmare.

"Sleep for me now, Zoey," he whispered. *"Sleep. And know when you wake up that everything's going to be fine. It was just a nightmare."*

It was much more than a nightmare, she knew. She just didn't know which part was real, and which wasn't. She didn't know and she was terrified to learn . . .

Chatham Bromleah Doogan the Third eased back from the bed and rested his elbows on his knees, watching Zoey painfully as Detective Sam Bryce stood still and silent at the bedroom door, her back to him.

How many times had he stood and watched this little imp over the past few years? She was intriguing, beyond beautiful, and she had mesmerized him from the first moment he'd seen her.

Whoever had done this to her would pay. He'd make damned sure they paid with their lives.

She was lucky Doogan was in town to meet with one of his agents, Graham Brock. Otherwise, Homeland Security as well as the Mackays might have found themselves involved in one hell of a mess.

But what would it have accomplished?

The young man in question didn't work for Homeland Security, officially. Unofficially, Doogan had provided whatever help the younger man needed.

Harley and Zoey were friends, though. They'd had a little spat a few days ago, Harley had laughingly told him. Zoey had come to his apartment and caught him with a young woman he shouldn't have been with. She'd been outraged. But they hadn't really fought, and she'd hugged him before leaving the apartment's parking lot afterward. Harley had indicated it was no more than a friendly disagreement.

Someone was determined to destroy Zoey with it, though.

On the bedside table were the vials of blood he'd drawn as soon as he'd arrived and the syringe that held the drug he'd used to ease the pain while he worked with the hallucinogenic he was positive had been used to convince her she'd killed her friend. And as he worked to reverse the nightmarish images planted in her head, his chest had ached while a dark, burning fury grew inside him.

What was it about those pale, pale green eyes and Zoey's pleas not to leave her, to keep her warm, that caused the break in his control and in the wall he maintained around his emotions?

Rubbing his hands over his face and blowing out a hard breath, Doogan forced back the regret, the stirrings of anger. If he was going to help her, if he was going to fix this, then he had to keep his head.

Without saying anything more to Zoey he rose from the bed, his movements drawing the detective's attention. Before she could speak, he motioned her to the other room.

He didn't want Zoey's memories further influenced by anything they might say between them. Her mind was so completely open at the moment, the effects of the hallucinogenic she'd been given at its height. Any suggestion, any discussion in her hearing could influence her thoughts and memories detrimentally.

Closing the door silently behind them, he pointed to the door of the guest room across the living room and followed her into that room. Once again securing the door, he breathed out heavily, wearily.

"Harley answer your text yet?" he demanded, keeping his voice low.

She gave a quick nod. "He asked to meet in another hour at Ziggler's All Niter, the convenience store at the north end of town. He said he was hunting at the moment."

Hunting. He was no wildlife hunter. Harley, despite his youth, was one of the best human trackers Doogan had ever had the discomfort of meeting.

Sam cleared her throat then, her hazel-green gaze wary, heavy with fear for the young woman now sleeping in her bedroom. Sam had a soft spot for the other young woman. It wasn't lust, or love, but her affection for Zoey ran deep.

"I checked her arm," he said, pushing his fingers through his hair. "There's evidence of several injection sites made in the past few hours . . ."

"Zoey does not do drugs, Doogan," she hissed, furious. Gathering the long curls that fell over her shoulder, she pushed them behind her as though preparing to battle.

"You didn't allow me to finish, Detective," he pointed out, berating her mildly. "As I said, the injection sites were made in the past few hours. She has all the signs of having been dosed with a powerful hallucinogenic. It literally rips the mind open and allows someone with the right training to convince the person something has occurred that didn't. In this case, that she killed Harley for trying to rape her."

Sam flinched.

She crossed her arms over her breasts, the gray ribbed cotton wife-beater tank she wore with loose gray shorts attesting to the lateness of the hour. She'd been asleep when the sound of a vehicle stopping outside her neighbor's small patio awakened her. At least, that was what she told her father, director of Homeland Security John David Bryce.

"Why?" she demanded.

To that, Doogan shrugged. "She's a Mackay; according to Timothy, trouble shadows them. Where's her sister Lyrica? Doesn't she have the apartment beside you?"

"She's staying the weekend with Kye Brock, Graham's sister." Sam paced across the room. Turning back to him she watched him suspiciously. "What the hell's going on, Doogan?"

Doogan pursed his lips thoughtfully. Sliding his hands into the pockets of his slacks, he leaned a shoulder into the wall and considered her question for a moment.

"You would know that better than I do. What could the Mackays be involved in that framing Zoey for the murder of a friend, would profit someone?" he asked.

"Murder?" the detective snapped. "I just talked to him by text."

"But Zoey believes she killed him. Harley said he was hunting," Doogan agreed. "Harley doesn't hunt four-legged prey, Sam. Despite his age, Harley's the best damned human tracker I've ever heard of. He came to me when he tracked a killer to Somerset. That's why he's here, tracking a monster no one has been able to catch."

Should he have anticipated this, Doogan asked himself?

But how could he have? Neither he nor Harley were connected to Somerset. His agents were based here, but Harley hadn't known the Mackays before following his target into the area. As for

Doogan, he'd seen Zoey only once, five years before. The target he and Harley were chasing couldn't possibly know she was a weakness to Doogan?

"Who?"

Doogan let a grin touch his lips. "That's why he's good, Sam. Harley doesn't know what his suspect looks like, he just knows the human 'tracks' his suspect leaves. He's been trying to identify him for over a year now. But framing Zoey for his murder wouldn't serve any purpose."

"He and Natches are friends," Sam pointed out. "Zoey's Natches's cousin and he'd never believe she killed him. Besides, she has an instant defense in her belief he was trying to rape her."

"Makes no sense." Doogan shook his head, one hand reaching back to rub at the back of his neck, irritation beginning to slip past his normally cool façade.

"There has to be a reason. Something we're not seeing," he muttered.

"Damn, Dawg will lock her in a hole so deep and filled with Mackay brotherly love she'll smother to death." Sam grimaced. "Hell of a way to die. So you can forget figuring out why anyone targeted her."

It was a running joke that the Mackay cousins, once the scourge of Pulaski County and surrounding areas for their sexual hijinks and penchants for troublemaking, made certain Dawg's sisters lived totally different lives. Completely innocent, virginal lives.

"Dawg can't know about this, Sam."

She froze for long seconds, simply staring at him.

"Are you kidding me?" she almost wheezed with wide-eyed disbelief. "Dawg finds out we held this from him, Doogan, and he'll kill both of us. And he will find out. Trust me."

It amazed him how terrified everyone was of Dawg Mackay and his cousins. They were formidable enemies, agreeably, and no doubt, they'd be enraged when they learned Zoey had been in danger. But they'd never kill a woman.

"And when she dies of brotherly love and overprotection? Or whoever did this to her tonight finds a way to get to her again and 'suggests' she kill herself? Herself and her family? Her nieces? Is that a risk you're willing to take?" he asked, barely managing to keep the cool, uncaring appearance he'd adopted over the past hellish year.

Could he bear seeing anything or anyone harming this innocent young woman? After all he'd lost, the thought of losing more threatened the hard-won control he'd managed to salvage in the past months.

Sam's nostrils flared and she glared at him in silent fury and denial. It was evident she had no desire to risk their wrath in any way.

"Hate me all you want to," he suggested, icy determination reflecting in his tone. "But before you go to Dawg, remember this. They got to her tonight. She's in her pajamas, so she was obviously in her room, asleep. Right beneath Timothy's nose they took her, Sam. They drugged her and tried to convince her she killed Harley Perdue. And if they convinced her, then she'll confess to it. She's a Mackay." Swiping his fingers through his hair, he knew no matter what he said, Sam would still go with her gut. "It's in their fucking blood or some shit."

And he had no doubt the little Mackay now sleeping in Sam's bed was a Mackay all the way to her soul.

He gave a short, approving nod when she said nothing more.

"Now, we have to get her back to her bed without anyone

being the wiser. Especially her brother. Otherwise, she'll never believe this was all a dream."

Sam shook her head, one hand slapping to her forehead in a gesture of utter amazement before glaring at him, the disbelief growing.

"Wow, Doogan, that's a hell of a fucking order," she snorted, her hands propping on her hips then. "Why don't we rob Fort Knox next?"

His brow arched mockingly. She could be a smart-ass, even as a child.

"I haven't finished the plan for that one yet. The plan for this one is easy, though. We have about four hours before the sedative I gave her wears off and she wakes up. We'll slip her into my truck and I'll get her to the inn, where Eli can help me do the rest."

A light brown, heavily mocking brow lifted slowly. "Eli hates you, Doogan. Worse than the rest of us do," Sam warned him.

Honest little bitch of late, wasn't she, he mocked silently.

"That's really not true." He denied the claim, amused. "But Zoey Mackay, he loves like a little sister and he hates what Dawg does to her. He'll help her, even if he does have a few issues with me. Now, go make that meeting. I'll take care of our little Mackay."

Her lips thinned, her eyes suddenly narrowing in suspicion.

"How do you just happen to have syringes, sedatives, and everything needed to draw blood samples, Doogan? And you're just conveniently here?" She held one hand out as her expression tightened with anger.

"I'm just prepared like that," he assured her. And he actually was. "Would you like to come see the other supplies I carry in my pickup? You might be amazed."

"I might want to shoot you even more than I want to do so now."

And that was possible.

"You have things to do," he reminded her. "I'll call Elijah and get him over here. Hopefully, this can be accomplished without too much trouble."

It was late morning when Zoey woke in her bed. Terror was a sickening taste in her mouth, the fear of what she would find when she looked around the room dragging a sob from her throat.

She didn't want to open her eyes, didn't want to see the carnage she was terrified awaited her.

Sitting up in the bed, she forced herself to look, though. Whatever had happened, whatever she'd done, she'd face it.

But oh God, she didn't want to . . .

Biting back a sob, tremors racing through her, she sat up and opened her eyes.

Then blinked.

There was no body, there was no blood. No blood on the walls, no blood on her blankets and sheets as she remembered. Her sheets were wrinkled and tangled, the comforter trailing to the floor.

A whimper left her lips at the pain throbbing in her temples and echoing through her muscles. She hurt so bad. Every bone and muscle in her body screamed in protest as she slid her legs slowly over the bed and forced herself to stand, to check the rest of her suite.

Stumbling, holding on to the furniture to brace herself against the weakness that made her legs feel like jelly, Zoey forced herself to the bathroom. In that far-too-realistic dream she'd thrown up, more than once. If she had, there would be something in the bathroom. Some proof of it, surely.

But there was none.

It was as spotless as it had been the night before. There was nothing out of place; nothing had been moved. The shower door was open as she always left it, her used towel folded in half and hanging on the glass door.

Backing out of the smaller room, her steps halting, tentative, she pushed through the door to the sitting room.

It was similarly neat. Her sketch pad lay where she had placed it the night before, the canvas she was working on carefully covered and sitting on the easel. The plastic wrapper that covered a new paintbrush still lay under the coffee table where she'd forgotten to pick it up. It hadn't been moved.

Forcing her steps backward again, Zoey returned to her bedroom and stood in the middle of it, shaking at the knowledge that whatever had happened . . . hadn't happened?

Fisting her fingers, she fought back the tears that would have fallen and looked down at her sore wrists. They were unmarred, no bruising, no scratches.

Covering her lips with one hand, Zoey bit back the scream tightening her throat. A whimper escaped, though. Low, drawn out, the sound was filled with fear.

Just a nightmare?

Zoey shook her head.

"It wasn't just a nightmare," she whispered, to assure herself she could speak. Because in those nightmarish memories, or dreams, she'd been unable to scream.

Something had happened, she just didn't know what. Or why.

But she knew to the depths of her soul, something bad had happened.

ONE

One year later

Music pulsed in a hard, throbbing beat, filling the exercise room on the ground floor of the small converted warehouse Zoey rented. The ground floor hid a twelve-foot-deep garage at the back that ran the width of the warehouse. A storage area hid the back garage, and then the gym was in front of it with its wall of mirrors, exercise machines, punching bag, and huge matted area she used for sparring with Eli, practicing the martial arts moves he was teaching her, or dancing to the oldies to tighten whatever.

She didn't get to dance to the oldies much, but the sparring and martial arts practice she managed to get in pretty often.

In front of the gym was the front garage, an area large enough for four full-sized vehicles, though only one was kept there. Her bicycle, moped, and small work area were walled off. The rest of the lower floor, about the full length of the other half of the building, sat empty and closed off from the areas in use. Zoey was still considering the best way to utilize it if the owner ever decided to sell the building to her.

The second-floor apartment with its huge living area, master bedroom, and three guest rooms, all with their private baths, boasted floor-to-ceiling windows spaced perfectly along the walls to let in maximum sunlight. When combined with the unique custom-made clear acrylic skylights set abundantly in the roof, it was like being outside.

Or, with the press of an icon on the computer-controlled program, she could darken every window, or just one. It was the windows and skylights she loved. She could open a whole wall in the room she used for her canvases, and the ceiling as well, and flood it with heat and light. She loved the feeling of painting outdoors while protected by the fact that she was actually indoors.

She wasn't painting now, though. She hadn't painted much, period in the past year. She'd been too busy dealing with damned nightmares and fantasies and getting them all mixed up in her head to the point that she felt tortured by both. The best Zoey had managed were several dozen dark, blood-soaked nightmares cloaked as fantasy images of death and betrayal.

They were selling, though. They were selling too well, considering they were born from the terrifying images that stole her voice and her strength in her nightmares.

Slamming her fist into the punching bag, she danced around with slow, rhythmic steps, ignoring the fact that she could no longer feel the jolting pain in her muscles and joints that she felt when she first began. She wasn't as weak or as vulnerable as she had been a year ago. She still had a long way to go, but she was learning.

She had learned to shoot and managed to purchase two Baby Glocks of her own. She was still learning to throw knives, but the expert at that was her cousin Natches's wife, Chaya. And Natches was so damned suspicious of everything that she rarely had a chance to convince her cousin-in-law to teach her more.

Thankfully, Chaya and Natches's daughter was becoming very interested in it, and Natches's objections had been swiftly vetoed by his wife. So hopefully, soon, there would be regular lessons.

She was learning martial arts, learning how to fight, and toning her muscles to enable her to protect herself in most situations.

Sweat poured down her face, dripped from the side of her neck, and dampened the long, jet-black hair pulled into an intricate braid along the top of her head before twisting into the heavy rope that fell past her shoulders.

Her brief sports bra was soaked, her skin damp with moisture, while the black shorts she wore clung to her skin. Still, her heartbeat wasn't up as it should have been, her pulse remained steadier than it had in past months, and her muscles weren't burning yet.

She couldn't stop, wouldn't stop until her body was ready to collapse from weariness and exhaustion. She couldn't. If she did, then she had to think, she had to remember the nightmares, and that she didn't want to do.

She slammed her wrapped fist harder into the heavy bag, her teeth gritting, desperation lancing through her senses as she began pounding at the punching bag. She didn't want to remember . . .

"It was a dream," the dark voice commanded, barely loud enough to hear but pulsing with the demand.

The shadowy image stepped into her dreams, his warmth wrapping around her, sinking inside her. She could feel him, and it made her ache to feel him closer. To feel him without the barrier of clothes, hot and naked against him while his powerful hands touched her.

"You're safe, Zoey. You're safe. Harley's safe. It was a terrible, terrible nightmare."

A nightmare.

A terrible dream.

So why hadn't anyone seen Harley since that night? He didn't answer his phone or his texts, nor had he returned to the apartment he'd rented. Several witnesses saw him that night at an all-night convenience store, after an obvious fight, gassing his truck. He'd even told the young woman he was seeing that he was leaving town and didn't know when he'd be back. But surely he would have answered calls to his cell phone, the texts or desperate emails she'd sent since that night.

It was just a dream, Zoey.

That shadowy image of the man who had taken her into his arms for such a brief time, danced with her, then left, haunted her. His voice, reassuring her and his arms holding her.

It was a nightmare. A terrible dream . . .

Damn, you were in trouble when your dream man lied to you in your dreams. There had to be some kind of psychosis that went with that. She had no doubt there was one. And it was just her luck to be afflicted by it. Because she knew he was lying to her, she could feel it. And she hated it.

"Zoey, do you hear me?" he urged her, that demand piercing her soul, pulling at her even now. It was just a dream, nothing more. And she believed it was all a dream. She really did.

"Don't ever forget you killed me, Zoey . . ."

Her fist plowed into the bag as a harsh sob tore from her throat. Did she believe it? She didn't know what to believe anymore. The nightmare of blood, death and pain, or the fantasy that stroked pleasure through her senses.

Holding on to the bag, her muscles trembling, Zoey closed her eyes, sinking into the memory of that nightmare, that fantasy, just as it had been before she awoke that morning.

"I'm scared . . ." She was terrified. Until his voice came.

Now it was a fear of being alone to face the demons once his voice was gone. The demons that raged and clashed inside her head and fought to convince her that she had indeed killed Harley.

"Don't be scared anymore, Zoey." Warm, callused fingertips eased from her temple to her jaw. "Listen to me, and everything will be okay."

She imagined she could make out a hint of his face, his profile perhaps. Strong features, dark eyes. His smiles were sad and filled with a loss of hope.

"Zoey. You have to listen to me so the pain will go away."

And that was all she had to do? Just listen to him? She didn't believe that. She could sense there was more, something he did that made the fragments of her brain come back together again and the pain fade away.

What had he done? She could sense it, she could feel the answer, but it drifted away now, before she could capture it.

"See, I'm going to make it better, no matter what you do, pretty girl," he whispered so softly she had to strain to hear him. Hunger filled his voice. Male hunger. The hunger a man feels for a woman, a lover. With no fear of the Mackays, no apprehension of what her brother might do. Just pure, carnal intent.

That intent filled her with pleasure. It stroked through her senses as his hands began stroking her body. Caressing her, stoking her need that much higher, hotter than ever.

"Isn't this part of the dream so much nicer?" His lips brushed over her neck as he laid her back, his naked body coming over her.

For a moment she tensed. Harley came over her to hurt her. But there was no pain here. The shadowy features of her lover didn't morph to Harley's features as Harley's did into a monster's.

"I always like this part of the dream better than I do the part that rips open my skull and leaves me wanting to scream, but I can't find my voice to scream."

He knew what it felt like.

He knew the pain, the agony, and she hurt for him while she dreamed. Ached for the sense of intuition that assured her he'd suffered in untold ways and still faced the nightmares. *"I hate that part of the nightmare too. See how much better this part is? See, that's how you know it's just a nightmare, baby. Because before it ends, if you don't wake up, then I'll be here with you and if I'm here, then the pain will go away."*

"Don't leave me. Hold me."

"Just for a little while, baby." His lips eased over her fingers. *"But I'll be back. If you promise me you'll know it was just a nightmare."*

She would promise him anything. "Just a nightmare."

"Sleep for me now, Zoey," he whispered. *"Sleep. And know when you wake up that everything's going to be fine. It was just a nightmare."*

"But it wasn't just a nightmare," she cried out as she pushed away from the heavy bag, her breathing rough and heavy, sweat soaking her skin.

Tearing off the tape wrapped around her hand, Zoey restrained the urge to kick something. She'd felt the anger burrowing deeper, growing stronger inside her since the night she dreamed she'd murdered Harley Perdue.

Her fingers found the plastic water bottle sitting on the cement ledge that ran along the outside wall. Gripping it firmly, she placed the straw in her mouth and drew on it, the cool water washing over her tongue, easing the dryness in her throat though the bitter taste of fear remained.

When she finished drinking she tipped her head back, squeezed the bottle, and let the water cool the heated flesh of her neck and shoulders before it ran into the already soaked material of the sports bra.

The music cut off abruptly. Swinging around, body bracing defensively, she immediately relaxed when she saw who had managed to slip into the gym with her.

Her sisters called him her hot, sexy roommate. He actually just rented one of the huge spare bedrooms at the other end of her apartment. He'd been the answer to a prayer in that first week after she moved in and realized she was panicking at every sound, certain someone was coming in on her.

He was always there in the evenings, never left the apartment at night, and he didn't creep around either. He walked like a normal person instead of a ghost like her brother, cousins, and brothers-in-law were prone to do. A person never knew when they were sneaking up on her.

"Cute moves with the water," he drawled, though his gaze was somber. "Give it some music and hippy twists and you have a winner there, Zoey." Elijah Grant gave her a little wink.

His amused voice wasn't so much a shock as a bit of a surprise. She gave a little snort at his comment.

"Sorry, bub, no stripping in my future so far. Check back next year."

"My luck." He shrugged negligently at the rejection before tipping his head to the side and watching her closely.

She hated it when he did that.

"Thought Graham had you working for the next few days.

Some hush-hush spy stuff." She grabbed the towel hanging on a peg attached to the wall and dried her face and shoulders. "I wasn't expecting you until later tonight."

His gray eyes watched her with thoughtful consideration. She hated it when he did that too. It meant she wasn't holding back the stress from the nightmares as well as she should.

"I finished up early." He finally shrugged before giving the punching bag a glancing punch, his gaze still on her.

Dressed in jeans, the bottoms of which were frayed behind the heels of his boots, and a dark T-shirt, he looked more like someone's kid brother than an agent for Homeland Security who worked with her brother-in-law.

"So why are you here if you're not working after all?" she queried, flashing him a mocking smile while looping the towel around her neck. "Can't find a date willing to overlook odd hours and last-minute cancellations?"

A wry grin tugged at his lips while his handsome features flickered with amusement. "Pretty much. But I was hoping I could get you to do me a favor."

"Anything." And she meant it. He'd saved her sanity more than once in the past year. And he'd never told her brother the secrets that mattered, even when he'd witnessed one of the horrifying nightmares in progress and heard her cries that she'd killed Harley.

"I have to go meet Graham's boss," he admitted with a grimace, hooking his thumbs in the front pockets of his jeans. "Bastard's always trying to pull me into one of his half-assed ops and get me shot at. If you went with me, though, I could just tell him I was out with you when Graham called, and since you're Dawg Mackay's sister, we have to run," he suggested with a hopeful look. "He wouldn't dare get you mixed up in anything dangerous."

Well, that wasn't nice. She would probably enjoy it for a minute.

She had to laugh at his explanation, though. "Really, Eli? I think getting shot at comes with the job description, ya know? Besides, I thought you were keeping me and your boss's boss far apart because of my wild hairs."

"Those wild hairs of yours are reckless and without a lick of sense, Zoey," he snorted. "But I think the whole Dawg Mackay threat will work just this once."

He always accused her of getting a "wild hair" stuck crossways in her brain whenever she decided it was time to slip away from Pulaski County and be someone other than Dawg Mackay's baby sister.

The trip actually sounded like fun, though. Something to take her mind off the nightmares that had only become worse in the past months.

"What time do we have to leave? I'll need a shower first if I have time." She strode across the gym, heading for the stairs that led to the apartment above.

"It was that easy?" He followed, the question faintly surprised.

"I told you it was," she reminded him, turning her head to glance over her shoulder at him. "Come on, Eli, I wouldn't have told you no if I wanted to and you know it. But we have to take the bikes. I haven't been out in too long and felt the air rushing around me. I'll kill two birds with one stone, so to speak."

"Leave the guns here?" Eli sounded so hopeful.

God love his heart.

"You know, Eli." Coming to a hard stop, she turned and faced him with a frown. "I practiced for three months before going for my license to carry and I passed with flying colors. I even make sure I spend at least two to three hours per week at the gun range. So what's your problem with my gun?"

The Baby Glocks just looked damned good too. Unfortunately, she had to carry them in her saddlebags or under her jacket rather than in the thigh holsters she'd bought for them.

"You're no superhero, Zoey." He repeated the same argument he always used. "You just look good enough to be one, okay? That's all. Freaky paranormal abilities do not come with the sexy leather you wear, baby doll."

She had to flash him a smile for that one. "Too bad you're not older, Eli, you have promise."

He kept telling her she needed a lover. Someone to keep her warm at night and chase the nightmares away.

"I'm not that much younger than you, Zoey," he pointed out rather eagerly as he followed her up the stairs again until they reached the second floor. "Come on, we're the same age but for a few weeks. I'd make a helluva fuck-buddy."

She threw her towel at him with a laugh. "Not this week, Eli. Sorry, bub."

"Man. Do a lottery or something; then I can at least cheat and make sure I win," he protested.

That brought her to a stop.

"A lottery for the position of my lover?" She was more amused than she should be.

His brows arched, a grin tugging at his lips. "Sounds good to me."

"What if I want more from my first lover? Some kind of commitment or promises?" Propping one hand on a hip, she flicked him a knowing look.

Eli did not believe in commitment.

He grimaced immediately, a mock shudder trembling through

his shoulders. "Stop trying to scare me. That's not right. Besides, who better to be your first than your best bud?"

"Keep dreaming," she suggested with a little wave of her fingers. "Now be quiet and don't break any of my stuff while I shower. How long do I have?"

"Long enough to shower and shimmy into that black leather you look so good in," he promised hopefully, his gray eyes filling with hope. "Come on. If I can't win the lottery, at least wear the black leather."

"Moron," she charged, striding to her bedroom. "We'll have to see about that."

Of course she would wear the leather if she was riding the bike tonight. The days of baggy jeans and shirts two sizes too big were over the night she'd dreamed of blood and death. Her research into protecting herself after that had suggested clothing that wasn't so easy to grab and restrain.

Showering and drying her hair always took far longer than Zoey liked. She'd actually been ready to have the mass of curls cut back to above her shoulders when her sisters had lost their minds over the idea. Now, she just dried it enough to get by with, laid several hair ties aside for later, and dressed.

The black leather pants slid over her skin like silk but hugged her toned legs and rounded hips like a lover's hand, while the black cotton tank hugged her from breasts to hips.

Her black leather riding jacket finished the outfit.

She slid her Baby Glocks into the soft holsters inside the jacket. One on each side.

A scarlet belt settled at her hips.

Pulling her boots on, Zoey adjusted the leather that rose just over her knee, grabbed her jacket, and hurried from her bedroom.

As she suspected, Eli was in her kitchen. He'd managed to sniff out her hidden stash of peppermint patties too. The ass.

"Stay out of my candy, Eli," she ordered, bracing her hand on her hip and narrowing her eyes at him.

He swallowed tightly, gray eyes widening to the point that they nearly bulged just before he coughed, the candy obviously stuck somewhere.

"Fuck, Zoey. Maybe the leather was a bad idea," he wheezed. "Change clothes. You'll cause the big boss to have a stroke or something."

"You're funny." She smiled indulgently. "Where are we riding to anyway?"

"The other side of Louisville," he sighed. "Do me a favor, though?"

She handed him the hair ties and turned her back on him, indicating he should go to work braiding the mass of curls.

They were silent for long minutes while he worked. She knew not to distract him while he pulled together the French braid weave that kept her hair tamed from her forehead to her nape.

"So what's the favor?" Once he started plaiting the hair from her nape to her shoulders, he was safe to speak to.

"When Doogan comes on to you—and he will come on to you, I'm afraid—just remember, he's the same rat who asked Eve out to dinner even when he knew Brogan was crazy about her," he said.

"What does that have to do with anything?" she asked as he worked quickly, efficiently, making the months and months it took him to learn how to do it all worth it.

"Well, it proves he's a rat, and that information might keep me in the running for the opportunity to cheat on that lottery," he snickered, securing the hair tie at the end of the braid.

Zoey dropped her head, shaking it and holding back her laughter. "You're a nut, Eli."

He patted her back consolingly. "You love me, Zoey. You know you do."

He was her best friend and as much a confidant as her sisters.

"Come on, Eli, let's go meet your boss's boss. Why are we riding to the other side of Louisville to do this anyway? Doesn't he know where Graham lives?" she asked in interest.

"Oh, he knows, and Graham's invited him in several times. He just says he's too busy. That's the same excuse he gave this time. So he's meeting us at a private airfield instead. The plane's landing just long enough for him to take care of some business and then he's leaving again."

Sounded a little too complicated to her. No wonder the government was short on money. They spent too much playing spy games in far too complicated ways.

Zoey led the way to the back of the apartment and the stairwell that led to the small garage she kept hidden from her family at the back of the converted warehouse.

The extra-wide metal door provided plenty of clearance for the Harley she stored there. Twelve feet deep but over a hundred feet wide, the full width of the warehouse. The garage provided plenty of room for her Harley and Eli's as well as her racing dirt bike, tool cabinets, parts, and a long workbench. The rest of the area she used to store both paintings as well as empty canvases.

Wrapping the tail of her braid around her head and securing it with a bobby pin, Zoey pulled on the full-head helmet and activated the radio in it.

"Test," she murmured into the link that connected to Eli's.

"Loud and clear," he answered, his voice low. "Ready to ride, girly-girl?"

"If you stop calling me those ignorant names. Really, Eli?" He was like a brother. An easygoing younger brother.

"Really, Zoey," he chuckled as she hit the remote on the bike to slide the door open and started the powerful motor.

Within seconds they were pulling out from the garage, the wide door closing behind them, security automatically activating and locking the entire building down while she was gone.

With the wind whipping around her, she pushed the nightmares behind her and let herself just enjoy the ride and the sense of freedom she found in it. A freedom she knew would be too short-lived and not nearly the adventure she would have wished.

TWO

The other side of Louisville turned out to be the Indiana side.

Not that she cared, but hell, he could have told her they were leaving the state. Sometimes, Eli had an odd habit usually attributed to Mackays.

Sneaky machinations.

She just didn't know yet what or who Eli was machinating against. Or for. But she had no doubt she'd figure it out. She'd gotten good at figuring out male games over the past years.

"We need to discuss your communication skills, Eli," she informed him drolly as they moved into traffic from the exit. "They're leaving a bit to be desired."

And how she would love to see his expression right now.

"I said the other side of Louisville." And didn't he sound so confused?

God love his heart, she was going to shoot him one of these

days. He was becoming rather too good at the male confusion thing, too. She knew him, though, and she knew better. Eli was anything but confused.

He didn't appear in the least confused either. Relaxed and enjoying the ride himself, he all but lounged back on the bike, the dark face shield of the helmet hiding his expression. And no doubt hiding the lack of confusion in his expression.

Confused? Not Eli. She could just imagine the smug grin on his face. The one that quirked his lips when he knew he'd pulled something off that he hadn't been so certain he could accomplish.

"This was needed information, you know." She tried to sound stern, but it wasn't easy. She didn't really care, she was just nosy about intended destinations when she was riding along. "What if I have something planned for tonight?"

"You have a date or something?" Eli chuckled knowingly. "I thought all your potential suitors were still cowering behind their mommies' skirts in fear of Dawg. You notice I'm not cowering."

She had to laugh at the comment, because she was well aware Dawg actually laughed himself at the thought of her sleeping with Eli. He saw the younger man as no more than a watch puppy willing to give up information whenever he directed a Mackay frown at him.

"I have noticed Dawg giving me credit for having better taste," she shot back. "He only lets you rent one of my spare rooms because he feels sorry for you. And because you're such a little narc. Kind of like a little golden retriever pup, I think. All playful energy and no bite."

"Golden retriever pup?" he exclaimed, outraged.

"A little Christmas puppy with a big ol' bow on his neck," she laughed. "Dawg's personal little tattletale."

He chuckled at that. "Never with the good stuff, though, and you know it, Zoey-cat. He'd kill me if he ever learned what I was holding back."

She had to wince at that.

Yeah, Eli would be in serious trouble if her brother ever suspected all the choice, juicy details Eli was deliberately hiding from him. They'd known when they worked out the details of his occupation, though, that Dawg would see him as easy pickings when it came to keeping an eye on his baby sister.

"Naw, he'd just hurt you real bad," she snickered. "Don't worry, I promise to install the handicap lift you'll need to get to your room. It's the least I could do."

"I appreciate your encouragement. Really. Just makes my little heart warm with affection, Zoey-girl." He didn't sound so affectionate, though. "We're taking the next exit. The airfield is just about fifteen minutes away."

The long stretch of interstate was basically deserted of businesses or even fast-food joints.

"Hell of a place to meet," she stated as they took the exit. "Ever heard of e-mail? It's great for all kinds of things. Pictures, videos, top-secret files. Phones are great too for oral reports. There's even video chats now, Eli."

Yep, it was no damned wonder the country was going bankrupt. All the clandestine, knotted routes their spies took no doubt cost a hell of a lot of money.

"And all are hackable, transferable, or otherwise vulnerable," he reminded her. "The big boss isn't the real trusting sort with top-secret stuff. He doesn't appreciate anyone else who isn't just as careful either."

The real suspicious sort. Like Dawg and her cousins. The way he talked about the "big boss," unlike the men in her family, he was more accepting of a woman fighting side by side with him. Eli once stated that the big boss was prone to even accept women on his security teams when he needed personal protection.

"The man's a real pain in the ass," Eli growled. "His family is even related to royalty somehow. I just never bothered to ask how. He's irksome enough as the boss."

"Well now, isn't he just special," she snorted in amusement. "Remind me to bow and be all ladylike if I have to meet him."

His head turned toward her as he gave a surprised spurt of laughter.

"You're wicked," he accused her. "But as much as I'd love to see that, be good. I need my job."

"No you don't, he just gets you shot at, remember?" she retorted in amusement. "If he fires you I'll pimp you out, hon. You should make enough to at least pay your rent."

"You don't charge me rent," he reminded her suspiciously.

"Yeah," Zoey drawled. "I didn't forget that either."

She laughed when he made the next turn without warning her. She was far enough behind that following him wasn't a problem, though.

The narrow blacktop lane led deep into the rolling hills bordering Louisville. They were in no way mountains, just gentle upraised slopes sheltering shallow valleys. The private airfield was located in such a valley. Several large hangars sat just back from the paved landing strip, appearing deserted and completely unassuming.

"He's in the first hangar." Eli pointed the large metal building out. "He has his own private jet and makes full use of it. Family money and all that shit."

"As I said, ain't he just special," she repeated, rolling her eyes. "Is this meeting going to take long?"

The boss's boss actually sounded like he'd be fun as hell to torment for a minute. Did he have a sense of humor?

Well, Eli was still alive, so he had to have a sense of humor, she thought in amusement. Even she considered shooting him once a week. He could be just that infuriating.

"It shouldn't take long. I just have to pass along some stuff Graham sent, find excuses not to accompany him on whatever harebrained op he's decided he needs me for, and then we'll be on our way."

She didn't believe him. It was that edge of resignation in his voice. The sound of a man who knows better than the explanation he was trying to force-feed her.

"Twenty minutes max," he promised.

"Hmm. I'll time you." Following him to the entrance of the hangar, Zoey drew the cycle to a stop beside Eli's and cut the engine.

Releasing her helmet, she removed it and hung it on the sissy bar behind her before shrugging the light leather jacket from her shoulders and laying it over the back of the seat.

"I promise, I won't be long." Helmet removed, his own jacket slung over the back of his bike, Eli watched her with a hint of discomfort now.

He so was not looking forward to this. It was almost amusing the way the big boss could intimidate him far better than her brother, Dawg, could.

"Go," she laughed, waving her fingers toward the jet parked in the hangar. "I'll wait, no matter how long. You can buy me a greasy cheeseburger later for my trouble."

He shook his head, a grin tugging at his lips, before striding to the steps leading into the private jet. "Those cheeseburgers will kill you, Zoe-Zoe."

"Not before I kill you for calling me all those damned sissy names," she warned him, though her gaze was on the jet.

Nice jet too, if she wasn't mistaken.

Dismounting the bike, she stood staring around the valley, stretching her legs for a minute before sitting crossways on the comfortable seat and straightening the small chains and charms that dangled from the zipper tabs of her boots.

She hated waiting. She wasn't the patient type unless she was hunting. She'd enjoyed that. Unfortunately Natches had ended the hunting lessons rather abruptly no more than a few months after they'd begun.

When he'd informed her they weren't going hunting anymore, she arched her brow, anger pulsing through her. *"Afraid I'll get good at it?" she'd charged him.*

Natches shook his head. "No, little sister," he sighed. "Afraid you'll get too good at it."

Hell, that was years ago. What had made her think about that?

Waiting, probably, she thought with a snort.

As much as she thought of Elijah, when the twenty minutes passed, she could feel herself becoming frustrated. She could feel herself beginning to think of things better left alone. That was why she hated waiting. She'd only gotten worse in the past year.

"It was a nightmare, Zoey."

"Always remember, you killed me, Zoey . . ."

"I'm Natches's heir . . . Natches will kill you . . ."

Natches's heir. Harley was a hunter; he talked about it all the time. Hunting and guns and Natches's new best hunting buddy? Well, that made sense, didn't it? As a former Marine sniper Natches would want an heir to teach what he knew, and his adopted son, Declan, had a tendency to laugh if someone suggested he go hunting with Natches.

Harley and Natches had been great hunting buddies, though.

"... *I'm Natches's heir* ..." *the voice of a nightmare whispered through her head.*

"... *don't forget you killed me, Zoey* ..." *Harley demanded in those bloody images, demanding she remember.*

Jumping from the seat of the motorcycle, she paced several feet from it, searching the area frantically for something to concentrate on, something besides a nightmare she just wanted to forget.

"Damn, Eli, is it going to take you all friggin' evening?" she snapped into the silence of the valley. "Let's hurry already."

"You could have come in with him."

Zoey swung around at the sound of the brooding tone, rife with amused mockery.

Her brows arched and she allowed a small smile to threaten the corners of her lips. Now, didn't he just look rather fun?

"Zoey Mackay?" A single dark brow arched, interest gleaming in his dark, chocolate-brown eyes.

He stood almost lazily next to the front wheel of her cycle, hands tucked into his black slacks, the sleeves of his white shirt rolled several cuff widths up his tanned, light-haired forearms, his longish, dark brown hair framing aristocratic, damned imposing features.

"And you are?" she asked warily, though she had a good idea who he was. The boss's boss. It was damned funny how even Eli refused to use his name. Like some kind of talisman that could hold him at bay.

He did look kind of dangerous, though, in a very aristocratic sort of way. In a very arrogant lord-of-all-he-surveyed way. And she had to admit, it was a damned arousing look.

She liked it.

A little too much perhaps.

Her eyes narrowed then. It had been years. Five years, to be precise. He was harder, his face sharper, his expression colder. But it was him.

She'd danced with him one sultry summer night, certain he'd kiss her once the dance was over. Instead, he stepped back, ran his finger from her temple to her jaw in a gentle curve, before turning and just walking away.

But did he know who she was? He didn't appear to recognize her, and it had been five years after all. Perhaps she hadn't made the same impression on him.

His lips quirked. "Who did Eli tell you he was meeting?"

Propping one hand on a leather-clad hip, she slid her gaze to the plane, then back to his amused features.

"His boss's boss." She wrinkled her nose with a hint of disdain. "Be careful of him, he tends to get his agents shot at, you know."

Casually, ensuring that the move appeared natural, Zoey lifted her jacket from the seat of the cycle and pulled it on once again. "Hopefully he doesn't get Eli shot at before we leave. I'm certain I have things to do tonight."

"Really?" The interest deepened in his eyes now. "Perhaps you can give him a few more minutes while you explain how you know so much about his boss?"

Lifting one arm, she checked her nails for a moment before lowering it once again and directing her attention back to him.

"I'm a Mackay, we tend to know these things. Instinct perhaps." She shrugged as though no more interested in the conversation than she was in the grass growing in the fields surrounding the airfield. "Think the boss's boss will be done with him soon?"

He turned and gave the plane a long look before turning back to her. "I don't quite think he's finished yet. You could come up with him if you like."

Uh-oh. That did not sound promising. For Eli at least.

"What's he doing?"

"A hundred push-ups for bringing a civilian along," he answered far too seriously. "And if I don't get back, he'll cheat on the count. There's cold drinks in the plane if you decide to join us."

"I assume you're the boss's boss, then?" she queried, knowing he was. "A name would be nice. Even my sister won't provide the name of the man who dared to invite her out to dinner while my brother-in-law was still trying to seduce her. I believe they consider saying your name bad luck. Rather like Rumpelstiltskin perhaps?"

She wondered if she should just tell him she knew who he was and how much she appreciated him taking her sister out. That was enough to piss her off.

That little twitch at the corner of his lips hinted at a smile of sincere amusement.

"Come along." As he angled his head to the aircraft, his gaze turned mocking again. "Eli can introduce us properly since he convinced you to come along with him."

"I just followed him," she retorted, grinning at his back now. "He does live with me, you know. And I was bored tonight."

"Get bored often, do you?"

Damn, she wished she could see his face when he asked that question.

"Only on Fridays," she assured him, wondering if the odd look he gave her was an indication that for her, every day was Friday these days.

"Today's only Thursday." Still, he didn't deign to let her see his expression.

"Oh well. I guess I started a day early, then. My bad."

She had a feeling she could have fun with this man. It might have had something to do with the little glimpse she caught of a grin he was trying to hide when she nearly caught up with him. Or the fact that he had a helluva backside.

"You're bad? Sweetheart, with the name Mackay, there wasn't even a doubt." He stopped at the steps leading up to the interior of the jet.

She took the first step, then paused and faced him. With the three-inch boot heels and the height of the step, she could stare him in the eye, and she liked that.

It put her close enough to catch the scent of his cologne, a bit of sandalwood, she thought. A very masculine, very intriguing scent that made her want to get closer.

A whole lot closer.

"Well then, at least you've been warned," she pointed out, lowering her voice and giving him a sultry look. "I, on the other hand, am still in the dark. Should I be warned as well?"

His hand lifted just enough to allow his index finger to insert itself under the sleeve of her jacket, where it then stroked over her wrist. A rasp of a callused fingertip against the sensitive flesh had the blood pounding harder through her veins.

"Oh God, Zoey, don't flirt with him." Eli barked the demand from the open door of the plane, horrified astonishment filling his voice. "I warned you what he was like. Do you really want to become a notch on his belt?"

"How very chauvinistic of you, Eli," she accused him lightly. "Maybe I'm thinking about making him a notch in my belt?"

Surprise gleamed in his brown eyes as well as a glimmer of laughter.

"You're crazy. Get away from him," Eli all but begged her. "He's like a damned plague where women are concerned. You never recover."

The boss's lips thinned, but she could see the grin he wanted to let free. Zoey leaned forward just a few inches and let a smile curve her own lips. "Why fight it? You know you want to."

His eyes flicked to her lips then back to meet her gaze.

"Oh, Miss Mackay, there are many things I'd love to do, but exactly to what are you referring?" Carnal, white-hot lust gleamed in his eyes now.

"The smile you're fighting." Stepping back, she gave a toss of her head and moved up the steps. "I bet you look really nice when you smile."

"He looks like an ogre when he smiles. All cracked, broken teeth and evil breath." Eli was waiting, arms crossed over his chest, his expression forbidding. "You never listen to me, do you?"

She couldn't help but laugh as she neared him.

"Only when you say something I want to hear." She reached up and patted his cheek fondly as she passed him. "So stop fussing. I'm just playing a little bit."

"With an alligator," he snapped. "Or a shark. You should know better."

"You're fired, Eli." The boss stepped in behind her obviously, his tone rich and deep, without a hint of amusement. He wasn't serious, though. She knew he wasn't serious.

Turning, she caught Eli's disapproving look as he glared at the other man. "Bullshit. Dammit, Doogan, stop firing my ass. You know our dads will just make you hire me back anyway, so why bother?"

"Because you irritate me." Doogan shrugged, turning to Zoey now. "He thinks because our fathers are best friends that I can't fire him. He's wrong."

"Suits me fine. Zoey already has a job lined up for me anyway," he shot back, his look daring her to reveal the nature of that job. "I won't have to worry about you getting me shot at."

"What kind of job might that be? Mackay jester?" Doogan snorted, though the barest hint of a wink as he passed her belied the seriousness of his tone.

"I really don't like you, Doogan." Eli was almost serious.

That was too funny. Eli didn't actually dislike anyone, but he obviously had a few issues with Doogan. She had a feeling that complications likely filled their relationship.

"He's annoyed with me right now." Doogan sat in the executive-style chair positioned behind a work area and facing the front of the plane. "He'll like me better once he doesn't get shot at this time before he gets back."

Now, that one gave her pause.

Zoey gave Eli a frown. "Before he gets back?" She turned the same frown on Doogan. "That's not going to work. I have to get back to Somerset before Dawg realizes I've disappeared."

Doogan lowered his head, his gaze on the open laptop, though she doubted his attention was there. He seemed to be choosing his words instead.

"You know the way back, I presume?" Doogan inquired then, his head lifting, his gaze locking with hers. "I didn't ask Eli if he cared to do it, I ordered him to do it."

"Go back by myself?" she asked, as though amazed he would make such a suggestion. "But I'm a Mackay. I'll end up in trouble before I'm halfway there and God forbid I should get a bruise and tell Dawg you sent me home alone." Her eyes widened, a pretense of sudden, fearful knowledge filling her expression. "I'd hate to see what happened then. He'd come looking for you, though."

Doogan's eyes locked on hers. "Then I guess you better stay right here until Eli gets back. It would be terrible if you caused your brother to end up . . . hurting himself. . . ." That wicked smile he flashed her was completely misbegotten. He didn't care in the least to stir up a little trouble, now did he?

Eli groaned, a defeated, painful sound.

"Eli. Go." Doogan's voice changed. It wasn't holding that playful little undercurrent any longer. He was dead serious.

Eli groaned again. "There goes my chance," he sighed.

"Your chance at what?" Doogan's tone deepened at the grin Zoey couldn't hold back.

Her gaze slid to Eli's, daring him.

"Living," Eli grunted.

A second later he left the plane, stomping down the steps like a two-year-old in temper. Though, admittedly, Zoey wondered if perhaps she should be a little worried herself.

"Sending him away really wasn't nice," she sighed. "He's terrified of your little side projects."

"Which is why he brought you. I'm no fool, Ms. Mackay," he told her with a softness that belied the steel beneath it. "Eli likes to think he can fool me sometimes. He doesn't."

There was more than a handsome playboy that existed beneath that implacable expression, she guessed. And far more than just the boss's boss.

"And I needed to know this why?" Crossing her arms over her breasts, she glared down at him, though she had a feeling if push came to shove, this man could steamroll right over her if she gave him half a chance.

The look he gave her was one of knowing exasperation.

"Have a seat, sweetheart." He indicated the chair in front of his desk. "Eli will be a few hours at least. You may as well make yourself comfortable."

She rolled her eyes at that. "I know my way home. I'm sure I can stay out of trouble that long."

Hooking her thumbs into the pockets of her jeans, Zoey tried to tell herself she could walk out anytime she wanted to and just ride home. No big deal. So why was she standing there? Why was she letting him hold her gaze, capture her senses?

"I'm certain you do, Zoey," he stated softly. "And I see the suspicion in your eyes. You can trust me, you know."

Uh-huh. Trust wasn't something she gave easily. It was even harder to attain with her than friendship was.

Turning away from him, Zoey stepped to the long couch behind the chair he'd motioned her to sit in and plopped onto the exquisitely comfortable leather seat.

"Trust you, can I?" she sighed. "And what would make me think I could? A single dance six years ago?"

Something shadowed his eyes then. Something dark, something hungry. It caused her heart to beat faster, a heat she'd only felt once before, to begin building inside her.

"We could start with that," he murmured.

It was about a year too late, she told herself morosely. If he'd shown up a year ago with that suggestion she might have had the option of considering it. She couldn't take that chance now.

"Nice plane." She grappled for a change of subject. "Yours or your agency's?" she asked, running her hand over the supple leather.

"Mine." The laptop closed and he relaxed his chest, regarding her with open, sexual interest.

"Hmm. Should I bow?"

His lips quirked. "It might be rather hard in that leather, but you can try."

"You'd be surprised what I can do in leather," she murmured, the wordplay more exciting than she'd ever known it to be.

Zoey liked to flirt; she liked pitting her wits against the so-called charmers who thought they could talk their way into her bed. This was more than just flirting, though. It was more than pitting her wits against a man she had no intentions of taking to her bed. This was a man she just might have considered giving her heart to at another time.

Maybe.

She crossed one leg over the other and relaxed into the giving cushions behind her. "I could have gone with Eli."

"You could have," he agreed with a short inclination of his head. "If I were certain of your ability to convince a bar full of bikers that you've seduced their favorite female lone wolf."

She grinned at that, reached up and removed the bobby pin from the tail of her braid, and let it fall over her shoulder. "I could totally do that," she assured him with a little wrinkle of her nose. "I have mad seduction skills, you know? All from watching Sam Bryce in action."

Sam was the shit when it came to seducing women. She could make a totally straight chick sit up and take notice. And give her more than a second thought.

His dark chocolate eyes gleamed with humor now. "Admittedly, Sam would be a capable teacher," he admitted. "I rather assumed it wasn't females you were into, though, considering the fact that she hadn't managed to seduce you yet."

There was the slightest hint of a question in his voice.

She gave a slow lift of her brows, playing with the braid hanging over her shoulder for a second before letting her gaze meet his again.

That knowing exasperation filled his expression again when it became apparent she wasn't answering his question. Before he could say anything, though, the ringing of his cell phone drew his attention.

Checking the number, he glanced back at her. "If you'll excuse me a moment," he said, rising from his chair, "I need to take this."

He disappeared through the door behind him without once ordering her to stay put.

She could just walk out and ride away if that was what she wanted to do. So why didn't she?

Instead, she removed her jacket, laid it across the back of the couch close to her, and waited instead. She who hated waiting was waiting for a man who her instincts warned her was far more dangerous than he appeared.

She wasn't certain how long he was gone, but it was long enough that Zoey ended up returning to the bike to pull a sketch pad free before returning to the plane. The need to draw wasn't as imperative as it had been a year ago, but she had a sudden need to sketch Doogan. To catch the subtle expressions on his face before she forgot them. To catch the hint of humor in his eyes and the steely determination in his savage features.

Time passed quickly then. Too quickly.

Lost in the world she became immersed in while drawing, she wasn't aware of the passing of time until the door opened and he returned.

"Sorry it took so long." His expression was harder, his gaze chilly. "That had to be taken care of."

Closing the sketch pad, she blinked up at him, taking a moment to process what he'd said.

"Did you get Eli shot at?" she asked, almost expecting an affirmative answer.

"Not hardly." The chill in his eyes warmed.

"That's good." She laid the pad and pencil on the small table beside her before turning back to him. "I've become rather fond of him."

The statement was actually true. Eli was like a younger Mackay, still fun-loving, not yet hardened or as stubborn as her brother and cousins.

"You're not exactly what I expected," he told her, making his way to the couch, where he took a seat with more than ample space between them. "Even six years ago. I have to admit, I wouldn't have thought you'd be quite so adventurous."

"And what did you expect?" Her heart was racing; warmth flushed through her, unbidden memories of the fantasy lover she'd created years ago flitting through her mind.

"I've met Eve and Piper," he stated. "Your elder sister is actually very quiet, very introspective."

"She's a writer," Zoey pointed out. "And I don't think I appreciate your efforts to seduce her the night Brogan broke up that little date with her."

He chuckled at that. "Had I wanted to seduce her, I wouldn't have taken her to the Mackay restaurant, sweetie. I merely wanted to push Brogan's possessiveness buttons."

She shrugged at that. "I'm not revising my statement."

"Piper's rather quiet as well," he stated then, as though the subject had never changed. "Though Lyrica is a bit more social, still." His gaze flicked over her, the lust in his gaze becoming more apparent. "My reports say none of them are leather-wearing, Harley-riding hellions."

"I'm a hellion?" She was rather pleased with the description. "Eli said I hadn't yet been promoted from troublemaker. I'm glad to see he was wrong."

"It's only an initial upgrade," he informed her warningly. "It could be revised at any time." She nodded sagely as though well understanding his dilemma.

"Ah well, I'm certain at some point my abilities have been overexaggerated," she agreed, though she couldn't imagine when. "Rather than underexaggerated." She gave him a quick, impertinent grin.

He didn't reply, merely stared at her, that gleam of hunger deepening in his gaze.

She'd never known a time in her life when she'd responded to a man as she responded to this one. When her pulse raced, her heart beat so hard it made her breathing harder, faster. Or when the look of hunger in a man's eyes had actually had her sex responding with slick readiness.

"Are you going to try to seduce me, Doogan?" she asked then, licking her dry lips quickly, her heart rate increasing further as his eyes followed the action. "I hear it's not quite advisable to allow you to do so. Eli would probably have a stroke. He gets rather upset where you're concerned."

"Try?" His lips quirked as one arm stretched out along the back of the couch, ignoring her observation on the other man. "I rarely try to do anything, Zoey."

Well now, wasn't he extremely confident?

"Think it's a sure thing, do you?" Clasping her hands lightly in her lap, she didn't balk at holding his gaze.

Her heart was racing double time now. And when his gaze flicked to the vein at her neck, she knew he was aware of the excitement flooding her.

"I'm quite certain it's a consideration on your part." His voice lowered, becoming a dark, brooding sound that stroked over her senses and had the oddest sensation attacking the girl parts that had rarely roused in the past year.

"A consideration?" she mused, adopting a thoughtful expression. "For a man I've not yet been properly introduced to? One I've only heard is prone to get his agents shot at? One who asked my sister out after that totally romantic dance with me where you never said a word or kissed me good-bye? A glancing thought is as far as I would go, perhaps."

He shifted closer. "I'm going to kiss you before you leave here tonight, Zoey Mackay. Then you can decide if you're just considering me or not."

It would be more than a consideration and she knew it.

"That would be rather rude, don't you think?" she forced herself to point out. "We're still at a first-name basis. I rarely allow such liberties so soon."

His gaze went to her lips again while the hand resting on the back cushion moved to tug at several curls that escaped her braid.

"Chatham. Bromleah. Doogan. The Third." He came closer with each word until his lips were poised over hers, so close.

Zoey felt hers part. Her breathing became short, ragged, but his wasn't exactly calm either.

"Can I kiss you now, Zoey?" he asked, but he didn't wait for permission.

His lips covered hers, took them, demanded her response and swept her into a storm she had never expected. A storm that crashed through her senses, pushed away barriers, and in a single moment, she feared, branded a hunger inside her she would never be rid of.

A hunger she wanted only to become more immersed in.

Wrapping her arms around his neck Zoey moaned into his kiss, swept away with such riotous pleasure that any thought of resisting him didn't have a chance. He was heat and overwhelming pleasure. Seductive energy and dark forcefulness and she was loving every minute of it. Loving it so much that even as he eased back on the couch and came over her, one hand gripping her hip, his knee easing between her thighs, she only moaned with the rising sensations.

She'd never wanted a man like this. She'd never known such a hard rush of pure lust as she did now. That complete "do-him-now" feeling that tore through her senses and left no room for even a whisper of resistance.

"Zoey!" Eli's panicked voice was a splash of reality washing over her. "Dammit. Dammit. I knew not to leave you with him! Where is your self-control?"

Doogan's head lifted and Zoey's turned, her gaze finally focusing on Eli's outraged expression.

"Eli, you're definitely fired," Doogan growled, lifting away from her.

"I think I better go." Scooting back from him, she grabbed her jacket, jumped from the couch, and all but ran to the door. "I'll wait for you outside, Eli. Hurry or I'm leaving without you."

She would too. As soon as she dragged her senses back and managed to make the world level out around her again. Or perhaps she was the one who needed to level out.

Oh, God, what was she doing? Especially with that man. The one man she couldn't have no matter how much she might want him. He was dangerous. Far too dangerous to her self-preservation. And she couldn't forget it. Lovers became too intimate. They wanted to spend the night and all that crap. And she didn't need the boss's boss of a federal agency realizing that the woman he was sleeping with was having nightmares of killing a man no one had seen since the nightmares began.

Sleeping with Chatham Doogan would be disastrous. And she couldn't ever let herself forget that.

THREE

Two Weeks Later

There were times in a man's life that a woman had the power to simply steal his breath. Times when the past and the present converged, and he found himself staring at a future he could have had, if he'd been smart enough to take the right turn rather than the left.

Or so he'd been told.

He'd suspected the truth of it six years ago when he'd been unable to deny himself a dance with Zoey Mackay. Just that small amount of time when he could hold her against him, feel her warmth, sense the innocence he saw in her eyes and ache with regret.

He'd never actually believed it though until two weeks ago when he'd held Zoey against him and felt a hunger burning through him like he'd never experienced before. She had stolen his breath then, and tonight, she stole it again and for a second he wondered if he'd ever get it back.

It was an interesting reaction.

Every bone and muscle in his body tightened and all the blood pushing through his veins stilled for a single moment in time. And for one precious second, he felt the convergence of what had been, what was, and what could have been, all in a single instant with all the anger, regret, and grief that came with it.

That loss of breath occurred the moment he saw her striding through the crowd, a smile on her face, her heavily lashed eyes bright and so filled with excitement. All those lush, lovely curls she possessed were once again tamed in a thick, heavy braid, leather cord binding it from her nape to where it ended just between her shoulder blades. There was no hint of the hand-tempting spirals that normally surrounded her head and fell to below her shoulders in wild abandon.

The curls might have been tamed, but the woman wasn't. As though binding her hair had caused some detour in the abandon that filled them, all that electric energy filled the woman instead.

Enough energy to singe a man's soul if he wasn't careful.

She strode to the graded track as Eli pushed a stripped-down dirt bike through a break in the stacked bales of hay surrounding it at the starting line. Another rider eased his bike alongside it, motor gunning, the young male riding it shooting Zoey a smug grin.

Nearing Eli, Zoey pulled the full-face helmet she carried over her head, securing the strap under her chin as the bystanders gathered in the clearing moved as close to the bales of hay as possible to watch the coming race.

The air of expectation and pulsing excitement that hadn't been there before Zoey's arrival was definitely there now. All eyes were on her, watching as she straddled the powerful little bike and brought it rumbling to life.

"She's gonna beat him one of these days." A young woman

spoke behind Doogan. "Maybe not tonight, though. Not until she finds someone with a little less fear to work on her bike."

"That Grant boy's gonna keep her from winning," a man remarked in reply. "He's too scared of the Mackays to ensure she has enough power . . ."

"Billy says her bike is off balance. Eli won't balance it. He's tried to tell her . . ." the woman remarked, her voice knowing and a bit irate.

The couple moved past him, eager to get to the edge of the barrier to watch the race, their conversation drifting away.

Doogan crossed his arms over his chest, remaining where he was, frowning as he listened to Zoey's bike revving, heard the distinctive sound, subtle though it was, that indicated a lack of necessary power, just as the couple had observed.

Narrowing his gaze on the stripped-down motorbike Zoey straddled, he could see where it would be off balance as well. And Elijah Grant had been working on that cycle? The young man knew motors and vehicles like most men knew a woman's body. Eli was much better with motors than what Doogan could hear in the sound of the bike Zoey was getting ready to race.

Eli was deliberately keeping her from attaining the ratio between balance and power she needed to race the rough, makeshift oval track, and that didn't make sense. It was definitely something he hadn't told Doogan about.

There was no way she could win against the other rider. It wasn't possible. The male racer knew it too. Doogan could see it in the young man's confident expression and gloating smile.

A slender young woman dressed in cutoff denims that nearly showed the cheeks of her ass and a too-snug red bikini top moved to the side of the track, a white handkerchief uplifted as she took a deliberately seductive pose.

The two motors revved, riders leaning forward, one leg braced on the track.

The young woman holding the flag gave a little wiggle, and the motors revved harder. When the white handkerchief went down they shot from the starting line. Zoey took the lead for a moment only. Half the track, then the other rider edged past with less than half a cycle lead. Four circles of the track later, going into the final lap, in the first of two turns, Zoey leaned into the turn, fighting to find more power, for the impetus to force her ride into the lead, but the lack of proper balance and power was her downfall.

He lost his breath again; of course, this time he was certain it had something to do with watching the little hellion wipe out as she took the sharp curve of the track. It was a laughable excuse for a raceway, but the sight of her losing control and plowing into the bales of hay stacked for just such an occurrence wasn't in the least amusing.

The crowd of onlookers gasped, no doubt aware every damned one of them would face her brother Dawg Mackay's wrath if the unthinkable happened. Or, if he or one of his cousins caught so much as a whisper of her weekend activities among their group and they hadn't been told, hell would explode over them.

Highly protective and all too aware of the dangers that could strike at his family at any given moment, Dawg Mackay, the eldest of the Mackay cousins, was known to become rabid where the females of his family were concerned. Especially in the case of his daughter, his nieces, or his baby sister, Zoey.

In Zoey's case it appeared he had more than one reason to foam at the mouth. She possessed more than her fair share of Mackay kamikaze traits, if this race was any indication. What else did the little spitfire get into that she was hiding from her family? For a moment the knowledge that it could be damned near anything that involved an air of danger had his teeth clenching in concern. The fact that Eli was supposed to be watching her back through her adventures and keeping Doogan informed of them indicated that the young agent was holding quite a bit back. For this alone, Doogan was about to become Eli's problem.

Jumping to her feet, Zoey jerked the helmet from her head. Snarling, she kicked at the downed cycle with the toe of her heavy riding boot, cursing worse than any sailor he knew if the words her lips were forming were any indication. Disgust curled the pillowy curves and tightened her delicate features as three young men ran to her in case help was needed. She didn't appear to need any help, though. At least, not in the kicking-cursing activity she was currently involved in.

Flipping the fingers of one hand toward the ride, she ignored their laughing comments. Stalking away, she left them to collect the bike while she made her way to the edge of the raceway, where Doogan stood, silently watching her.

The winner of that particular little race met her at the finish line, several feet from where Doogan stood, a smile curling his lips as he brushed the dust from his leather riding chaps and jacket.

"Girl, I told you that cycle wasn't balanced right." The rider laughed in pleased satisfaction and held his hand out, palm up. "Pay up, sweet thing. Man, I just love taking a Mackay's money."

Zoey pulled a wad of bills from her snug jeans, slapped them into his palm, and bared her teeth at him in feminine irritation.

"I can help you, sugar." The rider smiled playfully at the look. "For the right price."

"Keep dreaming, Billy Ray," she suggested with a little glare. "Your dreams are the only place where you'll touch my bike. Or anything else of mine."

It was said with grumpy humor, though. She was pissed at the bike, not the winner.

Billy laughed at the response. "Taking your money's good too, girl. Give me a call, though if you want some help. I think Eli's a little too spooked to give his best to it."

Striding away, Billy Ray moved back to his own bike, where several other men stood waiting.

Propping her hands on her slender hips, Zoey lowered her head and shook it in an air of resigned frustration before turning and facing Eli as he moved to her hesitantly. Doogan could have told Eli he gave himself away with the very attitude he was displaying.

"Eli, you and I are going to talk," she informed him, knowledge and barely hidden anger resounding in the low tone of her voice. "A very serious, perhaps painful talk."

"You're blaming me?" Eli's expression was surprised; his gaze hardly made it, though. His eyes couldn't lie with his face quite yet.

"Oh, Eli, I'm doing more than blaming you," she informed him with narrowed eyes and tightened features. "I'm going to kick your ass."

"Come on, Zoey, it's not my fault you can't beat Billy," Eli protested without the fire he needed to convince her of his innocence.

The young agent was almost amusing. Doogan barely managed to hold back his grin as he watched and listened to the confrontation. Eli wasn't convincing Zoey of anything because where it counted, he was actually scared of her.

He was more scared of her than he was of Doogan. Because he could actually lie to Doogan and make it convincing. That was faintly insulting, Doogan decided.

"Oh, Eli, you did not just blame me for losing that race." One hand went to her hip; the other clenched the strap of her helmet as though actually considering using it on the young man's head. "I know you're not that damned stupid."

Doogan himself would have already at least threatened to use the helmet on the young agent. Just because Eli was so damned scared of her. He deserved to have his ass kicked for letting such a tiny thing scare him like that.

"Well, I wasn't the one who lost it," he assured her, frowning down at her. "Come on, Zoey. It's not my fault."

She glared back at him. "I am not talking to you, Eli. Talking to you just pisses me off, so if I were you, I'd run."

"Zoey . . ."

"And run fast." Her voice lowered as he stepped back and actually turned and stomped off.

Now that was funny.

Doogan couldn't help a chuckle this time as he watched Eli get as far as the middle of the crowd gathered around Billy before he stopped and turned back to watch Zoey.

That was when Eli caught sight of him.

Doogan let his gaze meet the agent's and watched Eli's eyes widen in surprise.

"I could help you with that motor," Doogan offered as Zoey made to pass him, her head down, lips thinned angrily.

That brought her to a stop.

For a second, surprise and feminine hunger flashed in her gaze before it stilled beneath a sudden shadow of fear.

"Now, doesn't that offer just sound a little too good to be true?" she drawled, not bothering to hide that Mackay suspicion and mockery that ran deep and wide. "Why would you want to help me, Mr. Chatham Bromleah Doogan the Third? You might actually get grease on your royal hands. That would suck now, wouldn't it?"

He lifted a brow slowly. Well, he hadn't expected an open-arms greeting, but he hadn't expected such a confrontational attitude either.

"Do I have Eli to thank for this reception?" He nodded to Eli as the other man strode toward them, his eyes narrowed, disapproval lining his face. "I thought we were getting along rather good the last day we saw each other."

Eli was just determined to make sure the Mackay blanket of protection remained fully in place around the youngest sister, it seemed, despite the secrets he held where the past year was concerned.

Loyalty, he thought. Eli's loyalty had shifted far too much in the direction of the Mackays.

It seemed all four agents he'd sent to Somerset had switched loyalties from Doogan to the Mackay clan. Now didn't that just figure? And why hadn't he expected it? He should have.

"Zoey, you're going to end up locked in a damned convent for your own safety," Eli hissed at her, concern gleaming in his gaze. "You don't understand. Dawg finds out about this and there will be no way in hell he'll let it go. Especially if *he's* involved." He jerked a thumb in Doogan's direction.

Celadon-green eyes gave a mocking little roll, her expressive features settling into a warning expression. "Eli, I'm already not pleased with you right now," she warned him. "And I'm well able to decide who I let into my little circle of friends and who I don't."

"He's no woman's friend," Eli seemed to be reminding her.

Doogan had suspected the younger man had done all he could to douse the sexual response Zoey had shown on the plane two weeks before.

"Boy, you're pushing it," Doogan stated, icy anger overshadowing the fondness he actually felt for the younger man.

"She's going to get herself killed," Eli retorted, frustration creasing his face before he glared back at Doogan. "What do you want? What are you doing here?" His gaze flicked over Doogan in disgust. "And since when did you start dressing down?"

Doogan arched his brow and just stared back at Eli for long, silent seconds, the warning clear in his eyes. The kid was pushing his luck. Mackays might have his loyalty, but he was still an agent of Homeland Security and therefore under Doogan's command. And he was still family. Sort of.

"This is messed up," the younger man muttered, no doubt in response to the fact that he knew Doogan well enough to guess how deep his interest in Zoey extended. And Eli should damned well be aware of the fact that the need for additional protection was now imperative.

"Possibly," Doogan agreed, never taking his eyes off Eli.

Eli breathed out in resignation. "What? What do you need?"

He might remember who ultimately held his job in his hands, but the kid was doing so with a decided lack of respect. He was going to have to take care of that, Doogan reminded himself.

"I want you to assure Ms. Mackay I'm fully capable of helping her with her bike," he asked, pleasantly he was certain. "She's hesitant to believe I am."

Eli's eyes widened, sheer terror seeming to flicker for just a second before he rubbed at the back of his neck, a grimace pulling at his lips.

"Elijah," Doogan prompted warningly.

"He knows what he's doing," Eli agreed, turning to Zoey suddenly. "He's guaranteed to make every male in your family ready to lock you up, though, if they find out you're having anything to do with him at all. Walk away, Zoey."

She actually laughed at Eli and when her gaze returned, Doogan made damned sure the look she saw on his face reminded her of that kiss in the plane, and the hunger that burned between them.

And she remembered. The light flush on her face, the way her eyes seemed to darken just a little at the edges assured him that she did.

"Zoey, you promised to stay away from him," Eli groaned, resignation and exasperation mixing in his tone.

"Eli," Doogan murmured warningly, "keep it up and I'll shoot you myself."

It was enough to make him wish he'd never sent Eli to Somerset to begin with, no matter how much Grant Brock had needed him at the time.

"Don't threaten Eli now," Zoey chastised him sweetly. "I get to hurt him first. He seems to forget which Mackay he promised to be loyal to first."

Doogan arched his brow at her with mocking amusement before turning back to Eli. "Why don't I give you more power and less excuses, then? Unlike Eli, Dawg and his cousins don't scare me in the least."

"Shows how smart you're not," Eli muttered before glancing warily at Zoey.

The young agent rubbed at the back of his neck again, his need to further warn Zoey clear in his expression.

"Stop making your neck raw, Eli." She rolled her eyes again, obviously reading the look.

"You have a truck? I have to get the bike back to the warehouse." She turned to Eli, pointing her finger back at him demandingly. "Keep your mouth shut, Eli. Squeal, and I'll make bacon out of your ass, you got me?"

He actually looked worried, Doogan thought. Was it the threat, or the woman making it? He had a feeling it was Zoey causing all that concern.

"He doesn't have a truck . . ."

"It's parked on the other side of the trees," Doogan broke in before turning back to Eli. "Get her bike, Eli, and follow us." Without waiting for an answer, he lifted a brow at Zoey. "Need a ride?"

"If you don't mind," she answered with a pleased little smile. "And I look forward to seeing how good you are. With my bike." Impish, teasing, that smile did something to him. Something he didn't want to think about or look too closely into.

"You could be biting off more than you can chew," he warned her. "With the bike as well."

Her brow lifted with graceful doubt for a moment.

"Come on, show me your truck." She was laughing at him again. "We'll get my baby loaded and get her home. Maybe next month Billy Ray will be paying me."

Oh, that was a given, Doogan thought without a doubt in his mind. If Eli thought he knew electronics, motors, or cycles, then he had nothing on Doogan.

"You can count on it," he promised her. "Bet on it."

Leading the way from the illegal racing track, Doogan pushed back that odd surge of emotion he felt, when emotion was something he rarely felt. Instead he let the satisfaction he felt free instead.

Who could have guessed that Zoey would have been so easy to connect with again? Adrenaline junkie? It was more than apparent the youngest Mackay sister was still chasing the only edge of adventure she could find outside her brother's and cousins' circle of control.

Following her to the parking area, just far enough behind her to glance at the rounded curves of her ass, encased in snug jeans, her legs surrounded by riding chaps, he wondered how wild she could get.

"Dawg Mackay will neuter your ass," Eli hissed, pushing the bike as he came beside Doogan. "He will cut your balls off with a dull knife and you know he will. This is not a good idea."

Eli was far too frightened of Dawg Mackay and his cousins. Personally, Doogan believed the younger man should be more frightened of Zoey. He would be, he thought in amusement, if Eli wasn't lying about the proficiency she was attainting in the martial arts as well as the street fighting lessons he was giving her.

"You're so melodramatic, Eli," he drawled, rather than advising the agent of the error of his ways.

The boy definitely had a problem, Doogan thought, casting him a dubious look. Eli had been pissed ever since he'd stepped into the plane to see Zoey in Doogan's arms.

It wasn't jealousy, though. Doogan could have faced the jealousy and dealt with it. What Eli was trying to protect her from was a danger that seemed to be following Doogan as well. One Doogan was beginning to believe was behind the events a year ago that still threatened to destroy her.

"Don't worry, Eli," Zoey assured him, her voice light, easy as she threw Doogan a sultry look. "I promise I won't let Dawg neuter him. I imagine Doogan just wouldn't be his charming self without his balls."

It was her tone of voice. There was something about it that had him wondering if he should be wearing a cup of some sort. Perhaps one made of titanium?

"That is, if she doesn't do it first," Eli said just loud enough for Doogan to catch. "By accident even. She's dangerous. You don't know . . ."

Sliding Eli a questioning look, he wondered at that particular comment.

Eli was well aware of the importance of keeping Zoey from facing the punishment of a crime she hadn't committed. Just as he knew why it was so important to allow Harley Perdue to remain hidden and the suspicion of his death to remain intact. The prey Harley was hunting was back in town, according to the message Doogan had received, his attention once again focused on Zoey. The stakes had risen though, and the threat of arrest was in the very near future if Doogan didn't find a way to stop it, quickly.

John David had made certain he'd aided the Mackays' little plot to tie Doogan's agents up with the oldest sisters, but he'd known Zoey would never give in to the only agent Doogan had left in town. Even Doogan knew Eli was still far too young to be able to handle that little spitfire.

Eli knew it as well.

Just as they all knew that Eli wasn't the reason someone was conspiring to destroy her. Take out Zoey, and the ties between the Mackays and Homeland Security were destroyed. Especially if the agent looking into Harley's disappearance had his way.

"He doesn't know what he's talking about." It was all Zoey could do to hold back her laughter as she defended herself against Eli, having obviously heard him. "I promise, if I neuter you, it wouldn't be by accident."

Despite the laughter and her genuine amusement, Doogan was perceptive enough to see the fear Zoey was pushing back, though.

"Well, that's comforting." That fear wasn't going to stand in the way of his having her, Doogan had already decided that. He'd thought about nothing else, hungered for no one else, since that first taste of her. "Let's do our best to ensure it doesn't happen, either by accident or by design. I wouldn't be pleased."

Zoey's gaze flicked back to him, shadowed and undecided.

"I don't believe I'd be pleased either," she finally murmured, definitely too low for Eli to hear as they neared the powerful black king cab four-wheel-drive pickup Doogan had elected to use while he was in Somerset this time.

It was the perfect vehicle for the job he was there to see to. And perfect for her needs. As he'd learned before nearing the starting line, she had to rely on friends to slip her motorcycle from the garage on the lower floor of the converted warehouse she lived in to the races. Eli was most often elected, always late, and always complaining about the chances of getting caught by her brother, her cousins, or their friends.

Doogan had no intention of complaining.

"Load it up, Eli," he ordered the younger man before escorting Zoey to the passenger-side front seat.

Eli's muttered complaints were ignored as Doogan opened the door, gripped her waist, and lifted her effortlessly into the roomy front seat.

She was watching him closely, the smile gone, her unusual pale green eyes probing, intent.

"He isn't happy with you," she informed him, her hands sliding from his shoulders. "Or with me. He could end up blabbing to Graham."

It wouldn't matter; Graham would come to Doogan before he went to a Mackay, and Doogan knew it.

"I can kick his ass far more effectively than Graham can," Doogan assured her, wondering at the lingering suspicion in her eyes. "And he knows I'll do it if he blabs."

At least, Eli better know it.

Closing the door, he strode to the back of the truck, where Eli was strapping the cycle down, still muttering to himself about bosses, guns, and a new career.

Doogan stood silently listening, watching, until Eli finally turned to him with a dark frown.

"I could make certain that finding a new job becomes very difficult," he told the younger man. "I could actually make it impossible, Eli. And before you open your mouth to Graham, or to our fathers, you should check your e-mail and your new mission parameters from none other than Director Bryce himself. Don't force me to have you called in for refusing to obey direct orders."

"And let me guess." Eli glared at him. "One of those parameters is that Graham isn't to know about your sudden association with Zoey? Right?"

"Pretty much. At least until I inform him of it myself," Doogan agreed. "Do you have a problem with your orders, Agent Grant?"

Securing the last strap on the cycle, Eli jumped to the ground and slammed the tailgate closed before turning to Doogan again.

"I obey orders," he reminded Doogan. "Whether I like them or not. Don't worry, I won't tell anyone. That doesn't mean they won't find out."

"Then let's put it this way," Doogan stated softly. "If anyone finds out, by any means, I'll hold you directly responsible. What do you think about that?"

"That you suck." Eli's glare deepened. "You suck really bad."

"And it's going to suck even worse for you if anyone so much as realizes I'm in town before I inform them," Doogan promised him. "So you better figure out how to make certain that secret, along with Zoey's, remains carefully protected, Eli. Very well protected."

Eli glanced away for a moment. When his gaze returned it

was filled with grief and painful concern for the young woman he knew had become a target. "You'll get her killed. You know that being with her will only make the danger worse. They'll kill her just like they killed your family."

His family.

A faithless wife, a jealous brother, and the beautiful, innocent daughter Doogan would have given his own life to protect. The sister and niece Eli still grieved for and still blamed Doogan for the loss of.

"They can try," he snarled furiously. "But this time, I fucking know they're here, don't I? I know their target and I know how they work." Fury burned through him, the flames of rage nearly overwhelming him before he found his control and reined them back ruthlessly. "Now you can help me, Eli, or stand the fuck back and keep your mouth shut. But don't get in my way. Do that, and you'll be as much an enemy to me as they are."

With that, Doogan moved to the front of the truck, stepped into the driver's seat, and glanced at Zoey's knowing expression.

"Finished threatening Eli?" She shifted in her seat to watch him directly. "Shame on you."

He merely grunted at the amused chastisement. "He'll survive it. Maybe," he promised her, putting the vehicle in drive and heading for the gravel road that led to the clearing. "If he doesn't know how to keep his mouth shut by now, then he needs to learn."

Eli would definitely survive his threats. If he didn't follow his orders, though, he might not survive Doogan's foot up his ass. Or Director Bryce's anger. Zoey Mackay had become the boss's new pet project and if Eli or Graham interfered, then there would be more hell to pay than either Graham or Eli might survive.

FOUR

She was crazy.

Insane.

She'd lost her ever-lovin' mind, just as Eli had accused her as they rode home from the airfield two weeks ago.

Doogan was the biggest threat to her life, Eli had reminded her somberly. If Doogan learned Zoey was having nightmares about having murdered Harley, and he couldn't find Harley Perdue, then he could arrest her. And if he did, all favor the Mackays had found with Homeland Security would go to hell. It would become a war. One her brother and cousins couldn't hope to win, and she'd end up in prison.

Eli had watched her like a hawk for the past two weeks as well, as though expecting her to sneak out to meet his nemesis. It was amusing at times, exasperating at others. And the nightmares were becoming worse and more frequent. She wasn't getting enough sleep and her temper was getting testy. And she couldn't stop thinking about that damned kiss.

"Why are you in Somerset?" she asked as he pulled the truck into the back garage and came to a stop next to the motorcycles parked there.

She stared straight ahead into the darkened garage, uncertain if she even wanted to know why he was there.

"Does it matter why?"

She could feel his gaze on her, stroking over her profile, urging her to look at him.

"I don't know if it matters or not," she finally breathed out, rubbing at her arms, telling herself it didn't matter why he was there.

"I don't like what you're doing to me, Zoey," he said then, his voice dark, deep, the surprising statement pulling her gaze to him despite her best intentions not to face him.

He didn't like what she was doing to him? At least he had a wealth of experience in understanding how to deal with the hunger. She had no idea how to deal with it. Or how to deny it.

"What am I doing?" She'd stayed away from him. She'd even stayed away from Graham and Lyrica's when she'd learned he was there the week before. "How the hell am I bothering you?"

"Like this." There was no warning. One second she was glaring at him, the next he'd wrapped his fingers around her braid and pulled her head back, and his lips were devouring hers.

It wasn't an easy kiss. It sure as hell wasn't an exploratory one. It was wet and wild, filled with carnality and driving lust. It was his hunger pulling hers free despite her best attempts to push it back. His tongue pumped between her lips, stroked over hers, and with his free arm he dragged her closer to him.

Zoey had no intention of fighting him. For the first time in far too long it wasn't memories of nightmares or fears haunting her—it was reality. For the second time in her life all her senses were captured, engaged, reaching for the promise of even more pleasure than just this kiss.

"That's what you've done to me." He breathed heavily, his lips lifting from hers just enough to whisper the words over them with a savage growl. "Because I can't get the taste of you out of my head and it's driving me crazy."

It was driving her crazy. It was invading even her nightmares. His voice, his hunger touching her, reaching out to her to drag her from the horror of murder and death and into a fantasy of pure, raw pleasure.

He tasted her lips again, sipping at them, parting them with his tongue to fill her mouth and fill her senses with the possession.

"Fuck."

Before she'd had enough of the tempestuous pleasure, he pulled back from her, his hands rubbing over his face before they wrapped around the steering wheel and clenched it tight.

"Invite me up, Zoey," he growled as she fought to catch her breath. "Invite me into your bed."

"Doogan . . ."

"I'm not some kid who enjoys coming in his jeans," he bit out. "I'll give you all the foreplay you want, but by God, I won't walk away hurting afterward. I'll be inside you, and we'll both be dying from the pleasure."

"It's not that simple." She couldn't think, couldn't come up with an acceptable reason why she shouldn't invite him up.

"It's that damned simple," he insisted harshly.

"For you, maybe," she exclaimed, breathing in roughly. "It's not that easy for me. I can't afford to have you in my life."

"What the hell do you mean by that?" The edge of impatience

in his tone was almost amusing. "How will having me in your life cost you anything?"

"What do I mean by that? You don't want anything but a few nights of sex, Doogan. That's just a little less than what I imagined my first lover would give me. Leaving is the best thing you could do for both of us. Because you'll only hurt me, and I'll never forgive you for it." She didn't wait for a response.

It wasn't just his lack of commitment that would end up hurting her. It would be the actions he took if he was there to witness one of those damned nightmares.

Pushing from the truck, she slammed the door closed and rushed to the metal stairs leading to her apartment. Reaching the door into the second floor, she heard the truck start and a sob tore from her chest. Slamming the door behind her, she blinked back her tears, but there was no blinking back the hurt and aching need rushing through her body.

Two weeks. She'd spent two weeks trying to forget his kiss, and all she'd done was wonder how much better it could be. What his touch would be like, how his lips would feel at her nipples, between her thighs.

She needed him.

She'd just opened her bedroom door at the other end of the apartment when the door behind her slammed again. Twirling around, eyes widening, she watched as Doogan stalked up the dimly lit hall, his expression drawn and intent, lust gleaming in his dark eyes, filling his expression.

She wasn't going to deny him now and she knew it.

She knew she couldn't fight him, though she knew she should. If Dawg ever found out about this he'd go insane. Doogan was the scourge as far as the Mackays were concerned. To be avoided at all costs.

Avoiding this wasn't happening.

He swept her against him, covering her lips with his, stealing any chance of a refusal. Stepping into her room, his tongue pushing past her lips as her bedroom door was slammed shut, the lock snicking into place.

It was crazy, it was insane. It would end up breaking her heart and possibly destroying her life. But if she could have just one night of pleasure rather than nightmares, just a few hours of memories to hold against the darkness, then she'd be okay. She would let him walk away and she promised herself she'd count her broken heart worth it.

Just one night.

"I tried to stay away from you," he groaned, his lips sliding from hers to her neck when she wrapped her arms around his neck and melted into him. "For both of us, Zoey, I tried to stay away."

And she'd promised Eli she'd stay away from Doogan. She'd meant to keep her word, but she'd known she couldn't. Not if Doogan touched her again.

"Take that fuckin' braid out of your hair," he ordered, his voice hard, his lips wreaking havoc with her senses as he bent to her, his lips moving over her collarbone. "Do it, baby. Take it down. Let me see all those wild curls."

Her arms lifted to her hair. Pulling the tie free of the leather ponytail grip, she let it fall to the floor. As she struggled to hold on to her senses enough to do as he ordered, her fingers fumbled, tangled several times in the curls springing free of restraint, but finally managed to release them.

She was lifting her fingers free of her hair when Doogan caught the hem of her shirt and whisked it up, clearing her head and arms before she could do more than gasp.

"God, save me," he muttered, catching her wrists before she

could lower them, securing them in one hand and holding them over her head. "Look how sweet. I've dreamed of tasting those hard little nipples."

Zoey jerked against him, a surge of striking, exquisite pleasure erupting in the pit of her stomach and sending sensation to rush to her already swollen clit and slick sex.

With his free hand he released the front clip of her bra. As he brushed the lace cups aside, a rumbling groan left his throat, the sound stealing her breath and her strength.

Releasing her wrists, he brushed the straps of the bra from her shoulders and down her arms, leaving her naked from her hips up.

"If you're going to throw me out, do it now," he demanded. "Because I don't know if I'll be able to stop later."

He didn't wait to let her think about it either. He eased her back the several steps needed before the bed pressed to the backs of her legs.

"Lie down for me, Zoey," he urged her, his voice rougher, harder now. "Let's get these boots off you."

Zoey swallowed, a tight, nervous movement. Sitting down slowly, she let him ease her back until she was reclining on the bed. Staring up at him, in the dim light from the lamp she kept turned on across the room, she watched his shadowed features, watched the hunger growing in his gaze as he began releasing the buttons of his shirt.

"Touch your breasts for me." The shocking demand had her eyes widening. "Come on, Zoey. I can see all that wild hunger inside you, dying to be free. Let me show you how to release it. Let me show you how to be wild for both of us. Our own little adventure."

Their own adventure. And she did so love adventures.

Zoey licked her dry lips, her hands moving, cupping her breasts as he finished unbuttoning his shirt. The first touch of her fingers against the swollen flesh brought a smothered cry from her lips. It had never felt like that before. Her own touch had never brought such a rush of instant pleasure as it did while he watched her.

"See how much better it is." His voice was low, grating as he removed his shirt. "Hotter, the pleasure stronger when you share it."

It was. So much stronger, her senses becoming dazed with the rush of sensations building inside her now.

"What do you like?" Satisfaction filled his gaze, his expression. "Show me how you touch yourself when you think of me, Zoey. Let me see how you pleasure those pretty breasts. Do you touch your nipples easy? Or do you tighten your fingers on them to find that edge of pleasure and pain?" Sitting on the chair next to her bed, he dragged his boots free of his feet. "I bet you like the edge. I bet you love that little bit of fire streaking through the pleasure."

She gripped her nipples, working them firmly, a helpless, mewling little moan spilling unbidden from her lips. She didn't know if she could stand it. Sensations tore through her senses now, striking through her body, wrapping around the swollen bud between her thighs and clenching the untouched depths of her sex.

Rising from the chair, Doogan moved to her, bent, and unzipped her boots before pulling them from her feet. When he straightened, his hands settled on her denim-covered knees and stroked slowly, so slowly, from her knees to her thighs, his thumbs meeting at the apex and pressing firmly against the aching, engorged little kernel of her clit.

"Doogan." As she arched sharply, her fingers tightened on her nipples, the rush of searing sensation washing through her senses and drowning them with pleasure.

"Oh, Zoey," he breathed out, his lips lowering to her stomach, his tongue licking over her flesh. "It's going to be so damned good."

So damned good.

The metal tab and zipper of her jeans were released, the denim drawn down her thighs slowly before Doogan slid them completely off her legs, leaving her clad only in the white lacy panties she wore beneath them.

His gaze centered there.

"Hell," he breathed out, his voice rough, his fingers catching the elastic band and removing them as well, leaving her naked to his gaze.

His fingers feathered over the bare flesh above her clit, his gaze darker, gleaming with such hunger her breath caught at the sight of it.

"How sweet," he whispered, his gaze lifting to hers. "Do you know how much better it's going to be with your flesh bare and unprotected against my touch, Zoey?" His lips quirked into a smile of satisfaction. "So fucking good you'll scream with it."

She couldn't stand the excitement much longer.

The heated spill of slick moisture between her thighs, sensation tightening at her clit, torturous in the need filling it, drew a dazed moan from her lips.

When he caught her wrists and slowly drew her hands back from her breasts, a shock of painful need clenched at her womb, arching her hips.

One night, she reminded herself. She could have him. He'd be her first, and he'd hold her heart forever. But Zoey knew she couldn't have more. Not yet. Not until she knew the truth of her nightmares.

But she could have tonight.

She could be daring, adventurous. She could have the fantasies, the pleasure, and the lover she chose the moment she saw him.

She could have Doogan.

Doogan was watching her eyes when he saw the explosion of color in them. The pale, pale green became surrounded by a ring of emerald fire, glowing like cats' eyes as her expression became suffused with such sensual, feminine hunger that the sight of it had his cock pounding with the rush of lust shooting to his balls.

Hell, had he ever been so damned hot for a woman? A virgin at that. He'd never taken a virgin, never been the first to experience a woman's pleasure. For a reason. He had no future to give them, he had no right to that first taste of them.

Until Zoey.

The very thought of another man claiming her innocence made him crazy. The tormenting knowledge that another man could bring her to orgasm, could feel her snug pussy gripping, milking his flesh as she came for him, enraged him.

He had nightmares of another man mounting her delicate little body and taking her. Dreams that brought him from sleep, so furious he could barely stand himself for hours afterward, tormented him.

He couldn't sleep for the thought of it; he could barely work for it. She had become an obsession in the past year, one he had to exorcise. One he'd have to burn out of his system before he could go on with his life.

When she straightened, sitting proudly before him as he placed his knee on the bed to lower himself to her, Doogan stilled. The wild hunger that filled her expression held him spellbound, still and silent as he waited to see what she intended to do.

She didn't make him wait long.

"Damn, Zoey." His teeth snapped together as her lips pressed to his abdomen, parted, and let her teeth scrape over the taut muscles. Her fingers were slowly releasing the leather belt circling his hips as her hot little tongue met his navel, causing his hands to jerk to her hair and clench in the lush curls with a desperate grip.

What the hell was in her mind?

"Zoey, don't . . ." God, she was so young, she had no idea—

Sharp little teeth nipped at his flesh in retaliation.

Her expression was determined, and so free of artifice. Lush, spiraling midnight curls surrounded her, flowing around her body like a living cape, giving her a preternatural appearance that had a dark dominance raging inside him.

Tightening his hand in her hair, Doogan drew her head back, tugging at the strands firmly.

The catch of her breath was a sound of shocked pleasure. The sound a woman makes at that first, conscious realization that the mix of pleasure and pain had the power to excite. Keeping that sharp pressure on her scalp, he stared down at her, trying to gauge the strength of the hunger he could see in her face.

"I could lay you back and make sweet love to your exquisite body for hours," he warned her, making certain she understood what she was about to do. "But you go this route, I won't be easy on you until you've finished me. Until you've taken every drop of my cum down that sweet throat. Do you understand me?"

"Did I ask you to go easy on me?" she breathed out, shocking him, her breathy voice racking his senses with need. "It's my adventure too, isn't it?"

Their adventure, and yes, it was hers too. If this was what she wanted, then he'd give it to her. And he'd love every damned second he was filling her mouth.

In seconds he had his belt loose, pants undone and tossed to the floor.

Wrapping his fingers around the heavy stalk of his engorged penis, he reached out, flipping the light on next to her bed and stared down at her.

He nearly came at the first clear sight of hungry innocence in her face.

He had no business with her, like this, and Doogan knew it.

Not with this act, where instinct warned him he couldn't go easy on her.

"You asked for this, Zoey," he reminded her, his entire body clenching as she licked her lips in anticipation. "If you want to stop, I'll stop, at any time. But I won't go easy while you have your mouth wrapped around my dick."

Witchy eyes narrowed, the light green gleaming with challenge.

"Did I ask you to go easy?" she whispered breathlessly. "I could have sworn I didn't. All I'm asking for is tonight. This one adventure."

He moved to the bed, settling against the pillows, half sitting, half reclining on the bed. He waited then. Watching her closely. She would initiate this; he wouldn't.

A siren's smile curled her pouty lips. Sultry innocence, impish temptation filled her eyes, and a second later she moved between his thighs, kneeling before him.

He was almost holding his breath, anticipation burning through him.

The fingers of one hand threaded through her hair again, tightened in the strands, his breathing becoming harsh as her lashes fluttered at the little sting he created at her scalp.

"Slow and easy," he ordered, the sound of his voice, deep and guttural, warning him of the line he was crossing. "Make it real good, baby."

"Or what?" she whispered, the slumberous arousal and tempting hunger in her gaze making him crazy for her mouth.

"Or I won't show you just how thin that line between pleasure and pain can get."

Excitement flared in her gaze. Holding the shaft with one hand, Doogan pulled her head down to meet the broad, mushroomed crest slowly.

His self-control had never been so shaky and he knew it, even before he felt the touch of her shy, inquisitive little tongue licking over the thick crown.

"Ahh hell, Zoey." His head fell back against the headboard, his hips jerking toward her, desperate to fill her mouth with his hard flesh.

How long he could maintain his control enough to allow her innocence to accustom itself to such an intimate act he didn't know. Not for long was for damned sure. Because he had to watch.

Watch the innocence merge with the sensual, erotic thrill and dawning knowledge of exactly how good it could get. Whether she was doing him, or he was doing her, how fucking good it could be.

Instinct assured him Zoey was far more innocent than even her virginity implied, though. For all her bravado, her sweet mouth was as much virgin territory to a man's cock as her pussy, and he knew it, sensed it.

"That's it, baby," he encouraged as her hand brushed his away to grip the base herself, her tongue licking, loving the throbbing head.

The wide, thick crest pulsed a bead of pre-cum, the droplet

quickly caught by her eager little tongue as it swiped over the dark, sensitive crest.

Ropy veins pounded with blood; pleasure throbbed through the heavy shaft, swelling it further, harder. Delicate fingers had no hope of meeting as they caressed the iron-hard stalk, her tongue licking, playing. And he wanted nothing more than to watch, to feel those pouty lips stretching, reddening as the thick flesh pierced them.

"Look at me, witch. Open your eyes, let me see your pleasure," he groaned as she tongued the sensitive undercrest with delicious little licks, fraying his already thin control. "Let me see your pretty eyes."

Thick, long lashes lifted. Her pale green eyes, now ringed with the brilliant darker green at the outside of the iris, nearly did him in. Before he could cover her fingers with his own, showing her where to apply pressure to hold back his release, a pulse of semen spilled from the slit topping the crown to meet the heat of her tongue.

She stiffened; a breath later her mouth enclosed the throbbing crown with the sweetest, hottest pleasure he knew he'd ever experienced in his life. Just watching it, watching his brutally hard flesh stretch her lips, feeling her hot mouth close on him, was almost too much for his control.

As long as he'd been sexual, as many experienced women as had worked his dick over, he'd never felt such a blinding source of complete, white-hot sensation.

Her mouth moved over the throbbing head, her tongue tucking at that too-sensitive spot at the undercrest naturally, and she began to suck. Moving her lips over him, advance and retreat, the ring of emerald deepening at the outside of pale green.

"Fuckin' witch," he groaned, a hint of his Irish heritage slipping into his voice, his hands tightening in her hair, hips lifting to her, pushing the hard flesh deeper as he forced her fingers to apply the pressure needed to hold back the cum building in his balls. "That's it, fuck me with those pretty lips, witch."

The emerald ring brightened, the color like a thin ring of jewels, and she struggled for a second with the width of his flesh.

"Ah fuck . . . Zoey." Her fingers played at the base of his shaft, the pressure easing, increasing as hunger began overtaking innocence, and she followed his lead, learning far too quickly how to make him crazy with her mouth.

Her lips and tongue were destroying him.

Tugging at her hair, giving her that little sting, he was rewarded by her mouth sinking lower, taking him deeper.

The sound of a low moan easing from her throat was almost a vibration at the crest. His balls tightened at the thought of taking her deeper, of piercing the tight confines of her throat, of teaching her how to give him a pleasure no other woman had ever been able to push past the lessons of previous lovers to learn.

He was the first to own her mouth. She had no preconceived blocks, no memories of overeager lovers trying to take too much too soon.

His balls tightened at the thought, drawn so close to the base of his shaft that it was torture.

And he had to hold back. Ah hell, nothing mattered but holding back and watching her eyes as he taught her how to destroy him with her hot little mouth.

As he tugged at her hair again, her mouth slipped lower again. He was desperate now, as talons of excessive carnal need dug into his testicles with a merciless grip.

With his free hand he found the curve of a breast, his fingers gripping the hard point of her nipple. Watching her eyes, seeing the growing excitement as she realized where he was headed, Doogan held her mouth in place and pressed his cock further over her tongue.

"Deeper," he demanded, finding her nipple with his thumb and forefinger and exerting the lightest pressure.

The needy moan that slipped from her was all he needed.

Pulling back, watching her lips surround him, reddened and filled with his flesh, only deepened the hunger for more. To take more. To teach her the ultimate pleasure a woman could give a man with her mouth.

Pushing back inside, slow, feeling her mouth tighten, her tongue rubbing along the undercrest, dragged a groan from his chest.

"Take me deeper, baby. Can you do it, Zoey? Can you open that sweet throat enough to give me just a taste of it?" he dared her as her mouth tightened around the fiercely engorged crown. "Give me your throat, you little hellion. Swallow on my cock."

He gave her the pressure she needed on her tight little nipple, rolling it in a heated grip, releasing it, tightening as he watched her eyes grow dazed.

Her lips eased further past the blunt width filling her mouth, slowly, taking him by increments as she felt her way through the act.

"Breathe in through your nose, deep." It was all he could do to speak as she breathed in and he thrust deeper.

The heavy width of his cock head slipped to the entrance of that ultratight spot.

"Now swallow," he groaned. "Damn me, baby, swallow on me," he groaned.

She swallowed on the pressure, moaned, and sent racking shudders of violent pleasure ripping up his spine.

"Ahh fuck." He pulled her head back, watching, holding her in place with the pressure on her hair, tugging, giving her a little burn as he let his fingers tighten on her nipple.

As he gave her the fire he thrust deep again, her mouth tightening, throat opening. She swallowed, moaned, that ring of color deepening around her iris, excitement blazing in her expression.

She was loving it. Moving on his cock, slow and easy, learning what she could take, what she couldn't. And she was taking far more of him than the oversensitized flesh could bear.

Ah hell. He couldn't take much more. His balls were so tight, so full of his cum he couldn't bear it. When he released, it was going to be like touching death. Could he survive it? Would he recover from a pleasure that deep?

A harsh groan tore from him when her lips slid down again, his cock pushing in deeper . . . oh fuck, that little bit deeper . . .

"I'm going to cum, Zoey." He had seconds. Only seconds. "And you're going to take it," he snarled, hips bunching, self-control disintegrating. "Every drop, Zoey. Oh God—every fucking drop . . ."

Her moan vibrated on him, the sound a rush of sharp, brutal pleasure.

He was dying.

He sank that little bit deeper. Just that little bit, enough that when she swallowed and moaned, he lost his senses. Lost all control.

"That's it. Fuck, Zoey. That's it. Take me." He pulled back, thrust past her lips, watched her eyes, and fucked straight to that hungry throat again. Again.

Doogan watched that color of her eyes glow, her long drawn-out little moan sinking into the head of his dick, and he lost it.

"All of it," he rasped, the brutal sensations racking his body before shattering with such brilliant pleasure it tore through his senses.

Flames danced over his balls when she released the pressure at the base of his shaft. Lightning ripped up his spine. His cum shot from the throbbing, engorged head and she swallowed.

"God, yes. Swallow on me, baby . . . ah hell . . ." Swallowing, her tight little throat clenching on the end of his cock head, rippling over it, pulling another brutal pulse of semen to her throat.

Fucking moaned . . .

"Ah hell. Ah, Zoey. Sweet, sweet fucking mouth," he rasped, pulse after pulse of his semen spilling to her, his release so deep, so deep, so fucking sweet—and she was shuddering, racking tremors racing over her, shocking him as her cry pulsed around his cock and had the next jetting explosion of cum shooting from him with a violence that dragged a groan of pure agonized pleasure from his lips.

He had never, at any time, had a woman find her release from excitement alone, her orgasm rippling through her from the act of giving him such pleasure. Never had a woman taken him with a natural desire to give rather than take, to pleasure him and to find her pleasure while doing it.

Until Zoey.

Until she destroyed him with her hot little mouth and he was afraid, branded his senses in ways he'd never be free of. In ways he'd have to force himself free of when his job in Somerset was finished.

When the last agonized pulse of semen spilled to her greedy mouth, Doogan drew her head back, watching as she straightened before him, dazed, existing on instinct alone. His jaw clenched when she slid her fingers down her belly, moving for the swollen bud between her thighs. To finish finding her pleasure. To ease the pressure no doubt racking her swollen little clit.

"Oh hell no." He caught her wrist, drawing it from her body.

"Doogan, I have to." She tried again. "It wasn't enough. I need . . ."

His fingers tightened on her wrist. "I could tie you to the bed if that's what it takes."

Heat flushed from her breasts to her hairline. Her eyes widened and pure, raw hunger spiked her dazed eyes.

"Oh, Zoey, baby," he whispered, his voice hoarse. "You have no idea how good it can get . . ."

FIVE

What was he doing to her, to himself?

He'd asked himself that question when he'd taken her mouth. He'd known what he was doing to her when he'd taught her how to pleasure him in such a way. He was marking her, marking her innocence, marking each pleasure she experienced, each touch she learned, as his.

He was branding her sexuality.

Just as he knew what he was doing to both of them as he did so.

He was marking them both. Marking her with his hunger, with a soul-deep ecstasy he knew he'd never found with another woman. Knew he'd never find again. And he was marking himself with her innocence, with watching the glazed pleasure building in her eyes.

Instead of obliterating the sensual innocence, though, each touch, each pleasure seemed to heighten it.

Staring at her now, spread-eagle before him, her wrists and ankles secured loosely to the bedposts, he wasn't surprised in the least to find his cock rock hard again. As though he hadn't cum with a violence that shattered him as he shot his seed down her throat. He was just as hard, just as desperate to spill into her again.

As he knelt between her thighs, his hands stroked over her, priming her, sensitizing every inch of flesh further before he began building the storm he could glimpse in her eyes. Regret nearly tore a groan from his chest, though.

God, walking away from her wouldn't be easy and he knew it. Having her learn the truth would be even worse.

"Why are you teasing me like this, Doogan?" she whispered desperately, tugging at the bonds now, trying to increase the sensation of each light stroke against her body. "I'm dying."

She was so sensitive that even the lightest caress against her perspiration-damp skin drew a moan from her lips. The emerald ring around her iris was brighter, darker, mesmerizing if he wasn't careful.

"Doogan, please . . ." she demanded.

"Not yet. Soon," he promised, bending to brush his lips against hers as she panted for breath. "Trust me, Zoey. Let me give you this. You trusted me enough to tie you to your bed; trust me to know how to touch you, to give you the ultimate sensations and pleasure."

She moaned, her eyes still dazed, the arousal riding so high inside her that even her smooth, silken belly was flushed with it.

"Will I have a mind left when you're finished?" She stretched beneath him again, trying to arch against his touch as it trailed down her side.

"You will, but I doubt I will," he admitted, loving the feel of her sleek, lightly tanned flesh.

Trailing his fingers to her breasts once more, he leaned closer, caught his weight on one elbow, and cupped a swollen breast, his thumb brushing over the violently sensitive peak of her nipple.

"A woman can orgasm from only having her nipples stimulated," he told her, blowing a breath over the tight peak and watching the reddened color deepen at the brush of air. "Your nipples are so sensitive, so eager for pleasure. I bet I can give you another of those hot little orgasms by doing nothing more than sucking these hard little nipples."

Her pupils dilated, her body jerking with a rush of sensation that he knew would be peaking in her womb.

"Shall we find out?" Lowering his head the last inch needed, he lashed his tongue against the pebble-hard tip, her low, strangled moan his reward.

She was so sweetly responsive. The arch of her body, her broken moans, the way she loved every touch he gave her. It made him want to push her higher, give her more.

"It's good, isn't it, baby?" he whispered before letting his teeth rake over her hard nipple.

A cry tore from her, her body shuddering against him.

"It won't take you long, Zoey," he promised. "Once that little, lightning-quick pulse of release hits you, then I'm going to take my kisses to your pussy. It's going to be so wet, so wild by the time I get down there that you'll think you could cum so easy." The thought of it was killing him, making him ache for the taste of her wet flesh. "It won't be so easy, though. It's going to take so much more than you can imagine. That's when your body is so ready, so primed for that explosive edge of pleasure and pain that when I spank that pretty flesh you're going to beg me for more."

Her eyes widened. Before she could process the sensual threat, his lips surrounded her nipple, his teeth raked against it, and his entire body flinched at the sound of the little wail of deepening need that escaped her lips.

He'd end up killing them both with pleasure.

For damned sure, he was going to destroy them with the loss of it once it was over.

"Doogan, please . . ." Zoey panted, trying to arch beneath him, the feel of moist heat surrounding her nipple, drawing on the tender tip, heightening the brilliant arcs of sensation torturing her, nearly more than she could bear.

"It's so good," she sobbed, arching, writhing beneath the pressure. "More. Harder." She cried out her demand as his teeth nipped gently, and then his mouth drew on her more firmly.

He was killing her.

His lips moved from one nipple to the other, his mouth torturing one as his fingers applied a destructive pressure to the other. And it wasn't enough. She needed more.

More of the pleasure, more of those fiery lashes of intense sensation that made her clit more sensitive, made the moisture weep from her vagina.

"What do you need, baby?" he whispered against the throbbing peak, licking over it. "Tell me what you want, Zoey. What do your hard little nipples need?"

What did she need? Everything. So much more.

"More," she cried out desperately, shuddering, burning beneath him. "Please, Doogan. I need more."

His lips surrounded the peak again, drawing on it deep, his cheeks hollowing before the pressure released, his lips pulled back, and she watched his teeth catch the too-sensitive tip and worry it with nibbling bites that had fiery pleasure streaking through her entire body.

Why had she let him restrain her like this?

She needed to get closer to him. To touch him. To find a way to make him release the agonizing pressure building between her thighs. Her clit was so swollen, so sensitive she couldn't bear it. Moisture lay in a heavy, slick layer on the bare folds of her sex, sensitizing her further.

Racking shudders of sensations kept racing over her, clenching in her womb, driving her mad.

And he wasn't sucking her nipple hard enough.

The pressure was teasing, tormenting.

"Damn you, harder," she cried out, panting, barely able to breathe. "I need harder. You're killing me."

She was fracturing from the inside out with the desperate need for him, for more sensation, a higher level of pleasure. She could feel it, just out of reach, waiting for her, teasing her.

Until his teeth clenched around her nipple.

An involuntary wail tore from her lips, the fiery pleasure tearing through her and almost, just almost peaking.

"Doogan, yes," she cried out, trying to lift to him, to urge him to bear down harder. "More. Please, Doogan. Please."

She'd never known pleasure like this. Never experienced such deep, overwhelming waves of electric sensation that raced over her flesh like sizzling static. She twisted into each flash of it, writhing beneath the hungry draws of his lips, the feel of his teeth rasping, nibbling a sensitive tip as his fingers played with the other.

And no matter how much she begged, she couldn't find that sensation, that lash of deep, fiery pleasure-pain she knew would push her over the edge. Her fingers clenched, fisting, the shudders building through her as Doogan gave a heavy, hungry groan against her breast.

His teeth clenched on one tip; his fingers tightened on the other. Sensations lashed through the peaks like lightning tearing through her body and exploding with pleasure.

Another wail escaped her throat, racking pulses of ecstasy shuddering through her as that peak suddenly flamed around her, through her. Trembling, shaking beneath the racking tremors, she thought surely it would be enough.

But it wasn't enough. As the waves of searing pleasure eased, the growing pressure, the need built again. It tightened through her body, throbbed inside her vagina, and pulsed in a desperate ache at her clit. Shaking, trembling in such overwhelming need she thought it would surely destroy her, she sobbed in furious need.

Then he began licking, nipping his way down her body, burning a trail of sensual hunger to her thighs. She realized that despite the explosion of pleasure, the pressure building in her sex had only tightened. It throbbed in her clit, her vagina, to a tormenting level now, a fiery ache, such extreme pleasure, a roller coaster of sensations. She loved every one even as she fought to release the clawing desperation they built inside her.

Doogan gave a rough, pleased little chuckle as he nipped at her hip, his hands stroking her thighs, his body easing between them.

"I hate you," she cried out, staring down at him, trembling at the sight of the hunger in his eyes. "Untie me."

"Not on your sweet life, baby." His eyes were nearly black, his expression fierce with the sexual need raging inside him.

And dominant. There was a deepening, dark dominance tightening his features, turning them savage in their intensity.

Before she could make the demand to release her again, his

hand landed on the swollen folds of her sex, a quick little pat, amplified by the moisture lying thick and slick on her inner lips.

Zoey froze, the sensations that ripped through her body holding her mesmerized, eyes wide, her gaze locked with his.

"I'll untie you," he growled, his hand cupping her, his palm applying pressure to the swollen bud of her clit. "But if I do, I won't do this anymore."

His hand lifted, then landed again, the sharp, fiery pleasure surged through her, stealing her breath.

A hoarse, broken cry spilled from her, her hips arching, savage desperation rolling through her.

"Just a little more pleasure, baby," he promised. "Just a little higher. And then, when I push inside that tight little pussy you're going to cum for me at the first thrust. You'll tighten and ripple around my cock. You'll scream for me, and you won't stop coming until I've finished. Over and over, Zoey. So much pleasure we'll both die a little from it."

His hand landed again.

Her hips jerked upward as she sobbed, the sound strangled and harsh. Furious need burned through her. Sensation seared her. It traveled through her body, sending a rush of hungry demands zipping through her.

She would kill him if he pushed her so high she was unable to orgasm. If he did her as she had often found her own desires would do. Become so desperate, so aching that no matter how hard she tried she couldn't satisfy the hunger.

"Your clit's so swollen and tight." A waft of heated air blew over the painfully swollen bud, causing her to shudder at the caress. "And your pussy's so wet. So sweet and wet and so ready for me."

His tongue licked through the narrow slit. The slow, heated lick was a lash of pure ecstatic pleasure. Better than anything, the hunger for more clawing through her senses now. Her hips writhed. Bucking against the licking strokes that drove her into a storm so chaotic she wondered if she'd survive it.

"Damn, Zoey, your pussy's so sweet and hot," he groaned, the vibration of sound pulsing into her clit, making her crazy for more.

Doogan's forehead pressed against her thigh then, his breath harsh, his tortured moan filling the air around her.

"Just a little more," he snarled.

A second later his head lifted, his hand landing against the vulnerable folds again, then again, again.

"Doogan . . ." She screamed his name, each heavy caress sending such furious shudders of sensation racing through her that she wondered if she was losing her mind.

Fiery pleasure almost, oh God, just almost detonated inside her. She was dying. Crying. Begging him . . .

"Doogan, please." Her gaze locked with his, her breathing so hard, so harsh she could barely speak. "Please. Please fuck me now."

His expression was hard, his dark gaze filled with carnal hunger and desperate pleasure as he rose between her thighs. One hand wrapped around the heavy width of his cock, his fingers stroking the shaft once, twice, before he released the ties at her ankles with one tug of the cord restraining them.

"Bend your knees," he snapped, dragging a pillow from beside her head. "Lift for me."

Her hips lifted, anticipation shredding her senses as he pushed it beneath her, angling her hips upward, displaying her sex to his avid gaze and her shocked one.

"Watch," he snapped, coming to her and dragging her thighs

over his, his cock pressing against the clenched entrance he sought. "Watch, Zoey. Don't you close your eyes. Watch me take you."

Holding on to her thigh with one hand, he eased closer, the wide head parting her, pressing into her, stretching her with such flaming pleasure that Zoey felt the pressure expanding in her clit.

"First thrust," he snarled. "You're going to start coming, baby. You're going to die for a minute right here, my cock filling you, working deeper and deeper inside you. Let it have you, witch. No worries." His thighs bunched beneath hers. "No worries, give it to me . . ."

She watched.

He pulled back, the thick width of the crown gleaming with her juices, the heavy veins pulsing in the shaft. Pushing back, he hesitated at the entrance, a hard groan leaving his chest, and a second later, Zoey screamed.

He surged inside her. One hard, fast thrust and half the fierce, heavy width of his shaft was inside her and she was exploding. Her hips arched, dragging a snarl from him, another cry from her as she took the throbbing length deeper and the detonations exploded inside her with a violence that stole her breath.

She was coming for him, orgasming with such brutal pleasure that one explosion gave birth to another and released Doogan from whatever restraints held him back.

God, she was killing him.

Blinking the sweat from his eyes, Doogan stared at the point where his cock penetrated Zoey's once-virgin body. Fuck, she was so delicate, so fragile, and each jerk of her hips against his thick erection took him deeper, clenching her tighter around his cock and making her pussy slicker, hotter.

The fist-tight grip around his sensitive flesh milked him, each pulsing shudder of the pleasure detonating inside her pulling him deeper.

Dragging the agonized flesh back until only the crown parted the spasming flesh, he thrust inside her again, her scream of pleasure causing his teeth to clench, sending warning chills of release to race up his spine as her pussy locked on his cock with a tight, rippling grip that had his balls flexing in warning.

He wasn't going to last.

God, he didn't know if he'd last long enough to bury full length inside her before he began coming.

Pulling back again, he thrust harder, deeper inside her.

"Ah fuck. Zoey . . ." His hands clenched on her thighs as she jerked again, surging into the thrust, his shaft penetrating deeper inside the hot, fisted grip of her pussy.

Timing.

Fuck, he had to watch his timing. Had to keep the sensations that rocked her into each orgasm at their peak. It was timing.

Sweet Zoey. Ah hell, it was so good. So good he didn't know if he could hold on.

He pulled back, thrust deeper, harder.

"Ah hell, yes, baby. Cum again," he snarled.

He was almost there. Almost there. His hips jerked, slamming against her as she lifted to him.

A strangled scream of agonized pleasure came as her body tightened again, her hips lifting further, taking him, ah God, taking him to the hilt as he shafted her hard and deep. She tightened around him until moving was agony, such deep, furious pleasure it was killing him.

They were both at their limit. He could feel her peaking, feel that final, destructive release building inside her, waiting. Just waiting for him to move.

He came over her, one hand holding her hip, restraining her movements, holding her in place, and then he began moving. Hard, jackhammer strokes and such blinding rapture he thought he might have bitten her, but hell if he could be sure.

He was fucking her with a fury he'd never displayed before, rapture shattering his senses, drawing an agonized groan from his chest as he felt her lift, tighten, her breath still for precious seconds before she exploded with a sudden, all-consuming violence that jerked him into the storm with her.

Her pussy flexed, sucked at his dick, heated and spasmed around it until control wasn't even a thought. It was just gone. His semen shot from his cock, spilling inside her, jetting inside her pussy and destroying him with the sudden, agonized knowledge that nothing had ever been so good in his life.

He'd never cum so hard, so fucking deep. Never felt his lover's flesh milking him with such deep, internal shudders that she marked him as he knew he was marking Zoey.

And through each blinding pulse of release he was pumping his cock inside her, small, slamming thrusts that amplified each agonized pulse of his release, each gripping, milking flex of her pussy.

When the final, bone-jarring shudder shot through him, stole the last of his energy and whatever ability he had to function, he simply stilled. It was all he could do to breathe. Beneath him, Zoey had become boneless, pliant, long seconds before him, though he could still feel the little tremors that occasionally rippled through her pussy and drew a groan from his lips as her still too-snug flesh fluttered around his cock.

He didn't want to move. Didn't want to ease from her. He wanted to stay right there, right where he was, just another heartbeat longer. He wanted to feel her wrapped around him for as long as possible. His cock buried inside her to the hilt, possessing her, feeling her like liquid silk wrapped so tight around his shaft like he'd never felt . . .

No condom.

He was bare inside her, he realized, his seed filling her, and he knew he'd shot inside her with such violent pulses there wasn't a chance his seed hadn't made its mark if by chance there was a flirty little egg waiting around.

Fuck.

How the hell had that happened?

He'd never fucked without a condom before. Never. It was a rule. Instinct. He'd had one tear once, the result was the marriage to a viper and the birth of the daughter that stole his heart. The child whose death had all but destroyed him. So what the hell had happened to instinct, to his determination to never chance another such loss, where this woman was concerned?

Dragging himself from her, his hoarse groan joining her weaker one as he pulled his cock from her tight grip, Doogan rolled to her side. What had him hooking his arm around her and dragging her against his chest, he'd be damned if he knew.

"I think I might have bitten you," she mumbled, exhausted, now lying bonelessly against his side. "But I think you bit me too."

He grunted at the information.

He knew he'd bitten her, and he'd glimpsed the mark he'd left at the base of her neck as he rolled from her. Unmistakable, livid, a love bite guaranteed to get him killed if anyone saw it and reported it to her brother.

Hell, it was worth it. He decided. The brutal explosion of pleasure he'd experienced was like nothing he'd known before. Let Dawg kill him. He'd regret never having her again, but he wouldn't have wanted to die without knowing that pleasure either.

"Think I bit you hard." She sounded sleepy, exhausted. "It's gonna show."

"Yours too." He tucked her closer against him. "Give me just a minute, baby; I'll get up and find something to dry you off."

"It's okay." She was slipping slowly into sleep. "I want to wear you for just a little longer."

Wear him.

Something tightened in his chest at her words. She wanted to wear him for a little while longer. She had no desire to wash the scent of him from her as other lovers rushed to do after sex. Instead of hurrying to the shower she was curled against him, her breathing easing, slipping into sleep.

He felt the moment she gave in to sleep, curled against him, the fragile delicacy of her body warm and far too comfortable to him. With any other woman he'd have already pushed himself from the bed and washed as well before dressing and finding another bed to sleep in. He hadn't slept with a woman in his entire life. Even the wife he'd once claimed.

This one, hell, he didn't want to move. He wanted to stay right here; he intended to stay right there.

Dragging the comforter from the other side of the bed to pull over them, he tucked his head against the top of hers, his fingers burying in the wealth of silky hair now splaying out behind her.

Those curls were like living silk. Springy, so damned soft it was only rivaled by the feel of her flesh, and warm. Just as she was. And he refused to allow himself to consider how dangerous she was to his control, to the lock-down he'd placed on his emotions. He couldn't let himself consider what the result of this night could do to his soul if he wasn't diligent enough, careful enough to ensure Zoey's protection.

He felt his lips quirk as she moved, coming closer to him, flowing against him until she was close enough that not so much as a breath could slip between them.

He liked that. He liked it too much, he knew, and when it came time to move, to separate himself from her, would he be able to do it?

He would have to.

He couldn't stay.

He couldn't keep her.

That last thought as he slipped into sleep had his chest clenching in regret.

He had a feeling, if he wasn't careful, nothing would matter more than keeping her. That holding her forever could easily become his only thought, his only desire.

And both their downfall.

SIX

Zoey Mackay stood at the edge of the water as the small waves lapped at the bank, mere inches from her bare feet. With her legs bent, her arms wrapped around them, her chin resting atop her knees, she watched as the sun began to descend along the top of the mountains surrounding her brother, Dawg's, home.

She could hear the voices behind her, many raised in laughter as the Mackay family, relations and friends, came together. The family reunion grew every year. And it seemed to last longer every year as well.

Dawg's sprawling backyard was filled. Tables laid out with every food imaginable, the smell of hot dogs grilling, the sound of children playing in the pool rather than romping in the shallow water close to the bank, echoed around her.

The pool was safer for the kids, Dawg had remarked.

Not to mention a hell of a lot cleaner.

It was the usual sounds of the Mackay yearly get-together, and once again, Zoey found herself on the outside looking in.

She'd been on the outside looking in since they'd arrived in Somerset. Never quite comfortable. Never quite certain when her past would catch up with her, when it would destroy her life and hurt everyone she loved.

She'd tried, she thought. She'd tried to fix it, but the price had been far too high. She couldn't fix one betrayal by creating another, could she? She couldn't betray her brother, her cousins. Her sisters. That was the price of freedom, and realizing that she couldn't pay that price was destroying her.

"Hey, munchkin. What are you doing out here by yourself?" The question came as bare feet stepped up beside her, the ragged edge of a pair of men's jeans brushing against the sand.

"Nothing. Just watching the sun set." She moved to get up.

"Please don't, Zoey." Dawg touched her shoulder as he moved to sit next to her, his larger body dwarfing hers. "Here, have a beer."

He extended the chilled bottle as Zoey turned to him warily.

"Thank you." Accepting the bottle, she turned back to the lake and took a sip before sitting it on the sand next to the nearly full beer her cousin Natches had given her earlier. That bottle was sitting next to the soft drink Rowdy had brought her.

What was up with all the drinks anyway?

"You know," he sighed, long minutes later, "when you and your sisters first arrived at the marina, I had a second I wished Chandler was still breathing so I could kill him myself. Especially when I saw you. All that wariness and fear in your eyes . . ."

"Do we really need to go over this, Dawg?" She sighed. "We're here, we're safe. It's over."

That usually managed to get him to back off. At least for a few months.

"Yes we do, little girl, and by God, this time you can give me the courtesy of looking at me while I'm talking to you," he ordered, his tone lowering, darkening, causing her to jerk around and stare at him in surprise.

This was not the gentle giant she was used to. Dawg never spoke sharply to his sisters. Ever.

"What did I do?" She frowned back at him.

Dawg wiped his hand over his face before staring back at her, the firm, commanding look giving way to a loving exasperation that always made her feel as though she had no chance of measuring up.

"You didn't come to me," he answered then, and for a second she saw a flash of pain in his eyes. "Even your sisters come to me when they need me. But when it was important, you didn't do that, Zoey."

God, no. He couldn't know. There was no way he knew.

She jumped to her feet, aware that he was moving just as quickly. So quickly that as she moved to rush past him, he still managed to get to his feet and catch her by her arm. Gently.

"Let me go." Pushing the words past clenched teeth as she refused to look at him, Zoey fought back the anger, the betrayal she'd kept a handle on for a year now.

"Why didn't you come to me, Zoey?" he questioned her, the command in his tone once again. "Why didn't you tell me what was going on instead of hating us . . ."

"Is that what you think?" Jerking away, she turned on him, anger still a force that raged through her with such strength she had no idea how to contain it sometimes. "Do you think I hated you, that I blamed you somehow?"

Confusion flickered across his expression. "I would have helped . . ."

She laughed, a broken, bitter sound that caused her brother to flinch. "What would you have done, Dawg? What do you think you could have done?"

"Zoey, what have we done to you?" He gentled then. Reaching out, he pushed back a heavy fall of curls that trailed down the side of her face, until he could meet her gaze fully. "What have we done, baby sister, to make you think we'd not protect you?"

She trembled at the question. She couldn't stop the tears that filled her eyes or those that overflowed to run down her cheeks.

"I love all of you," she tried to reassure him. "You haven't done anything. Nothing is your fault."

"Why not tell him what you did, Zoey?"

Dawg jerked around, dragging her behind him as his big body blocked hers from the sight of the man stepping from the tree line.

Elegant. So handsome he made her heart break every time she saw him. The one man she'd prayed she could avoid just a little while longer.

The day of reckoning was here, though. She couldn't hide from it any longer. She couldn't fight it any longer.

He may have betrayed her. He may have lied to her in the worst possible way, but it was her fault. She had no one else to blame.

"I'm so sorry," she whispered at Dawg's back, laying her forehead against him as a sob tore through her. "I'm so sorry, Dawg."

"Doogan, what the fuck are you doing here?" The sound of his voice was savage, like a predator determined to protect its offspring.

"Ask your sister, Dawg." Doogan's voice was quiet, intent. "Ask her why I'm here."

"Dawg, do we have a problem?" Natches asked the question.

"Doogan, this is a family party," Rowdy stated calmly. "You weren't invited."

"And you're sure as hell not family," Timothy, the man she often wished had been her father, stated with that razor edge of innate arrogance he always carried whenever he felt his family was being threatened in some way.

"Thank God," Doogan drawled then, the amusement in his tone causing her to shake. He was at his most dangerous now, his most cunning. "Why not tell them why I'm here, Zoey? Or are you going to force me to do it?"

"No." Pushing away from Dawg she forced herself out from behind him, trying to move in front of him, trying to stop the tide of destruction before it began. "Stop this," she demanded, anger raging through her now, shaking so hard now she wondered how she was still standing. "Don't do this, Doogan. Don't turn this into a war."

"Natches." Dawg's tone was the warning. Unfortunately, she wasn't fast enough.

Natches pulled her to him, against his side, holding her firmly as she struggled against him, staring back at Doogan, begging him silently, knowing it wouldn't do her a damned bit of good.

"Go to the house with Natches, Zoey," Dawg ordered firmly, never taking his eyes off Doogan "We'll discuss this there."

"Where you can surround me with Mackay males, and the agents you so carefully pulled away from me?" Doogan chuckled as though amused by them all. "That was an excellent move by the way, arranging to have my agents fall head over heels for the women they believed they couldn't have. What better bait than to make a man think he can't have a woman he desires? Ah Dawg, you're good. You, Rowdy, and Natches are really good . . ."

"Better than you know," Natches assured him as Zoey stopped struggling, shocked by her cousin's declaration. "Good enough to have already figured out exactly what you're doing here and why

Zoey was terrified to come to us when she realized she was in trouble."

"Really?" Doogan drawled. "And why is that?"

Zoey shook her head slowly, holding his gaze, bitter, hollow rage destroying her from the inside out.

He was destroying her and he knew it. He would destroy her and her family and there was nothing she could do to stop it.

"Get the hell out of Somerset, Doogan," Tim demanded then. "Don't turn this into a fight. It's one you won't win and you know it. Not against me."

Chatham smiled. "Perhaps, perhaps not." His gaze never left hers.

"You know this is wrong." Helpless, desperate, she knew begging wouldn't help. Doogan would only see weakness in a plea. "We had a deal . . ."

"But you reneged on your side, sweetheart." He stepped forward slowly, his gaze pinning her, forcing her to remember, forcing her to make a choice.

"I didn't renege," she all but screamed back at him, hating him, hating herself more. "You lied to me, Doogan. You lied."

"Don't do it, Doogan," Dawg warned him softly. "You'll regret it."

Doogan only stared back at her mercilessly. "Zoey Mackay, you're under arrest for the murder of Harley Perdue . . ."

Then all hell broke loose.

Zoey came awake with a hard, brutal punch of awareness, her breath catching, the dream so surprising, so shocking it made very little sense.

Why would she dream something like that?

It made even less sense than the nightmares she so often had.

Hell, it made about as much sense as her life had in the past year. She would call it a comedy of errors, but there had been far too little comedy and far too many errors for the description.

As she rolled to her back, a little moan left her lips at the unique tenderness of her body that reminded her far too well of the hours past and the sexual exhaustion that had gripped her somewhere in the early hours of the morning.

She glanced at the bed beside her, and a folded square of paper had her reaching out. Picking it up and unfolding it, she couldn't stop the pleasure that tightened her chest.

Had a few meetings this morn. Will be back to work on the cycle. As well as another project I'm considering.

She bit at her lower lip; still, a smile curved it and she couldn't help but reread the letter and wonder what he had in mind for another project. She couldn't imagine he'd top the night before. The things he'd made her feel, the pleasure that had exploded through her, still amazed her.

So why the dream? What was it that made her dream such a thing after experiencing such ecstasy at his touch?

As she glanced at the clock, her eyes widened.

Damn, Lyrica would be arriving in only a matter of hours. Zoey had promised her sister the painting she'd finally completed of her family. Graham, Lyrica, and their three-month-old twins. She had the painting ready and she knew her sister wouldn't accept putting it off. Dammit.

Forcing herself from the bed to the shower, she made a mental note to make certain to inform everyone she was painting for the next week or so. That would keep them away; it would make certain no one bothered her while Doogan was there. She doubted he'd be there long; she couldn't afford for him to stay long. But she wanted every touch she could take as her own, every moment she could steal with him before she had to let him go.

Elijah could feel the bullet Natches was going to

put right between his eyes, bearing down on him. He was so dead and he knew it. The Mackays were going to kill him. It was his job to keep Zoey safe, no matter what she got into, or if he couldn't do it, then he was to call one of them.

Her brother, Dawg, knew he was pushing Zoey away from him by being so overprotective with her older sisters. He was trying desperately to give her the freedom they hadn't had, and to keep her from running from Somerset. She was the only one who didn't threaten to do so, and the only one who withdrew from the family completely whenever she went head to head with her brother or cousins.

And they were right. She would leave. She wouldn't run, she'd simply pack up, tell everyone good-bye, then be gone. That was why he'd agreed to help them. That was why he'd accepted her invitation to use the guest room when she'd offered it.

Then Doogan had called that night, just days after the Mackays secured his promise to watch out for her. And he'd seen what could happen to her, even while she was living within one of the most secure homes in the county.

Drugged, convinced she'd killed a friend, her mind so vulnerable, so open, he and Doogan had to remain completely silent, communicating with hand signals alone while slipping her back into her suite at her mother's inn.

He'd watched her hold on to Doogan as he laid her back in her bed, heard her quiet sobs as Doogan eased her arms from around his neck.

"Don't leave me," she'd begged him, as though aware Doogan was more than the dream she'd been told he was. "Please don't leave me."

And he'd seen Doogan's face too. That tormented, dark regret that creased the other man's face and filled his dark eyes. He'd never seen that look on Doogan's face before, and he'd known the older man nearly all his life.

Eli knew him well enough to know that Zoey had somehow taken a hold on him, and it was one Doogan hadn't been able to free himself from in the past year. But that didn't mean Doogan wouldn't shred her heart and leave her broken.

Eli had become fond of Zoey in the past year. And he'd found more than one reason to regret the promise he'd made her brother. If he betrayed Zoey, she would hate him. There would be no forgiveness. And if he didn't? What would happen to Zoey if he didn't find a way to protect her from Doogan and the enemies now focused on the woman someone had realized the other man cared for?

Hell, Eli knew Doogan was already in her bed. His truck had been in the garage, but the spare guest room was empty and Doogan hadn't been anywhere else. As Eli had stood in the living room, he'd heard the faint sounds from Zoey's bedroom. It was as well soundproofed as most of the bedrooms; still, the slightest sound had escaped and Eli had made himself leave the apartment entirely.

Hell, he'd ended up dozing in his truck until daylight. Now, he had to figure out what to do.

He should have never obeyed Doogan's order to bring her to Louisville with him. He should have told the bastard to get fucked.

It wasn't like Doogan could really fire him for it. But Eli hadn't been able to get the memory of the torment on Doogan's face that night out of his mind.

And now, Eli told himself furiously, he was fucking paying for it in spades.

He liked to think he was a fairly intelligent man most days. He might not agree with Dawg and his cousins where Zoey's protection was concerned, but he understood why they did the things that so enraged the sisters. Over the past several years he'd seen the danger Zoey's sisters had faced. If it hadn't been for Dawg and his cousins' determination to protect Dawg's sisters, then they would have died.

He didn't always agree with how they did it.

This time, someone needed to know what was going on, though. He was going to have to tell someone, some way. Warn them and at least make sure someone suspected she could be getting into trouble.

Unfortunately, if he told, Doogan had the power to lock him in a deep, dark hole and throw away the key.

Damn, this whole situation was making his guts cramp. Zoey had been vulnerable enough after the man determined to kill Lyrica a year ago had broken Zoey's arm while trying to force her to betray where her sister was hiding. The arm had barely healed before Sam found Zoey huddled in front of Lyrica's apartment, drugged out of her mind and convinced she'd killed someone she considered a friend.

A year. He and Doogan had investigated the incident for a year, and still they didn't have a single suspect. And they hadn't been able to find Harley after Sam's meeting with him that night, after Zoey showed up outside her apartment.

Harley was alive, Eli knew he was alive. But proof was another thing entirely.

This wasn't a motorcycle race or a little backwoods party where Zoey's presence was more amusing than a reason to call the Mackays. This was Zoey's life. And whoever, whatever had tried to destroy her a year ago, Eli suspected was trying to get to her again. That was why Doogan was there. Because of the two attempts to break Zoey's security and Eli's certainty she was being watched.

He shouldn't have called Doogan. Dammit, he should have just told Dawg.

And Zoey would have hated him. She would have given him that look of broken trust and he would have always wondered if there had been another way. If Doogan would have been the better choice.

He was so screwed.

"You're pacing, Elijah," Graham announced, entering the kitchen, a twelve-week-old twin cradled in his arm. This infant was wearing a dress. The girl was actually more active than her laid-back brother. A scary indication of the future, Eli thought.

God, the kid was a Mackay, despite being Graham's kid. Eli was ready to fucking leave Somerset. Mackays were a pain in the ass, pure and simple and that boy was a future pain in the ass. He just didn't need the headache.

"So why are you pacing?" Graham probed again when Eli forgot to answer him the first time.

Did he dare? God, Doogan would murder him.

Zoey would hate him and the Mackays would skin him alive. A terrifying thought no matter which he considered.

"A new security design." Elijah pushed his fingers restlessly through his hair.

"I see." Graham just stood there watching him as though expecting more. He suspected more, Eli thought. Could he somehow at least warn Graham?

"I think we need to update the security systems now that the rug rats are here." He tried to grin as he nodded to the infant in her father's arms. "Make certain everything's working right." Fuck, surely he could have come up with something better than that?

"Hmm," Graham murmured. "You know, Elijah, the only time I see you that nervous is when Doogan's around."

"Doogan's here again?" Had the bastard arrived at Graham's and Eli hadn't seen him? Fuck. Surely it was too early for the bastard to be lurking around again. And Graham had promised to warn him first.

"I don't believe so," Graham chuckled. "Keeping up with Doogan isn't exactly easy, though."

Oh, Eli knew where he'd been until daylight at least.

"Bastard," Elijah muttered, resignation churning his gut. If he kept his mouth shut and Zoey got hurt, then he'd hate himself.

"Come on, Eli, what's got you wearing tracks in my kitchen floor? New security designs just make you hyper. Get it off your chest, you'll feel better."

Feel better? He wouldn't go that far.

Grimacing, he faced the other man, more a friend than his superior. Graham had always known when to hold his tongue and when to act. Maybe . . . "Graham, do you think the Mackays, or anyone for that matter, has the right to protect their sisters the way they do?"

Graham paused as he opened the refrigerator door, then glanced back at Elijah. "Zoey hurt herself at the race last night?"

Amusement lit Graham's gaze as Elijah just stared at him. How the hell had Graham known about the races?

"No." Elijah drew the word out, waiting to see how much his commander knew. "She wasn't hurt."

Graham pulled free several bottles of water before closing the door and facing Elijah again.

"As for your question." The other man leaned against the counter, watching Eli carefully. "I think they go too far. They're intelligent women and have enough sense to know when they need help. It's Dawg's habit of going too far at times that's made the girls seem a little wild. Especially Zoey. She's always wanted more, loved the adrenaline too much for his comfort level. It's going to backfire on both of them one of these days." His gaze sharpened on Eli then. "If it hasn't already?"

Zoey's sister Lyrica chose that moment to step into the kitchen, her son resting against her breast as she took the water Graham opened for her.

She shot Eli a hard look, and he knew he was in a shitload of trouble if he said anything more.

"Don't be tattling on Zoey, Elijah. She'll make you pay for it," she advised him, lifting the water for a drink. "And trust me, I'll narc you out so fast it'll make your head spin."

This was such fucking bullshit. He was damned no matter what he did.

"What if someone has taken an interest in her . . ." he tried.

Lyrica glared at him and he swore he felt his balls shrink at the promise of retribution in her gaze.

"Unless he's a suspected criminal element, let it go. If he is, then talk to Zoey first," Lyrica advised him, her tone warning. "Of all of us, Zoey will be the one to hate you for tattling on her, and you know it. She doesn't keep friends she can't trust."

And Zoey already didn't have many friends, especially those she felt she could trust.

It always amazed him how the sisters never, ever seemed the least bit interested in knowing what the others were doing. They loved each other and were incredibly loyal. But they never seemed to question anything the other was doing.

As Elijah glanced at Graham, his lips thinned as the other man gave a small shake of his head. Keep his mouth shut? Fine, he could keep his damned mouth shut, and when she ended up hurt then he'd remind them all that he'd tried.

"Fine. Whatever. I have work to do." Turning, he jerked the door open and left the kitchen. Stepping onto the back deck, he let a curse slip past his lips. "Don't blame me when it all fucking backfires," he muttered, though there was no one to hear him.

Dammit. Doogan was trouble by himself. Having him and Zoey in the same place was like throwing a match on gasoline. It was guaranteed to start a fire. Or in this situation, a fucking catastrophe.

He couldn't just remain silent. He had to find a way to tell her cousins or Graham what Zoey was facing. Before she ended up dead.

"So who's interested in Zoey?" Graham watched his wife, his fascination with her as strong now as it ever had been—no, stronger.

Lyrica laughed at his question. "I really have no idea. She hasn't told me yet."

But she would, Graham knew. He, Brogan, and Jed were aware of what Lyrica and her sisters' brother hadn't seemed to guess yet. The sisters kept very few secrets from each other. Actually they probably kept no secrets from each other.

"And if she tells you?" he asked curiously, watching her expression closely. "Would you tell me?"

She was at least considering the option, he could tell, as her emerald eyes stared back at him thoughtfully.

Taking a seat at the kitchen table, she cradled their son close to her breast and pursed her lips for a moment before speaking.

"Give me the name of one man you know who is not a criminal, but one you'd kill if he became interested in Kyleene. Unmarried, but completely unsuitable."

"Doogan," he growled, remembering the other man's apparent interest in her other sister, Eve, and Brogan Campbell's reaction to it during the first days of his relationship with Eve.

Lyrica grimaced at the name. "Fine, as much as I dislike him myself. Doogan. If I told you Zoey was seeing Doogan, would you find a way to tell Dawg or someone who would tell him?"

Graham had to admit she had a point. "Probably," he sighed. "I know Doogan. He'd break Zoey. Hell, he'd break any woman with a heart."

"And I wouldn't want you in a position where you felt you had to look out for her emotional safety," she sighed. "Besides. Eve, Piper, Zoey, and I swore to each other, unless it was life or death, we'd never tell anyone, even Momma, certain things. So if Zoey is seeing someone, no matter who it is, I can't tell you. She's my sister, Graham, and I swore. She kept my interest in you a secret even when Dawg all but interrogated her. If she hadn't, Dawg would have tried to stand in my way every time Kyleene invited me here to the house."

And if he had, Graham knew, then Dawg might have kept them apart far longer than Graham's own ignorance had.

"They just wanted your safety," he sighed. "Each of you has been at risk for one reason or another. It would kill them if anything happened to any of you."

The mocking smile she shot him had his brows lifting curiously.

"Rowdy once said if we wanted to have a relationship without interference, then choose a nice, safe man to have a relationship with," she revealed. "When I told Zoey that last year, she tried them on it. Stanley Kelly, the accountant in town? Remember him?"

Graham grimaced. Stanley was a boring little man but definitely a safe one.

Lyrica laughed at his expression. "Stanley left town for nearly a month when Rowdy informed him he wasn't good enough for Zoey. When she protested, he laughed and told her to find a man he couldn't frighten away. Then told her Stanley peed himself that day. Zoey felt horrible. She and Stanley were actually friends. He won't even speak to her now." Humor filled her eyes. "Kyleene thinks Dawg and the cousins do all this crap to ensure that the men we're with love us and will protect us. But Zoey, of all of us, will not tolerate it, Graham. Better yet, she'll make damned sure they don't find out until she's been married a year and ready to have that first child." Lyrica laughed, then sobered. "That or she'll just leave us and go far enough away that they can't interfere, period. And that would break all our hearts."

He didn't know about what Zoey would do, but he did know that the Mackays, Timothy Cranston, and several of their friends were definitely involved in manipulating the sisters into the arms of the men they'd chosen for them. And he knew the candidate they had in mind for Zoey didn't have a hope of keeping up with her.

"Do you think Zoey would actually keep a relationship hidden that long?" She'd be smart to do just that, he thought, amused.

"I hope she doesn't," Lyrica revealed with a heavy sigh. "We've been keeping the wedding gown Piper finished for her a secret for years. Eve and I both agreed Zoey deserved the only gown Piper would have time to dedicate herself to. And it is a fairy-tale dream. A fairy tale Zoey painted years ago. I'd cry if she didn't get to wear it."

The Mackay sisters were hopeless romantics, Graham knew. He just hoped the man Zoey eventually fell in love with would be just as romantic.

Maybe he should have a talk with Billy Ray and his step-brother, which would effectively keep Eli from Zoey's vengeance. Billy and Jack Clay were Zoey's co-conspirators. They gave her a chance to hit that adrenaline high and kept her from getting hurt while she did it. Not that she'd hurt Eli if he told, but she was damned picky about loyalty; Lyrica wasn't lying about that. Zoey would expect Graham to poke his nose in, though.

"Don't do it, Graham." His wife watched him with a knowing, somber gaze. "Don't put that between me and my sister. If you find out anything and she learns you told anyone but me, then that will always be there between us. If Dawg destroys a relationship that means something to her, she will never forgive her brother. Please, let it go."

Please.

He let out a hard breath and gave her a slow, accepting nod.

"But." She grinned. "If you find out who it is by accident before I do, you can tell me. I'll keep your secrets, hot stuff. You can trust me."

That was his wife.

God, he loved her . . .

SEVEN

Zoey was in the front garage when Lyrica drove up to the open bay doors. Stepping from her pickup, her sister shot her a chiding smile.

"I want to grow up and be you," Lyrica laughed as they headed for the steps leading to the second floor of the converted warehouse. "Especially after seeing how totally scared you have Eli of you. I swear, he's like a grumpy rattler."

"Eli's having issues," Zoey snorted. "And he better keep his mouth shut."

"Oh, he'll keep it shut," Lyrica promised without turning back. "But it's killing him." The second Lyrica actually got a look straight at her, Zoey knew there would be no evading her sister's questions. The bite mark she was sporting at the base of her neck was rivaled only by the one she'd left on Doogan's neck.

She'd glimpsed the one she left on Doogan before exhaustion

dragged her into sleep the night before. The one he'd left on her was just as bad.

Reaching the door, Lyrica stepped through ahead of Zoey, then came to a hard, shocked stop, nearly causing Zoey to plow into her back.

Not that she blamed her sister; Zoey was suddenly rather speechless herself.

Doogan stood in the middle of her kitchen with nothing but a towel secured at his lean hips and the hickey from hell marring the right side of his neck, incredibly close to his jugular vein. He was obviously headed back to her bedroom with a cup of coffee.

His dark hair was damp; sunlight gleamed across the dark strands, picking up lighter highlights that she hadn't noticed the night before. Tight, taut abs tightened above the towel while the light mat of hair on his chest looked far too inviting.

"Well, hell." He frowned, his brown eyes cool as his gaze slid from Lyrica to Zoey, regret flickering in his gaze. "I thought you were alone, Zoey. I'm sorry."

"Oh my God. Oh my God," Lyrica whispered, waving her hands in front of her face as she stared at him, eyes wide. "Dawg's gonna have pups when he finds out about this. Doogan, you can't . . ."

"Lyrica," Zoey said softly, warningly.

"I'll just get dressed." Doogan gave his head a little shake and strode to her bedroom. "Sorry, Zoey."

They watched him disappear, the door closing quietly behind him.

Zoey bit her lips and lifted her gaze to the skylights above them. No way Lyrica missed that hickey on his neck.

"Oh God. You slept with him . . ." her sister wheezed.

Zoey cleared her throat uncomfortably. "Well, we didn't sleep much."

Lyrica's smothered squeal had Zoey's gaze jerking to her in shock at the sound. Her sister was staring at her, hands pressed against her flushed cheeks, her green eyes dancing with sheer disbelief.

"Oh my God," she choked.

"You said that already, Lyrica." Zoey glared back at her. "What's wrong with him?" Hell, Zoey thought, she hadn't found a damned thing wrong with him.

"Oh my God, that look on your face," Lyrica exclaimed.

"What look?" Ducking her head, Zoey stalked away from her sister and headed for the kitchen. "I need coffee."

"Oh, Zoey, please don't let Dawg find out," Lyrica whispered. "That so wasn't his pick for you."

They'd seen enough, heard enough to know that Dawg, Rowdy, and Natches, as well as Timothy and several of their closest friends, had been playing matchmakers in the oddest ways where Dawg's sisters were concerned.

"Yeah, well, his choices sucked anyway," Zoey snapped. "And if I wanted one of the men he's lined up I could have had them at any time since the day we arrived in Somerset. Stop worrying, Lyrica. I have a handle on it."

"Oh, Zoey," Lyrica sighed pityingly. "Haven't we warned you about lying to yourself? I was so certain we had—"

"Shut up!" Zoey demanded. "And stop worrying. Now, where's the babies? With Momma?"

"Zoey, listen to me," Lyrica demanded, pressing the heel of her hand to her forehead. "Honey, you don't understand. If anyone asks, Graham, or Brogan, who the one man was that would send them straight to Dawg if he's seen with you, the answer is him." She pointed to the bedroom door. "He gets people shot at. Hell, even Brogan wants to shoot him. But, Zoey . . ."

"Well, I just want to do him, and I'd prefer to do him in peace if you don't mind," she snapped back, watching Lyrica's eyes widen a second before her lips parted, closed, and then she shook her head with a groan.

"God, Lyrica, shouldn't I be able to choose who my first lover is . . ."

"But Zoey, honey, he'll break your heart," Lyrica whispered.

"I know." And she did. "But he's my choice, Lyrica. Isn't that what counts?"

"You love him," Lyrica said softly, surprised. "Zoey."

And she'd had enough. Turning from her sister, she all but stomped to the coffeepot. "You want coffee or you want to get all weepy and maudlin on me? Really? You'd think I could have what I want, just once, without worrying about big brother."

Just this once, let her have something for herself, just in case life as she knew it, was over soon.

"Oh my God, Zoey. If big brother finds out, he'll hurt Doogan. Of any man on the face of this earth, Doogan is the one he'll lose his mind over," her sister warned her.

"That's when I'll leave, Lyrica." Turning back to her, Zoey knew if Dawg did one thing to ruin this for her before Doogan left on his own, then she'd leave herself. And she'd never come back.

"Oh, Zoey." Lyrica knew what Zoey had already accepted.

Dawg would find out and he would, as she said, have pups. But if he interfered, she'd make sure he never interfered in any other choice she ever made again.

Doogan lowered his head as he heard Zoey's promise to her sister.

Listening to them through the small earbud he was testing the listening devices with, Doogan shook his head wearily. Zoey admitted she knew he was going to break her heart, and still she wanted him. He was her choice, she stated. He wasn't her brother's pick but hers alone. As though Eli could handle her. The other suspected pick was Shane Mayes, the former sheriff, Ezekiel Mayes's son. And though Shane was a fine man, one Doogan wouldn't have minded having as an agent, he was still a far cry from a match for Zoey.

He gave a mocking sneer at the thought of the men Dawg chose before disconnecting the earbud as Zoey and Lyrica's conversation turned to babies and Lyrica's marital bliss. What kind of husband Graham Brock was didn't concern him in the least.

He was a little perturbed with himself, though, for not making certain Zoey was actually alone when he heard the door open. The bright spot in that was the comment Lyrica made indicating that the sisters refrained from sharing each other's secrets with anyone else. Which explained why they managed to actually get so many things past their brother and cousins. Finishing his coffee Doogan dressed in jeans and a narrow, white striped gray shirt. Sitting at the edge of the bed he pulled on well-worn leather ankle boots, laced them, then rose to his feet and left the bedroom. Where he once again faced Zoey's wide-eyed sister.

"I'll be in the garage, Zoey." Damn Lyrica; he'd waited to get back, shower, and have another taste of Zoey. He hadn't expected her sister to show up.

"You don't have to leave, Doogan," she said softly, a hint of concern flashing in her pale green eyes. "Trust me, Lyrica won't even tell Graham about seeing you here. Though Eli will probably tell him about seeing you at the race."

"Not this morning he didn't," Lyrica revealed. "I talked to Graham just after Eli left and he had no clue."

"Eli and I talked last night," Doogan assured them. "He won't say anything."

Lyrica still watched him intently, a small frown at her forehead as her gaze raked over him again before pausing at the mark on his neck. Zoey's mark.

"I'll be in the garage, then." He nodded to Zoey and her sister before moving past them to the hall leading to the end of the second level of the building and the metal staircase they'd used the night before.

He wanted to make certain the bike was at peak performance, while also ensuring it provided the best balance to weight for Zoey before that next race. She was small and delicate without the strength to manhandle the machine as the male racers did. He had a few ideas to fix that. There were also items he needed to purchase for her riding gear to ensure her safety. A new helmet for sure. The one she had wouldn't protect her hard head effectively, and he didn't want her risking more than a few bruises.

Bruises were a necessary part of life, he thought; anything more serious wouldn't be tolerated, though.

"What's with all the funny looks?" Zoey demanded as Doogan could be heard moving quickly down the metal staircase.

"Hell, Zoey, he walked out dressed like a normal person." Lyrica blinked back at her as she leaned her elbows on the counter, where they were sitting across from each other. "If I hadn't known who he was, I wouldn't have recognized him."

She liked the way he looked, Zoey decided. She'd seen him all GQ proper two weeks before, and though he'd looked damned good, he looked even better in jeans.

"Maybe Dawg will have the same problem if he sees him, then." Zoey could only hope.

"Eli says he always manages to get himself or his agents shot whenever on a mission," Lyrica told her, obviously worried. "He acts scared to death whenever Graham has to send him to meet with Doogan."

"I'm not one of his agents," Zoey pointed out.

"Why is he here with you, Zoey?" her sister asked, leaning forward worriedly. "Whatever he's in Somerset for, it's not to work on your bike or because he just couldn't stand another day that he wasn't in your bed. And if it was because of a case or an investigation, he would have met with Graham, and I would have known he was in town."

"It's not to get me shot at," Zoey assured her, but she had to admit that question had bothered her throughout the day as well, despite his answer the night before. "It's probably just spy stuff," she finally told her sister. "No one knows he's here, though, and he won't be here long. Stop worrying."

"One of us has to," Lyrica objected, lifting her coffee cup to her lips. "It's obvious you don't intend to."

"Lyrica, sometimes I'm very scared it's too late to worry about that. I just want to live, just in case those nightmares aren't nightmares. And I want to experience the touch of a man I can't say no to . . ."

"That man can have you locked up, baby sister," Lyrica warned her softly. "Those nightmares ambush you. You never know . . ."

"I know that." Raking her fingers through her hair, Zoey turned quickly from her sister.

"Zoey, I'm scared for you," Lyrica whispered.

"I trust him." Zoey didn't know why, couldn't explain why. "He'll break my heart, I have no doubt." She turned back to Lyrica slowly. "If he left right now, my heart would shatter, Lyrica. But he'd try to protect me. I know he would."

"Zoey . . ."

"It was a nightmare," she whispered, and she had no idea why she kept telling herself that. "We know it's a nightmare. Right?"

"Zoey." Lyrica reached out and covered her sister's hand gently. "It was a nightmare. You know that. He was seen that night leaving town, and you said yourself when you woke up, you were in your own bed at the inn. Come on, no one can get into those rooms without the cameras showing something. You checked the cameras, right?"

"And he hasn't been seen since," Zoey whispered. "Something happened that night. I don't know what, I don't know why I know it, but I know it did. Something bad."

She could feel it. Everything inside her assured her there was a reason for those nightmares. Yet, as Lyrica said, Harley had been seen leaving town late that same night. Even the woman he'd been sleeping with had seen him at the convenience store along with dozens of customers, including Samantha Bryce, a detective on the Somerset police force.

But Lyrica was right. Zoey had checked the cameras as soon as she'd had a chance. A few squirrels had slipped across the porch, moths had slapped against the porch light, but no one had slipped into her room, or out of it. The same for the hall camera. Zoey had watched a mouse her mother was unaware they had run along the baseboards, but no one had crept to her room or out of it.

There was nothing but Zoey's certainty that something had happened.

Nothing made sense or added up. She was actually worried enough that she was somehow crazy that she'd created a bucket list. A list of adventures she wanted to experience before losing her sanity completely. Or being arrested.

"It was just a nightmare," Lyrica objected. "If it hadn't been, honey, you wouldn't have woken in your own bed, in your pajamas. Remember that. You didn't hurt anyone, Zoey. Come on, you know you didn't hurt anyone."

When she was awake, she knew it had to be a nightmare. She'd gone to sleep in her bed; she'd woken in her bed. But the nightmares . . . God, the nightmares were like memories, so vivid and so messed up she woke screaming, terrified.

"Zoey." Lyrica reached out, her hand covering hers, concern filling her emerald eyes. "Please, please talk to Natches about this. If anyone knows where to find Harley . . ."

"No." Jerking her hand back, Zoey moved quickly from the counter, panic suddenly tearing through her, the certainty of danger, of a gun sight aimed at her almost overwhelming her.

The nightmare threatened to become a delusion, a hallucination. A waking hell she couldn't escape.

"Zoey . . . ?" It was her sister's voice, filled with an edge of fear that had Zoey pushing those visions back, fighting to escape them.

"This has nothing to do with Natches." She forced herself to control her breathing, to push back the fear. Natches wouldn't hurt her. He would never hurt her. But he didn't need to know about this.

"Okay," Lyrica agreed hastily. "That's fine. We'll figure it out another way. I promise."

She promised. Her sisters never broke their promises to her. It was going to be okay, because they'd find another way to locate Harvey. Natches didn't have to know . . .

Zoey stepped into the garage area quietly several hours later, her gaze finding Doogan hunched next to the bike as he finished tightening something inside the motor.

He was tall, powerful, but without the bulky muscle most powerful men possessed. Doogan's muscle was lean, appeared more natural, denser, and harder than that of his bulkier counterparts. He was at least six three, his dark hair a bit long.

"Eli has strangled the power in a variety of ways," he told her as she continued to watch the muscles of his back flex as he worked. "If one weren't aware of his particular genius, then the entire bike would have had to be stripped and everything replaced."

A costly project, Zoey thought, thinking of the amount of money she now had in the motor, electronics, and various running parts.

"It's fixable, then?" she asked.

"Fixable," he assured her. "It shouldn't take long either. A week, maybe. I'll have it ready in plenty of time to win that race next month."

She had at least a week. At least six or seven nights with him.

"You're sure I'll have a chance of winning?" she questioned, tilting her head to watch his profile.

"If you can control the power, which I believe you can." He shrugged. "Once I balance the bike sufficiently, there shouldn't be a question of winning. I'll find a proper area where you can test it before the race, though."

Her brows lifted. Eli fought her tooth and nail whenever she attempted to test the bike before the races. And without his truck, she had no way of testing it without Billy learning exactly how the bike performed.

Eli had helped her keep the bike running since she'd begun riding in the private races Billy Ray and his friends put together every month. She knew Eli had deliberately cut back the power the motor was capable of, though, and once Billy had informed her of it a few months ago, it had done nothing but piss her off.

She'd suspected it before Billy had come to the garage and

confirmed it. Billy had even offered several times to help her. But he'd use his knowledge to win each race as well. There was no fairness in that any more than there was any fairness in what Eli had done.

"I need to get a few parts," Doogan stated as she stood watching him. "Nothing too expensive. And I have a few ideas to fix your weight-to-balance ratio. The items I'll need for that I'll have to run a search for. I checked a few places in Louisville just before you came in. I may have to get them out of state, though."

Straightening, he moved to the toolbox, replaced the ratchet he was using, then moved to the small sink to wash his hands. Drying them, he turned back to her, his gaze curious as it settled on her.

"Figures. I keep losing it in that curve as I hit higher speeds," she told him, leaning against the back of his pickup and tucking her hands in the pockets of the cutoff shorts she wore. "Never matters how I balance it, it wipes out there."

"You're too light to balance and make up for the impetus you need to get around it, even with the speeds you can actually attain." Facing her, he nodded to the cycle. "It's fixable, though." Then a little grin tipped his lips. One of those wry, almost amused curves. "So did your sister lecture you properly about me?"

Lecture her? She and her sisters tried hard to never lecture each other; they heard far too much of it from their other family members. Especially their brother and cousins.

"Lyrica and Eli say all your agents live in fear of working with you," she admitted. "You get them shot at."

He leveled a look of superior mockery in her direction.

"Eli?" His brow arched with a hint of inborn arrogance. "He forgets his job description includes such things. Working with Graham has made him squeamish."

Squeamish wasn't the description she would have used. Eli wasn't a coward.

"Eli isn't the gung-ho sort," she pointed out. "He's more cautious and methodical."

"Young." Doogan nodded. "Eli doesn't always understand that often a sudden strike versus slipping in is the only effective way to act. A strike team strikes. It doesn't tippy-toe."

"And you're a strike team?" she asked.

"I normally head a strike team," he amended. "Eli's been assigned to those teams a time or two. He dislikes bullets more than most agents, though."

For some reason she had the feeling that bullets didn't concern Doogan, and she wondered if they ever had.

"Eli doesn't seem particularly fond of you personally, though," she pointed out. "I thought he was going to demand to drive me home himself last night."

Eli didn't actually dislike Doogan, but Zoey sensed the younger agent rarely agreed with him.

"He may have made that demand of me," Doogan admitted, crossing his arms over his chest. "I simply reminded him of the definition of *boss*."

Zoey winced. Eli wouldn't have appreciated that at all. He was young, but he had plenty of pride.

"He tends to get his feathers ruffled easily." Doogan shrugged.

"Why are you really in Somerset, Doogan?" She asked the question before she could stop herself. "And don't pawn me off with that excuse you gave last night."

She was smart. Intuitive. Doogan had known that all along. Just as he'd known Lyrica's knowledge of his presence in Zoey's home would ensure that Zoey began questioning why he was there as soon as her sister left.

He was prepared for it.

"I'm here to oversee an active investigation," he finally answered her, trying his damnedest not to lie to her. "And that's all I can tell you."

"All hush-hush, huh?" She peeked up at him from between thick, sooty lashes. "Are you going to get me shot at, Doogan?"

She was teasing him, and he was damned if he'd expected that from her.

"Not if I can help it." The thought of getting Zoey shot at was terrifying. And not just because her brother would kill him.

"Well, at least you didn't try to lie to me." Full breasts lifted with a heavy sigh beneath the tank top she wore with the cutoff denim shorts and cowboy boots. "I would have never believed a full-out 'No.' Not with your reputation."

He arched his brow curiously, finding it particularly hard to keep his eyes off those tempting breasts.

"My turn," he stated.

Zoey inclined her head, indicating her agreement.

"How do you know so much about the agents operating in Somerset? I know for a fact Eli hasn't given you that information, and you know a hell of a lot, even for a Mackay."

"You know that old saying 'the walls have ears'?" she said softly. "Farmhouses have really thin walls."

His arms went across his chest, his brows lowering broodingly. That wasn't a good sign, but she could go with it.

"I know for a fact when Dawg remodeled the bed-and-breakfast, the walls were rebuilt as well."

Zoey lifted her brows and gave a heavy sigh, accepting the fact that she could give up a little information. "I stole some of Dawg's bugs. God love his heart. He just keeps misplacing them." She gave a shake of her head, her eyes widening innocently. "It's pitiful. Old age, I think."

Dawg would have a fit if he heard her say something so outrageous. Hell, it was all she could do to say it and keep a straight face.

Doogan's eyes narrowed now. "My bullshit detector just exploded," he warned her. "Want to try again?"

"I've been known to cause that." She sighed, blinking at him with false remorse. "Dawg's always having to replace his too."

He just stared back at her, those brown eyes watching her as though not quite certain of the response he should give to pull her back in line.

Yeah, Dawg had that problem too, she thought, reining in her laughter.

"So, do you want to make a parts list for me?" she asked him as though there weren't a question on the table to answer. "I can pick everything up for you this afternoon when I go out."

"And no one will question why?" He was going to let it go, Doogan thought, surprised at himself. Leaning against the sink counter, Doogan tried to keep the arousal from building in him and fought to keep his cock from becoming fully erect.

It was no wonder her brother and cousins were finally going gray. If he looked close enough he'd probably find a gray hair himself now.

"That was last year," she stated with a little wave of her hand. "The parts store employees finally stopped calling Dawg when I convinced them I was picking up parts for friends while they were at work. Dawg couldn't find a reason to suspect otherwise, so he let it go."

Doogan grinned at that. "You let him suspect before ever going close to one of those races, didn't you?"

Once his suspicions were aroused, Dawg would have had the races watched or been on the lookout for a title in her name.

"Guilty," she admitted. "So you want me to pick them up or what? I assume you won't want to risk Dawg learning you're here."

"You assume correct," he assured her, uncrossing his arms to brace them on the counter behind him. "I'll make a list for you. I may have to leave before daylight in the morning to meet with a contact, but I should be back before too late. I'll be out till late tonight, though. It'll be morning before I finish going over the bike and making that list."

"Thanks for letting me know." She nodded. "Remind me when we get upstairs and I'll give you the spare security fob."

Doogan nodded, watching her closely. "Are you sure you want me to stay?" he asked then, watching the frown that fitted at her brow and the somber disquiet in her gaze.

"It's a little late to ask that question, don't you think?" she asked him, swallowing tightly.

"I don't want to hurt you when it's time to leave, Zoey, so don't fall in love with me, please. For both our sakes. Because I'd feel like a complete bastard if I broke your heart." Why he felt the need to warn her he wasn't entirely certain.

"Consider me warned." She shrugged, but instead of looking at him, her gaze moved to the motorcycle he'd been working on. "I made my decision last night, though. I don't regret it, and I won't cry when you leave. How's that?"

But she didn't say he wouldn't break her heart. She didn't assure him she wouldn't fall in love with him.

There would be no walking away without ripping at what was left of his emotions. He knew when that time came, she would cry. She would wait until he was gone. She wouldn't let him see the tears, but they would fall.

Moving to her, he gripped her waist, lifted her, and set her cute, perky little ass on the lowered tailgate of the truck. Pushing between her thighs, Doogan wedged the erection he'd been unable to stop into the notch of her thighs, gripped the hair at the back of her head, and pulled her head back to stare into her oddly colored eyes.

Surprise and lush anticipation softened her features as he watched her and felt her soften against him.

"Ask me to kiss you, witch," he demanded, brushing her lips with his.

"Ask you for it?" Her hands tightened where they gripped his biceps. "Why should I have to ask? You're going to kiss me anyway."

"So we both know what you want," he answered softly, the sexual need riding harder, faster inside him. "Besides, it can be incredibly sexy when you know you have only to ask your pleasure and it'll be given to you."

The very thought of her asking for other, far more intimate acts had his cock straining against the zipper of his jeans.

"And if I ask, you'll give it to me?" Sharp little nails pricked past the material of his shirt as she asked the question.

"Whatever you want, Zoey. Whenever you want it."

"What if you're not here?" Her breathing was tighter, faster now. "If I really want something and you're away?"

"All you have to do is text me. Call me," he promised, watching her eyes. "And whatever you want, however you want it." The very thought of it had his voice darkening, the need to give her whatever she desired, sexually, tightening his balls. "And I'll make sure you have it."

"Kiss me, Doogan. Hard and deep . . ."

He didn't wait. He couldn't wait.

His lips covered hers, hard, his tongue pushing past her lips, stroking against hers, and he made zero allowances for the inexperience he knew she still possessed. One hand cradled the back of her head, the other cupped the delicate curve of her neck, and he ravished her lips, his tongue fucked her mouth.

When she asked for hard and deep, he'd seen the lack of knowledge in her eyes for what she was asking. There was such innocence . . . and he wanted to replace that innocence with knowledge. With sensual, sexual confidence that he alone gave her.

As he worked his lips over hers his tongue thrust past them, teased hers, tasted it until he swore he was becoming intoxicated by her, high on her kiss alone and loving every sweet, forbidden moment of it.

Soft, kittenish little mewls left her throat, the sound of them sparking a deeper, hotter hunger inside him, thoughts of all the sexual acts he could teach her racing through his senses.

For a moment he eased the intensity of the kiss. He had every intention of releasing her from the sensual, sexual spell deepening around both of them. He would have given her a reprieve, a chance to catch her breath. As he moved to pull back, sharp little teeth nipped his lips as her fingers jerked to his hair, tangling in the strands, tugging at them, nipping his lower lip again to demand more.

The innocent, playful act was like a match to gasoline. The dominant, dark core of male sexuality he possessed broke free, and even the small allowance he'd made for her innocence was forgotten.

He would brand her senses with him. No other man, or woman, would be enough. No other kiss would ever seem quite right. No one but Doogan would ever be enough when he was finished. This sweet, sensual little witch would always be his alone.

Zoey's senses exploded with pleasure.

One hard hand gripped her hip, pulling her to the edge of the tailgate and holding her in place. A second later the hard, thick width of his jeans-covered cock ground against her sex as his tongue speared past her lips, pumping in and out of them in the same slow, destructive rhythm he used between her thighs.

He wasn't just kissing her, he was fucking her with his tongue, possessing her with a kiss that had her vagina rippling with each push into her mouth, each hard thrust against her mound.

His lips slanted over hers, holding her in place with the delicious, explicit act before the hands in her hair began pulling at the long strands he held captive.

Sharp, intense pulses of sensation shot through her womb, straight to the depths of her core. Moisture eased along the passage, hot and sleek, spilling to the sensitive folds beyond.

Each thrust of his tongue against hers, each tug of her hair and driving thrust of his hips against the mound of her sex sent harsh, shattering arcs of sensation driving through her vagina. Her inner muscles clenched and spasmed, moisture wept slick and heated, coating her flesh, inside and out, preparing her, sensitizing her while her clit throbbed in peaked, painful need for touch.

And in the next second it was gone.

He stopped.

EIGHT

As Doogan pulled his head back, his hips stilled, the tightened sensations building in her clit pulsing in painful denial.

She ached for him. The pleasure of the night before hadn't been forgotten and she wanted more. Needed more.

"Look at me." The dark guttural sound of his voice had her eyes opening, her gaze connecting with his.

"You're like a fucking drug that has hold of me," he rasped, the brown of his eyes like deep, dark chocolate. "All I want to do is taste you, fuck you until we're both drowning in the pleasure."

"No one told you not to." The breathy sound of her own voice surprised her.

Sliding her hands from his chest down over his abs to the leather belt cinching his hips, Zoey began working it free. Once it was loosened, she unbuttoned the metal tab, then moved her fingers to the zipper holding the material closed.

His hand caught her wrist, the other pulling at her head, dragging her head back again. "I came inside you last night."

She blinked up at him in shock. "What?"

"I forgot to wear a condom, Zoey." His voice, his expression, was iron hard. "I came inside you so fucking hard I thought I was dying, and I did it without protecting you."

Her lips parted. "You do that often?"

"I have never fucking done something so irresponsible," he snarled, his gaze burning into hers. "Never."

"I'm protected." She could barely breathe. It was the look on his face, in his eyes. He wasn't angry, nor was he fighting any possible consequences, and she didn't want to question why.

His jaw tightened. "I don't have a condom with me now."

She fought for breath now, excitement surging through her.

"I'm protected," she repeated.

A second later she gasped when he lifted her again, her knees gripping his hips. He stalked around the truck, jerked open the door to the back, and placed her on the edge of the seat. A second later her shorts were pulled from her and the iron-hard width of his cock was pushing past the already slick folds of her sex.

Zoey couldn't help but watch.

Thick, dark, the plum-shaped crest parted the swollen, juice-laden nether lips wide.

He paused then, pulling her gaze up to him.

His shirt cleared his head without the first button being undone. She was pretty sure she saw several of the small white buttons flying from the material, though.

Then he caught her beneath her knees and angled her hips up to him.

Zoey fell back, catching herself on her elbows, watching the broad cock head as it began pushing inside her. Slowly.

"Hard," she begged, feeling the stretching bite of a pleasure-pain that wasn't nearly enough.

"Not yet," he groaned. "Let me watch, Zoey. Watch your sweet pussy open for me. Take me. Slow and easy."

He worked inside her, just as he said, slow and easy, stretching her inner flesh, sending fiery lashes of sensation racing through her system.

Working inside her, push, retreat. As he pulled back, the thick coating of her natural lubrication clung to the thick, dark shaft. It glistened, covering his flesh even as it clung to hers.

"That's it, little witch," he groaned as the throbbing crest disappeared inside her again, parting her, the intimate folds hugging the stalk with a sheen of slick moisture. "Milk my cock inside you, Zoey. You're so tight. So fucking hot and tight."

One hand lifted, slid to the hem of her tank, and pushed it over her breasts, his glaze burning hotter as he stared at her swollen curves, the puckered, pebble-hard nipples.

He came over her then, his lips moving to the hard point of a nipple as his hips gave a hard, shallow thrust. Fiery pleasure pulsed inside her, that pleasure-pain sensation dragging a cry from her lips and shuddering through her.

His lips, teeth, and tongue worked over her nipples, one to the other, sucking deep and hard, nibbling with exquisite heat, and licking over them with hungry demand.

"Doogan." The cry tore from her as he began thrusting harder, deeper inside her.

As he plunged the wide crest and broad stalk deep, the heavy veins throbbed with blood, rising beneath the silken flesh and creating an intense bite of sensation with each pounding stroke.

Blinding, white-hot flashes of raw sensation began wrapping around her senses, burning through them, pushing her into that incredibly erotic storm beginning to build inside her.

Each lunge of his hips buried his flesh deeper, built the exquisite sensations churning through her. Lifting herself to him, writhing beneath him, Zoey buried her fingers in Doogan's hair. Her neck arched, moans spilling unbidden from her throat as he began taking her harder, faster. Driving inside her, each fierce thrust sent piercing lashes of desperate need tightening in her womb, spiraling through her senses and pushing her deeper inside the chaos building through her.

"That's it, baby," he groaned, his lips lifting from her breasts, stroking them over her neck, brushing against hers, his breathing as harsh and labored as her own. "Take me, Zoey. God, you're so sweet. So fucking tight."

Pulling back, thrusting inside her again, again, until he buried to the hilt, the fiery stretching burn stealing her breath and tearing a groan from his chest.

"Ah hell, Zoey. I love your sweet pussy." The hand at her hip tightened, his lips covered hers, his tongue sinking past them as he began moving, each driving impalement a shock to her already oversensitized flesh; each stroke, each blinding furious thrust drove her higher until she was crying out his name and exploding into ecstasy.

Deep racking shudders raced through her body. Her internal muscles clamped down on his cock, tightening around it as he pushed in to the hilt and growled her name against her lips, finding his own release inside her.

It was like flying, being flung into a storm of pure, raw sensation, and Zoey knew she was becoming hooked on him. On this pleasure he gave her, the warmth that surrounded her, and the sound of his voice as he whispered her name.

When it was over, sweat-dampened and boneless she lay beneath him and pushed away any thoughts of what the future would bring once he was gone. She couldn't let herself think about tomorrow. Couldn't let the thought of losing him spoil the time she had with him.

Not yet. Not until she had no other choice.

"Come on, witch." Lifting her into his arms after fixing his jeans, Doogan strode up the stairs and carried Zoey to the sun-splashed bedroom.

Depositing her on the bed, he stared down at her, watching as she lifted those thickly lashed eyelids just enough to stare up at him.

"We could take a nap," she suggested, a tempting smile curling her lips.

"I'd love to," he said regretfully. "Unfortunately, I have to take care of some of that spy stuff you mentioned earlier."

A little wrinkle of her nose and a sensuous stretch of that far-too-tempting body had his dick twitching in renewed interest. He was going to end up fucking them both to death if he wasn't careful, because all he wanted to do was live inside her.

"You be good," he ordered, bending to catch those pouty lips in a quick kiss.

Then he lingered.

She mesmerized him. She made him so damned hungry it was all he could do to function for the need to have her again. To sink inside her, feel that tight pussy gripping him, pulling him inside her.

If he wasn't careful she'd end up owning him.

That thought had him pulling back, breaking the kiss, breathing out roughly and straightening once again.

"You're dangerous," he told her, knowing she had become far too important to him at a time she wasn't even aware of. What she was doing to him now could become far more than a simple hazard to his self-control.

"Well, I lost a lot of sleep last night." Celadon green peeked up at him through lush, heavy lashes. "I think a nap is definitely on my schedule today."

He bent to her again. He simply couldn't help himself. Brushing back a tangle of long curls from her cheek, he let his lips brush against hers again. "Dream of me, baby," he whispered, letting his gaze touch hers, assuring her silently that when he returned, they would definitely play again. "I'll be back soon."

"I'm sure I'll be waiting." She laughed up at him. "The hickey on my neck assures it."

As he straightened, his gaze went to her neck, the mark he'd left on her clearly visible. Just as visible as his was. And he couldn't help the surge of satisfaction the sight of hers brought him, even knowing the consequences it could bring.

"Sleep well, witch," he said softly.

He had to force himself to leave her. After changing clothes and arming himself, he had to force himself to the garage, and even as he drove away, leaving her nagged at him. He wanted to stay. He needed to stay. And needing Zoey wasn't supposed to have happened.

The black pickup Graham was watching for moved into view. The lights went out on the truck when it reached the side of the bar. A short distance later Doogan pulled into a spot protected by ornamental trees and shrubs that extended from the back of the bar to the side door, providing complete anonymity for anyone with the proper code to get past John's security and the bouncer just inside.

"Lyrica thinks Zoey will drop the racing once she wins," he commented, rather than informing the other man that Brom Doogan had arrived. "She says it's just one of Zoey's little adventures."

Eli looked up with a glare. "She tell you what's next on Zoey's little bucket list?"

"She has a list?" Graham assumed she had one, he just had no idea what was on it. Or even why she had it.

"Oh, she has a list," Eli growled. "Once she wins the damned race, her next adventure is to lose her virginity to someone who will make her family scream the loudest. And so far, the candidates she's listed give me nightmares . . ."

"She's already decided on the candidate I do believe." Brom Doogan walked in, his gaze going to Eli as the young agent jumped immediately to his feet. He only shook his head sadly at Eli before turning to Graham.

Marriage was being damned good to Graham, Doogan thought. His friend's face was more relaxed and his gray eyes had lost that shadowed look.

"'Bout time." Graham grinned, gesturing to the chair next to the desk. "Have a seat and tell me what the hell you're talking about. And here I thought Kye causing trouble in the bar tonight was going to be my biggest worry."

"Yeah, this is guaranteed to be a good one," Eli snorted mockingly.

Doogan figured he'd had about enough of the young agent's smart ass. "Agent Grant, get out there with Kye and keep her out of trouble before you end up fired."

Eli turned to Graham, his gaze fierce, questioning.

Doogan arched his brow at the older agent. "You get a promotion the director didn't tell me about, Graham?" he asked pleasantly. "Congratulations. Should I start calling you sir now?"

As far as he knew, Graham had turned down the offer Doogan had accepted as director of operations.

Graham lowered his head, hiding a smile as he shook it briefly. "Nope. No promotion here, Brom."

"Would you like to be reassigned, Agent Grant?" Doogan asked softly. "It can be arranged. Before the hour is out, actually."

"No sir," he bit out with the barest civility.

"Then get your ass out that door and into that bar. Once there, you will stick as close as possible to Miss Brock until your commander or your operations director informs you otherwise. Are we clear?"

"Yes. Sir." Animosity filled the young man's tone now, but he left the room, closing the door with a controlled snap as Doogan turned back to Graham.

His friend was watching the closed door with brooding thoughtfulness.

"His insubordination is straining my patience, Graham," Doogan informed him. "This is your fair warning, just as I promised. One more time and our friendship won't save his job."

Graham nodded slowly, his expression still contemplative.

"You've put up with him longer than I would have under the same circumstances, Brom. I was hoping he would have softened by now. I'll take care of it."

Brom. Graham called him Doogan when others were around, mostly. He was one of the few Doogan allowed the privilege.

"Now." Graham narrowed his gaze back at him. "What's this about being at the top of Zoey's list of potential first lovers?" He grimaced worriedly. "That's not a safe place to be, my friend."

Reaching into the light jacket he wore, Doogan pulled free a white envelope and handed it to Graham. "Perhaps this will explain things better. It's from Director Bryce himself."

"Why do I have a feeling this letter is just going to end up pissing me off?" Graham sighed.

With an inclination of his head and a wry smile, Doogan took the chair Graham had offered moments before and watched as the other man sat back down at the desk.

Propping his ankle on the opposite knee, Doogan turned his attention to the security camera as Graham opened the envelope and pulled the letter free.

As Graham read, Doogan watched Eli via the security camera placed behind the bar. The younger man sat at the bar, watching Kye in between glares at the camera.

Doogan was trying to be patient with the boy. He knew why Eli had a problem with him, just as Graham did. Because of it, he'd let the young agent get away with far more than he should have.

Eli refused to see the truth of the events that instilled that resentment in him. No matter the times Eli's father had tried to make him understand, and no matter the attempts Graham had made, that resentment lingered.

"Oh, fuck," Graham groaned as he finished the director's letter. "Doogan, you don't want to do this."

No, he didn't want to do it, but there was little choice at this point. Somehow, another agent had learned Harley was missing and was under the belief Zoey had killed him. Neither Doogan nor Director Bryce had yet to learn the agent's source of information.

"If I don't do it, then the assignment will go to Collin Westfield." Doogan leaned forward as Graham's eyes narrowed in surprise. "My own initial investigation revealed the rumor that Natches Mackay beat up Agent Harley Matthews aka Harley Perdue and demanded he leave town because of his cousin, Zoey Mackay. That's the rumor here in Somerset. According to Westfield, he was contacted by an anonymous source who revealed that Zoey Mackay killed Harley, then somehow managed to hide the act. Rather than investigating, Westfield requested immediate arrest. The director refused the request, but that hasn't stopped the agent from threatening to go over his head. If that happens and Zoey's arrested, then all the hard work the rest of us have done since Timothy Cranston began courting the Mackay clan as DHS support is shot to hell."

"Arresting any Mackay will start a war between a hell of a lot of powerful men and DHS," Graham admitted. "The director will lose quite a few damned good agents as well. I can think of four of us right off the bat."

"Five, just in case I wasn't a consideration," Doogan amended coolly. "The problem is, Westfield won't care. That's why I'm here myself, because I do care."

Graham wiped his hand over his face, then stared back at him in disgust. "That letter." He flipped the paper in contempt. "Orders me not to tell my wife jack shit, Doogan. That's her sister we're talking about."

"And your wife's baby sister doesn't do a damned thing that your wife isn't well aware of, Graham," Doogan informed him mockingly. "Are you aware Lyrica knows Zoey is tortured by nightmares of killing Harley?"

Graham stared back at him in shock. "Not possible. Lyrica would have told me."

"I stayed at Zoey's last night and bugged her living area. I actually overheard the conversation this afternoon. Lyrica's certain it's some nightmare Zoey can't distinguish from reality, whereas Zoey is convinced there's more behind it. Incidentally, it would have happened before he was seen at Ziggler's convenience store at the edge of town. But if Westfield ever gets so much as a whisper of that little nugget of information, then hell is going to explode at DHS as well as in Somerset."

Graham shook his head. "Harley's not dead. I saw him for about two minutes after I was released from the hospital last summer. He made the shot that killed Jimmy Dorne. That was months after he was seen leaving town."

"He has to come in, Graham . . ."

"Good fucking luck," Graham snapped. "He won't even come in for Natches, and they were tight as hell. Hell, until he took that shot at Jimmy, no one had seen or heard from him since he'd disappeared."

"Does Natches have any idea why?" Doogan asked him.

"None." Graham shook his head, and he wasn't lying.

As Graham tapped the letter against the desk, his expression creased with worry. "You'll break her heart, Brom," he said, meeting Doogan's gaze again. "She doesn't deserve that. She's a good kid."

"Better a broken heart than what Westfield would do." He pinched the bridge of his nose wearily. "If he arrests her, he'll send her straight to Gitmo or a black site outside the U.S. to be held before anyone can stop him. By the time Matthews showed himself and she's released, she wouldn't be the same. You know what would happen to her, Graham. She'd never be the same woman who was taken."

"And if he tries it anyway?" Graham asked, knowing the war that would erupt if anything even approaching that scenario happened.

"Then he'll receive a similar order to yours," Doogan informed him. "This operation is top-level covert and under not just my direction but also my command. If he tries anything after that, then I get to kill him myself." He stared back at Graham with icy determination. "And I will kill him."

Collin Westfield's vendetta against the Mackays was becoming a problem even the director was concerned with. It was getting harder and harder to block his bullshit and keep knowledge of it from reaching Dawg, Natches, or Rowdy Mackay. Their contacts in the law enforcement field were far reaching and went even deeper than the director knew. So far, between himself and Bryce, they'd kept the other agent contained. That wasn't going to last much longer.

The Mackays' strength, loyalty, and dedication to their county and country had changed the face of several once-suspected small, emerging family-backed militias. And not just in Kentucky. Those clans were now allies to the agency. If it appeared DHS was betraying the Mackays, then they'd lose far more than one family's loyalty.

"Westfield's not stupid, Brom. He's already prepared," Graham mused. "He wouldn't have expected you to take the assignment yourself, though. He'll be trying to figure out a way to work around you."

Doogan drew in a heavy breath. "Be careful, Graham, because someone close to the Mackays is funneling information to him.

Just before I headed out he went to the director with a request to come to Somerset to follow up on a contact's report regarding questionable Mackay activities. Bryce set his ears back with an ass chewing that's only going to hold him back so long."

"You think it was Eli?" Graham's fingers closed into a fist where one arm rested on the desk.

"Actually, no, I don't." Sitting forward once again, Doogan narrowed his eyes at the security camera to watch Eli edging closer to Graham's sister Kye. "But someone's trying to make it appear it's Eli. His animosity toward me is well known, and Eli doesn't always watch his back properly. Perhaps we should partner him with someone we trust. Someone who will watch his back."

Graham sat back in his chair and looked up at the ceiling for several moments before straightening and nodding slowly. "I know who I can use. Eli's assignment has been Zoey, but I've been thinking . . ."

"Take him off Zoey, Graham," Doogan ordered him softly. "I'll kill him if you don't."

Graham grunted in reply but shook his head. "I don't think that's how we want to do it." He sat forward slowly, eyes narrowed thoughtfully. "How much do you know about Eli's interaction with Zoey?"

"That he fucks that bike up to keep her from winning." A dumb move on the kid's part. "She's ready to kick his ass."

A small, rueful grin tugged at Graham's lips then. "I assume you're going to fix that?"

Doogan merely stared back at him blandly.

"That's what I figured," Graham chuckled. "Look, let me put him with a deep-cover contact here in town. He's working with another DHS agent that only Bryce knows about. He's older and he's damned good with younger agents. He'll make sure whatever changes you make on the bike stay. Eli trusts him, Doogan, and Zoey does as well. Let's give it a chance."

"Who? It won't work if I don't know who he is." He loved getting to know the black agents Bryce kept hidden on the books.

"Zoey's landlord," Graham admitted. "Lucas Mayes. He's former SEAL and he's been working with me ever since an injury sent him home. I'll talk to him, apprise him of the situation. He knows how to keep his mouth shut with the Mackays too, but he's damned protective of all of them."

It could work. If Eli didn't learn to contain his animosity toward Doogan and the director learned of it, the repercussions wouldn't be pleasant.

"We'll try it." Doogan nodded. "Let Mayes know I'm aware of his status. And he has my contact info." He grinned. "I've known of him for a few years now."

"Figures," Graham snorted. "Now, how 'bout dinner tomorrow?" An amused glint filled his friend's eyes. "Come on, you have to meet the twins before they're grown. You never stay long enough to see them. You're going to be their godfather."

Doogan just stared at him for a long moment.

Godfather? Hell, he could feel his guts burning with the onset of acid reflux already. Godfather to a Mackay? He just barely contained a shudder.

"I must have misunderstood you . . ."

"Nope. Godfather." Graham rose to his feet. "Come on, Sam just arrived and Kye's getting pissy. She'll start a fight."

"Uh, Graham, about that . . ." Doogan was a bit slower to rise.

Godfather? No, that simply wouldn't work.

"Brom." Graham turned, his look somber now. "They're my

kids. My soul. You'd protect them if the worst happened, I know you would."

"But . . ."

"This just makes it official. Come on, you know I'm not going to change my mind. Stop protesting. Let's go help Sam get Kye out of here."

Godfather? Kye and her bar fights and Samantha Bryce all in one night?

He could feel karma's teeth on his ass and it wasn't pleasant.

Not in the least.

NINE

She was restless.

By the next evening, Doogan still hadn't returned to the apartment, and though Eli had been there the night before, he was gone early the next morning.

Dreams had haunted her sleep, and they haunted her after she woke. Like flashbacks, the colors icy blue and emerald green, something scarred and something gold.

Working out in the gym didn't alleviate the restlessness this time, nor did it ease the constriction in her chest; the certainty that there was something she had to remember, something imperative eluding her, was driving her crazy.

Her fists slammed into the punching bag; she kicked at it, pummeled it with all the fury and certain knowledge that time was running out.

The nightmares were becoming worse, but they were changing. How they were changing she couldn't remember.

"You killed me, Zoey . . ."

But he wasn't dead. He was glaring at her, emerald-green eyes so like Natches, filled with anger and hatred.

She couldn't fight him because she was restrained. Her wrists and ankles were tied to her bed, panic and horror raced through her.

Slamming her fist into the bag, Zoey collapsed against it, her ragged breaths half sobs as pain exploded through her head, nearly taking her to her knees with the force of the agonizing strike of sensation.

She didn't know what to do. She couldn't talk about the nightmares; the pain became worse and sometimes just thinking about it was enough to fill her with agony. She just wanted it to stop. The nightmares, the fear, the certainty that there was far more involved than just her overactive imagination playing with her were growing by the day.

But there were no answers.

Even her sisters believed it was just a nightmare.

Even Sam . . .

"Come on, Zoey, let's get you inside before someone sees you . . ." Sam picked her up, the warmth of her body a shock against Zoey's icy flesh.

"I'm so sorry . . . Tell Momma I'm so sorry, Sam . . ."

The other woman laid her in a bed.

"Here, you're so cold, Zoey. Let me turn the heat on, honey. Let's get you warm . . ."

"I killed Harley, Sam. I killed him. I have to tell you. I killed Harley." She gripped Sam's arm, trying to hold on to her as the agony in her head refused to dim.

Then the warmth was surrounding her. It didn't touch the iciness inside her, but it eased the painful cold on the outside.

So cold . . .

She was going to throw up.

The pain was too much; it was blinding now, like needles piercing and ripping through her brain, cracking it open.

". . . pop your little head like a grape . . ."

She went to her knees, her hands gripping her head, fighting the pain and the roiling in her stomach as ice seemed to encase her entire body.

She'd never relived those images outside her nightmares. Why now?

A punch of pain erupted in her skull again. She was cold. So cold that shudders began jerking through her, uncontrollable, violent tremors she couldn't still.

Pouring with sweat, her breath heaving from her lungs, Zoey fought to catch her breath, to stop the ragged, broken sobs and terrifying shudders. What had happened that night?

A jagged scar . . .

Intense, white hot, the pain drove her to the floor, her shoulders meeting the mat. Curled into a fetal position, gasping cries falling from her lips, she fought to live now. The agony was ripping her brain to shreds, destroying her . . .

"Zoey!"

No.

Oh God, not Doogan . . .

"Zoey, baby. Come here."

Son of a bitch. Whoever had done this to her was going to die! By his hand, they would die.

"I'm here," he whispered softly, so softly he knew she'd have to concentrate to hear him. "I'm with you, baby. Right here."

The suggestions he'd made while she'd been under the influence of that powerful mind-control drug were subtle but all the stronger for it.

He was there. The pain would go away.

"I'm right here, Zoey. You're warm. You're safe."

The shudders began easing, the iciness of her flesh warming as he wrapped himself around her, holding her firmly to his chest, his head against hers.

"I have you, baby."

He wanted to snarl in rage. He wanted to kill the bastard who'd done this to her.

"I'm so scared." Her whimper sent rage clawing at his senses as his chest tightened with the pain of what he knew she was feeling.

"No fear, baby." He kept his voice low. So low she had no choice but to concentrate on it to make out what he said. "No more pain, Zoey. No pain while I'm here."

Her arms tightened around his neck. She burrowed closer to him, her hands sliding into his hair, holding him to her.

"You danced with me," she whispered. "You didn't stay. You didn't come back."

Six years. It had been six years, six brutal, guilt-soaked years since he'd danced with her.

"I know." Brushing his lips over her temple, Doogan stroked his hands down her back, regret flaying his heart.

"Why?" The pain was easing from her voice, hunger edging into it instead of pain and fear. "Why didn't you kiss me? You wanted to."

He'd wanted to.

He'd wanted to eat her kiss, stroke and taste her sweet body before devouring her pussy. The fantasies he'd been helpless against the moment his eyes locked on her that night had destroyed him.

"I wanted to kiss you," he agreed. "I wanted to consume you. To fill my senses with you."

Her breathing was still hard, fast, but not from pain.

"I waited for you." Breathy, filling with such intense hunger that it constricted his breathing, her voice held him almost spellbound.

"What were you waiting for?" Lowering his lips to her shoulder, he let his tongue taste the sheen of perspiration on her skin and groaned at the salt and sweet taste of her.

"I'm a very bad girl in my fantasies," she whispered, as though it were a secret. "But you're very, very bad. Always so hungry for me and determined to teach me how to please you."

She was becoming lost to his touch now. No nightmares existed for her at this second. Only his touch, his lips, the pleasure he was building slowly within her.

Doogan nipped at her shoulder, then eased the little flash of heat with his tongue.

"How are you a bad girl?" He let the seductive hint of Irish into his voice then and felt the little shiver of pleasure that rippled up her back. "Come, love, tell me how you get bad with me in your fantasies. Tell me what you want me to teach you."

The thought of the acts he could teach her had his back teeth clenching to hold back a groan.

"Teach me to take your cock deeper in my mouth," she whispered. "I've read about it." She nipped at his neck, low, sharp little teeth sending fire lashing at his senses.

"Fuck. Baby." Doogan cupped the back of her head, holding her in place. "Now ease the burn. Lick over your bite."

She licked. Kittenish little flutters of her tongue stroked over the bite.

"Now tell me more," he demanded, his fingers clenching in her hair and pulling her head back. "Tell me about all those hot little fantasies." One hand went to the zipper securing her exercise bra. "And I'll suck your hard little nipples until you cum for me."

Pushing the bra over her shoulders, Doogan eased her back to the mat before coming over her. Inserting his knee between her thighs and pushing it firmly against her pussy, he watched that emerald ring darken around the paler green color of her eyes.

"Doogan." Moaning his name, Zoey arched when he brushed his thumbs over her distended nipples.

"Tell me more, Zoey." Crooning, teasing, he demanded to know what she wanted, what she dreamed of. "Do you touch yourself in these little fantasies?"

"Oh God, yes," she groaned.

"Did you ever use any toys?"

He watched her face, watched the emerald color deepen.

"I wanted to be able to please you," she moaned, crying out as he gripped her nipples lightly, tugged at them.

"What did you do, baby? You bought a toy?" he asked softly.

"Harder," she panted, arching into the tug of her nipples. "Make them burn, Doogan. Grip them tighter."

"Tell me." He all but snarled with the need to know. "Tell me what you did with that toy you bought."

Lowering his head, he took one swollen, sensitive nipple between his teeth and let his teeth tighten on it, tug at it.

"Oh God, yes," she cried. "I read how to take you deep if I ever had the chance. I tried to learn. Taught myself how to a little bit . . . Doogan." She tried to scream, nearly erupting in release when her words, the images they evoked, had him tightening his teeth on her nipple and raking it with his tongue.

As he released the tip, satisfaction surged through him at the ruby flush of the tight tip.

"You want my cock deeper in that tight little throat?" Moving his knee back, Doogan pushed one hand beneath the tiny shorts she wore to the saturated heat of her pussy.

"Deeper," she panted, twisting beneath him when his fingers found the clenched, rippling entrance to her pussy.

Damn her. He was ready to blow any second. Never, not even once had another woman driven him so hard, so fast into a hunger he couldn't control.

"I'll cum in your throat again," he groaned. "Is that what you want, baby?" He rimmed the entrance, feeling the silky slide of her juices against his fingertips.

"Yes. Oh, Doogan, I want that. I want to hear you cry out my name like you did the first time."

His finger pushed inside the gripping heat of her inner body in one hard, bold thrust.

For a second, just a second, he was certain she would explode before he wanted her to.

"There, baby," he whispered, licking her nipple as each breath she took ended in a lingering little whimper.

Retreating, dragging the slick dampness from inside her, he eased his finger lower, finding the tight puckered entrance he sought.

Hips lifting, she whimpered his name each time he dragged her body's lubrication to the closed, extremely tight portal of her rear.

"I'll buy you a toy, Zoey," he promised, slickening her further, wishing he'd had the foresight to bring what he needed to teach her how to take the pleasure he could give her there.

"Then, while I'm fucking your tight little throat, I can fuck you right here as well." He pushed his finger to the first knuckle inside the gripping entrance of her anus and nearly came in his jeans when she screamed his name and demanded more.

"Deeper," she cried. "Oh God, Doogan . . ."

She writhed on the penetration, bearing down, taking him to the next knuckle.

Twisting his wrist Doogan sent a finger thrusting inside her pussy, his lips covering a nipple, consuming it, nipping and licking and growling with demented hunger.

He couldn't take much more.

God, he had to get inside her.

Pulling back, he ignored her shattered cry, her demand to give her more. Loosening his jeans, he drew the engorged length of his shaft free before gripping her wrists and pulling her into a sitting position.

"On your knees," he snarled.

He didn't wait for her to move. Wrapping one arm around her hips, he lifted her, turning her. When she caught her weight on her hands and knees, he jerked the brief little shorts over her shapely ass to her knees, gripped his cock, and, as he watched, pressed it against the glistening, swollen curves of her pussy.

"I'm going to come inside you again," he breathed out in anticipation. "Like I did before. Damn, Zoey, it's incredible how good it feels to pump my release in your snug little pussy. To feel you surrounding me . . ." He pressed forward. "Ah baby, so hot and wet. So tight and sweet."

Her inner muscles bit down on him, tightening, rippling around the advancing intruder, milking him deeper, sucking at his flesh with such incredible pleasure that holding back was killing him.

Sweat trailed from his temple, beaded the rest of his face. Teeth clenched, a groan pulling from his chest, he pushed inside her further. His balls tightened, his cock throbbing. And the sweet heat enclosing him was like a silken vise tightening around his cock.

Still, he pushed in with slow, measured thrusts, watching her flesh stretch around him, seeing her juices clinging to his shaft as he pulled back. Then in again, groaning, his thighs bunching to hold back his release as her inner muscles sucked at the too-sensitive head of his cock.

She was killing him. She was ripping his soul open, tearing down the defenses he'd spent years building, and reminded him, with each look, each second he spent with her, why he'd nearly broken a sacred vow one hot summer night, just to have her.

"Ah Zoey, I love how you take me," Doogan groaned behind her. "So hot and tight, sucking my dick in . . ." His hips jerking, driving him deeper, harder.

A desperate cry spilled from her lips.

She needed harder, deeper. He was killing her with the exquisitely slow thrusts and retreats. Sensitizing her to the point that the pleasure was an ecstatic agony.

Excitement raged through her, making breathing harder, each breath becoming a moan as he stroked inside her. The callused fingers gripping her hips kneaded her flesh; she felt beads of his sweat drip to her back, felt his cock throbbing inside her, the heavy, ropy veins rasping against her inner flesh, the broad, mushroomed head driving her crazy with each thrust before the heavy shaft lodged inside her, pounding with each beat of his blood racing through the throbbing veins.

"You're killing me," she cried, her shoulders collapsing to the mat, her nails digging into the tough canvas. "Stop torturing me, Doogan . . . Oh God . . . Doogan, please . . ."

Slow, so slow she could feel every heated stretch of her inner muscles as the broad crest eased inside her. Flexing, rippling in need, her pussy clenched on the invader, milked it, fought to hold him inside her.

It wasn't enough.

Each slow impalement only built the need higher, increased the storm beginning to rage through her senses. Lazy, steadily tightening spirals of sensations lashed through her while each slow thrust, each retreat, had her crying out the need for more, for harder, for relief from the steadily building intensity that was driving her crazy.

"Sweet Zoey," he crooned behind her, that hint of the Irish accent so damned sexy it just made her wetter. "Ah babe, how I love the feel of you."

"Doogan, I need you. Now," she groaned, her fingers fisting, perspiration dampening her hair now. He was burning her alive, the flames searing her senses, racing through her body like wildfire. "Please let me cum. Please . . . Fuck me, Doogan."

A sudden, slamming thrust nearly triggered the explosion she was begging for. As though his control merely slipped for an instant. He stilled as the hard, fast thrust buried him to the hilt, his hands clenching on her hips, a rough groan tearing from his chest.

"I love you fucking me," she whispered brokenly as he eased back, retreating by slow degrees. "So thick and hard inside me, so hot . . ."

Hard, shocking, white-hot pleasure suddenly snapped through her as he thrust inside her hard and deep, not just one, twice, three times . . . Oh God, she was so close, and he stilled.

"Fuck me. You little witch. You'll pay for that, love," he groaned, his breathing harsh, heavy.

"Willingly." Clenching on the flesh stretching her with such brutal pleasure, Zoey whimpered, stretched on a rack of such pleasure she didn't know if she'd survive the release. "What pay . . . oh God, what payment?" She groaned as he moved against her, stroking her internally. "Fuck me, Doogan. Deep and hard and the next time you get your dick in my throat—" She screamed.

Or rather she tried to scream.

One hard hand buried itself in the hair at the back of her head, tugging, pulling at it as the other tightened at her hip and the control he'd just had a handle on slipped completely.

Coming over her, Doogan settled at her shoulder, his teeth clenching at her flesh like an animal and pushing her higher as he began thrusting inside her with such hard, deep lunges she felt the ecstasy gathering like supercharged particles. Increasing, moving faster inside her, hotter, tightening . . .

"Oh . . . Doogan . . ." She cried out for him when it overtook her.

Heady, white hot, blinding her with the intensity of the orgasm that detonated inside her with such force, such steadily increasing pleasure she swore for a second she might have died from it.

"Ah hell . . . Zoey . . . Damn you, Zoey . . ." Fiery, lashing, the jetting pulses of his release inside her only added to the ecstasy. Each pumping ejaculation increased the sultry splendor and the orgasm she could feel invading every part of her.

Her breath caught, held just before the racking, uncontrolled shudders of rapture began tearing through her again. And Zoey swore she felt a part of her very spirit open, felt the pleasure invade it, and felt Doogan mark her there even as he marked the flesh he held captive at her shoulder.

As the brutal shudders of ecstasy eased away, she collapsed beneath him, breathless, exhausted.

"Witch," he groaned, pulling from her as their too-sensitive flesh reacted with a sensation far too close to renewed need. "You'll kill me."

She grinned. "Hmm, good way to go, huh?"

Lying beside her and pulling her into his arms, he gave her an odd, almost amused grin. "The best, sweetheart. The best way to go."

So why, she wondered, did he sound so damned somber and filled with regret?

TEN

The next evening Zoey couldn't stand the isolation of the apartment any longer. The mark on her neck hadn't yet faded enough for her comfort, and the fact that she was confining herself to the apartment to ensure her family didn't see it, was only pissing her off. She couldn't have a life that entailed anything her brother disapproved of. She couldn't have a motorcycle that he knew about because it was just too dangerous. And don't even think about having a lover. Unless he chose that lover for her. She hated it. Hated having to hide so much of who she was and what she wanted. Working out again lasted no more than half an hour. She couldn't concentrate on the painting she'd started weeks before. And she needed to escape. The restlessness was only growing and she didn't know why. Why was it tormenting her now? Why did her apartment seem too closed in, her mind her enemy and her life racing out of control?

And why the hell was she hiding, too damned scared to leave

because someone might tell her brother she had a hickey? It was making her crazy.

Dressed in jeans, tank, and sneakers an hour later, she escaped and headed out of town in the little roadster she'd managed to buy off Billy Ray the year before. The restlessness she couldn't seem to do anything with was like an itch she couldn't scratch, simply because she couldn't find it. Irritating as hell, impossible to ignore. That feeling that she was forgetting something important from those dreams was like that itch. She knew it was there, it was making her crazy, but she just couldn't locate the right spot to scratch.

Eli wasn't even around to distract her.

He hadn't returned yet, and he'd been acting damned strange since Doogan had begun sleeping with her. She rarely saw him and she found she actually missed him a little. Especially now, when the need to burn away the restlessness required at least a good sparring match.

Driving to her sister Lyrica's, Zoey grimaced at the sight of Natches's car parked in the driveway as she neared the turnoff. Graham's Viper was absent and she had no doubt he was meeting Doogan somewhere. It was nearing dark and she had no idea what Doogan thought of as late, so she had no idea when he'd be back to the apartment.

Being alone was preferable to having Natches interrogate her, though. He'd been doing that for a while now whenever he saw her. What had she been doing? Who were her friends, was she dating anyone yet? She felt like a damned teenager again.

Rather than pulling into the driveway and dealing with her cousin's questions and general nosiness, Zoey continued along the back road as it wound along the edge of Graham's property before circling along a tributary of the lake and heading back to town.

As she came to a stop sign before turning onto the main road nearly twenty minutes later, car lights suddenly flicked on, a motor racing, before a vehicle tore from a graveled side road and barreled toward her.

Instinct had Zoey hitting the gas, the car's motor that her cousin Natches kept in peak condition responding immediately. The tires bit into blacktop and threw her forward, the back end fishtailing before she righted it and managed by inches to keep the truck from running over her. Cursing, she glanced at her rearview mirror, the lights of the other vehicle gaining on her fast once again.

"I don't need this," she snarled. "You've had it, Billy. I'll kick your ass for this." Right after she called his stepbrother, Clay.

Dawg would go apeshit if Billy actually managed to touch the bumper of her car.

Just as she neared the turnoff to Graham and Lyrica's home, the truck's horn sounded behind her, raucous and strident. Red and green trim lights flicked on along the grill of the truck, assuring her she hadn't been wrong about the identity of the asshole behind her.

That boy had a few screws loose, and that was all there was to it. Slowing, she let the moron race around her only to groan at the sight of Natches standing on Graham's front porch through the trees separating the house from the main road. There was no doubt he'd heard Billy Ray, and he'd have definitely recognized the sound of her car, motor revving and tires screaming as she tore out of the side road. If she didn't stop, he'd be at her place within minutes of Graham's arrival, which would probably coincide with Doogan's arrival at her apartment.

Turning onto the narrow road again Zoey made the turn into the narrower lane leading to her sister and brother-in-law's home.

Turning off the ignition, Zoey slid from the car and headed up the walk.

"Okay, sis?" Concern filled Natches's emerald-green eyes when Zoey stepped to the porch.

He was her cousin, but Dawg, Natches, and Rowdy were often mistaken for brothers by those unaware of the Mackay family history. And she loved them like brothers. Overprotective, affectionate, always loving, brothers.

"The little moron." She rolled her eyes at Billy Ray's antics as his hand settled at her back, leading her into the house.

"Where's Lyrica?" she asked.

"Her room, with the babies," he answered, his voice relaxed enough, but there was an edge of tension in his expression that warned her that Billy Ray's future could be in question. "That was Billy Ray tearing around you, wasn't it?"

She heard that carefully bland tone and knew it for what it was. It wouldn't be much longer before Billy was sporting Mackay bruises.

"Dammit, Natches, they're friends. Let it go," she demanded, turning to face him as she entered the hall, knowing if she didn't confront it now then she'd only have to deal with it later.

"I heard you tearing onto the road a mile away, Zoey," he refuted, concern flickering in his gaze. Concern and no small amount of anger. "The way the motor was screaming, you were scared. Don't deny it."

She didn't hesitate. One never hesitated when it came to Natches. Going to her tip toes, she shoved her finger in his face, anger tightening her expression.

"If you, Rowdy, or Dawg or any of your cohorts lay one hand on my friends, Natches, I swear I'll head straight to California. Seth and Saul have promised I could stay with them any time

I want. Keep pushing me, Natches, and my 'want to' just may get real deep and intense. Know what I'm saying?"

The Navy SEAL August twins had made the offer more than once after hearing about her brother's and cousins' attempts to protect the sisters.

It distracted him, though. His gaze had strayed to her neck, where she'd pulled her hair over her shoulder to hide Doogan's mark. At least, she hoped it was still hidden.

"That worries me?" he snorted. "Hell, Zoey, those boys of Cade's and Marley's are a hell of a lot more protective than we are."

Natches might have to redefine their ideas of protection.

"And I wouldn't forget, cousin," she reminded him with a fierce glare. "The Mackay sisters and the August brothers are just kissin' cousins, and those are some fine-lookin' Texas boys."

Natches actually stepped back in shock before he blinked as though he couldn't believe she'd said something so outrageous. "You wouldn't . . ."

Well, no, not now she wouldn't. But he didn't have to know that, now did he?

"The Mackay cousins could when they were my age," she reminded him. "Do you think I wouldn't get happy-happy with two of those bad boys if you dared me, Natches? Push me and find out."

Walker's Run Bar

Doogan saw the confrontation, outrage and pure white-hot, livid lust surging through him at the threat she made to her cousin.

"Oh, fuck!" Eli snickered as he watched the live feed from

Graham's security camera on John Walker's large-screen television. Lyrica had called her husband the second Zoey had stepped
into the hall and laughingly told him to pull up the security feed.

"Damn, Zoey." Natches rubbed at his chest, the camera catching his wince and that expression of disbelief on his face.

"Acid reflux," Graham guessed, chuckling as he glanced at
Doogan. "This is about to get good."

"You're making my acid reflux burn," Natches grimaced.

"Test me, Natches." She bared her teeth, heavy black lashes
narrowing over her pale green eyes. "Not a single bruise."

"You wouldn't . . ."

"Winter gets real cold," she reminded him softly, and the faint-
est hint of sensuality flickering over her expression had his teeth
grinding. "A set of those twins would keep me just nice and warm,
don't you think? You know how much I hate the winter. You really want to test me on it?"

Oh, like hell.

Doogan could feel every bone and muscle in his body tightening in outrage as he watched. Natches blinked. If her cousin's
expression was anything to go by, he was just as outraged. And
furious. Not to mention fucking speechless.

"Not even one bruise," she snarled. "Not by you or any of
your friends, or you just watch me."

Elijah and Graham were choking on their laughter. Doogan
was grinding his molars to nubs.

Graham stood, legs braced and arms crossed over his chest,
head covered as his shoulders shook. Eli leaned against John
Walker's desk, moisture building in his eyes as he tried to contain
his mirth.

"Is she serious?" John questioned, barely getting the words out
as Natches seemed to pale on the large screen.

"Oh, she would do it or die if he pushed her," Graham chuckled. "And Natches knows it. If any Mackay or his friend touches Billy Ray, she'll head straight to Seth and Saul. And they'd go head to head with anyone dumb enough to stand between them and a woman they took as a lover. Even a Mackay."

Doogan felt his lips tightening. Thankfully, he wasn't a friend of Billy Ray's or the Mackays'. He could beat the shit out of the little fucker.

"I'm going to assume we're finished here?" He'd had enough of the show Lyrica had informed her husband was being played out in their home.

"Now, I'm going to go see Lyrica and the babies," Zoey stated. Settling back and taking a deep breath, she pushed the hair back from her face before giving her cousin a sweet smile, even as she flashed the dark mark he'd left on her lower neck, almost hidden by her curls until she flipped them back. "And I still love you, cuz," she promised. "No matter what you push me into doing."

Natches actually flinched, but not at her reminder. He'd seen that mark himself, and Doogan swore he paled further. There was no mistaking the fact that Natches's gaze had lingered just that second too long on her neck or that he swallowed a little tightly, no doubt biting back his outrage.

"Well, Zoey, I love you too." Natches cleared his throat. "But I really don't want to kill one of those August brats."

"Might be interesting to see the attempt." She frowned, and Doogan wondered if she noticed Natches had a slow, deep burn rousing his notorious Mackay temper. "Navy SEALs. And they look pretty tough to me. You might have a fight on your hands there."

Turning from him, Zoey moved quickly up the stairs while Natches blew out a hard breath and shook his head as though to clear it.

"Damn," Elijah breathed out in amazement. "Fuck me. She won."

"She usually does," Graham assured him thoughtfully.

"Good night, gentlemen." Doogan headed for the door. "Perhaps tomorrow the three of you can keep your minds on the meeting."

He intended to be waiting when Zoey arrived home. He'd just have to see how firm her resolve was in having that pert little butt spanked and then penetrated. Those August boys never took a woman alone, and greatly enjoyed taking their women anally.

Hell, Doogan thought, she'd probably blow his mind there too.

Several things were for damned sure, though. If she even considered heading to Texas or California, then she'd deal with him. And he'd be having a talk with Billy Ray very soon.

Very damned soon.

Leaving Graham, Eli, and John to chortle over Natches mumbling now, Doogan headed back to Zoey's. Before turning onto the street that passed the converted warehouse, he parked beneath a heavily leaved oak tree on the street bordering the apartment. Shutting the motor off, he reached behind the passenger seat, removed a set of night-vision goggles hanging from it, and pulled them on over his head.

As thorough as he was, still, he nearly missed the single presence positioned just across from the front entrance of Zoey's apartment. The heat signature he caught sight of was watching the front lane leading into the building, his profile to the back entrance of Zoey's home, though any lights would draw his attention.

Positioned on the roof of the discount store, cleverly tucked between two vents, Doogan would have missed him if the watcher had settled into position just a few inches deeper into the small area.

Well now, who was so very interested in Zoey tonight that hadn't been interested in her before?

Fortunately, there was something very familiar about the height and demeanor of the watcher. Doogan knew the men he worked with, especially those he'd sent out for shadow ops training as he had that one.

There was no way to get his truck up the lane to the back of the warehouse without being seen, though. And until he was certain if the watcher was an enemy or friendly, then he'd just as soon remain hidden. Leaving the vehicle parked where it was would draw attention as well. Mackay attention no doubt.

That left maneuvering it, in the dark and without lights, along the narrow path sheltered by heavily leaved oak trees that bordered the back of the property. It was doable, if he was lucky. And he was feeling lucky.

Securing the night-vision glasses to his head, Doogan slid the vehicle into drive, the sound of traffic among the nearby streets hopefully enough to cover the smooth purr of the motor as he used the trees to hide his turn onto the sidewalk, then along the property bordering the warehouse until he came to the line of sheltering trees.

Keeping a wary eye on the watcher's position, Doogan eased the truck along the tree line, then into the garage with surprising speed. Using the fob Zoey had given him, he ensured that the security was reset, turned off the truck, and stepped from it.

Careful to keep the lights out, he moved quickly and quietly up the metal stairs, the night-vision goggles firmly in place. He made his way quickly through the upper level to Zoey's room, where he'd have a clear view to the roof across the clearing. Tearing the goggles off as he reached beneath the bed, he pulled the rifle he'd stored there free and stepped to the curtained window.

Zoey'd be returning soon and he'd be damned if he'd let some bastard take her out. Even if it meant revealing himself in her life to her brother and cousins. He eased the barrel of the weapon to the edge of where the curtains met and adjusted the night-vision sights.

His lips thinned at the sight of the watcher in clear view now, night vision attached to his head as well and staring back at Doogan.

His cell phone vibrated with an incoming text.

I got this, the message read.

Got what?

Your back, bro! the watcher typed back. *Your back!*

"Fuck!"

We need to talk. Now! Doogan demanded.

Later. Don't get distracted. Protect Zoey!

No! Now! Doogan demanded. *Will come to you!*

Later, bro!

Have to talk . . .

There was no answer. The message waited; the icon indicating that it was unread stayed next to it.

"Damn you!" He checked the rooftop again, but it appeared deserted. Son of a bitch, what the hell was Harley up to?

Later, bro, his ass. That damned kid was going to end up pissing him the hell off. And his mood was already iffy after hearing Zoey's threats to head to California.

Dammit. Those August brats were family to her. Third or fourth cousins, he was certain.

Kissing cousins.

Like hell.

Pacing the bedroom, he waited for her return; the thought of her allowing those damned women-sharing bastards to touch her was more than he could tolerate. He'd be damned if he'd allow it.

Raking his fingers through his hair in frustration, Doogan refused to delve into the reasons why he was so damned pissed off over it. Because he'd never cared before who or what a woman was doing. If he found himself disapproving of a woman's actions or interests, then he simply moved on. There were plenty of women in the world.

There was only one Zoey Mackay.

And that thought didn't set well with him at all.

Sam Bryce stepped from her pickup; the glimmer of a vehicle parked on the dirt path behind the evergreen shrubs at the far end of the parking lot drew a heavy breath from her.

God, she was tired, and she knew damned good and well that the owner of that car wasn't out to just check out the scenery. He had far better things to do with his time. And he had a key to her apartment. She had no doubt he was waiting for her.

Striding across the narrow strip of grass to her patio, Sam slid the patio door open and entered the apartment. Just to find out how very wrong she was.

"Let the light out, Sam." Chaya Mackay rather than her husband stood leaning against the counter separating the kitchen and living area, a glass of Sam's favorite wine held loosely in her hand.

There was a weapon clipped to her waist, a sheathed knife strapped to her thigh. Chaya wasn't there for friendly conversation or tips on a new cookie recipe, she guessed. Son of a bitch, Mackays were getting on her last nerve.

"You know, you're about as ballsy as any Mackay," Sam groused, sliding the door back into place with a heavy push.

Chaya lifted the glass and sipped at the moscato Sam was so partial to. The look wasn't one Sam found any comfort in either.

"You sleeping with Zoey?" Chaya asked as she lowered the glass and stared into the clear, perfectly balanced sweet wine for a moment.

When her gaze sliced back, piercing and curious, Sam wondered if somehow that Mackay arrogance had rubbed off on the wives. Maybe it was contagious. She'd make a note not to get too close to any of them from here on out.

She arched her brow mockingly now, though. "Is she in my fucking bed, Chaya?"

She tossed the shoulder pack she carried to a chair before stomping to her bedroom and removing her weapons. She locked the Glock as well as the smaller backup strapped at her ankle beneath her jeans in the wall safe, while she tried to figure out why the hell Zoey's cousin's wife was there.

"Come up with an explanation for what I haven't asked yet?" Chaya stood in the doorway, her voice amused, her golden-brown eyes like amber ice.

"You haven't asked a question yet," Sam snorted. "Ask. Then I'll worry about the answer."

She toed off her sneakers and pushed them beneath the chair next to the wall. The cap she wore came next before she began working the hair bands from the ponytail she kept her hair confined to while on duty.

All the while Chaya watched her with such clinical detachment it was unnerving. The other woman's years away from DHS hadn't weakened her stare in the least.

"I think you were fifteen the last time I saw you," Chaya commented long minutes later. "All long legs, long hair, and a chip the size of Texas on your shoulder." She sipped at the wine again while

Sam waited. She didn't have to wait long. "John David still hasn't accepted the fact that you'll never marry and give him grand-babies, has he, Sam?"

Sam shot her a hard glare before pushing past her and stalking to the kitchen, where she checked the empty bottle on the counter before pulling another from the fridge.

She normally detested wine, but the moscato she'd discovered had become one of her new favorite drinks. She'd tried a lot of drinks in the past year. Remaining silent as she worked the cork from the bottle, Sam cursed Doogan to hell and back. Somehow, he'd fucked up. He'd had to. Otherwise, the former agent wouldn't be here drinking the last of one of her few remaining bottles of wine.

"The next time I arrive home to find a Mackay camped out in my fucking apartment, someone's going to regret it," she stated, pouring half of the bottle into a wineglass.

The bottle held two good glasses and that was it. She had a feeling she would be drinking both rather quickly.

Finishing her wine, Chaya placed the glass on the counter, braced her hands flat against it, and leaned forward slowly, her expression cold.

"Zoey," she said softly. "It's explanation time, Sam. Did you put that rather deep mark on her neck, or did Doogan do it?"

Sam stared at the wine filling the glass. Yeah, she just might end up breaking out her reserve bottle. Tipping it to her lips, she drank half the glass, the light sweetened fruit taste washing over her taste buds and sinking into her senses.

Lowering the glass, she turned her gaze back to Chaya. "I'm not sleeping with Zoey. And I don't know about any damned mark on her neck."

The bastard. The least Doogan could have done was remained

consistent. For the first time in as long as she'd known him, it seemed he'd marked a lover's neck. He never did it. He claimed it was against his sexual policy or some shit.

Chaya eased back, though her expression didn't change.

"You know, Sam," she drawled as though amused, "I'm in a rather odd mood tonight. Why don't you just tell me a little fairy tale? A story I might be interested in. Natches finds it rather amusing to try to get his ass out of trouble like that. You can give it your best shot if you want to."

"Suck my dick, Chaya," she muttered. Lifting the glass, she finished it, then refilled it.

Did she even have enough wine to make tonight palatable?

Chaya chuckled at the sarcastic demand.

"Penis envy doesn't become you, Sam," she chided her gently. "Now, you know, it's always better to give me the explanations I'm asking for. Otherwise, I can become a problem. Do you want me to become your problem, Sam?"

Sam grimaced at the threat. She remembered the first time Chaya had made that statement.

"I'm not a kid anymore, and you're damned sure not my fucking bodyguard these days," Sam informed her.

"No, I'm Zoey's fucking family." Chaya's voice sliced like a frozen dagger. "Don't turn this into a battle. I'm better at it than you are. And we both know damned good and well you've had something you've wanted to tell me for a year now and can't get up the nerve to do it."

Sam rolled her eyes. "You think I'm scared of the Mackays, Chaya?" She had to laugh at that. "Don't fool yourself. I highly respect all of you, but I'm not scared of a single damned one of you."

"Then you're not near as smart as I thought you were." Chaya crossed her arms over her dark T-shirt. "Is Doogan sleeping with Zoey? And if so, why?"

"Why would any man sleep with her?" Sam shrugged, trying to ignore the little flare of cutting jealousy. Not that she'd ever had a chance with the black-haired little imp, but hell, she cared . . .

"Sam." Chaya's expression warmed for a second, compassion shadowing her eyes. "Don't you think I know how much you care about her? And we both know Zoey's in trouble. A trouble you can't fix for her."

No, she couldn't fix it. God knew she wished she could. Hell, she'd even tried to. Wished it had been her Zoey had responded to, that those pale green eyes had lit up at the sight of her, rather than the sight of Doogan.

"Something happened last year," Chaya continued, her tone softer now. "Something that's eating Zoey alive and causing you to camp out in your car and watch her place far too often. Now Doogan's here apparently, sleeping with her. I want to know what's going on."

"So you can tell Natches and her brother?" Sam snarled. "So they can lock her down so deep and bury her in so much protection she runs from all of us? That would get her killed faster than keeping my fucking mouth shut."

Chaya's expression never changed. "You know better. But push me on this and I will go to Natches. Trust me, and I'll do what I always do with her. Ensure her protection myself without alerting the men in the family. And before you play so charmingly dumb, I know about Zoey's little hijinks with Clay's group of bikers. I know about the races, the motorcycle, the black leather, and the fact that she has horrible nightmares of killing a friend." Fury flashed in her gaze. "Now tell me what the fuck is going on before I kick your ass myself."

The problem was, Chaya Mackay, despite the fifteen years she had on Sam, could probably do just that. Kick her damned ass.

Sam pulled free the last bottle of wine and jabbed the corkscrew into the cork. God, she should have bought that bottle of whiskey she was considering just after Doogan showed up.

Rather than using a glass, she tipped the bottle to her lips and took a long drink. Setting the bottle carefully on the counter, she stared back at Chaya silently, thoughtfully for long minutes.

"She was drugged last year," Sam stated then. "A hallucinogen used to brainwash the victim into believing they had done something they hadn't done, according to Doogan."

Chaya stiffened, her expression turning completely emotionless. "Go on." She nodded.

Sam swallowed, the action difficult as her throat tightened with remorse and regret.

Briefly she explained the state she'd found Zoey in at her sister's patio door that cool spring night. Icy cold, dressed in a pair of pajama shorts and brief sleep tank. Her suspicion that Zoey had been drugged had her calling her father rather than an ambulance. The Mackays were like royalty to DHS. She had no doubt they could pull diplomatic immunity if they put their minds to it.

Her father's orders to hold tight, that Doogan would be there, had infuriated her. But Zoey had been adamant that she had to confess to murdering Harley Perdue. An act Sam knew Zoey simply wasn't capable of committing.

The blood Doogan had taken from Zoey that night had affirmed his certainty of the drug used on her. Sam's meeting with Harley at the convenience store had assured her Harley was indeed alive. Then he'd disappeared and Sam hadn't been able to reach him since.

"He has breakfast with us at least twice a week," Chaya revealed. "Though Natches doesn't even tell Dawg and Rowdy about it. When we found him, probably just before daylight after you met him that night, he was barely alive. Someone had tried to carve his insides with a knife. And came damned close to doing it. They also managed a few hard blows to his head. He barely remembers what happened. Two men attacking him, the knife slicing him up, but little else."

"Wonderful." Sam pushed her fingers through her hair, her fear for Zoey increasing. "Chaya, he has to show himself to Zoey. She has to know he's alive."

"We have to figure this out first," Chaya retorted. "Why is Doogan sleeping with her?"

That one, Sam was really hesitant to answer.

"Don't play with me, Sam," she snapped. "Why is he sleeping with her?"

She blew out a hard breath, stared over Chaya's shoulder a long minute, then met the other woman's eyes.

"Probably because he's in love with her and too damned stupid to realize it," she stated heavily. "Crazy in love with her. He'd kill for her, Chaya. But I also think he'd die for her."

And she couldn't blame him.

The problem was, Doogan refused to see what he felt for Zoey. The past six years hadn't been easy ones for him. The bitter years of his marriage had caused him to shut down. With the death of his wife, his daughter, and brother two years ago, Sam had feared Doogan would never let anyone past his defenses again.

Chaya tipped her head to the side thoughtfully.

"And you know this, how?" she asked.

Sam shook her head. "I guess you'd just have to know Doogan. I know Doogan. And trust me, I've never seen him mark a woman's neck, and hearing that he has shocks the hell out of me. Even during his wilder days, he never left a mark on a woman's skin. He claimed it was a very intimate, very primitive way of shouting 'mine.' And he wasn't stupid enough to ever claim a woman as his. It was like asking her to shred his guts."

"Wonderful." Chaya reached back and rubbed at her neck wearily. "Natches will blow a gasket once he learns who's sharing her bed. He saw the mark earlier when she showed up to see Lyrica. It's about to kill him, not being able to figure out who's daring to claim his baby 'sister,' as he calls her."

Sam shrugged, lifted the wine bottle to her lips again, and finished it. Tossing the bottle to the trash, she stared at the can for long moments.

Yeah, Doogan loved Zoey. But Zoey loved Doogan too. Sam had seen it that night when he first spoke to the younger woman, easing her drugged hysteria, calming her instantly. Zoey didn't trust anyone instantly, drugged or not. She was wary, temperamental, and as explosive as hell. And she never trusted easily. Not like that.

"He was married when he first saw Zoey," Sam said softly. "A party at Clay's about six years ago. He watched her for hours, Clay said." She shook her head, wondering what loving someone like that would feel like. "Doogan ordered the DJ to play something slow until Doogan left the dance floor. When he did, Doogan went to Zoey and pulled her against him. They danced for an hour, Clay told me. He thought he was going to have to kick Doogan's ass before the night was out because he was messing with Zoey while he was married. Then, at the end of a song, Doogan stepped back from her, returned her to her friends, then left. He made certain to stay away from her after that. Until last year."

"Interesting," Chaya murmured, her tone thoughtful. "Tell me, Sam, do you love Zoey too?"

Did she love Zoey?

Sam frowned at the question, then slowly shook her head. "I care for her. I'd do her in a New York minute. But no." Lifting her head, she met Chaya's look directly. "I'm not in love with her. All I care about at this point is keeping her alive, Chaya."

ELEVEN

Doogan was back.

Zoey checked for the truck after parking in the front garage and moving up the metal staircase leading to the kitchen side of the living area more than two hours later.

Lyrica had been watching her confrontation with Natches on the television in her and Graham's room as she nursed her son. The kid might have been the quieter of the twins, but he ate so much that Lyrica had been forced to supplement his diet with baby formula.

As she nursed her son, Lyrica was all but howling with laughter. Natches had remained standing in the hall where Zoey left him, staring up the stairs, anger and a hint of confusion filling his expression.

He'd appeared not to know exactly what he should do at that point. It had been amusing, yes, but she hadn't quite seen the hilarity in it her sister did.

"Tell Graham and I'll never speak to you," she'd informed her sister.

Lyrica had only laughed harder. "I swear, I won't have to. He was watching at Walker's Run. Along with Doogan."

And now she would be facing Doogan. The thought of it excited her rather than filling her with the caution she knew it should.

As she entered the second level, the dim wall lights flipped on and Doogan stepped into the doorway of her bedroom, tucked his hands into the pockets of his black slacks, and watched her silently. The sleeves of his pristine white shirt were rolled above his wrists, the black tie hanging askew at the unbuttoned neckline.

Yep, Doogan was pissed.

She'd known he wouldn't be pleased when Lyrica had revealed that Graham and Doogan had seen her confrontation with Natches. That meant Elijah and John Walker had seen it as well.

"Did you just get in?" she asked, dropping her shoulder pack to the table at the top of the stairs. "I assumed you'd be later."

"Yet another miscalculation on your part tonight," he drawled mockingly. "And here I had hoped common sense would prevail at some point."

Common sense? Oh, he was getting into dangerous territory now. Snide, arrogant, and far too mocking, he was working on getting his ass kicked out of her apartment.

"Brom," she said sweetly, using the name Lyrica had revealed Graham sometimes called him. "Please let Doogan come out to play again. I like him much better."

The last thing she wanted to do was deal with the same asshole tendencies her brother and cousins felt the need to display.

"Tell me, Zoey, seeing as you've only recently taken one man as a lover, what makes you think you're ready to move into the big leagues with two, baby? Especially two Augusts? Have you experienced what it's like to take a man anally yet? Let alone have one filling that snug little pussy at the same time? I'd suggest allowing a single lover to initiate you first. Just to be certain it's an act you'll enjoy."

Zoey swallowed tightly, the suggestion paralyzing her as the thought of Doogan initiating her hit her imagination. She couldn't breathe. Excitement flooded her, her body sensitizing, nipples hardening, her sex becoming slick and heated.

"Perhaps. But I'm only accepting applicants with a bit more in mind where a relationship's concerned than it seems you do," she informed him sweetly. "It's that whole intimacy and trust thing, ya know?"

"Long enough to keep you warm this winter?" he growled, his tone low, brooding. "I'll make sure I show up every time it snows."

She laughed. The comment was so outrageous. If she didn't know better she'd think he was jealous. Unfortunately, she didn't think Doogan was into jealousy.

"My arguments with my cousins are none of your business," she informed him, knowing it was the wrong thing to say even as it slipped past her lips. "They can be morons and they make me insane."

That tacked-on little excuse wasn't helping, if his expression was anything to go by.

"Yet another erroneous assumption, sweetheart," he assured her, the smooth icy tone causing her teeth to clench in irritation. "When it comes to another man, or men touching you, then I'm making it my business."

He was making it his business? Really? And just who the hell did he think gave him permission to do that?

"We need to stop this now . . ." She actually tried to smooth things over rather than letting her anger, or her perverse sense of humor, get the best of her. Either one wouldn't be a good idea at this point.

"Tell you what, baby," he suggested smoothly. "I have a bit of experience in sharing a lover. Come to bed and I'll give you a taste of what you're asking for."

Her eyes narrowed, arms folding across her breasts to keep from throwing something at him. Something like the fake fruit Natches had carved for her and placed in a collectible basket for her dining table. Large apples, oranges, bananas, and clusters of grapes. They were heavy, just the right size to throw at dumbasses.

"Would you really?" Her brow arched as the question slipped past her lips with heavy sarcasm. "Well, how kind of you, Doogan, but I really couldn't let you put yourself out like that. I mean, after all, you barely know me."

Brooding lust filled his expression, darkened his eyes. "No worries, baby, I'm sure when I get my dick up that cute ass of yours, we'll know each other rather well."

Oh, would they now?

Arrogant jerk.

Not that she'd mind experimenting with the act, but his attitude left something to be desired.

"You can just keep your dick out of my ass." Her body was highly protesting that statement. "I won't be owned by you, my brother, my cousins, or any other man. And I sure as hell won't be berated for a confrontation that was none of your damned business, *Brom*."

She moved to stomp past him into her room just to have him step in her way, his gaze burning with lust.

"*Brom*." She emphasized his name again. "Don't start."

"Oh, Zoey." He shook his head slowly, his smile slow and lazy.

"I'm not your brother or your cousins. Pulling that Mackay arrogance on me simply doesn't work."

Well, that wasn't fair.

She'd perfected Mackay arrogance.

It even worked on Mackays.

Sliding to the side, she put the dining room table between them, grinning at his chastened look.

"You really don't want to tangle with me after I've just finished a fight with Natches," she warned him, narrowing her eyes at the pure arrogance that settled over his features. "It's a really bad idea, *Brom*."

"The sarcasm in your tone offends me, Zoey," he informed her coolly.

Irritation flickered over his features, pulling a small laugh from her. "Those power clothes you wear like a second skin offend me, but hell, each to their own, right? They make you arrogant and cold. Put your jeans back on. Let Doogan out of lockup and we'll discuss additional sexual privileges and who I allow to have them."

Mockery tilted his lips, gleamed in his chocolate gaze.

Damn him, she just loved his eyes. Even when they were cold and assessing as they were now.

Stepping around the side of the table, he stopped as she shifted to face him again, frowning. "I'm not into children's games, Zoey. Stop moving around the table."

She grinned. "Now that would just be too easy. I'm not all about your caveman tactics. You want me? Catch me."

Pure male dominance lit his expression. "Zoey baby, not a game you want to play."

She laughed at that, careful to keep the table between them. "Well, I'm sure it is. I'm playing it, aren't I?"

Dark eyes narrowed on her. "When I catch you," he said softly, "I'm tying you down to your bed, and once I've finished making you so damned hot you'll swear you're on fire, then I'm going to show you exactly what it feels like to take two men at once."

She couldn't help but grin smugly. "There's only one of you, Doogan."

"One of me, and the very erotic toys I've purchased just for you," he promised. "Everything's already laid out and ready."

She blinked back at him. He wasn't serious. He couldn't be serious.

Then, before she could anticipate the move, he vaulted over the table, hooked one arm around her waist, and dragged her to his chest.

"That's cheating," she cried out, laughter getting the best of her.

Not that he paid much attention to the accusation because a second later she found herself tossed over his shoulder and he was striding to her bedroom.

"Doogan, you so are not getting away with this," she squealed, part laughter, part outrage. "You're crazy."

Seconds later she was tossed to the bed, bouncing lightly, the laughter getting the best of her as her hair flipped around her face, the long, loose curls tangling and blocking her sight.

By the time she managed to push it behind her, he'd gripped her feet and removed her shoes and socks, and all she could do was stare at him with sudden, blazing arousal.

He was already naked, and fully aroused. The wide, dark crest and thickly veined shaft arrowed toward her, pre-cum glistening on the tip and reminding her how very erotic it was to take him into her mouth.

"Hey . . ." Her gaze shot to his face as he removed her jeans with simple expediency.

How had he managed to release the low-cut band around her hips so easily? And he'd taken the thin silk thong she wore with them.

Without answering her, Doogan moved to the bed, straddled her legs, and gripped the hem of her shirt. His position placed the straining length of his cock at just the right level. The perfect position to push it into her mouth.

"Give me the shirt." His voice was a hard, rough rasp as he pulled the tank to her breasts. Zoey licked her lips, lifted her arms, and let him have the tank top and then the lacy bra she wore.

He could have the damn clothes. She wanted him. She wanted him in her mouth, wanted him taking her, possessing her.

Her tongue swiped over the broad crest as she leaned forward those last few inches.

Doogan's response was immediate.

A low, harsh groan, the fingers of one hand bunched in the hair at the back of her head, holding her back, allowing her to taste him with her tongue alone. Lifting her gaze to him, Zoey licked what she could touch of the broad crest, loving the heat and the taste of him.

He had one knee bent next to her, his foot pressing into the mattress as the other rested on the bed. The perfect position for one hand to stroke up his thigh, her nails rasping lightly until they came to the taut sac at the base of his cock. His testicles drew tighter as she let her fingertips and her nails play against them.

"Think that's going to distract me?" he asked, his brown eyes completely wicked. "That your sweet mouth will make me forget just how many times I've dreamed of taking that sexy little rear of yours?"

"Hm. Possibly," she murmured before stroking the crest with her tongue again.

"Not a chance, sweetheart." The promise in his voice was the only warning she had before he moved, pushed her back on the bed, and then came over her.

His lips covered hers, owned hers, the kiss so hot, so carnal that her toenails wanted to curl with the pleasure. He held her wrists easily, stretching them above her head, holding her restrained as he worked her mouth, his tongue teasing hers, drawing her deeper into the mesmerizing eroticism sweeping through her.

So intense was the pleasure, the sheer excitement he caused with his touch that when he pulled back and she moved to wrap her arms around his shoulders, it took her a minute to realize he'd managed to restrain her.

She tugged at the bonds. The restraints on her wrists were soft, supple. Securing her wrists directly above her head, he'd have no problem putting her in whatever position he wanted her in. On her back . . . or on her stomach.

"Sneaky," she panted, breathless at the sensation of his lips at her neck, his hands stroking along her side to the swollen mounds of her breasts.

The raspy chuckle whispered against her skin as his kisses moved lower, his lips on a direct path to her breasts.

Her nipples were tight, hard, aching for attention. They were so sensitive that when he blew a soft breath over one, sensation heated the tip and dragged a moan from her lips. Chills of pleasure raced up her spine seconds later when he brushed his lips over the straining bud.

"This restraining-me stuff is going to have to stop," she moaned, because he was teasing her to death and she was loving it. Dying from the need for more sensation and arching closer, all but begging for more of the torment.

"We can discuss it later," he promised, the words whispered over the straining nub of the opposite nipple.

"When later?" She was panting, her voice filled with a pleading note.

"When your pussy's not dripping within seconds of being cuffed to the bed." His fingers were suddenly between her thighs, running through the narrow slit to prove his point.

She was so wet, so slick that the moisture lay in a thick, heavy layer over the swollen folds.

Once his fingers dipped into the lush, slick juices, they didn't retreat. Rather, his lips parted, drawing the hard tip of her breast into his mouth and drawing on it with fiery pulls of his mouth. His fingers slid lower, drawing the slickness back to the smaller, tighter entrance he sought. There, he rubbed the tightly clenched opening, the tip of his finger pressing and massaging it, stealing her breath with the forbidden, erotic caresses.

With each slight penetration of his fingertip, her senses became awash with a slight stinging pleasure as he parted the puckered flesh. Deeper, though, inside the feminine, sensual core of her, she could feel something more.

"What are you doing to me?" she whimpered, unable to tell him to stop, but not so certain of the stirrings of emotion that made little sense to her.

"God, Zoey." Releasing her nipple, he brushed his cheek over the highly sensitive nubbin of flesh. "I'm destroying both of us. Do you feel it, baby?"

Forcing her eyes open, she stared at the tightly drawn features, the heavy, carnal need, and in his melted chocolate gaze she saw shadows of some emotion she had no idea how to define.

"Tell me to stop, Zoey," he demanded, his lips moving to the opposite breast. "Tell me to let you go. Or neither one of us will be the same later."

Not be the same? It wouldn't be any different than when he took her virginity. How could any sex act be more momentous than that first time, that first lover?

Hazy sensuality surrounded her, filled her. When his head lifted she stared back at him, the pleasure drugging her.

"You're not going to do it, are you?" he groaned. "You won't tell me to stop, will you, Zoey?"

She could feel his cock pounding against her thigh, see the vein at his neck pounding in excitement.

"Maybe," she answered him breathlessly, stretching beneath him and letting a smile touch her lips. "Let me think about it a minute, 'kay?"

Let her think about it?

Let her think about it?

Doogan narrowed his eyes on her, seeing the challenge in her gaze, the hint of a dare and shadows of that destruction in her oddly colored eyes.

She was so fucking innocent. Too innocent.

She had no idea what she was tempting by allowing him to take her in this way.

"Time to think is over." Surging back, Doogan flipped her to her stomach before she could protest, glancing at the cuffs on her hands to be certain the toggle on the chain securing them to the bed turned with her wrists.

She gave a throaty little laugh filled with hunger and such a complete lack of fear that his chest clenched. She trusted him. At this moment, before she realized exactly what he was about to do to her, she trusted him completely. And once he was finished, that trust would go to her soul.

"How pretty." His hand smoothed over the curve of her rear. "So pert and well rounded. The first time I saw you, your back was to me and all I could think was how bad I wanted to spank that pretty ass."

He watched, anticipation and hunger exploding through him as his hand landed on the curve of her rear in a heavy caress, lifted, and he saw the first, erotic blush stain the satiny flesh.

Zoey stilled.

Her breathing was harder now, her fingers gripping the chains of the cuffs and holding on tight.

Giving her a moment to anticipate the next caress, he drew free the items he'd laid out earlier on the bed and covered with one of the pillows. The tube of lubrication and a vibrating dildo not quite the size of his own cock.

This had nothing to do with showing her what it would be like to take two lovers, though.

Smoothing his hand over her rear again, Doogan stroked her to her lower back before moving to grip her hips and pull her to her knees.

The sight of her juices lying heavy on the bare folds of her pussy caused his dick to clench in demand. He was so damned ready to fuck her. Where he was dying to fuck her required a bit of preparation, first.

"Doogan?" She whispered his name, the breathless, almost questioning pitch of her voice bringing a hard smile to his face.

She'd been so certain she could weather this as she had their first night together. Being a woman's first was an honor to any man, he'd always thought. But this . . . He let his fingers caress along the narrow crease, his fingers once again finding the puckered little entrance he intended to be the first to take as well.

"So pretty." And she was. She was so damned pretty. He'd

never forgotten her after that dance six years ago. And his hunger for her had only grown. "And you have the sweetest ass, Zoey."

His hand landed against the curve of her rear, the helpless moan that fell from her lips causing his teeth to clench as he fought for control.

As he lowered his head, his lips brushed over the slight blush his hand created, feeling the muscle tighten, feeling the little shiver that raced up her back. Holding her hips in place, he let his lips wander along the shallow crease, his tongue stroking, teasing until reaching the puckered entrance.

"Doogan . . ."

"Getting scared now, baby?" It wasn't fear. He could feel the way her body pushed against him, then eased away, hesitant in the face of caresses she'd probably never considered.

"Scared? Never," she scoffed, then whimpered in pleasure.

Flicking his tongue around the clenched entrance, he rimmed it teasingly as he lifted one hand and lowered it again in another of the heated little caresses.

She wasn't frightened, not in the literal sense, but Doogan could sense the feminine instincts rioting as he touched her so intimately. Just as he could feel her pleasure in the soft, silky slide of moisture coating the intimate folds just below his lips.

She was so wet, so slick. For the first time since he'd begun having sex, he could feel his self-control fraying with the need to just fuck. To fill her, pump inside her, and ride them both into the storm of carnal hunger and need building inside him.

Controlling this woman's passions and that instinctive Mackay arrogance and temperament would never be easy. She would always be a challenge. She would always be looking for a challenge.

Pulling back, he applied a heavy measure of the lubrication to his fingers.

With his free hand he caressed the rounded curve of her ass, tapped it again, just enough to create a sensual heat in the sensitive flesh and unlock the heart of the woman who would be his destruction.

Oh God, what was he doing to her?

Zoey gasped, her breath coming in hard pants, panicked excitement building in her. Arcs of fiery sensation detonated beneath the flesh of her rear, then raced through her bloodstream to a previously unknown depth of her sensuality.

This was crazy. With each little tap to her backside she was craving more. She ached for more of the heat that rode a line of pleasure and pain and only built a demand for more. His hand, broad and callused, tapped one cheek, then the next before returning and starting again. His tongue raked over that forbidden entrance, shocking her to her core, stealing her breath and tensing her body with an instinctive need to protest.

"Scared, Zoey?" The challenge in his voice, the dare she sensed in it, forced back the words she would have spoken, the plea she would have voiced that he release her.

She wasn't scared.

She was . . .

"Oh God, Doogan," she cried out at the feel of his finger, heavily lubricated and shockingly cool, pressing against the entrance now.

What was he doing to her?

"Should I stop, Zoey?" The knowing tone of his voice had her breathing in deep. The next tap to her rear had her back arching, fingers clenching into the blankets beneath. While her senses were locked in processing that new, fiery pleasure, that wicked finger pressed inside her, retreated, returned.

Like a thief, in that moment she felt him steal some part of her. A part of her she didn't know was hiding, waiting to be taken.

When his finger returned, more of the cool slick gel coating his finger, easing its penetration inside her, Zoey couldn't hold back her moan any longer. When his hand landed on her rear again she cried out at the twin sensations of white-hot pleasure. One feeding off the other before combining and lancing her senses with a need for more.

Always more.

Her body was greedy, each sensual storm only building the burning need to push higher, to let the spiraling sensations amass until they consumed her.

"So pretty, Zoey," Doogan groaned, his finger retreating from the narrow channel.

When he returned, her entire body tightened, back arching again as she felt a wider, hotter penetration. It was shocking. Sensations were detonating through her senses with sudden, ricocheting force, giving her no time to consider the implications, to build any defenses against the confusing pleasure and pain that only made her greedier.

She couldn't even touch him. She wanted to touch him, wanted to feel him.

"Easy, baby," he crooned behind her, that hint of Irish in his voice so damned sexy it would make any woman beg to give him whatever he wanted. "There you are, love. Damn me, you're so fuckin' pretty, Zoey. So hot and sweet."

As he spoke, his fingers moved inside her in slow, measured thrusts. Each impalement sent that hint of fire streaking inside her, but with each little thrust the fire would dim and she needed more. She wanted that fiery burst of white-hot heat and pleasure back again.

Opening her thighs wider, Zoey pushed back into the thrusts, taking his fingers deeper, harder, moaning at the carnal need building inside her and her inability to dim it.

"Like that, baby?" he crooned, the lyrical flow of his voice deepening. "That little bit o' bite? The way your pretty little rear burns and gets greedy for more?"

She whimpered at the intensity of those sensations.

With each thrust inside her, his other hand delivered a heavy pat to the rounded curves of her butt, each heated caress intensifying the burn beneath her skin and inside the far-too-sensitive channel his fingers were working inside.

"No. Don't stop," she demanded when his fingers slid from her entirely, leaving her aching, that entrance flaring with a demand that he return. As though the sexuality he was unleashing inside her were a force all its own, the building hunger no more than an extension of it.

It was terrifying, exhilarating. Like an adventure itself. One far more extreme and dangerous than she'd ever known before.

"Oh, sweet, I've no intention of stopping," he promised her. "Not until your body is lying limp and exhausted beneath me and my cum is spilling deep inside your sweet little ass."

A shudder raced through her at the warning, then shook her when his fingers returned. Slicker, the cool gel was worked inside when he returned with a less burning thrust. A single finger working the slickness inside her, over and over again, pushing in deep, past the ultratight ring of muscles where he teased the nerve endings there, built the increasing hunger for more before retreating again.

"Ah, sweet Zoey," he whispered. "Ya look so pretty with my fingers stretching your tight little rear. I wish you could see how sweet, how fucking hot it is when I see this."

Stretching. Burning.

Zoey wailed at the additional force of the fiery pleasure attacking the clenched entrance when he returned.

"You stretch so sweet and tight around my fingers," he breathed out, his voice rough. "You're almost ready, love. Almost ready to stretch around my cock and milk me inside. Almost, baby."

His fingers lodged inside her, stilling for a moment. That didn't mean he had any intention of giving her a chance to adapt to such destructive pleasure. Doogan had little mercy in him when it came to pushing her into the heart of the storm building inside her.

As his fingers stilled, she felt the broad press at the entrance to her pussy, then a slow, deep vibration as Doogan pushed the vibrator inside her.

"Son of a bitch," he groaned. "That's it, sweet love, take it. Let it fill your sweet pussy."

His fingers began stretching inside her, scissoring apart slowly, pulling back as they remained widened, until he slid free of her entirely.

That buzzing inside her, the vibrating pulse of the dildo worked further inside her, distracting her. It was thick and heavy, almost as thick as his cock, but not nearly as warm and satisfying.

His fingers returned again. All three, pressed close together but still so thick, so wide . . .

Zoey tried to scream as the vibrator was pushed to the hilt, the flash of intense, rocketing pleasure blazing through her senses a second before Doogan sent his fingers tunneling inside her rear, driving in deep before spreading apart again. The stretch of that inner ring, so tight and sensitive, had her clawing at the blankets.

She wanted to demand he stop. She needed to demand he give her more. Her hips moved, pressing back, rocking against the dual penetrations, pressing into them, her senses out of control with the lashing bursts of rapid-fire pleasure-pain.

"That's it, Zoey." His voice was rife with gathering lust. "Fuck back into me, baby. Damn me, when I get my dick inside your tight ass I'll be lucky I don't spill inside it on the first thrust."

His fingers jacked inside her, a short series of rapid little thrusts that had her wailing his name, burning from the inside out and eagerly awaiting each intense flare of agonizing pleasure.

"Now." She had to force the words past her lips. "Please. Doogan, please. Now."

He shouldn't talk to her. Each time he did, she lost more of herself to him.

Rather than giving in to her demand, he pulled the vibrator back, worked inside her again, pushed his fingers back in another, blistering thrust.

She should kick his ass for torturing her, but instead she was pushing back into each thrust, low, desperate cries spilling from her as instinct began to demand, and her body's response began tightening, nearing her orgasm.

Doogan chuckled, his fingers easing from her. "Not yet, my Zoey. You'll not cum yet. Not until my cock is buried balls deep and I'm shooting inside you with a force that may kill me with the pleasure."

TWELVE

Zoey fought her rocking senses as she felt his fingers retreat. The vibrator wasn't retreating, though. With surprising speed he anchored it firmly inside her before she felt him rising behind her.

Her body was a mass of sensations, fiery pleasure and intense demands.

"There, love." Doogan's lips pressed to her hip, one hand reaching beneath her, and a second later Zoey cried out desperately, the buzzing vibration filling her vagina, rippling through it and sending tremors of desperate sensation rocking her body.

"Now, baby." His voice was hoarser, deeper. "Now, I get to fuck that pretty little ass. Do ye know how often I've dreamed of it, love?"

The broad, blunt crest tucked against her back opening, the pressure blooming through the nerve endings building as the heated cock head began pressing in slowly.

So slow.

"Oh God . . . Doogan . . ." She pressed her forehead into the bed; her body shook, shuddering as she felt the opening parting, stretching around him with a slow, fiery buildup of agony and ecstasy. The most pleasure she'd ever known mixed with a desperate, white-hot burn she eagerly accepted. Accepted and sought more of.

Doogan didn't ease back, he didn't allow the flames attacking her senses to falter, he only stoked them, built them, let them begin consuming her.

"Doogan. Please . . ." she begged, crying out desperately as the slow, stretching burn began to consume her, to build in her flesh.

Like a drug. This pleasure was like a drug. She couldn't possibly survive . . .

"Should I stop, baby?" he crooned behind her. "Damn me, you're so pretty. You're opening for me love, flared around the tip of my cock, parting so sweet. And it's like flames beginning to wrap around my dick, you're so fucking tight."

Steady, stretching, burning, pleasure and pain and the heavy vibration destroying her senses, leaving her to exist for nothing but the increasing detonations of sensations so deep and intense her entire body entered a state of hypersensitivity.

"Ah, Doogan." She cried out his name again as the full width of his cock head slid inside, her muscles clenching with a spasming response and a surge of static sensation raced up her spine.

Her buttocks clenched furiously, involuntarily, the tissue locked beneath the blunt force rippling, working furiously to adapt to the invasion.

"That's it, baby." Guttural, rasping with pleasure, the hint of Irish, a shadow of emotion, he encouraged her acceptance as the tighter, more sensitive ring of tissue began flaring around the crest.

She couldn't take more.

Grinding her forehead into the mattress, she sobbed out at the increasing demands whipping through her, the heightened sensation, her flesh stretching, pleasure-pain building, taking her . . .

Inside her pussy the vibrator's deep, internal strokes and teasing caresses only aided the steadily rising, remorseless burn and demanding intensity overtaking her.

It wasn't pleasure. It wasn't pain. It was such a mix of both, so heightened, built to such a level it should have been terrifying. Should have been. If not for Doogan's soft croon, one hand steadying her hip, the other stroking, caressing.

"Now, love," he warned her gently. "We're almost there, sweet. Just here . . ."

Zoey screamed.

That place she existed within burned white-hot, with sensations fracturing inside her, pulsing with such a violent overriding response that she knew that when it was over, she would never be the same.

He hadn't been certain she would take him, Doogan realized as he forced his eyes to focus on the point where his body became a part of hers. The responsive tissue hugging the base of his cock rippled and pulled at his shaft. Inside, the bite of the inner ring of muscles locked down on his erection and rippling around it was nearly too much pleasure to bear.

It wasn't the first time he'd taken a woman's ass, but it was the first time he'd heard that scream of surrender and felt a woman give herself to him like that.

He could feel it. She was open to him, taking every moment of pleasure, every shocking second of carnal hunger into her woman's soul and locking around it while she gave a part of herself to him.

"Zoey, baby . . ." He wanted to sob for both of them. Because he felt her inside his soul, a presence so subtle he hadn't even realized what had been spurring the hunger for her until now.

He shook his head.

No. Emotion wasn't allowed. He could regret, hunger, he could even care. Love wasn't reality. It was a fantasy. A fucking chimera . . .

And it was digging into his soul like talons.

A hard shake of his head didn't clear it, no more than it cleared the beads of sweat stinging his fucking eyes.

Gripping her hips with both hands, Doogan concentrated on the pleasure, rather than the coming agony. Nothing mattered but this. The sweet lancing heat he could feel surrounding him, spilling from her, easing him.

Pulling back, watching the slick width of his cock stretching her flesh, he was still amazed she was taking him, stretching for him and begging for more. She was so tiny, so delicate . . .

He pushed inside her again, watching her take him. The need to cum was agony. Holding back wasn't going to last . . .

Fuck.

Fire and lightning surrounded his erection, whipped through the sensitive flesh and arrowed so deep inside his chest he wondered if it had struck his soul.

She was so damned tight.

His fingers clenched at her hips, feeling her tighten further, her flesh rippling around him, the vibration of the erotic toy lodged in her pussy echoed to his cock, making each sensation stronger, deeper.

Ah God.

Sweat dripped into his eyes as he focused on that point where she stretched around him, watching her hug his cock, feeling her flex and tighten around him as he moved. He couldn't stop moving. He had to fuck her, had to feel her like this, take her, bind her . . .

Whatever he'd meant to do when he began this, what he ended up doing was ripping away the lies she told herself and revealing a truth she feared would destroy her before it was over.

The sensations rocking her body, what he was doing to her, was more than just the physical act. The implications of it she might have enough brain matter left to ponder later, but she wondered for the briefest second, if she even wanted to consider them.

Restrained, at his mercy, nothing to hold on to but the instinctive awareness of trust or fear, Zoey learned she had the ultimate trust in Doogan.

The preparation, the penetration, and now the hard, heavy lunges of his hips, his flesh burying inside hers, rocking her to the core with so much burning pleasure she didn't know if she would survive the coming cataclysm. But she didn't try to avoid it either.

The explosion began in her clit, where Doogan tucked his palm between her thighs, allowing her to ride the sensations, to stroke the highly sensitive bud against his roughened flesh. That first detonation was all-consuming by itself. It ripped through her, jerking her body against his and setting off the explosion deep inside her pussy.

Her muscles clenched tight, dragging a groan from Doogan as he thrust into her rear channel, stroking the suddenly tense tissue despite the rapid-fire shudders and primal tightening of her body. When the powerful, soul-deep eruption reached its peak she screamed—or she tried to scream. Racking, heaving spasms attacked her as sensations so deep, so cataclysmic that they ripped through the very heart of her began setting off mini explosions of white-hot rapture.

She was flying through a storm of pure sensory awareness. Her body felt everything. The hard, jetting pulses of Doogan's release shooting into her rear, the rasp of his flesh with each jerk of her body that raked her too-sensitive clit against his palm. The brush of the air. The feel of his heart racing against her back, the feel of his cheek against hers, his weight held from her by the strength of his arm next to her.

He didn't mark her neck this time, but he didn't have to. There was no reason to leave a mark for others to see ever again. He'd left his mark inside her, in her soul, and that would keep any other man from her bed far more effectively than a mark to her skin.

Then she couldn't sense anything but the tidal wave of sensations as they converged and stole her ability to do anything but feel. The pleasure, the emotions suddenly running rampant through her heart, and the man behind her. And what she sensed there, she couldn't hide from either. A man who refused to acknowledge that he could feel, that he could love.

The man who would break her was far too broken to ever be put together again.

Doogan lay with Zoey spread across his chest like a living blanket, boneless, recuperating after he'd released her, wiped the moisture from her body with a damp cloth, then dried her skin.

She might not be moving, but she was thinking, and she was thinking hard.

He'd known during that time he waited for her to return from her sister's what he was going to do. Why he was doing it, he had refused to delve into at the time.

It wasn't because she'd threatened her cousin with the possibility of a complete move and a relationship with two men known to give little mercy where the sensual pleasures they could give a woman were concerned.

It wouldn't have mattered if she'd threatened to move in with one man, two, or a whole fucking unit. When the words slipped from her lips that she'd dare to allow another man to touch her, Doogan had existed on autopilot. Get to Zoey, take her, establish himself in the most intimate, the most instinctive way possible.

By marking her sensuality.

By owning it.

"Doogan?" The drowsiness in her tone was real, but he could feel what he had known was coming even before he'd touched her.

"Yeah, baby?" God, what had he done to both of them? He couldn't, he wouldn't lie to her.

"If I were really cold and called you, would you come keep me warm?" There was a note of amusement to her tone, as though it didn't matter the answer. He knew the answer mattered, though.

"Every time," he promised, knowing he would, knowing he'd be helpless against her need.

God, she'd slipped in when he hadn't meant to let her in. Stole right past his determination to keep her out of his heart.

"Why did you wait so long to find me again, then?" She kept her head against his heart, and he wondered if she heard what was left of it break. "Why did you wait?"

He forced himself to swallow, forced himself to answer her.

"Because I was married."

Zoey froze.

A chill washed through her. Where she'd been lazy and warm but a heartbeat before, she could now feel the icy fingers of fear invading her.

"Are you still married?"

"No, I'm not still married," he assured her, his hand stroking down her shoulder. "And it takes more than a piece of paper to make a marriage, I believe."

"Yeah, that's what Dawg says." Frowning, she tried to decipher the odd, dark note in his voice. "Did you divorce?"

"No. She died two years ago, the same day our daughter Katie was killed when she was struck by a car."

That tone, it was pain. Regret. And Zoey sensed there was far more to it than the brief explanation.

"I'm very sorry, Doogan," she whispered, pressing her lips to his chest, just over his heart. "That's a terrible loss."

"Yes, it was." Something in his voice had her heart breaking for him.

He'd lost the woman he loved and their child; where did that leave her where the future was concerned? The man she loved . . .

Dammit. She was in love with him.

That sucked.

His heart belonged to another woman, a dead woman. A woman who'd had his child, and that child was taken as well.

"Sleep, baby," he whispered, stroking her shoulder once again. "I have a meeting in an hour or so. If you wake and I'm gone, I'll be right back."

Lifting her head, Zoey met his gaze, the somber, dark eyes watching her intently. "Super-spy stuff?" She arched her brows playfully, aching to take just a little of that too-serious, dark regret from his gaze.

"Super?" he snorted. "Not hardly. Boring, tedious follow-up. The life of a super-spy isn't always guns blazing and cars racing."

No kidding.

She was actually trained for guns blazing and cars racing and still hadn't experienced it. The bad guys didn't often get to Somerset.

Yawning and settling against him again, she curled into his warmth and let her eyes close. "Wake me when you get back. I have things to do."

"Sleep, baby." His lips brushed over her forehead.

As she closed her eyes, her last thought was the painful realization that Doogan had far more secrets than she'd ever imagined.

THIRTEEN

"I have the information you requested earlier." Eli was angry. "Do you want company?"

Doogan nodded. "Wait in the truck till I get there. I have a few things to check before we head out. Text me the information and I'll be down when I've finished."

Eli nodded. Glancing to Zoey's door, he gave a shake of his head before turning to leave the living area.

"Eli?"

The young agent turned back to him slowly. "Yeah?"

"Stay angry all you want, but the insubordination is going to begin causing problems soon," Doogan warned him. "It's time to let it go."

"Let it go." Eli stared at him bitterly. "You think it's that easy?"

"I didn't kill her, Eli. I didn't frighten our daughter to the point that she ran out in front of that car nor did I put that bullet in

Catalina's head. And I didn't ask her to lie to her family. She was your sister, and I've tried to be patient because you were a fine brother-in-law. But it's going too far. Protecting Zoey is all I care about at this point, and I need to know I can trust you to do that. I'd hope your anger toward me won't affect that."

Catalina's lies and deceit during his marriage to her had nearly destroyed him. He hadn't given a damn. Katie had been all that mattered to him by then, and she'd known it. Because of it she'd tricked the brother that resented him and tried to steal the child Doogan had loved.

"Zoey's my friend," Eli stated simply, and Doogan heard the loyalty he felt toward her.

"Let's find out what the hell's going on here, fix it for her, and then we'll deal with the past," he suggested. "Until then, let's see if we can get along and do this right."

Sliding his thumbs into his front pockets, Eli stared back at him for long, silent moments before he gave a short, decisive nod.

"Understood." Eli nodded. "I'll text that information as soon as I get downstairs. I'll suit up and wait for you."

Within minutes Doogan had all the information he needed and had dressed in the protective black mission clothes such as the ones Eli would be wearing.

Thigh holster, weapon, and extra clips were secured in place as well as various other backup weapons. Grabbing the rifle, he laid it on the bed and pulled his phone from the secured pouch attached to the thigh of the pants opposite the holster.

Pulling up the earlier contact, he texted.

Have a meeting. Cover Zoey, he ordered the shadow that had stood watch earlier. He knew it was Harley. Hell, he was 100 percent positive it was Harley, and he'd kick the boy's ass once he showed himself.

Don't you ever sleep? He could only imagine the quarrel-some tone.

Now!

Bullshit.

Doogan sighed, shaking his head.

Not debatable. Leaving in 20. Will inform Natches of your refusal should she be harmed, he informed the other man.

Fuck you! Will inform Natches of your sleeping arrangements! Zoey won't like that! 18 and counting, Doogan texted.

Not your fucking backup. The reply came quickly.

17, Doogan counted.

Fucker! The insult only had Doogan shaking his head.

AWOL, he reminded the other man. *16.*

Been in place, asshole. Know you!

That had been Doogan's assumption all along.

Never did like your ass!

Doogan snorted at the last message, shoved his phone back into the pocket, collected his rifle, and left the guest room where he'd stood it. Retrieving the earbud he'd connected to the listening devices and tied into his sat phone, Doogan secured it in his ear and strode to the staircase leading to the garage at the back of the warehouse where Zoey kept her motorcycle hidden.

He had a meeting with Billy Ray. From what he'd heard during Zoey and Natches's confrontation, the bastard had crossed a line Doogan would make damned sure wasn't crossed again.

"We have a problem." The agent Doogan rarely saw in Eli snapped into place with a suddenness Doogan hadn't expected as he eased the truck, lights out, along the back alley leading to Ray's Garage and Motorcycle Repair.

"The truck isn't here," Doogan murmured while confirming the location of Billy's phone. "Billy Ray's inside."

At least his phone was. Eli was certain Billy never left without his phone.

Flipping the truck's lights on, Eli accelerated out of the alley onto the street at the end of the block and into the next narrow lane across from it.

"Would Natches have taken the truck?" Doogan questioned him, pulling the phone free of his mission pants.

"No way. They'd let their fists discuss the matter with his head and leave it there," Elijah answered.

Know Billy Ray's truck? Doogan texted quickly.

Just pulled in the lot.

Stolen.

"I'm calling Billy." Eli had his phone in hand as he drove quickly through the back streets.

"The truck just pulled in at the store across from Zoey's," Doogan stated.

"Dude, what's your truck doing at O'Riley's?" Eli snapped. "And Natches will rip your ass for trying to run Zoey down earlier."

Frantic shouts could be heard coming across the line.

"Not you?" Eli laughed; the amused sound was a sharp contradiction to his expressions. "Hell, son, you better collect that truck and get with Natches right real fast, you feel me? Looks like you're gettin' a hard-on for his niece that has nothin' to do with the happy-happy."

A second later Elijah disconnected the call.

"Billy just woke big brother." Eli grimaced. "Not good."

"In what way?" Doogan pulled his weapon, checked the clip, and snapped it back into place before chambering the first round.

"Big brother?" Elijah snorted. "Billy's stepbrother is Jack Clay, a big-assed tattooed biker Zoey rides with from time to time. Badass."

Doogan snorted as a text lit up the screen of his phone.

"Two men just exited the truck. Driver and passenger," Doogan told Elijah.

Eli accelerated, sped through another alley, then turned quickly onto a silent residential street.

"We're close, how do you want me to go in?" Eli questioned. "Billy Ray, Jack, and God knows who else will be about a minute behind us."

"Pull onto the street next to Zoey's," Doogan ordered. "No doubt Dawg and the others will be there before long. I need to hide my presence there before they go searching the place."

"Won't happen, but I'll go in and make sure Zoey stays put." Eli breathed out roughly. "They'll check on her, but they won't check the place."

"I would," Doogan growled. There wouldn't have been a chance in hell he would leave without checking the entire building, just to be certain.

"Trust me." Eli grinned. "Better yet, bet me. I'm broke. Hundred bucks says they check on Zoey, period. They won't search the place."

The confidence in the younger agent's tone had Doogan's brows arching in doubt.

"They catch me there, you'll be out of a job. How's that?" Doogan countered as the truck turned onto the street he'd used earlier.

Grabbing the rifle from the back, Doogan moved from the vehicle as Eli slowed the truck. Using the trees as cover, he ducked and moved for the apartment. Slinging the rifle over his back as he ran, Doogan pulled his Glock from the holster and headed to the back of the warehouse.

He was slipping up the stairs at the back of the apartment after doing a quick check of the garage, when a heavy, booming knock began sounding at the front door, echoing into the earbud he wore.

Hell, Mackays hadn't had enough time to get there.

Doogan was beginning to think Zoey's life was far too exciting, even for him.

Ducking into the unused guest room, he slid into the large closet, removed the mission clothes, and grabbed his jeans, grimacing at the hard blows to the metal door he could still hear through the listening device.

Jerking the denim over his hips, he headed quickly back.

"Son of a bitch!" Zoey cursed as the sound of movement in her room assured Doogan the pounding at the door had finally woken her. "Billy Ray? I'll kill your ass!"

She was definitely awake.

Moving to the door but keeping it closed for the moment, Doogan let a smile tip his lips. At least her life wasn't boring . . .

FOURTEEN

Stomping to the front door, Zoey was ready to rip Billy Ray's head off his shoulders and shove it up his ass. Or at least make him feel as though she had. Until she flipped on the security monitor and glimpsed the man actually pounding on the door while Billy Ray yelled at her again. Why the hell was Jack there?

Sliding the inside bolt free and keying in the security code, Zoey threw the door open.

"Jack." She frowned up at the hard, tattooed all-around bad boy fiercely. "What the hell are you pounding on my door at three in the morning for?"

"Sorry, Zoey." Jack frowned. "Had to make sure you were okay, sweetie. Can we come in?"

It was too early for any of this to make sense.

"You can." She shot Billy a glare. "He can keep his ass outside for all the trouble he's caused me tonight."

Billy rolled his gray eyes at her, though concern filled his expression. "I didn't do a damned thing, Zoey; you always think the worst."

"Because you usually do the worst," she snapped as Jack moved around her, striding into the apartment. "And what are y'all doing in my house at this time of the morning?"

Turning, she moved quickly along the short hall when she realized Billy's stepbrother had disappeared.

Gripping the front of her knee-length robe, Zoey looked around the living area and, not seeing him, swung on Billy.

"Where did he go?" she demanded suspiciously.

Billy shrugged, frowning. "Probably checking the garage or something. Dammit, Zoey, we got problems here."

"Dammit, Billy, *you* are a problem here, and evidently so is Jack." Dammit, Doogan's truck was in the garage.

"Zoey, it wasn't me that tried to run you down tonight." Billy stepped quickly in front of her, his expression creased in concern. "Listen to me, someone stole my truck and it's been sitting in the store lot across the road, facing your place. Someone used my truck to try to hurt you."

It hadn't been Billy? She stared up at him, feeling shock rolling through her.

"It wasn't you?" she whispered. "You weren't just trying to play one of your stupid pranks?" Fear tightened in her belly.

"Dammit, Zoey, I wouldn't do that to you," he protested, his expression darkening painfully. "You know I wouldn't do that to you. Elijah saw the truck when he drove by earlier and called me. Jack called Natches to let him know we thought someone was watching your place. That's when Natches threatened to rip my dick off and shove it down my throat for trying to run you over earlier." A shadow of remorse flickered in his gaze. "Zoey, girl, you know I wouldn't even act like I was going to hurt you. You should have known that wasn't me. Come on." His voice lowered. "We're friends, Zoey. I'd fight for you if I even suspected who did that."

It wasn't Billy? He hadn't pulled out behind her and nearly run over the ass end of her car?

For a moment, shadows whirled through her mind and pain lashed at her senses, nearly stealing her breath.

"Get out of my house." She could barely breathe enough to force the words past her lips. She had to get them away from her. Get Billy out before panic set in.

Turning, she moved to rush across the room to the metal staircase she assumed Jack would have used, when Billy gripped her arm and pulled her around.

"Don't touch me!" Crying out, Zoey jerked away from him. "Get out, Billy. Now."

"Zoey, listen to me . . ." He grabbed her arm again, confusion filling his expression.

At the sound of her cry, Doogan's bedroom door flew open and before she could process how quickly he moved, he had Billy's wrist in his hand, forcing him to release her before placing himself between them.

"Who the fuck are you?" Billy snarled.

It wasn't Billy who had her attention, though. Jack Clay stood in the doorway, having obviously been in the room as well.

He'd known Doogan was there. He had known and they were obviously just chatting it up, no doubt about her and Billy's stolen truck.

"Get them the hell out of my house, now," she ordered Doogan, fear and fury clashing inside her. "Now. Or I will call Natches myself and have all of you thrown out."

Fists clenched, her voice harsh from the tightness of her chest, she turned, stalked to her bedroom, and slammed the door closed.

Leaning against the closed door, Zoey dragged in a shaky breath. It was okay, she assured herself. This was all okay. Whoever stole Billy's truck must have thought she'd realized it had been stolen. And leaving it at the store across from her home was coincidence. That was all. It was a deserted lot, dark and easy to slip away, perhaps steal another truck. It didn't have anything to do with her. It didn't have anything to do with the nightmares that seemingly had no basis in reality.

So why was she shaking? Why was panic tightening her chest and making it so hard to breathe? Why did she suddenly wish Doogan would just hold her and make it all go away?

Just for a little while . . .

Jack Clay, the tattooed biker, had arrived earlier than Doogan had expected. He hadn't expected the other man to be in town for several more days. Before heading to Somerset, Doogan had called in markers rather than agents and favors over agency resources. His team was compromised by Mackays. That was a weakness now rather than the strength it would have been otherwise. He needed allies in Somerset outside the Mackays.

Mackays were damned fine allies whether they liked who they were backing or not. As long as the battle they were fighting was a mutual one, then Doogan knew they could be trusted. To a point.

This battle? Their love for Zoey would be a detriment. They'd jerk her away from him and hide her so deep he'd never find her. But they trusted Jack. Trusted him enough that when Jack called regarding his stepbrother's truck and Jack had learned she and Natches had disagreed, as Natches described it, over how to approach Billy, Jack had suggested checking on her himself.

When Zoey had learned it hadn't been Billy who had attempted to slam into the back of her little car, Doogan had seen those oddly colored eyes flash with a deep haunted fear.

Just as he'd feared last year, that sheer Mackay stubborn will and determined strength was overcoming the drug she'd been given and suggestions posed while she was under its influence. She was beginning to remember, but just enough of those suggestions remained that she was as yet unable to talk to anyone that could really help her.

The experts in that particular drug all agreed that all Doogan could do was ensure her trust in him and be there when the memories returned. When the trigger needed to push aside the suggestions and reveal the truth engaged, that he be there to help her through it. To help her distinguish between memory and fear. Something he'd been too late to do with his brother.

Damn Catalina and her traitorous lover. The bastard had ensured her guilt over the death of her daughter didn't convince her to betray him by putting a bullet in her head. He'd killed her before escaping himself, his identity still unknown. All Doogan knew was the bastard had eventually made his way to Somerset, and to Zoey. The last person that could be taken from him. And he still didn't know why. All he knew was that she was in danger because of him. And if he didn't save her, then saving himself would be impossible. Losing her would be the final blow. It would kill him.

FIFTEEN

Zoey hadn't slept well, but at least she hadn't over-slept. She was awake and dressed far earlier than she needed to be for a meeting with one of her buyers in Louisville the next day.

Meeting him alone wasn't something she wanted to do, though. The past few years hadn't been the safest for Dawg Mackay's sisters.

Glancing at the clock, she sighed heavily. Doogan was gone, Eli hadn't answered her earlier text, and everyone else in the family was gone to pick out supplies for the family reunion. That didn't leave a lot of options.

Picking her phone up, she considered the only other male she knew who could be the least bit intimidating if he had to be. And after the night before, he owed her favors in spades.

"Zoey, you okay?" Billy answered on the first ring, his voice concerned.

"I'm fine," she informed him shortly. "Look, I need a favor."

"Whatever you need," he promised.

"I have to meet a buyer with a few of my paintings and this is my last chance to sell to him. I'm not comfortable meeting him alone. Everyone else is busy . . ."

"Can I drive your car?" Eagerness filled his voice.

Everyone wanted to drive the little roadster she'd bought with its powerful little motor, especially Billy. He'd rebuilt the motor and customized the interior for himself before he was forced to sell it the year before. He jumped at every chance he could get to drive it. Hell, he begged to drive it sometimes.

"You can't speed in my car, Billy." She was resigned to this. The few times she'd asked Billy to go anywhere with her, the price was always her car. "I'll drive over to your place. Give me twenty minutes."

"Gives me time to clean up nice for you," he laughed. "See you in a bit."

She still had to wait for him, but not as long as she had to wait last time.

"Zoey, you're my favorite girl-buddy," he laughed, sliding over the door instead of opening it and settling into the driver's seat.

"Knowing that makes my day," she snorted. "I'm meeting the buyer in Louisville, and then we'll stop in Danville so I can deposit the check."

"Sounds great." Running his hands over the leather steering wheel as a sigh of pleasure passed his lips. "Aint she just so pretty. Damn, Zoey, letting this beauty go hurt."

"So you keep telling me." She shook her head though she couldn't hold back her grin. There was a reason why she let him drive the little car. He might get a little fast in it, but she knew he'd never risk actually wrecking the car he put so much time and love into. "Good thing you like driving her I guess, you'll be behind the wheel for a while today."

"Awesome," Billy sighed, sliding the car into gear and accelerating away from the curb. "Man, I am so glad everyone else was busy."

With the top down, a hard rock station on the satellite radio, and Billy's smile of pure delight as he drove the sleek, little black two-seater, Billy headed out of town. It usually took a while for him to get over the boyish giddiness at driving the car. He wasn't much for chitchat during those times. But Zoey found she wasn't much for it herself. The night before had been too damned unsettling.

Her brother had made it to the apartment before Jack left, his pale green eyes somber and intent when he pulled her into his arms for a hard hug. Doogan had made himself scarce, making calls, he'd told her, while Dawg was there. Dawg had been unusually quiet though, his expression heavy, concern for her or suspicion she wasn't certain. When he'd left he'd made her promise to call him if she even thought she needed him.

"Let me help you, Zoey," he'd whispered as he hugged her, his voice quiet at her ear. "I swear, we'd work things out however you need. Don't hide from me, sweetie."

She'd wanted to sob against his chest, wanted him to help her. The closer she'd come to doing so, the heavier the pressure had built in her head, though.

The pain made no sense. Almost as though it were a programmed response.

The pressure was there now, just behind her temples, threatening to develop into the agonizing strikes of sickening pain.

Programmed.

Rubbing at her temples Zoey fought to find a way around it.

Natches and Chaya played a little game whenever they couldn't tell each other something directly. They proposed a little story to the other. A "what-if," their daughter Bliss had laughingly confided. Zoey understood imagery, imagination, painting words into pictures, but she couldn't find an image to push past the pain to the truth. If she could, she'd sketch it, paint it, give a picture to the hell she knew waited beyond the pain, then she'd do just that. She could face it, if she knew for certain what the truth was. Was it blood and death? Or was it a voice whispering in her ear, painting memories into her brain that weren't really memories?

The pain was building in her head, sapping her strength, her ability to think.

Pushing back that particular angle of the problem facing her she turned back to Doogan instead.

He was there because of an investigation, he'd told her. Top-secret stuff she'd thrown at him, irritated at the answer. Somber, filled with regret, his gaze had remained on hers as he nodded at the description. Then he'd pulled her into his arms and drew her to bed. Not for sex, though. How he'd known she'd needed him to just hold her, just protect her for a few hours while she slept, she didn't delve into at the time. But he'd done just that. He'd held her, his arms wrapped around her, her head tucked against his shoulder as he sheltered her while she slept.

Her thoughts held her until Billy pulled into the parking lot behind the gallery and activated the retractable roof to slide into place.

Davis Caston was waiting for her, just as he promised, a check already made out to her when she turned over the paintings. He eyed a quiet, brooding Billy warily.

She had to give Billy credit, though. Every time she'd asked him to accompany her anywhere, he'd always played Mackay bodyguard perfectly. Just as he did this time. Albeit silently. Mackays rarely did so silently.

Thanking the gallery owner as well as the buyer, Zoey felt satisfaction fill her. It had been months since she'd made a really good sale. And this one rated there at the top. She might even be able to squirrel a little away.

"We did good then?" Billy flashed her a smile as he opened the car door for her.

"Yes, we did. I can now officially pay my bills next month," she stated happily, sliding into the passenger seat of the little convertible.

"And your loss in the race." He winked cheerfully, closing her door and striding to the driver's side. Minutes later, the top down once again, they were heading out of town to the bank Zoey used. One outside Somerset, and she always hoped, her family's nosiness.

Billy cleaned up good, she admitted. Black jeans and a dark gray cotton shirt buttoned conservatively, the cuffs rolled back only twice and neatly at that. Dark blond hair, a little long with the slightest wave. At twenty-three, he was considered one of Somerset's newest bad boys. Zoey considered him a friend, except on race nights.

On race nights she didn't let friendship interfere.

"I'm going to beat your ass next race," Zoey promised, smothering a yawn.

"Sure you will," he laughed, glancing at her as she leaned her head against the headrest tiredly. "Take a nap, Zoey, I swear I won't speed. I'll wake you when we get to Danville."

"Make sure of it," she muttered, letting her eyes close as she slid her dark sunglasses over her eyes. "Or I'll tell Natches."

"You'd think those boys would get weaker as they got older," Billy sighed. "I think they get stronger as they get older."

Zoey had no doubt in her mind. They also got more protective and confrontational. Not to mention more nosey.

The lack of sleep the night before and the pure irritation had exhaustion tugging at her. With the easy speed Billy kept the car at and the warmth of the day, she was nodding off, slipping into a light nap despite her best intentions.

How long she'd slept, she wasn't certain, but before she knew it they were pulling into the bank's parking lot. Depositing the check, she glanced around the bank casually. She swore she could feel someone watching her. No one in the bank paid any attention to her, though. Shrugging the feeling away, Zoey collected her receipt and returned to the car. Once Billy got on the road again, she slipped back into a light nap.

She could hear the music, and Billy's low voice as he sang along with it. She was comfortable, the music soothing. For a while.

"Fuck! Fuck!" Billy suddenly yelled, fury pulsing in his voice as the car surged with speed and her eyes snapped open in alarm.

"What . . . ? What the hell?" Zoey came awake in a snap as she was suddenly staring at a hole in her windshield.

"Get down!" Billy screamed furiously, shifting gears and pushing the little car harder.

Turning her head, Zoey peeked between the two sports seats, eyes wide as she saw the car racing behind them and the male passenger aiming at them with a handgun.

"Oh God!" Flipping around, she stared at Billy in horror. "Dawg . . . they're all out of town, Billy. Dammit, I didn't bring my fucking guns either," she cried, suddenly terrified.

"Jack. Call him." Tossing her his phone, his hand went back to the wheel, the other one shifting gears as the little car screamed around the curves. "He has friends close. Call!" he screamed as another shot hit the windshield.

"Billy?" Jack answered, his dark tone curious.

"Jack, help us!" Zoey yelled above the whine of the motor as the windshield shattered in front of her face. "We're about three miles past the county line heading back from Danville in my car . . ."

The line disconnected.

"He hung up on me." She turned shocked eyes on Billy. "He hung up on me."

"He's getting help!" Billy was fighting the steering wheel, pushing the car as hard as he could, the back end fishtailing around a hard curve. "Jack don't waste time."

She wished she'd texted Doogan before she left. Hell, now she wished she'd had Dawg go with her after all. No one would have dared attack her in this way.

Billy's phone rang.

"Jack . . ." she answered desperately, nearly crawling into the floor as a bullet whined close to her ear.

"Zoey, listen to me." Doogan's voice was calm. "Billy's coming up on a side road on his right. Take it."

"Side road ahead on the right," Zoey cried out as more shots rang out. "Take it."

"Oh man, that road will kill the car . . ." he moaned.

"Take it!" she screamed as a bullet shattered the dash between them.

Billy cursed furiously as he slung the little car into the turn. The back end fishtailed as Billy fought the wheel, the veins in his neck standing out, a snarl on his lips.

"Jack there?" Billy yelled.

"He's here," Doogan answered.

"Yes," Zoey answered, bracing herself with one hand on the dash, her feet digging into the floor as the car rocked, tires sliding before biting into asphalt and propelling the car forward.

"Oh, my poor car," she cried as more shots rang out, pelting the back of the car as the pitted road banged the undercarriage.

"Zoey, ask Jack if he remembers what happened in San Diego," Billy yelled.

Before she could ask, Jack's voice came over the phone.

"Tell him I got it," Jack growled. "You're almost there, Zoey."

"We're almost there . . . Billy!" Turning, she saw his head slump. "Billy!" she screamed. "Oh God. Doogan . . ."

The car was still racing hard and fast as dozens of cycles poured from the trees bordering the road. Zoey ignored the sound of return gunfire and a crash of metal behind them as she fought to control the steering wheel.

Suddenly, a tall lanky body jumped from one of the cycles to the back of the car and lifted Billy, tossing him literally on top of Zoey as the other man slid into the seat and seconds later brought the roadster to a smooth stop.

Peeking over the unconscious Billy's shoulder, she stared at the biker. Frosty blue eyes filled with joy, he was young, maybe Billy's age. A do-rag covered his hair; a teardrop was tattooed beneath his left eye.

"Motor still sounds good." His deep baritone voice was a complete shock. "The body, though." A crooked grimace pulled at his lips. "Maybe Natches's boys can fix it." He grinned. "Come see me if they can't, we'll work something out." A wicked wink and he brought his boot-shod feet up to her seat and launched himself smoothly from the car.

Helping hands pulled Billy from her, rushing him to a van as Doogan strode across the small clearing toward her.

He was in Brom clothes, dammit.

He moved to the car, leaned against the frame of the shattered windshield, and crossed his arms over his chest. "Dawg is probably going to have those pups now," he stated calmly.

She craned her neck to stare behind her at the men being dragged from the other car and thrown over the shoulders of two of the larger members of Jack Clay's group and carted off.

Zoey's teeth clenched. "The world just ain't right anymore."

"Hmm." He nodded. "I guess we better get the blood cleaned off you before Dawg . . ."

Blood?

There was blood?

It was everywhere. So much blood.

Zoey screamed.

The blood was on her hands, on the knife. . . .

Harley.

She couldn't escape the sight of the scarlet fluid. It soaked his shirt, her hands.

She screamed his name. The knife fell from her hands and there, coating her palms, was the crimson proof of her crime. Or was it?

She stared at her hands, only vaguely aware of Doogan rushing her from the car and into the cool silence of the woods surrounding them. Jack Clay moved ahead of them, his expression hardcore pissed off from what she saw of it. When she saw it.

The images shooting through her head like crazy fireflies were far more terrifying than the nightmare. They flashed between nightmare and memory, strangling her with fear and pain, paranoia and fury.

Tied to the bed, helpless, gagged. The syringe pushing into her arm, the drug the color of sunlight as it was pushed from the plunger into her vein. And once it hit her system, it boiled in her blood, like lava inching through her, ripping through her mind with agony. She tried to scream, but the sound was blocked, smothered by the gag over her mouth. Instinct had her fighting, her fingers curling into claws, fighting to reach the smirking, malicious face of the bastard staring down at her.

She stared into the eyes of the man drugging her. Ice blue, a jagged scar running down his face. She knew him. He'd been there at the party the night she had danced with Doogan. There hadn't been a scar, but she remembered his face and his eyes, and the malevolence that filled them.

And when his partner stepped to the bed and straddled her, she stared into his green eyes, into a face from the past. He'd smiled. He'd enjoyed her pain, enjoyed making certain it hurt as much as possible.

He wasn't Johnny Grace, the cousin Natches had been forced to kill sixteen years before. He was Johnny's clone. Or his son. In his twenties, his gaze malicious, his voice filled with hatred.

Her stomach cramped as the memories poured over her. Pain lanced her head, tearing through her temples with brutal punishment, just as he'd warned her. She couldn't remember anything but what they told her, she'd been instructed. She would only know what they told her, nothing more. And as the drug began speeding through her system, she hadn't been able to fight it. She'd tried. She'd fought . . . and then the real pain had begun.

Stumbling, collapsing against Doogan now, Zoey fought to breathe, to let the memories just pour in. As though they belonged to someone else, not her, she let them spill over her. She would be angry later. She would cry later when she could deal with it. For now, she just wanted the truth.

She hadn't killed Harley, but she was terribly afraid they might have. They planned to. They knew where he was and they were going after him next. After they dumped Zoey on her sister's patio for Sam Bryce to find.

So she could confess to killing Harley, and Sam would have to arrest her. When she did, the Mackays and all their friends would lose favor with Homeland Security and lose the protection they'd gained over the years. As well as the power base they'd built not just in Kentucky but within the law enforcement agencies as well. And once that was done, not just the Mackays would be taken care of, but Doogan as well. She hadn't known then who Doogan was or why it would affect him.

"Killing you won't hurt Doogan near as bad as destroying you. You, your family, his power base. Too bad he let the wrong person see how much he cared, isn't it? Now, Doogan and the Mackays all lose when they lose you. . . ." The words filtered through the agony, through the images of blood and death flashing through her mind.

"Too bad . . ." another voice echoed through her head. *"Too bad you had to choose the wrong man. . . . Too bad . . ."*

Jarring, horrifying, the pain dug into her head, breaking the words off, shattering the memories as she felt herself collapsing into Doogan's hold, her strength stolen by the slicing pain saturating her head.

"They were so confident," she whispered, as she found herself cradled in Doogan's arms, his back propped against a tree as Jack Clay crouched beside them. "One, he had green eyes, like Natches. He's Johnny Grace's son. He said Natches would pop my head like a little grape, just like his father, Johnny. I couldn't go to my family; I had to confess to Sam, because he said Natches would kill me. His partner called him Luther. But I've seen him before. His eye color was different." They were aqua before. The aqua eyes had thrown her off. She'd seen his face, seen him somewhere. "The other, he worked at Natches's garage for a while. Scar, cold blue eyes. Luther called him Rigsby."

"Tom Rigsby. He's actually former DHS. He worked in inter-rogation, which explains how he knew about that drug. Luther Jennings would be Johnny's boy, I guess," Clay said softly. "Tom was driving the car that chased you and Billy. I recognized him. He and Luther hooked up a few years ago when Tom was kicked out of DHS for failing to pass a polygraph. And you're right, Luther's eyes were aqua when he was here in Somerset a few years ago."

"He stayed at the inn." Zoey held her head; the pain was bad, but it wasn't as bad as it had been. "He was always trying to flirt with me. Creeped me out."

It was the way he looked at her. His gaze hadn't been hateful or mean, but something had lurked behind his smile and in the eyes that seemed far too calculating.

"Did you catch Rigsby?" Doogan asked.

Zoey stared at Clay, praying, oh God she prayed they'd caught both men.

Instead, Clay shook his head slowly. "Rigsby was killed by one of my boys. The shooter with him was a two-bit hired bully out of Louisville." Concern filled his eyes. "Luther won't be happy to learn his buddies are dead. And if Luther's anything like Johnny, then he's as mean and cunning as a damned rattler."

"We have to tell Dawg," Zoey groaned, laying her head on Doogan's chest as she felt him tense. "Oh God, that's going to be so bad."

"So bad doesn't describe it." Moving to his feet, Doogan helped her to rise, keeping his arm around her as they stared around the sheltering forest before turning his gaze back to Clay. "I need wheels. We have to get back to the apartment and I have to make some calls first."

"Take my bike." Clay nodded to the Harley parked on the dirt lane cutting through the valley. "I have a call out to Sam and she'll take care of everything here. Let me know when the Mackays are coming to call if you want me there." He didn't sound so eager to be there, though. Not that Zoey could blame him. Hell, she didn't think *she* wanted to be there. Doogan kept his arm around her, holding her close to his side. And it was a damned good thing, because Zoey didn't think her knees were strong enough to hold her up yet. She could feel herself shaking from the inside out and she hated it. She hated it to the point that her teeth were clenched, her muscles tight with the effort to hold back the shudders.

"What do you have to do and what kind of calls do you have to make?" Zoey asked him as he helped her onto the back of the cycle. "Why did a former agent help Johnny Grace's son try to convince me I'd killed Harley?" When he didn't answer, she grabbed his arm before he could turn from her. "Talk to me, Doogan. Tell me what's going on."

"That's why I have to make some calls, Zoey. Hell, I didn't even know Grace had a son or that Rigsby was involved in this. If I had, I might have been able to stop this before it started." He handed her the helmet before straddling the Harley himself and starting the ignition.

"Hold on, baby," he warned her through the helmet headset.

Gripping his waist, Zoey held on as he sped back to town, the Harley eating up the miles. She could feel the tension in his body, feel the anger pouring through him, and wondered, when it was over, where it would leave her in his life.

SIXTEEN

Doogan drew the Harley to a slow crawl as he started up the lane to Zoey's apartment, his eyes narrowing on the sheer number of vehicles parked in front of it.

"We might have a problem, Zoey," he murmured into the Bluetooth headset. "A big one."

She snorted at the understatement. "Ya think, Doogan?" she asked. The sarcasm in her voice would have made him grin at any other time. But her brother, Dawg, and cousins Natches and Rowdy were waiting at the head of the group, their glares trained on him.

Damn. This was going to get dicey. He could feel it, like an itch at the back of his neck.

"Zoey, don't let them pull you away from me. We don't know what the hell's going on yet." And they would try. He could see it in their set expressions. "And I'll be damned if I'll watch them drag you off and lock you down tighter than Fort Knox."

"They look really pissed," she muttered.

Pissed wasn't even close. It wasn't just her brother and cousins either. Her brothers-in-law, Graham, Brogan, and Jed, stood behind them while Timothy Cranston leaned against his truck and glared at the motorcycle as it inched up the drive.

"Dawg looks really mad, Doogan," she pointed out.

"We could always turn and run," he suggested, watching the other men as the back of his neck started to itch with a sense of rising danger.

"Where's your backbone?" She pinched his waist lightly. "They're all bark . . ."

"Bite," he amended, grimacing as she gave him a light, though concerned little laugh. She was nervous herself, she couldn't help it. She'd never had every damned male in her family waiting on her like this before.

Pulling the cycle up to the group of men, Doogan eased his helmet off slowly, aware of Zoey doing the same. His gaze locked with Dawg's immediately. Zoey's brother was beyond pissed. The fury burning in his gaze made the celadon green appear to swirl with a hint of emerald.

"Dawg? And friends." He nodded to them a bit mockingly. But hell, he felt as though he were being ambushed. "What can I do to help the lot of you?"

"Get off the bike, Zoey," Dawg ordered, his voice harsh. "Eli will take you back to my place . . ."

Zoey's hands tightened at his waist. She was tense behind him, wary.

She laughed without so much as a hint of nerves, though. "Really? No explanation, just pack up and go?"

"I didn't mention packing," Dawg informed her, his voice icy. "I said go."

The tension in the air grew.

"I don't think so. Not without a damned good reason."

"A damned good reason," Dawg snapped, his arms dropping, his shoulders going back confrontationally. And he did present a hell of a powerful impression. That fist was going to hurt when it struck, Doogan knew. "How's this for a reason. You go or he'll end up in the hospital tonight. You don't want that, Zoey."

"No, Dawg, *you* don't want that." There was steel in her voice, a core of pure, tempered titanium that surprised Doogan for a moment. "You want to get in your truck and drive out of here and come back later, while you're calmer, and Christa can accompany you. Otherwise, I promise you, I'll make damned sure every one of you are on your knees begging me to leave this county within three months."

"That's an awful big threat from such a little girl." Natches stepped in. "That will never happen and we both know it."

God, she wasn't in the mood for this. First some bastards ambush her on a perfectly nice drive back from a killer sale, and now, her brother thought he could just order her about? Was it Pick on Zoey Day?

"You have any other threats in your arsenal?" Doogan muttered, evidently doubting the fact that her brother was bluffing.

"I don't need any other threats," she assured him, though she had to admit, she was becoming a bit concerned when Dawg simply flicked her the same look he gave his daughter when she was acting up. "Zoey, get off the damned cycle and go." Dawg took a single step forward.

"Dawg, get off my damned property until you can treat me like an adult," she demanded, hurt feelings, wounded pride, and anger mixing with the other emotions ripping at her now.

"Then act like an adult." His hands went to his hips, disgust lining his face as he pinned Doogan with one of those insulting, superior Mackay looks.

Doogan was ignoring the confrontation for the most part, or at least pretending he was. As she and Dawg jockeyed for dominance of her life, he was sitting back on the Harley's seat, one booted foot propped on the footrest, the other braced on the ground as he studied the area silently. Curiously.

At Dawg's demand that she act like an adult, he tensed once again, though, his head lifting, and Doogan's expression was anything but friendly.

Stepping from the bike, Doogan turned, his eyes like chips of ice, his expression savage. "In the apartment. Now."

She swung from the bike, took his hand, and let him lead her through the wall of male bodies to the garage door at the front of the building. Swiping the security card through the reader, she waited for the metal door to lift, surprised when Doogan ducked and pulled her inside the second it was high enough to do so.

"They're following us," she informed him, aware of the press of male bodies behind them.

"Of course they are." There was something dark and knowing in his tone. Some sense of coming upheaval that had her tensing in dread.

"Eli, get the fucking door secured once they've finished posturing and filed in," Doogan barked, leading Zoey to the stairs. "Then I want you and the Three Stooges to make sure this damned building's secure."

"Three Stooges?" Graham wasn't the least pleased with the description.

"Stooges." Pulling Zoey up the metal staircase behind him, Doogan glanced back, his gaze connecting with Graham's.

"Jed, Brogan, check this level," the other man ordered. "The Mackays and I will check the upper level before we have this little talk with Doogan."

"He doesn't give the orders here, Graham," Dawg snapped, his glare meeting Zoey's gaze, the anger and concern riding side by side.

"In this he does," Graham refuted, then nodded back to Doogan. "Let's make sure the building's secure before we get into this, Dawg. Make sure Zoey's safe first."

Make sure Zoey was safe first. What the hell was going on?

Tossing her hair over her shoulder, Zoey pushed at Doogan's arm with her shoulder, indicating her insistence that they keep moving. Get it over with and get everyone out of her house. She needed to recoup; she needed to figure out how to handle the memories that had been shrouded in nightmares and the nightmares that hid the memories.

"Graham, get hold of Sam; I want her here now." Doogan pulled Zoey behind him as he indicated that the other man should follow him in the direction of Zoey's room. "She has twenty minutes. I'll check Zoey's room, then meet the rest of you in the living area." He turned to Zoey as he stopped at her doorway, his expression commanding. "Stay here, let me check it out, and then you can shower or whatever you need to do."

"And let you have all the fun by yourself?" She mocked him. "I don't think so."

For a second, an amused grin tilted his lips. "Fun? Is that what we're calling your family today?"

The low, almost intimate tone of his voice soothed that rising panic inside her just enough to allow her to give him a little smile in return. Her stomach was still jumpy, though, nerves eating at her self-control, and it was all she could do to keep her hands from shaking.

"I'll check your room. Wait here for me." Doogan drew her to the wall next to her bedroom door. "This will take just a few minutes."

She almost rolled her eyes. "Really, Doogan?"

"Really, Zoey," he assured her, a glower beginning to darken his expression. "This has nothing to do with ability and everything to do with someone trying to force you into destroying yourself. Admit this is a battle you need help with."

Pressing her lips together tightly, she watched as her brother and cousins carefully checked the rest of the apartment. Rowdy and Natches were slipping into the spare guest room while Eli stepped cautiously into his own. And they were all armed. Just as she should have been.

Her bedroom door opened and Doogan stepped out, his expression still somber, his dark brown eyes still worried.

"It's clear," he promised, stepping back and allowing her inside. "Why don't you let me take care of this, Zoey?"

A mocking laugh fell from her lips. "When did you decide you had a death wish?" She shook her head, glancing into the apartment to see her brother and cousins converging in the kitchen. "No. You don't handle the Mackays, Doogan. That was your first mistake." She turned her gaze back to him, betrayal slicing at her as vague, barely-there memories of him and Sam began filtering through the shadows of her mind.

His jaw clenched, his gaze becoming hard and cool once more. "Of course you do, darling," he drawled. "The same way you handle any other wild animal. Look it in the eye, growl deeper, and be prepared to bite harder."

She would have laughed if she'd had anything even approaching humor left inside her right then.

"Try honesty first," she whispered painfully. "It works wonders."

"Does it really?" His fingers curled firmly around her upper arm as she started to turn away from him, holding her in place and sending a rush of pleasure from his touch racing through her.

She was so weak. Why did his touch affect her as it did? Why couldn't she deny him as she'd denied so many other men in the past?

"I hate to disagree with you, sweetheart, but honesty doesn't work with that fucking drug they pumped into you that night or the suggestions they left in your very complicated little brain," he informed her, his voice gruff. "So until you've remembered every fucking whisper they planted there, don't assume you can judge me, or my level of honesty toward you. Doing so could well end up being disastrous."

Her heart was racing, his suggestion causing her head to ache further, the disjointed memories to slip through her mind like shadows, there then gone, never staying in one place long enough to force them to make sense.

Doogan stepped back, the icy chill in his gaze only growing deeper as Rowdy stepped to the doorway.

"Sis?" he questioned her, the compassion and concern in his voice and expression causing her heart to clench.

He and Natches had taken her and her sisters to their hearts just as Dawg had. They weren't cousins in the Mackay males' eyes. They were sisters to all of them, just as they were more brothers than cousins.

Doogan held her gaze; the warning she could see in the dark depths caused her throat to tighten and trepidation to rise. This wasn't over by a long shot. And she had a very bad feeling that she still hadn't remembered nearly enough.

"You have five minutes," Doogan told her. "But have no doubt, Zoey, the days of protecting those men in there from their own natures is over, as far as you're concerned. They're big boys. It's time to let them face the fact that you're probably more of a Mackay than any of your sisters ever thought to be. That, or put your damned head down and deny everything you've fought for in the past five years. Marry their choice of man for you and settle down to having babies and being the nice, safe sister Dawg dreams of."

Zoey flinched at the suggestion. "You're an asshole, Doogan."

"And I take great pride in the fact." His gaze sliced to Rowdy before a hard smile tugged at his lips. "But then, I'm not alone, am I?"

Doogan strode from her bedroom, his shoulders straight, his expression so arrogant and damned confident it made her back teeth clench.

"Zoey?" Rowdy stood at her bedroom door, his worried expression causing her breathing to hitch painfully.

"Why are you guys even here, Rowdy?" Rubbing her hands over her face, she wondered if her life would ever come close to making any sense at all.

"Because you're in trouble," he answered her without hesitation. "And like him, we'll always be here whenever you're in trouble, Zoey, whether you want us to be or not."

Whether she wanted them to be or not.

When it came to her family, she had no idea what she wanted and what she didn't. Staring beyond Rowdy's shoulder, she glimpsed Doogan as Eli stepped to him. The secrets those two probably shared would make grown men shudder. Eli resented it sometimes, felt anger in it other times, but watching them now,

Zoey could see the innate trust the younger man felt for Doogan, despite his anger.

"I need a few minutes," she told Rowdy. "Please don't let them hurt him before I get back."

"So you can have that privilege?" Rowdy grinned.

Zoey shook her head, sighing deeply. "No, so I can protect him from himself and that death wish I'm still convinced he has. Why else would he ever consider taking on a Mackay?"

Why would anyone choose such a completely irrational battle?

Doogan was furious, and he knew it was a mistake to allow the anger to grow inside him as it was. He wasn't at his most rational when he couldn't control the dark, building fury that could burn deep and far too hot. And when dealing with a Mackay, a man had to be at his most rational, with no anger marring the logic he had to use to keep them under control.

Not that anything or anyone completely controlled the wayward impulses that came with that particular bloodline.

"Tell me where you lost your mind, Doogan, because this is going to get you killed." It was Graham who approached him once he stepped into the living area, preparing himself to face the less than rational male family members.

Graham was a good man; Doogan had known that the first time they met, in their early twenties. And he was a hell of an agent. Of the three agents to have married into the Mackay family, Graham was the one Doogan had depended upon the most.

"What is the 'this' you're talking about?" Doogan questioned, wishing Eli would hurry with the files he'd been sent for.

"Zoey," Graham answered, his voice low. "Letting her remain in danger . . ."

"From the moment I learned she'd been targeted, she was protected far more than you know." Doogan's head snapped up, that anger he always fought to keep chilled with logic slipping its leash a bit. "Never doubt that for a moment, Graham. And remember one damned thing, it wasn't my security those bastards slipped past to threaten her to begin with."

"No, it wasn't. That failure's mine." Timothy Cranston's admission as he stepped to them earned him a glare from Doogan.

As much as Doogan liked the other man, they still clashed as often now as they had in the past.

Dammit, he hadn't meant for Timothy to hear that. This was why he fought to control his temper rather than letting it free.

Doogan sighed wearily, rubbing at the back of his neck. "What do you know, Timothy?" he asked as he let his hand drop, glimpsing Eli moving from the guest room with the box of files and written reports he'd kept over the past year.

The others were now standing around the dining table, Dawg and Natches glaring while Brogan and Jed watched him suspiciously.

"Not nearly enough, it seems," Dawg answered for him. "According to an anonymous phone call this morning, there's plenty you know, though."

Anonymous phone calls, a man had to love them.

"Such as?" The box Eli set on the table drew the interest of the other men now.

"Why Zoey's about to be arrested for murder." Natches watched him with murderous intent. "You know we're not going to allow that, right?"

Doogan guessed that was a rather mild statement. His lips quirked at the thought while he faced Zoey's family.

"If I intended to arrest Zoey, I would have already done so rather than giving even the weakest lawyer a perfect defense instead," he assured them all, sliding his hands into the pockets of his slacks while watching them closely. "Are you aware Johnny Grace had a son before he was killed?"

The looks of shock on their faces assured him they were unaware of it. "He was perhaps ten when Johnny died, well hidden by Dayle and his sister Nadine Mackay Grace and raised by a couple Dayle chose himself."

"Well, isn't that just wonderful," Natches drawled, the mockery in his voice slicing. "Good ol' Dayle. The bastard."

There had been little love lost between Natches and his father, even when Dayle had been alive.

"And let me guess." Dawg crossed his arms over his chest, his expression dark, bordering enraged. "He has a grudge."

Doogan inclined his head in agreement. "Did your anonymous tip inform you that a year ago Timothy's security was breached and Zoey was drugged and taken from her room at the inn?"

Their shocked faces assured him they were unaware of that.

Briefly Doogan filled them in, aware of the gathering storm building in each man as he told them the hellish images planted in Zoey's mind and why. Rigsby and Luther Jennings hadn't felt the need to watch what they said, or worry about what to allow Zoey to overhear as they bragged of their intelligence. Just as they had never guessed the strength of the woman they were attempting to destroy.

Even Doogan couldn't have guessed how quickly Zoey would overcome the suggestions implanted in her complicated little brain.

As he gave them what he knew and answered the questions they had, Zoey stepped from her bedroom to his side. The position she took, next to him rather than a family member, wasn't lost on the other men if Dawg's glare was any indication.

When he informed them of the afternoon's attack and Rigsby's death, he could feel the tension explode through the room. Every protective instinct the men possessed became heightened, and more dangerous than before.

"Zoey, you can't stay here." Dawg looked pale now. "Get packed, sweetie, and we'll take you somewhere safe."

"I'm safe right where I'm at." The hardened determination in her voice assured every man in the room that Zoey wasn't about to be ordered.

Unfortunately, the men she was facing hadn't survived without learning a few tricks of their own.

"Then I'll just throw your ass over my shoulder and take you somewhere safe," Dawg snapped; his eyes, identical in color to his sister's, turned brooding and determined. "Your choice."

"And my choice is to stay right where I'm at." The inflection of her tone didn't change. It didn't become heated or angry, it just became harder.

Natches gave a low, mocking chuckle. "She's so cute, Dawg. She actually thinks saying no will work."

Doogan wondered if Natches saw the hurt that flashed across her expression at his comment.

"Enough, Dawg." Timothy's voice was harder, colder than Doogan had ever heard it. "Get your heads out of your fucking asses for a minute and ask yourself why? Why did they target Zoey?"

"Because Johnny's little bastard is as crazy as he was?" Natches snorted furiously. "What other explanation is there?"

Doogan stiffened. What other explanation? He turned slowly, pinning Zoey with his eyes. There was another explanation and it was one he simply hadn't had time to consider earlier. Jack had been trying to tell him something last night, though, when he and Billy had shown up after the theft of Billy's truck. Something Zoey had interrupted.

Son of a bitch, he was going to kill Jack and Billy, and then he was going to paddle her damned ass.

"Doogan?" Rowdy's tone was wary and Doogan could feel the tension in the room shifting, growing thicker as he watched her.

A little pout formed at her lips, but Doogan saw her eyes. He saw the pride, that flash of accomplishment, and God help him, it made him hotter than hell. Still, he shook his head slowly, wanting to deny it. Begging fate and God to please not let it be.

"Zoey, it's time." Tim stepped behind her, his voice heavy, his expression filled with pride.

Fuck, he was going to have to kill that little bastard. This time, Doogan admitted, Timothy Cranston had to die.

"Time for what?" And that was definitely fear in Dawg's tone and expression.

As though guided by instinct and a desire not to collapse straight on his ass, Dawg lowered himself to a chair instead and just stared at Zoey.

She sighed heavily. "In two weeks, renegotiation for an alliance between Homeland Security and six of the biggest biker gangs in the nation begins. The original agreement was signed last spring, just before Rigsby and Jennings drugged me. I was the mediator for that agreement. Without me, there will be no renegotiations and no further information gathered by the members of those gangs and sent to DHS."

The other men took their seats slowly as well, leaving only Timothy, Doogan, and Eli to stand with Zoey.

"Not possible." Brogan, Zoey's brother-in-law, denied the explanation. "That pact was mediated and negotiated by a woman three of those gang leaders knew personally. And none of them are from Kentucky."

"And neither am I," Zoey reminded them. "And my brother and cousins like to forget that before we came here, we weren't exactly angels. Slipping into the biker bar close to our home was a normal occurrence for us. We couldn't have done that and remained safe there if we hadn't been protected by more than one of the customers. And they wouldn't have been so loyal to us without a reason."

"And what exactly was that reason?" Brogan was rubbing at the back of his neck as though trying to remove actual skin.

"Because a twelve-year-old girl with more guts than brains slipped into an old warehouse and helped three of her friends escape when they were attacked by a rival gang trying to move into the area," Timothy explained. "One of those young men was the son of a gang that controlled that area. His father gave Zoey lifelong protection by the gang and made damned sure everyone knew he wouldn't think twice about killing for her. When she moved, he and three of his friends, now leaders of two other gangs, rode out to check on her. That was the summer you were invaded by bikers and going nuts trying to figure out why." The former agent smirked.

"Witchy." Dawg nearly choked on the name. "You're Witchy."

Zoey smiled easily. "Wow. That was easier than I thought it would be."

Doogan sat down slowly himself and shook his head. He should have known. Sweet Lord, he should have known.

"Where's the whiskey?" he muttered.

Natches was on his feet and hurrying to the kitchen. He pulled the bottle from one cabinet, the glasses from the other. He looked as stunned, as shocked, as Doogan felt.

"You're dead, Cranston," Doogan assured him. "Officially dead."

"Officially," Dawg agreed.

Rowdy snorted. "And none of you suspected? You surprise me."

"And I guess you did?" Natches sneered back at his cousin.

"Who do you think helps protect her at those negotiations, Natches?" Rowdy said softly. "One of those bikers is a friend. And he's smart enough to know which of us to come to. Three of the gangs would very well kill for her, but there's three other gangs, smaller and wanting a larger cut of the pie than what they received in initial negotiations. Unfortunately, Zoey didn't tell any of us about her nightmares, and Doogan was too dumb to let any of us know what the hell was going on in his own life. Doogan spearheaded the first negotiation when he learned that influx of bikers that year was because of one person the bikers called Witchy. He assumed she was an adult. Rigsby tried to destroy Doogan first." Compassion filled Rowdy's voice. "When they didn't, they came looking for Witchy instead." Grief filled his expression. "I'm sorry, Zoey, we didn't know you'd be found, sweetheart."

Zoey shook her head. "And it wasn't your fault either."

"What are we looking at then?" Doogan ran his hands over his face, the look of rage and pain in his eyes causing Zoey's chest to clench in regret.

"Jack won't be able to keep my friends from hearing about the attack today, either," Zoey injected. "If I don't meet with them soon, then you'll be invaded by bikers again. Pissed-off bikers. And I don't want that."

And there she was. Zoey stood strong and proud in front of them. She didn't have to raise her voice and she didn't have to force her point across. She was Witchy. Everyone listened.

Everyone but the one man determined to see her destroyed.

SEVENTEEN

Witchy.

He'd called her his witch, but Doogan assured himself he hadn't suspected who she was, and he knew that next night he'd been lying to himself.

He'd known the night he asked her to dance, and he'd known she belonged to him. He'd been in Somerset that summer to identify the woman known only as Witchy. He'd had no description, no way of knowing who she was, but when he met Zoey's gaze across the room, he'd stopped looking for her. He hadn't searched for her since. He'd sent messages to her, read hers in reply, but he hadn't accepted what he knew inside.

He also pretty much figured out that Eli had known who she was all along as well. The younger man had kept her secrets, watched over her, worried and took the weight of those secrets with silent acceptance.

How in the hell she'd kept a secret like that, he wasn't entirely certain. He was just amazed it had taken this long for someone to figure out a way to strike out at her. Whoever orchestrated it, he rather doubted it was Luther Jennings. The background he now had on Johnny Grace's son showed a rather ineffectual little bastard with barely enough intelligence to stay out of Kentucky and out from beneath the Mackays' circle of knowledge.

Jennings just wasn't smart enough to put something like this together. That impression was confirmed after Doogan got off the phone with yet another contact he had reached out to for information. Luther Jennings dreamed of glory but had very little drive to attain it.

He was a coward, just as his father was, just as his grandfather was. And he was always blaming someone else for that cowardice.

"You have to do something about this," Dawg hissed as he stepped into the garage where Doogan was working on the racing bike rather than dealing with her family, who refused to leave.

"And what do you suggest I do?" Looking up from the finishing touches he was making to the motor, he arched his brow curiously. "I've worked with Witchy for five years now, Dawg, albeit long distance. She's damned good at what she does."

"Damned good at what she does?" Dawg plowed both hands through his hair, stomped to the metal doors, then back again. "At dealing with cutthroats, drug runners, and murderers?"

If ever a man wanted to hit something out of pure rage, then it was Dawg.

"Dammit, even Rowdy kept this from me." The note of anger in his voice had Doogan shaking his head.

He was damned if he wanted to play therapist to the Mackays. Where the hell was Timothy when he was needed?

"Rowdy's a little smarter at some things than you and Natches are." He shrugged. "You could learn from him."

"Learn how to let our daughters jump from the frying pan into the fire?" The other man's voice was strangled with outrage.

"This is about your daughters?" Doogan asked, rather surprised. "I thought it was about Zoey. But I guess the same advice could apply." Bending to access a mounting bolt, he tightened it carefully. "They're not children all their lives. Zoey grew up."

"Has nothing to do with it," Dawg countered furiously.

Straightening, Doogan stared at the other man thoughtfully as he cleaned the ratchet he'd gotten oil on and placed it carefully in its designated slot in the case.

"What the fuck are you doing?" Dawg looked at the case, then to Doogan. "Are you fucking cleaning your tools?"

Surprised, Doogan looked at the case and back to Dawg. "You don't clean the oil from yours?"

Dawg glared at him. "It's oil. Keeps them from rusting."

Doogan looked at the tools carefully. They were rather old, and he'd used them quite often actually. "Mine aren't rusted." He shrugged. "As to Zoey and your daughter, I suggest you take a few nerve pills a day and let them live their own lives. All of you will be happier for it."

"What the fuck do you know about it? You don't have kids," Dawg snapped.

But he'd had a child. A perfect, beautiful little girl with dark eyes and an angel's smile. So delicate he'd been terrified to hold her, certain if he breathed the wrong way she'd break.

"I guess I don't," Doogan had to admit bitterly, grief welling inside him. "What the bloody fuck do I know? And why the hell am I even trying to talk to you? Why don't you just rant and rave and I'll do as everyone else does, nod and agree with you and then do as I fucking please when your back's turned?"

Snapping the lid of the tool case closed with a force that slammed it in place, Doogan clipped the locks, grabbed the handle, and all but threw it in the backseat as the image of his daughter taunted him, shadowed him.

"Why don't you get the fuck upstairs, Mackay, and out of my damned face?" He slammed the truck door, anger surging inside him. "It's more than apparent you already know everything you need to know, so I can't tell you anything that would help you. Correct?"

Dawg tipped his head to the side for a minute, his gaze curiously haunted. "I'm sorry, Doogan," he said simply, the words and the tone sincere.

"For what? Being a fuckin' bastard where your sister's concerned?" Yeah, he should apologize for that one. To Zoey.

"For your loss," Dawg stated instead.

His loss. Doogan froze.

"And where do you get that?" Doogan knew he hadn't said anything.

A shrug of heavy shoulders and Dawg swallowed tightly. "You have the same look on your face that I felt in my gut when I learned Christa lost our first child."

"That is not a discussion we're having," Doogan warned him softly. "Not now, not ever. We clear?"

Laying his forearms across the top of the truck bed, he stared back at Dawg.

"We're clear," Dawg agreed. "But you ever need an understanding ear . . ."

"You can't keep doing this to Zoey," he stated reasonably, ignoring the offer. "She'll be the one that hates you for it. Of all your sisters, she'll not forgive what you take from her."

Dawg looked away. "I can't help it. If something happened, and I knew I could have stopped it somehow . . ."

"It will break off your soul, it will rip your guts to a thousand shreds," Doogan finished when Dawg couldn't. "But you'll know you didn't fail her, Dawg. You didn't make her play with Barbies when she wanted to learn how to throw a ball when she was three. You'll know that when she wanted to learn to ride a bike at four, you didn't buy her a Big Wheel instead." His throat felt tight, strangled. "You'll know you let her be who she wanted to be, who she needed to be, even if it was Witchy, when she was killed because her mother promised her a bike if she would go to the park with her. Then the bitch let her run across a busy street when she became frightened of the man whose car her mother tried to force her into. Because if she had trusted me to let her ride that god-damned bike, maybe she wouldn't have gone with her mother when she knew she wasn't supposed to." He all but yelled the words back at Dawg, his fingers curled into fists, rage eating at his soul. "Stop worrying about your own fucking comfort level all the time, Mackay. Let them ride their goddamned bikes."

He was finished with the bastard.

Pushing from the truck, he was stomping around it when Dawg's hand shot out and clasped his shoulder.

Not to restrain him. Not to argue or disagree, but in sympathy. Something no one had done; even after the death, during the funeral and burial, Doogan had stood alone.

"I'm sorry, man," Dawg said again. "Clear to my fucking soul, I'm sorry."

He forced himself to swallow, to breathe. "Yeah, so was I,"

Doogan said then, breaking the contact and heading for the stairs. "So was I."

Zoey covered her lips as she stood in the dark en-trance from the storeroom beside the garage. The narrow, shadowed gap between a tall shelf and the wall was a perfect doorway to the rest of the garage, so she'd just left it.

When she'd heard Doogan and Dawg talking from where she'd sat amid the boxes and discarded furniture, she'd used it to hear what they were saying.

What she heard destroyed her. How had he borne it? And why did he take such blame for it on his shoulders?

"Eavesdropping, sis?" Of course, Dawg would know she was there.

Holding back her tears wasn't easy. Moving into the garage, she stared up at her brother, her grief for Doogan's loss tearing at her heart.

Dawg sighed heavily. "I'm sorry," he whispered as she met his gaze. "I wanted you safe, Zoey. That's all."

Her lips trembled. "There's no way to tell him." Her voice shook. "It wouldn't have mattered if he had taught her to ride the bike or not. Until she realized her mother was taking her away from her father, and that her father was her real security, she wouldn't have fought. That was her mother." Her breathing hitched. "I would have given Chandler a chance, even then, if he'd found a way to convince me he truly wanted one. A little girl always believes it's her fault when a parent doesn't love her, Dawg." A single tear slipped free, because that had been her belief until she came to Kentucky, until she learned what a monster Chandler had actually been.

"Hell, Zoey." His arms went around her and he pulled her to his chest just like he always hugged his daughter. Close to his heart. "I'd kill him all over again, myself if I could, sweetie."

"I know." She nodded, barely holding back the rest of her tears. "And if I could give Doogan back his daughter, I'd do it, Dawg, just because I love him that much."

He stilled for a second, and then a heavy sigh passed his lips. "That wasn't who I picked for you," he groaned. "Damn, Zoey, Eli was the perfect match."

"Don't make me hurt you, Dawg," she laughed, though she knew the weariness in the tone wasn't very well hidden. "And for that one, you owe me."

"You want us to leave, don't you?" he asked. "You think because I actually like the bastard, I should let him live now?"

She listened to her brother's heartbeat; it was strong, steady, just as he was. "Yeah, I do," she agreed. "It's time to let go, Dawg. It's time to let me grow up."

"Hell no," he objected immediately. "Nine or ninety, it's all the same in my eyes, little girl. It's time to let you learn how to ride your bike, though. I can do that. And when you skin your knees, if that asshole doesn't make it all better, then I get to kill him."

She didn't say anything; she couldn't. The knowledge that Doogan had lost so much had changed something inside her as well.

"Do you know what Rowdy said when he found out what I was doing and agreed to help me?" she asked her brother then.

"What's that, baby girl?" He petted her hair, stroking it gently, like he stroked his daughter's. "He said he was only helping me because he didn't want the adventure to hurt me. And that he knew, one day, I'd find the adventure I was really looking for." She looked up at him, sniffing, realizing she'd actually lost the battle with her tears. "I found the adventure I was looking for, Dawg."

"Yeah, I think I already knew that, sis," he sighed. "Hell, I'm not stupid. But I still say Eli was better."

"Because he's your narc." She gave him a watery laugh. "That's why you like Eli so much. He's scared of your ass."

"'Course that's why." He grunted, giving her a look of mock surprise. "I'm no dummy, honey."

He made her laugh. She couldn't help it. No matter how mad he made her, no matter how many times she swore she was leaving Somerset because of his or the cousins' antics. At the end of the day, she loved him.

Just as he loved Rowdy and Natches.

And she loved Doogan. Doogan was her adventure; she'd just had to be there to find him, or for him to find her.

"Well hell, let's go upstairs then and tell the family we're leaving," he sighed. "But you have to stay safe, Zoey. Stay safe. You're too damned important to lose."

"We'll lose you first," she snorted. "You'll worry yourself to death."

He chuckled at that. "Gotta hang around a while longer, girl," he promised her. "Who else is going to keep those little pricks you girls keep marrying in line? Now my sweet little Laken done promised her daddy he could pick out her husband all he wanted to."

Satisfaction filled his voice, but Zoey stared at him in horror.

"She was five when she made that promise, Dawg," she burst out, horrified. "Oh my God, you can't hold her to that. Besides, you made her promise."

He shot her a mild glare. "Promise is a promise," he told her gruffly. "Laken knows that."

"No, Dawg . . ." He moved quickly up the stairs at her protest. "No, listen to me. That doesn't count . . ."

Poor Laken.

It was almost dark when everyone left.

Checking the clock on the wall, she frowned, realizing Doogan was still in the gym. He'd gone down just after she and Dawg had entered the living room, and he'd no doubt realized she must have been downstairs somewhere.

He hadn't looked at her, hadn't spoken to her, just disappeared down the front stairs, the most direct route to the gym. And he was still down there, no doubt furious with her for eavesdropping on him and Dawg.

But if she hadn't, she wouldn't have known. She would have never known how he'd lost his daughter, or the wife she thought he loved had betrayed him. Of course, the fact that she hadn't known was telling. If he'd intended to stay, if he meant for her to be a part of his future, he would have told her, wouldn't he?

She'd known when she let him into her bed that he wouldn't stay, that her time with him would be limited. She'd warned herself of it more than once. And it hadn't helped. She hadn't been able to keep him out of her heart, no matter how she tried. And she had tried. She had fought it, she had told herself it wouldn't happen, refusing to admit it already had. It had happened six years ago, at a time when having him was impossible.

Stepping into the gym, she stood in the doorway watching him at the punching bag. The way his fists slammed into the heavy weight, the sound of power smacking into canvas. Sweat gleamed on his naked chest and shoulders, beaded on his face, and ran in rivulets down his powerful back to the band of his sweatpants.

His expression appeared to be one filled with concentration until she glimpsed his eyes, glimpsed the pain and rage that filled them, darkened them.

Leaning against the door frame, she watched somberly. He knew she was there. Was he hoping she'd just leave? That she wouldn't be here, hoping to make that bleak pain she'd heard in his voice go away?

Straightening, she kicked off her sandals. He saw the action, his gaze flicking to her shoes before he turned his back, his fists still striking the bag. Moving into his line of sight once again, she unbuttoned her jeans and shimmied out of them, before leaving them discarded at the edge of the mat.

He paused this time, his gaze going over the brief tank top and white panties she wore.

"Panties or shirt next?" she asked, the throaty tone of her voice filled with hunger.

"You don't want this right now, Zoey." Pure steel filled his voice, but pain raged in his eyes. Just as lust was beginning to rage through him. His erection was clearly visible behind the cotton material of his pants.

"You think?" She gripped the hem of the top and pulled it up her body, over her head.

Before it fell from her hands a sharp, pleasure-filled cry tore from her lips.

Heat, rasping, hungry damp heat surrounded her nipple; the force of the pleasure, the rough, desperate need in his sucking lips, the hard hands that lifted her to him, and the male groan that surrounded her instantly pushed her into blinding, chaotic wantonness.

Sexual heat rose like wildfire, overtaking her senses, surging through her bloodstream and filling her with a voracious need.

She needed him. She needed the fiery hedonism she'd only ever experienced at his touch. At the ravenous, ravishing hunger he touched her with.

"You shouldn't have come here," he groaned, his lips lifting from one nipple, moving to the next. "You should have left it alone."

His lips surrounded it, sucking it into his mouth, exerting a firm, heated suction that sent electric pulses of frenzied abandon to sweep through her. Her womb clenched; heated moisture spilled from her vagina, coating the outer lips with a slick lubrication that only made her hotter, her clit more sensitive. And it made her wilder. The silky slide of it along sensitive tissue was like a teasing caress, a hint, a shadow of what she needed.

"I would have stayed away from you," he breathed out, his voice so rough and filled with carnal intensity that it stole her breath.

"Why?" Her nails rasped down his side until they reached the elastic band of the pants circling his waist. "Take them off, Doogan. Pleasure me."

So she could pleasure him. So she could steal the sorrow and the loneliness she'd glimpsed in him for just a few moments. For the space of time that he was a part of her, that he was as lost in the pleasure they created as she was.

"God, yes," he muttered, his lips moving to her neck, his tongue licking, tasting her, his teeth rasping and nipping. "Let me pleasure you, Zoey. Let me give to you. Give to you . . ."

Her panties were ripped from her hips. A second later the band of his pants cleared the thick, throbbing head of his cock. Zoey gasped as he lifted her, pushed her against the wall, and slipped between her thighs.

"Put your legs around me." The order was followed by a nip to her neck and the fingers of one hand lifting her thigh, guiding her legs into place around his hips.

She lifted her legs, curled them around him as the broad crest of his cock parted the folds of her pussy and began pressing inside.

Zoey ground her head into the wall behind her, lips parting as she fought for breath, her lashes nearly closing, so heavy as sensual weakness began flooding her. Pleasure and pain clashed and merged as the iron-hard width of his erection began pushing inside her, slowly. So slowly. Stealing her breath and her mind with the incredibly erotic sensations.

"Doogan." She whimpered his name, her eyes locked with his as he took her, pushing inside her, stretching her, killing her with the need for more.

"You're so sweet. So tight and wet." Pulling back, pushing forward, taking more of her with each thrust, his expression tightening with each cry that spilled from her.

She was dying for more of him and he wanted to take his sweet time entering her?

"Look at your face," he groaned, his voice growing guttural, his thrusts deeper. "So pretty. You're so fucking pretty, Zoey."

Her fingers tightened on his shoulders, her thighs clenching desperately at his hips. She lifted, settled against him, used the powerful muscles braced between her legs to anchor herself as she moved against him.

"That's it, baby." His fingers gripped her rear, moving her, lifting her until only the broad crest remained inside her, stretching her. "Now, take me, Zoey. Take all of me."

"Doogan." She cried his name, nails digging into his shoulders, her neck arching as the engorged width thrust partially inside her.

His expression twisted, a grimace pulling at his lips.

"You like that, don't you, Zoey? All that pleasure and that bite of pain?" He pulled back, his hands tightening at her rear again, holding her still for just a second before pushing harder, deeper inside the clenched tissue.

A wail spilled from her lips, shudders tearing through her as rapture threatened to explode through her senses.

"You love giving it," she panted, her pussy rippling around the intruder, milking the hard flesh throbbing inside her. "You love it, Doogan. Every second of it," she sobbed.

"Love it." Something flashed in his gaze. Something gentle, something filled with regret as he lifted one hand, cupping the side of her face and lowering his lips to brush against hers. "Hold on to me, Zoey. Let me give you more."

His hips bunched, pulled back, and in the next breath his hips slammed forward, his cock burrowing hard and deep, filling her to the hilt and dragging a keening wail from her lips as she felt her orgasm explode with brutal strength through her pleasure-tortured senses.

"Doogan . . ." The shattered cry tore from her lips, the feel of hard, desperate thrusts extending the ecstasy, pushing it higher and forever binding her pleasure to his touch alone.

She felt it. Felt the invisible brand that went inside her, and accepted it.

"Fuck. Zoey. Baby. Ah hell . . ." His lips buried at her neck, his cock pulsing, spewing his seed inside her.

His hips jerked with each ejaculation, pushing his cock deeper inside her, the flex of the wide crest stroking her internally. Holding to him, Zoey buried her head at his shoulder to hide the tear that escaped, spilling it against his skin, knowing he'd never know, never realize how much of her he owned. That she'd given him all her heart, all her soul, and watching him walk away would tear both to shreds.

"I'm sorry," he whispered as she lay against him long moments later, fighting to catch her breath. "I'm so sorry, Zoey. I never wanted to hurt you."

She lay still, silent, waiting, feeling it coming.

"You know I have to leave," he finally whispered. "We agreed. Just for a while . . ."

"Just remember, you promised to come to me when it snows." The sobs were held back; the hoarseness of her voice could be excused by the aftermath of pleasure. "Don't forget me when it snows, Doogan. I get cold . . ."

Breathe. Just breathe. She was dying inside. Every dream she'd tried not to build around him was exploding inside her.

He released her slowly, letting her legs slide from his hips until she had her feet on the floor and he stepped back from her.

"Zoey? Please don't cry," he whispered, turning her face up to him, his gaze tortured.

Zoey shook her head, forcing a smile to her lips. "No tears, Doogan," she promised, though they were tearing her apart inside. "No tears."

Stepping away, she gathered her clothes and left the gym. She felt exhausted, drained. The tears she'd promised she wouldn't shed were choking her, strangling her with every breath she took.

She forced herself upstairs and into the shower. Forced herself to step beneath the heated spray of the water before she let herself break the promise she'd made him. And there, in the corner, water raining down on her, Zoey slid to the floor, her forehead resting against her knees, silent sobs shaking her shoulders as she let herself accept the fact that it was almost over. He was almost gone, and when he walked away, it would kill her.

EIGHTEEN

His pants once again around his hips, his entire body drained, Doogan sat on the wide bench next to the rack of weights close to where he'd fucked Zoey against the wall.

Hell, he hadn't even kissed her. He'd just pushed her against the damned wall and fucked her like he was dying.

Resting his elbows on his knees, he wiped his hands over his face and tried to make sense of the emotions ripping him apart. This was why he tried to stay away from her. He was damned if he could sort through everything she made him feel, and all the regrets he'd fought to bury when he'd buried his baby girl.

Just the thought of walking away from Zoey tore him apart.

She was too damned innocent, too damned sweet for the likes of him, and he knew it. And still, he hadn't been able to walk away from her. Hadn't been able to stay away from her.

And he was beginning to fear that might well be the only way to protect her.

Dragging herself out the shower, Zoey quickly dried
her hair before braiding it, then pulling on a pair of shorts and a
T-shirt to sleep in. She didn't expect Doogan to be up anytime
soon. Hell, she didn't really expect him to be up at all. He was too
busy trying to find all the reasons why he shouldn't be with her to
see all the reasons why he should be. And Zoey could have fought
anything or anyone else to be with him, but him. At this point, she
wasn't going to fight him for it.

Leaving the bedroom, she had every intention of dipping into
a bottle of wine and turning on some sappy, romantic tearjerker.
She made it halfway across the living room when she came to a
slow, stomach-churning stop.

"Well, it was hard enough getting in here." The voice was
pleasant enough; the expression was pure evil, though.

Smiling, the emerald-green eyes were like ice, his expression all
the more dangerous for the amused derision in his gaze.

"Dawg's baby sister," he sneered, the dull gleam of the gun he
held on her terrifying. "I had such plans for you and Dawg. Rigsby
was so certain that drug would work." Fury flashed in his gaze.
"All he was concerned with was that pact. All I was concerned
with was seeing you in prison and Dawg suffering."

Luther Jennings looked like his father, except for the eyes. The
odd brilliancy to the green eyes marked Mackay blood. He had
that. The eyes would have actually been pretty, if they weren't so
marred by hatred.

"You look like his daughter." He stepped fully from the corner
of the room where he'd been standing, his head tilted to the side
thoughtfully. "I want you to know, that actually made this harder.

For some reason, striking at a child revealed a conscience I wasn't aware I possessed. Though it would have been easier to mess with Laken's young mind, I guess."

Zoey could feel the oily, noxious feel of the terror she'd felt that night washing over her now. She remembered his threat to rape Laken, to hurt her.

"You won't get away with this, Luther," she warned him, stepping back, trying to get as close as possible to the metal steps leading to the ground floor.

Doogan was still in the gym. He would hear Luther if she could just get him closer to the entrance to the room where she'd left Doogan.

Luther smiled in vicious amusement. "Your boyfriend left. Pissed him off, did you?"

"What are you talking about?" Doogan hadn't left. He wouldn't have left her there alone. And even if he'd had to, he would have told her first.

"Chatham Doogan," he answered, his voice filled with contempt. "He left. I watched him slip from the back entrance. Didn't he tell you he was leaving?"

He hadn't.

Why would he leave her alone?

She couldn't conceive that he'd actually desert her. Or that he'd slip away without even warning her.

"No," she finally answered, still backing away from Luther. "He didn't tell me."

He wouldn't have done it. That just wasn't Doogan. He was too protective, and he cared too much for her. He might not love her, but she meant something to him, she knew she did.

"Keep trying to run, little rabbit." He laughed at her with a low, evil chortle. "There's no way to escape, you know. The security system won't work now until I release it. And I won't release it until I kill you."

Yeah. Right. Eli had created that security system for her and he'd thought of that. There was a safeguard. A simple, quick release of the locks that had nothing to do with the electronics. It was a safeguard only she and Eli were aware of.

"Just to hurt Dawg." She shook her head at the knowledge that anyone could be so vicious. So utterly merciless and evil.

"Just to hurt Dawg," he agreed, hatred flashing across his expression. "Just because he's the reason my father was killed, the reason my grandfather was killed. If that bitch Chandler Mackay was married to hadn't been so conniving, then my father and my uncle would have had the inheritance they deserved. It should have belonged to my father."

The child of an incestuous relationship. Johnny Grace's parents had been Dawg's father and his aunt, Nadine Mackay Grace. And after Chandler's death, she had been her other brother's lover as well. Some said the two brothers shared her before Chandler died in a fiery vehicle accident.

"That wasn't Dawg's fault, nor was it mine," she tried to point out logically, working her way slowly around the dining room table.

"It was Dawg's fault my father was killed," he sneered, watching her carefully, like a jackal moving in for the kill. "Natches killed my father to save Dawg and his whore wife. He didn't give him a chance to live, didn't give me a chance to know him." Rage filled his voice. "He didn't have to kill him."

Johnny Grace would have never stopped. Leaving him alive would have ensured that Dawg and Christa faced the same danger later. And possibly Natches and Rowdy as well. Johnny's hatred was just as deep and just as all-consuming as Luther's was.

"And who will you blame for killing me, Luther?" she cried, as though fear were getting the better of her. "There's no one here to brainwash. No one to take the fall for killing me."

"But you'll still be dead," he snarled, his lips drawing back from his teeth, the dark blond of his hair falling over his forehead carelessly as he gave his head an enraged shake. "It doesn't matter who takes the blame or if no one does. You'll be dead, Zoey."

"Because I'm the only one you could get to?" Just a little farther.

She just had to get closer to the end of the table.

Luther laughed at the accusation. "You were easy, I'll admit. As I said, though, Laken would have been easier, but no challenge. She's just a child, after all. What challenge would a kid be?"

He lifted the gun, aiming it at her heart. "Stay still, Zoey. Let's not make this more difficult than it has to be."

The utter ridiculousness of the statement astounded her.

"What? You want me to make killing me easy for you?" She questioned him incredulously. "Are you serious, Luther?"

He frowned at the question. "I'm actually very serious. There's no need to make this harder on both of us. You'll only upset me and cause me to hurt you further. There's no need for that."

She blinked back at him. Standing completely still, Zoey tilted her head and frowned back at him. "Were your parents siblings as well? Because that's completely crazy."

A dark, heavy flush washed from his neck to his hairline as fury snapped into his gaze and contorted his expression.

"I'm not crazy," he yelled, his tone defensive, so much so that she guessed she must have hit a nerve. "You didn't even know who I was. No one knew who I was."

She had to laugh at that. "Luther, everyone knows who was behind what happened to me last year, just as they know what you tried to do. Did you actually believe Rigsby could make me stay silent about it?"

"No . . ."

"He told every secret the two of you thought you could keep." Lifting her arms from her sides, she watched his gaze jerk to the movement. "I didn't forget it, as he told you I would. All his bragging ensured you would fail. Why do you think he tried to kill me?"

"I told him not to do it." A pout pulled at his lips, though the weapon never wavered. "I warned him not to try it, even when he followed you and Billy. That little bastard's too good a driver. I warned him of it."

"And his brother's always close, ready to protect him," she reminded him. "Clay and his pack killed Rigsby and his hired gun. And they're looking for you now. Do you really think you can hide from him? Or from the three men who called me their little witch?" She finally asked gloatingly. "That's four biker packs, Luther. And three of them are renowned for their mercilessness when they go hunting out of vengeance. They'll make you hurt, for a long time, before they kill you."

Something flickered in his gaze then. Fear. Uncertainty.

Zoey remained quiet. Gloating further, threatening or warning him further would only harden his resolve. Let him think about it a minute.

"You think you're so smart," he accused her, about a minute later actually. "You think that's going to keep you alive?"

She looked heavenward with a sigh, then glared back at him. "I think you should have introduced yourself before you decided to become my personal headache, because you're every bit as damned stubborn as any other Mackay male I've ever met, Luther," she snapped, propping one hand on her hip and gripping the edge of the table with the other hand. "You would have gotten along with the rest of them fine."

The gun lifted.

"I wouldn't," the dark, inherently murderous tone of voice suggested from the hall. "It could get you killed."

Doogan.

He hadn't left her. He was still there. She wasn't alone with a crazy Mackay. A Mackay male was bad enough. A crazy Mackay male was worse than a rabid animal.

Anger, fear, and a flash of that crazy filled the aqua eyes.

"I hate you," Luther suddenly shouted, though the weapon never rose farther as he glared at Zoey.

Her eyes widened. "You're breaking my heart, Luther," she informed him intractably. "You think I didn't figure out you hated me?"

"I didn't even hate you then," he cried. "I just wanted you arrested. I didn't really hurt you. I wanted Dawg hurt. He's the reason I was sent away." The crazy was beginning to become enraged.

His hand trembled, his finger tightening on the trigger as it lifted just a little farther. She jumped to the side, throwing herself to the floor. Doogan jumped for Luther, slammed his body into the smaller man's, and took him to the floor. The gun was flung across the floor, skittering beneath the table. Zoey scrambled for it, grabbing it quickly and coming to her knees before she realized Luther was unconscious.

Resting on one knee, Doogan flipped Luther to his stomach, jerked the other man's arms behind his back, and secured his wrists quickly with a pair of nylon restraints Luther himself had carried.

"He's crazy," she whispered, staring back at Doogan wide

eyed. "How does someone so crazy manage what he and Rigsby managed?"

Staring at the now-silent Luther, Doogan rose slowly to his feet before turning to her.

"Evidently, Rigsby was the brains of the two," he grunted.

He was still tense, though, too tense, his gaze warning, something about his demeanor filling her with dread.

It wasn't over.

Tightening her grip on the weapon she'd snapped up from the floor, Zoey rested it against the padded seat of the chair she knelt beside.

"Unfortunately for Zoey, that's not necessarily true, Doogan." Jack Clay stepped from Zoey's bedroom then, his gaze hard, his expression, though, regretful.

"Jack." She whispered his name in shock.

Not Jack. He couldn't be involved in this. He wouldn't hurt her. They'd worked together for so long. For more than five years.

"You were supposed to die on the way back from Louisville," Jack sighed, the gun he held not trembling in the least. There was nothing crazy in his expression or his gaze. Just determination.

"Billy knew?" she whispered.

"Billy's probably the only reason you're still alive," Doogan said then. "Jack wasn't expecting his brother to be with you."

Jack's lips quirked at the statement. "Very true," he sighed. "I actually expected Dawg to make that trip with her. At which point, I would have been in place myself to take his head off with my rifle, and Rigsby would have taken care of Zoey." He shrugged negligently. "I really hadn't wanted to kill Zoey myself."

"You wouldn't have been any less guilty," she whispered, her voice hoarse.

"Still, I wouldn't have put the bullet in your head myself. Then you just had to call Billy to go with you." His smile was rueful. "Mackay intuition?"

Zoey swallowed, the movement difficult. "Everyone else was busy. I promised Dawg I wouldn't take trips out of the county alone."

He chuckled at her answer, though his attention never faltered from Doogan as he stood in position to keep them both in sight. "Fate, then? How fucking appropriate. That bitch seems to like your family far too much, Zoey."

She'd heard that accusation before.

Turning her wrist, she aimed the gun she held, pain racing through her. She didn't want to kill him.

"That bastard Rigsby shot Billy, though." Jack shook his head. "He would have died for that alone. Now, I have to kill both of you myself." His gaze flicked to the unconscious Luther. "I thought for sure he was smart enough to take care of this. Crazy enough to do it, anyway. I didn't anticipate him being soft where you're concerned."

"Most people are," Doogan assured him coolly, drawing Jack's attention from Luther. "You're not going to get away with this, Jack. It won't happen."

"Sure I will," Jack assured him, his gaze somber. "I'm going to hate having to do it myself, but I accepted last year that it had to be done. I can't let that pact go through, Doogan. Those three bastards who are so loyal to Zoey would destroy my own little business. I thought at first that killing your brother and kidnapping your kid was enough, but Rigsby couldn't even get that right could he? He was smart enough to cap Catalina, and your brother was nice enough to put a bullet in his own head, but you were still pushing, still working, even through the grief. But you were soft on Zoey. Real soft on her, and I knew it. Destroying her would have finished you, wouldn't it?"

"Why Jack?" Doogan asked coolly. "How did any of this really help you? My daughter was innocent, Zoey was innocent. How does killing them help you?"

"They weren't supposed to die." Jack sighed, weariness filling his expression. "You just don't understand. You can't stop the changes coming. A revolution is building, man; fighting it will only get you killed. Sometimes you just have to go with the flow and profit from it where you can."

"Fuck, Jack," Doogan sighed wearily. "You're behind the arms thefts in Fort Knox, aren't you?"

"A nice little sideline." Jack shrugged. "The real money is information, though. The Army Human Resources Center is a beehive of information, Doogan. You don't know the sensitive information on service members that goes through there, or the profit to be made in it for the right person." A smirk touched his lips. "I guess I'm the right person, and several of the members of my pack work inside it. People aren't always as careful as they should be, I guess."

"Why?" Doogan's voice hardened. "Why betray your country like that? Everyone you know? And Billy? This will kill him, Jack."

Zoey was careful to remain quiet, the weapon she held trained on him, though she'd have only one chance to hit him, and then that shot would be below the waist.

"Billy will never know." Icy control and determination tightened Jack's face. "If you'd actually killed Luther, I might have been able to let this go." He glanced at Luther. "But you intend to question him, I guess. I have a feeling he'd break easy. Don't you?"

Doogan simply stared at him as Zoey felt tears burning her eyes. As he said, this would kill Billy. He idolized Jack. Their parents were dead and they had no other family. Billy would feel lost without Jack, and Zoey wouldn't blame him.

"Sorry 'bout this, Doogan . . ." Jack lifted his arm, fully intent on firing.

Zoey's finger tightened on the trigger. A second before she would have fired her own shot, Jack's eyes widened and the sound of a weapon discharging exploded through the shadowed apartment.

Doogan threw himself toward Zoey as she ducked, the gun still gripped in her hand when Doogan grabbed it from her and rolled to his back, aiming at the hall entrance across from them.

Peeping beneath the table, she saw Jack's fallen form stretched out on the floor, blood pooling beneath his body, his lifeless gaze directed toward the back of the apartment.

"Are you okay, Zoey?" Billy's voice came from the hall, low, and filled with aching pain.

Billy had killed his brother. Her friend had looked up to his brother just as Zoey looked up to Dawg; killing him would be ripping Billy's heart out.

"Toss your weapon where I can see it, Billy," Doogan ordered him.

The gun clattered across the floor. "I found Harley outside," Billy said, his voice hollow. "He's hurt pretty bad, but he was able to tell me who 'bout killed him tonight. Mackays are on their way. Jack wasn't going to wait any longer, though, was he, Doogan?" Billy was still hidden by the wall that extended beyond the kitchen.

"He wasn't going to wait," Doogan agreed.

Reaching for Zoey, he drew her to her feet as he rose, keeping her carefully behind him.

"That's what I thought." Billy sounded almost dazed.

"Billy, I need you to show yourself," Doogan ordered, his gaze and his weapon never wavering as Zoey pressed her head to his back, shaking it slowly.

"Is Zoey okay?" Billy asked, rather than doing as Doogan commanded. "He didn't hurt her, did he?"

"Zoey's fine. Do as I said, Billy." Doogan's tone hardened, his body tensing.

"Can't do that." The weak, hollow sound of his voice caused Zoey to clench her hands at Doogan's back.

"Why not, Billy?" Doogan wasn't relenting. His fingers gripped her arm when Zoey would have moved around him, holding her back.

"Hell, I don't think I can stand back up, man." A heavy breath filled his voice. "I followed him. I heard him on the phone. Heard him say Zoey had to be taken out." The disillusionment was horrible to hear. "I followed him after he left. Slipped in the garage door behind him. Hell, Zoey, did you give him your code?"

A sob broke from her voice. "He had the code to the back garage," she answered as she followed Doogan's slow advance to the edge of the kitchen.

Sirens could be heard racing closer now. The cavalry was coming, but they were coming far too late to save Billy from the most horrible decision Zoey could imagine he'd ever had to make in his life.

"I'm so sorry, Zoey." Billy's voice was low, weak.

"Hurry. Please," she begged Doogan. "Don't let anything happen to him, Doogan. Please. He's my friend."

He was one of the few friends she'd claimed in the past year. One of the few who had never run to her brother to tattle on her.

"Stay here." Low, hard, the order was a lash of inner rage that sent a chill racing down her spine as he stopped her only inches from the entrance to the hall.

Doogan stepped to the edge of the wall, looked down it slowly, and then with a low "Come on," he moved to Billy's fallen form.

Sirens and flashing lights filled the apartment as Zoey rushed to Billy, kneeling beside him. The wound where the bullet had been dug from his side had torn open. Blood stained his T-shirt and dripped to the floor. Pale, weak, he stared up at her miserably as Doogan rushed back to the kitchen.

"I'm so sorry, Zoey," he whispered. "I'm so sorry."

Holding his hand, Zoey patted it gently, aware of Doogan hurrying back, a stack of her dishcloths in his hand.

"I'm still beating your ass in that race at the end of the month. That scratch on your side won't save you." It was impossible to keep the tears from her voice or from falling down her face.

His head lolled to the side, resting on her shoulder as Doogan worked to stop the bleeding, his eyes so hard, so cold, it broke her heart.

He was distancing himself, pulling away from anything he might feel.

"I killed my brother, Zoey," Billy said, misery spilling from him. "I killed him."

"No, Billy, you didn't kill your brother." Doogan's head jerked up, that inner rage so reflected in his gaze that Zoey flinched. "Trust me, the man you killed, killed your brother. He wasn't your brother when he made the choice to betray everyone who trusted him. He ceased being your brother in that single second. You hear me?"

"Like *your* brother?" Billy asked, the words sending shock racing through Zoey. "When he betrayed you?"

"Like my brother," Doogan agreed, the rage, the flash of pain, all of it receding beneath the ice as he stared back at Zoey.

He'd lost so much and she hadn't even known. He hadn't

shared any of it with her, no part of himself but the pleasure they'd shared.

"Makes you dead inside?" Billy sighed as the security system to the doors activated, notifying the intruders tearing through the house that law enforcement had been called and they were now being recorded.

Mackays, their in-laws, and their friends were filling the rooms; EMTs rushed behind them and Zoey's world became chaos. And through it all, she knew the one thing she would remember most was Doogan rising to his feet, turning his back, and walking away.

Walking away from her.

NINETEEN

Three weeks later

Doogan stepped into the shadowed, cold stone walls of the Doogan ancestral home, and for the first time in far too long, he didn't feel as though he were smothering from the loss of his daughter's laughter ringing through the halls.

The pain was still there, bittersweet, regretful, and tinged with guilt. He'd always blame himself for his sweet Katie's death and the confused horror he knew she must have felt that day. She'd known she wasn't supposed to leave the house with anyone, but her uncle Regan had come for her. Her nanny wasn't around; of course she hadn't known Uncle Regan had locked the nanny in a closet, and her "unca" promised her it was all right to leave.

Her uncle promised her that her mommy was waiting to give her the bicycle she wanted so bad, and of course he'd already told her daddy. It was fine. And his sweet, trusting Katie had left with him.

And then her mother and her uncle Regan had tried to make

her get in the car with a strange man. A man whose face frightened her. One she knew her daddy wouldn't want her with. She hadn't known Rigsby, but she'd seen the evil in him.

Katie had broken away from them. Her flight was caught by a security camera on a nearby business. The fear in her face, the tears, and her mother's and uncle's rage as they tried to catch her. She'd run in front of the car before anyone could do anything. There had been no way the driver, whose speed had been clocked at no more than six miles under the speed limit for the residential street, could have seen her. Still, it had been too fast to stop, to keep from slamming into the little girl racing from between the parked cars.

Doogan hadn't even been able to tell her good-bye.

The driver said Regan had been inconsolable, that Katie's final words had destroyed him.

"Why, unca? Why did you let me get hurt? My da will miss me, unca. I want my da." Then Katie's sweet eyes had closed and never opened again.

Katie's grave had been placed next to her grandmother's, where she would rest secure between loving grandparents when Doogan's father passed. Doogan's plot was below his baby girl's; her nanny had asked to be buried above her. The middle-aged woman had passed in her sleep six months later when her heart had just stopped beating. Another death Doogan laid at his bastard brother's and traitorous dead wife's feet.

His wife's lover had killed her before the day was out. A gunshot to the head. Doogan had found Regan later in Katie's room, the gun he'd used to kill himself lying on the floor beside him. The grief and guilt, he'd written before taking his own life, was more than he could bear. He'd believed Catalina. Believed Doogan was divorcing her to be with another woman and taking Katie from her.

Breathing in deep, he strode through the vaulted entryway and through the family room to the office on the other end of the room. His father's call that he had visitors had pissed him off. The old man refused to tell him who the visitors were, only that they were friends, and someone Doogan needed to see.

There was no one person he wanted to see. The only person he needed to see, he assured himself, was better off without him.

Zoey.

She was better off without him, but letting her go proved to be impossible. He was the last person she needed in her life. A man who couldn't protect a five-year-old child could never hope to protect a woman who loved adventure. And his Zoey loved her little adventures.

Pushing through the partially opened door to his office, he came to a hard stop, staring at the men awaiting him.

"There you are." Chatham Doogan rose to his feet, his headful of thick gray hair standing on end in places, his expression surprisingly less somber than normal.

At sixty-seven his father ruled the Doogan mansion with an iron fist after his wife's death. He told anyone who cared to listen that his precious Illy, Illandra Doogan, would never forgive him if he allowed her home to fall to ruin.

"Father." Doogan nodded, though he didn't take his eyes off the man that rose when Chatham did to face him.

"I thought you said visitors, in the plural?" Doogan asked his father.

Closing the door, he strode behind the desk and sat down heavily, watching Graham suspiciously.

"Well, the other three decided they could wait to see you." His father scratched absently at his head, his gaze questioning. "They didn't say why."

"The Mackays felt the meeting would go more peacefully if they weren't here," Graham admitted, glancing at Doogan's father. "Can I have a minute with him, Chatham? I'll make certain we finish catching up before I leave."

"Of course." Chatham nodded, his gaze moving to Doogan warningly. "Don't start another fight in here, Bromleah. Your mother will be screaming through the halls again if ye do so."

The Irish was as thick and pure in his father's voice as it was the day he stepped on American soil as a young lad in his mother's arms.

"I'll do my best," Doogan assured him. "I never throw the first punch, though, if you remember."

"You just piss a man off enough to do the job for you," Chatham grunted. "Try not to piss young Graham here off. He's likely the last friend ye have left in this world."

No doubt, Doogan agreed silently, watching his father leave the room. When the door closed behind him Graham sat down, his gaze faintly amused.

"He never changes much," Graham chuckled. "Always as opinionated and determined as ever."

"Determined to run my life and have an opinion on every mistake he believes I've ever made," Doogan agreed, though fondly. "The world's a better place with him in it, though." He sat back in his chair, watched Graham for long minutes, then shook his head. "This isn't a good time, Graham . . ."

"Yeah, walking away from a woman and tearing her soul out at a time when she needs you most makes things a little iffy when you're in love with her." Graham nodded sagely.

Doogan could feel his molars grinding instantly, his jaw clenched so tight.

"You don't know what the hell you're talkin' about," he gritted out.

Graham sighed heavily. "That Irish only comes out when you let those tightly held emotions of yours slip. Funny thing, though," he pointed out. "I never heard that accent slip once when you were married, unless you were talking about Katie."

He'd married Catalina when he'd learned she was pregnant. Love had never been part of the equation. He'd never told anyone that, though. He'd never allowed his memory of his daughter to be marred by the fact that she was conceived before his marriage to her mother. In his youth, he'd felt his child would be hurt by such knowledge.

How stupid he'd been. He should have divorced the day Katie was born and paid off the judge for custody. Had he known then what he knew now, he would have done just that.

"Is Zoey okay?" He pushed the memories back and focused on now. Focused on another loss so deep, so painful that dealing with it was taxing his patience.

"She's fine." Graham nodded. "Grieving. Missing you. Living with Dawg."

Doogan sat up at that news. "Why is she livin' with Dawg?"

That fucking accent was about to piss him off, Doogan thought, unable to control it just as he was unable to control the hell his life had become without Zoey in it.

"She's grieving, missing you," Graham repeated with a snort. "It broke her heart when you walked out and just disappeared. A few phone calls a week won't heal it, dumbass."

He just stared back at the other man, refusing to comment.

When he said nothing, Graham sighed heavily. "Dawg was

right, it was best they not be here, because you're determined to keep punishing yourself and Zoey right along with you."

"You made a mistake comin' here, Graham," Doogan warned him, the anger he was trying to hold back slipping free in the low throb of his voice. "Perhaps you should leave."

"Yeah, for now." Graham rose to his feet. "But wait too long to fix this, Doogan, and I swear to you, I'll help the Mackays run your ass out of town when you do return. Then you'll understand the mistake you're making."

"Meanin'?" he snapped, rising as well. "And you'll run me from no place that I decide to be, boyo. I promise ya that."

The hard sneer that curled at Graham's lips had his fists wanting to curl, to meet flesh and expend the fury rushing through him.

"You think your friends didn't know why you married that bitch?" Graham snapped. "That we weren't well aware she deliberately let herself get pregnant to trap the Doogan heir into marriage? That when she didn't have a boy and you refused to touch her again, that she didn't begin conniving to force you into paying her off for the rest of her fucking life?"

It was the truth. It was the reason he and Eli could never get along. Her younger brother had never wanted to see what his sister had become. He'd become estranged from his family when his parents refused to have her grave blessed, when Doogan refused to allow her to be buried next to the daughter Eli thought she loved. Just as Chatham Doogan had refused to allow his bastard son, Regan, to be buried in Doogan ground, swearing he'd sell every inch of the land if the 'illegitimate spawn of evil' was placed anywhere close to the child he killed.

Doogan understood, though. Eli hadn't seen his sister's spiteful nature; he'd still been too easy to use. She'd been certain he only saw what she had wanted him to see. Only believed what she'd wanted him to believe. That Doogan had broken her heart, taken her daughter, and left her with nothing.

Eli should have the truth by now. Doogan had allowed the file he'd ordered withheld made available to the agent. Eli wasn't a boy, he was a man. If he couldn't use a man's intelligence to see what his sister was, then so be it.

"I don't want to fight you, Graham," Doogan snapped, forcing his fingers to uncurl. "Leave this be."

"She cries all the time. She's like a ghost. She turned the remaining details and the position of overseer of the pact over to another agent and isn't even interested in it now." The surprising information had Doogan staring at Graham in confusion now.

"Why would she do that?" he questioned the other man. "It makes no sense."

"She said she's done with it." Graham shrugged. "Hell, she's a Mackay, who knows why they do things. And as you said, it's none of my business." Contempt filled his voice. "The day will come when I'll tell you the same damned thing, though. She's none of your business. And you'll listen. I promise you that, I'll make sure of it."

Before Doogan could question him further, Graham stomped from the office and from the house. He didn't stop to keep his promise to the old man, Doogan thought, sitting back down wearily. No doubt, he'd catch the blame for that one eventually.

Because it was his fault.

The thought had him glowering in brooding anger at the fireplace across the room. Empty, cold; the dark bricks looked like the yawning mouth of empty fucking dreams from where he sat.

Fuck.

"Yer makin' a mistake, boy." His father stepped into the room, watching him with that patient, somber expression Doogan hated.

"That woman was drawin' ya even before Katie was taken from us. Even I heard the way ya spoke of that woman causin' havoc in Kentucky whenever. And it was no coincidence ya petitioned your godfather for the annulment when ya did. Ya knew ye couldn't stay away from her, didn't ya?"

He'd petitioned his godfather, a bishop in the Catholic church, for an annulment. Catalina was fighting it though, swearing they shared a bed, when they hadn't.

Doogan stared into the fireplace with the desperation of a man searching his soul rather than the empty space that only rarely held the warmth it was created for.

"Ah, Brom, yer mother will be yellin' at ya later, ya know," his father warned him. "Call it drafts in an old house all ye need to. We both know the sounds of her wailing and tears, don't we, son? Tonight, they'll keep us both awake, aye?"

Yes, his mother haunted them. He'd accepted it the night of Katie's death. They eerie sounds of his mother's cries had sent chills racing up his back. He only prayed tonight wouldn't be one of those nights, though he knew better. He swore he could feel her staring at him now, her Irish temper ready to erupt.

"She was a fine woman, yer mother." Chatham sighed heavily. "Loved to do the things that made a man terrified for the loss of her, she did. Rode those horses hell fer leather, laughin' with joy when they reared and thought to take the reins from her. And she'd loved that wee little girl a' ours, didn't she? I thank the Lord daily she left us before Katie was taken. We'd have lost 'em both had she not."

"Stop . . ." Doogan snapped.

"Stop, ye say," his father grunted. "Stop, Da. I'll hear na more, Da," he snarled. "Well, ye'll be hearin' your mam tonight, ye will. Mark my words. When the midnight hour opens the doors betwixt here and heaven, she'll be a-ragin' at ya. Mark ma words she will be."

Doogan came to his feet furiously. Casting his father an irate glare, he stomped from the room, determined to escape the truth.

"Run, boy, all ye like. She'll be waitin' for ya when ya return," Chatham yelled at his retreating back. "And ya know she will be."

Run? Hell. He'd stopped running from his mother's temper when he was a lad. Because his da was right. She was always waiting when he returned.

Two Weeks Later
Cumberland, Kentucky

Zoey pulled her suitcase through the house, the padded wheels almost silent, the weight of the bag negligible with the ease of movement.

Good thing, she thought; now wasn't the time to be carrying it.

With that thought, she entered the kitchen to face the family that had gathered around her, supported her, comforted her. And now, she hoped, was willing to let her leave.

Sitting with the various Mackays, in-laws, and out-laws as she liked to call them, was Harley. Harley Matthews though, rather than Perdue. Leaning back in a kitchen chair, his shaggy dark brown hair lying around his face, his blue eyes quiet and intense, he gave her a little wink when he caught sight of her.

He'd been a little worse for wear the night Jack had tried to kill her and Doogan, but his head was harder than anyone imagined, it seemed.

"Hey, sis," Dawg greeted her gently. "Everything good?" He asked her that every morning. He worried, and in the time she'd spent with him, the hours they'd spent talking, she understood why. Just as, she hoped, he understood why she'd felt smothered and restrained by that worry.

"I hope the cleaners are finished at the apartment because I'm going home." Zoey faced her family in her brother's kitchen as they sat around the huge table drinking coffee.

Dawg, Natches, Rowdy, and their wives; Timothy and her mother; her sisters and their husbands were all present that evening. Timothy had arranged the meeting after receiving the final report on the status of the pact between the three motorcycle packs. Zoey had turned the negotiations over to the female agent who had assisted her for the past two years, her heart no longer in the adventure.

With the report on the pact were the final reports on Jack's activities and the events that led to his death at his brother's hand.

Billy was home from the hospital and under the care of several medical techs provided by Homeland Security. The motorcycle pack Jack had led was finally released with the exception of Jack's three co-conspirators and the firing of several human resources employees from Fort Knox.

The past weeks had been hell. She just wanted to go home, hide, and figure out what to do after the news she'd received herself that day sank in.

Everyone stared at her silently, their gazes moving from the suitcase at her side, then back to her face.

"You don't have to leave, Zoey." Christa spoke gently from Dawg's side. "You know we've enjoyed having you here."

"I'm ready to go home." She couldn't rage here. She couldn't cry, grieve, or let herself find the comfort she'd learned that morning that Doogan had given her before he left.

"All right." Dawg nodded, shocking her with his answer as well as the somberness in his gaze. "Do me a favor, though?"

"What?" she asked warily. He'd agreed far too easily.

"Let me and Natches come over in a few days and redo the security. I'll never sleep at night worrying about you and the baby otherwise."

She froze for a second before her gaze jumped to her sisters. But they were just as shocked. They hadn't told. Then Zoey turned slowly to her mother.

Her mother, Mercedes, stared at Timothy, a frown on her face, her arms crossed over her breasts.

"Timothy?" she questioned him warningly.

"Not me." Tim's hands went up, denial creasing his face and filling his eyes. "Stop glaring at me."

"I knew you were at the doctor's office this morning," Dawg sighed. "Jenkins is an OB/GYN, Zoey. I'm not a fool, sweetheart."

No, he wasn't a fool.

"You are not to tell Doogan," she informed him, suddenly afraid he would do just that. "None of you are."

"Zoey." Graham drew her attention. He was Doogan's friend, the one person in the room who would call him the quickest. "That's not our place, sweetheart. If you want Doogan to know, then you can tell him. We're here for you, though. However you need our support."

However she needed their support.

She needed Doogan, ached for him, missed him desperately. He'd called her several times a week since he'd left, checking on her, sometimes just discussing the day when he called late at night. But he hadn't mentioned coming back. He hadn't told her why he left as he had.

And she didn't want a man who had to be guilted into her bed. She hadn't told him her suspicions and she wouldn't tell him they were confirmed now. She would slowly stop taking his calls, let him disappear from her life as he so obviously wanted to disappear.

"Thank you." The tightness in her throat was nearly impossible to swallow around.

Before leaving there was the round of hugs, her sisters' tears, her brother's and cousins' regret, and Graham's whispered "I'm sorry, little sis."

It wasn't his fault; it wasn't Doogan's fault.

She'd loved having him inside her, loved the feel of his release heating her, extending hers, and the intimacy it had given her. A false feeling of intimacy, it seemed, but still, the belief that there was a bond building between them, that he cared for her, had filled her with warmth.

Finally, her suitcase stored in her newly rebuilt roadster, Zoey was pulling from her brother's driveway and heading home. She had to fight her tears every step of the way when she had so wanted to sob against her mother's shoulder. She wanted to scream and rail and let free the tears that she'd held back for so long.

She wanted Doogan.

She wanted him to hold her, wanted him to touch her, and she so wanted to feel at least a suspicion that he wouldn't hate her for being pregnant, for forcing him to face the risks and dangers he'd no doubt think of if he learned of her pregnancy.

She wanted to share her joy with him, because the knowledge that she carried their child gave her the kick in the ass she needed to get her life back in order and to leave her brother's protective embrace.

She had bitched about him for so long, hid who and what she

was for so many years, when Lyrica had been right. She should have gone to him and Natches, asked them to back her. Because they would have. She'd seen that gleam in their eyes when she'd met with the leaders of the motorcycle packs she'd known since she was a teenager.

The three leaders of the largest packs to sign with Homeland Security, Tigen, Black, and Forest had been surprised to see them there, but Zoey was the one who had been shocked to learn the lengths the three men had taken to get to know the Mackays once Zoey and her sisters were moved to Kentucky.

Dawg, Natches, and Rowdy had seemed years younger as they escorted her into the Louisville bar where the meeting was held. Armed and dangerous, their gazes watchful, their still muscular, powerful bodies ready to move if they had to.

According to Black, the pact would have moved much faster if her family had been involved simply because protecting her would have been an assurance they wouldn't have had to double- and triple-check. They had never trusted Jack or his pack to protect her. And it was probably a damned good thing.

They were willing to protect the pack Jack had left, though. The suddenly orphaned men and women who had made the pack their family and support network had been at a loss, just as Billy felt. Forest had agreed to move into the area and allow Jack's to integrate with it. The men and women who followed him could also integrate easily into the surrounding counties and their work-force, just as they did wherever Forest led them each season.

They were like modern-day Gypsies, she'd always thought. Waiting, subconsciously searching for that one place they could call home. Maybe Lake Cumberland could become home for many of them.

The packs weren't drug dealers, thugs, or murderers. They were like sentinels without backing. Hard fighting, rough talking, less than respectable, but sentinels all the same. Though they didn't take anyone's shit. A few were suspected to have killed; there were quite a few who slipped and smoked, shot up, or snorted their drugs of choice. But they kept to a code that their leaders enforced with unflinching swiftness. Those members knew better than to get caught, because Tigen, Black, and Forest would beat their asses and leave them lying.

Pulling into the parking space in front of her garage, Zoey hit the remote and waited for the door to lift, then eased the car inside. The heavy steel panels rolled back into place, locked down, and left Zoey sitting alone in the dimly lit interior.

She thought it would feel lonely, that the emptiness of her home would close around her. She hadn't looked forward to that. That wasn't what she felt, though. The warmth she'd felt while Doogan had filled her life was still there. It wrapped around her; the memory of his touch, the sound of his voice, the excitement he filled her with, warmed her. It didn't ease the incredibly hollow pain that throbbed inside her.

"Time to figure things out, huh?" she said softly, one hand pressing to her lower stomach.

Of course, the baby wasn't aware of the world around him or her yet. Still, speaking to the child resting there made her feel not so lonely.

"What are we figuring out?"

Doogan.

Her head jerked to the metal staircase, eyes widening at the sight of Doogan sitting on a wide step, watching her curiously.

He looked tired. He couldn't have gotten much sleep since he'd left. From the looks of it, not much more than she had.

Stepping from the car and closing the door, she watched warily as he rose and came toward her. That confident swagger, the powerful presence, and the far-too-wicked glint in his eyes had her breath growing heavy, her body softening, the flesh between her thighs moistening.

"What are you doing here?" She sounded like some weak-kneed ninny without the strength to tell him to go to hell.

Wait, she didn't have the strength to tell him to go to hell. The desire to wasn't even there.

Still, she eased away from him, watching that wicked gleam in his eyes intensify as she tried to escape to the door of the gym. She made it as far as the front of the car before he stopped her.

"I missed you, witch." His hands settled at her hips, holding her in place as she felt his erection pressing into her stomach.

"You missed having a fuck toy," she accused him, still no heat in her voice, no strength.

She was such a pushover where he was concerned.

"A fuck toy," he murmured, his hands sliding from her hips, beneath the sleeveless top she wore, to the naked skin of her waist. "I think it's gone far past the toy stage, sweetheart. I think we're heading into much more dangerous territory."

Callused, rasping against her flesh, stroking, his fingers sent heated lashes of pleasure racing through her. She could practically feel her senses melting for him. The inner flesh of her pussy was definitely trying to melt for him. Slick and heated, her juices spilled from her, weeping to the swollen lips and engorged clit throbbing for his touch.

"Doogan . . ."

His lips stole whatever she was about to say. They covered hers, his kiss instantly ravenous, his tongue plunging inside and rubbing against hers.

Oh God, she'd missed him.

Wrapping her arms around his neck to hold him to her, Zoey tangled her fingers in his hair, moaning at the exquisite sensations racing through her, sizzling through her senses and wiping everything from her mind but the need for him. A need she couldn't, wouldn't fight.

TWENTY

She didn't know why he was there, and for this moment in time she wouldn't let herself care. For right now, the need for him, the need to have him touch her, hold her, one more time, was all that mattered.

"God, I missed you, baby," he breathed out, his voice rough as his head lifted.

His hand slid to her hips again, lifted her, and laid her back along the still-warm hood of the car, his hands going to the snap and zipper of her denim shorts.

"I do have a bed, remember?" She frowned up at him, but her hips lifted, a moan spilling from her as he drew the material down her legs. "This is completely decadent, Doogan."

His smile was knowing. "No, baby, this is completely tame," he assured her. "We'll get to decadent real soon, though."

Well, at least he was staying around long enough for decadent.

She wondered how far from decadent this was in his opinion, though.

"I haven't forgiven you yet." There wasn't a damned thing for her to hold on to. Her fingers curled, reaching above her, finding the rim of the hood and gripping it desperately as he pulled her boots from her feet and dropped them to the cement floor.

"Let's see if I can convince you to forgive me a little faster." The dark growl in his voice was the only warning she had before his lips lowered, his tongue swiping through the swollen folds and sending her senses into flames.

Dark, almost black eyes stared up at her as he licked at her, his tongue rolling around her clit, rubbing at it, tormenting the little nub with striking flares of desperate pleasure. And it was so good. So good she could only lift to him, moan and whimper for more. More sensation, more of the whipping, whirling sensations that made her feel him all the way to her ragged soul.

A heated, sucking kiss to her clit had her hips jerking to him. When his head lifted, she was ready to wail in protest.

"Take the fucking shirt off," he groaned. "Let me see your pretty breasts, Zoey, and those hard, tight little nipples."

Still watching her, he flicked his tongue over the sensitive nub of her clit, then massaged it with a slow, rolling little move of his tongue.

She all but tore her shirt and bra from her, tossing the material to the floor, uncaring of where it fell. Immediately her fingers gripped her nipples, tightened on them, tugging at them as brutal fingers of overwhelming sensation tore straight to her clit.

"Fuck." He pulled back, his gaze moving to her clit then to meet her eyes. "Your little clit's throbbing for me, Zoey. Pushing against my tongue. So eager. It's so damned eager to cum for me."

"Then let me cum." Lifting her hips, her fingers pinching at her nipples, she rode a wave of such intense pleasure she almost lost her breath.

"Not without me, baby." As he pulled back, one hand gripped the iron-hard length of his cock that he'd already released from his pants.

Thick, heavy veins ran over it, blood pulsing through them in a throbbing rhythm. The plum-shaped head was dark, imposing in its width, and tucking against the weeping center of her body.

"I can't wait, Zoey." Hard, callused fingers gripped her thighs. "I can't wait, baby."

She licked her lips, fighting to breathe. "Don't wait, Doogan. Fuck me . . . Oh God, Doogan," she cried out at the first, hard push inside her gripping depths.

The tissue convulsed, clenched around the intruder, stroking and milking the hard flesh that came to a stop only a bare few inches inside her.

"Fuck. You're tight," he snarled, his teeth baring, extreme pleasure tightening his face.

"Take me hard, then," she demanded, reaching behind her again to hold on to the rim of the hood. "Give me all of you, Doogan. Show me how to fly again. Make me burn . . ."

The groan that tore from his chest came as he drew back, paused, poised at the rippling entrance as his gaze locked with hers.

"Fuck me, Doogan," she breathed out, her juices spilling from her aching pussy to meet the wide crest of his cock. "Hard . . ."

She needed him, ached for him; she'd been dying without him.

"Hard, baby, just like you want it."

"Doogan . . ." She tried to scream his name.

Her body bowed, hips arching, her breath stilling in her throat as he thrust inside her, still not to the hilt, but he wasn't finished yet.

The next thrust buried him balls deep inside her, pushing past the muscles hugged tight around his shuttling flesh as he groaned her name, the sound of hoarse male pleasure rasping over her senses.

"Have mercy," he breathed, the hard rasp pushing her higher as he began the rhythmic strokes she knew would send her exploding into rapture.

And it wouldn't take long. She was climbing, muscles tightening, the spiraling sensations building fast, burning bright as he came over her.

One hand gripped her hip, the other curved around the mound of a breast, his lips covering the hard point of a nipple as he sucked it into his mouth. Firm, deep draws sent fingers of fiery sensation rushing straight to her vagina. The convulsive clench of her inner muscles around each hard thrust inside her dragged a groan from his throat, a cry from hers. His teeth rasped and nibbled at the tight bud; his pelvis scraped across her clit with each thrust as his cock throbbed, the head burying deep. Each stroke inside her, each slamming thrust parted sensitive tissue, caressed it, stoked the sensations burning so bright and hot inside her.

"Doogan, Doogan please," she cried out as his arms slid beneath her legs, lifting them, pushing her knees back, his hips moving faster, harder.

Completely open to him now, the snug, clenched muscles of her pussy tightened, flexed, and in one blinding second Zoey felt the world explode around her and inside her.

She jerked in his arms, her cries echoing around her, joined by the hard, harsh growl of her name and the feel of his release spilling inside her. Hard, pulsing ejaculations shot his seed to the depths of her pussy, filling her with him and sending her racing into the fiery center of ecstasy.

Catching his breath took a while. Long enough that Zoey dozed beneath him, warmed by the lingering heat of the car's motor against the metal hood and his body. Sprawled beneath him like a sexual sacrifice, all those unruly black curls spilling around her, framing her flushed, sated features.

He wanted to smile at the sight of her, but to allow that one small measure of happiness free too soon could destroy him later, if she decided his baggage was too much, his memories and his mistakes more than she could handle in the coming years. Because once he had his ring on her finger he'd be damned if he'd let her go. And he wasn't waiting too damned long to put that ring there if she fucked up long enough to agree to it.

Easing back, he grimaced at the excess pleasure raking along the head of his cock as he pulled free of her. Her little protesting whimper assured him that same pleasure had stroked across her senses as well.

"Come on, wildcat," he whispered, lifting her slight weight in his arms and carrying her up the stairs to the apartment.

She curled against him, her head resting against his shoulder, her arms looped around his neck, and he didn't miss the fact that she felt as though she'd always belonged there. Right there, against his heart, held in his arms.

Entering her bedroom, he moved to the bed, placing her in the center of it and stretching out beside her. She draped herself across his chest, relaxed, drifting, he knew, in a sensual aftermath he hated to ruin.

Hated to, yet he knew if he didn't tell her what he needed to, then he never would.

"The night we danced," he told her softly, pressing her head to his chest when she would have lifted it. "I told you I was married. I married Eli's sister when she told me she was carrying our child. For six years, I lived like a fucking monk. I took the vows, I kept them. The night I met you nearly broke that resolve, though. I wanted you with a hunger that nearly broke me. And I had no choice but to walk away, because you deserved so much more than a man who would have had no choice but to lie to have you."

And he'd nearly done just that. If Jack hadn't been watching him with that disapproving frown, if he hadn't known Dawg Mackay would kill him and he'd break her heart and forever lose the belief in him he'd seen in her eyes, then he would have taken her.

But his wife was fucking a path through D.C., his daughter was still a baby, and he knew that keeping her if he divorced her mother would probably be impossible. He was a grown man; he'd made his bed, and he wouldn't have his daughter pay for his need to escape that cold, hard rock he'd made for himself.

So he waited, kept track of her, watched her, ached for her from afar until Katie turned five and he'd filed for an annulment. His wife had left with her lover, Rigsby, and with Regan Doogan Moore's help had attempted to take his daughter.

His breath caught when he told her how Katie died. He felt her tears on his chest, her silent sobs in the shudder of her shoulders.

"Less than six months later, Harley had tracked Catalina's lover, her killer, to Cumberland; we just couldn't figure out his identity or why he was in Kentucky. I left Harley here to find the bastard, see what he was up to." His fingers clenched in her hair for a tortured moment. "The next thing I know, Director Bryce is on the phone telling me . . ." He had to stop, swallow past the lump in his throat. "Telling me you were in trouble and for me to get to Sam's. And God as my witness, I had no idea Rigsby was behind it. I suspected his presence here had something to do with the weapons thefts from Fort Knox, but I had no idea anyone knew what I felt for you. And I never suspected Jack, not with his ties to the Mackays."

Luther had filled all the blanks in. How Rigsby had known about Zoey, used her to distract Doogan and Harley while he and Jack continued to steal information on high-level military teams currently abroad on assignment. Luther Jennings was unaware how he was being used as a distraction if he was needed. Then Doogan had returned to Cumberland, his interest in Jack's pack making the two men far too nervous.

He'd known more was going on than a threat to that pact when he'd arrived; he'd believed the threat was to Zoey, though, not the human resources information they'd found access to. He'd been distracted. That mistake had almost been a fatal one. He'd almost lost Zoey.

"I knew I loved you, Zoey," he whispered. "I knew if I lost you too, I couldn't live. Losing you would break me."

"I was right here, Doogan. I was always here, waiting for you," she whispered, finally able to lift her head to stare down at him.

And in his eyes she saw the pain, the rage, the man who had to face the fact that he could only run for so long, and that the time for it was over.

"Yeah, you are," he whispered, reaching up to cup her face. "Graham came to see me a few weeks ago," he said then.

She nearly stopped breathing. God, he'd promised . . .

"He told me if I waited too long to come for you, then he'd make sure when I got over my dumb and came back later, he'd make sure I left just as fast." His lips quirked. "He'd do it too. I figured I better get my ass back here and claim you while your family was willing to let me."

Her brow arched. "You need their permission?"

"Not anymore." He tugged at her hair, pulling her to his kiss, whispering the words over her lips. "I belong to you, witch. Heart and soul. There's no way in hell I can live without you."

Her smile lit up his heart. Filled with love, with a promise that met the one in his heart.

"Welcome home, Doogan." And her lips lowered to his, their kiss one of shared promise, of shared love.

When it was over, he tucked her against his side again. "Damn, I'm tired, honey. You wear a man out."

"Better get your rest," she murmured as he let his eyes drift closed. "I figure you have about seven months to recuperate."

His eyes jerked open, panic flashing through him for about two seconds.

No, he told himself desperately, she didn't mean . . .

"Zoey . . ."

"Did Graham tell you I was pregnant, Doogan?" she asked, her tone perfectly reasonable. "Because if he did, you walk your ass right back out of here. At least until it snows."

He blinked up at the ceiling. He tried like hell to swallow.

Slowly, he sat up, telling himself his hands really weren't shaking. He wasn't ready to pass out because he couldn't breathe past the tightness in his chest.

"What did you say?" he wheezed.

That siren's smile, those witchy eyes. Emerald circling celadon. So damned beautiful she could steal his breath even when he wasn't in shock.

She caught his hand and dragged it to her still-flat stomach. "I warned you," she reminded him. "I just didn't realize the pill I was on was low dose. My doctor figures I'm about six weeks pregnant."

He stared at his hand where it covered her stomach, realizing what she hadn't told him.

"You weren't going to tell me." He turned his gaze to her, glaring back at her. "Were you?"

"No, I wasn't," she admitted, stubbornness flashing in her eyes. "If you didn't want me without a baby, then you could do without me. I wouldn't have kept our baby from you, though." Regret filled her expression. "I would never punish our baby, Doogan. I would only love it, and you, and always regret what hadn't been."

His Zoey. His witch.

"I love you, but I'm spanking your butt for that one," he promised her.

A little roll of her eyes was followed by a smothered yawn. "Later, I might let you."

Later.

But he could kiss her. He could let his lips whisper over hers and he could thank God he got over his dumb in time to claim her. And their child.

Their child.

Damn. When he'd felt as though he'd come home the night he'd danced with her, he'd been right.

Zoey was home.

His heart.

His soul.

The mother of his child.

His sweet seductress and his life.

And for the first time in his life, he was complete.

EPILOGUE

Two Weeks Later

"That is so not fair, Dad." The teenager's voice could be clearly heard outside the office door as Zoey Mackay pushed into the Mackay Marine Convenience store from the rental and fuel office attached to it.

Whatever her father said was muffled, but there was no mistaking the edge of frustration in the quieter response.

"I'm fifteen, not a baby," Annette Mackay cried out. "And you don't let me do anything."

Zoey winced as she turned to Annette's mother, Kelly Mackay, to see her propped back on a stool behind the sales counter, sneaker-clad feet resting on the counter, arms folded beneath her breasts, a look of long-suffering patience on her face.

Whatever Annette's father, Rowdy, said in reply to the accusation had his daughter jerking the door open moments later and stomping into the store, tears turning her summer-green eyes the color of brilliant jewels, though not the first drop fell to her sun-tanned cheeks.

Shoulder-length, ribbon-straight black hair was pulled into a ponytail, her pretty features set into an expression of stubborn teenage fury, her fists clenched at the sides of the white sundress she wore over her bathing suit.

"Momma, you have to do something with him," Annette cried out, her heart shattered into a million pieces if her voice was anything to go by. "He's being completely unreasonable."

Kelly dropped her feet from the counter, slid from her barstool, and glanced at the open doorway where her husband stood, amusement gleaming in his eyes, before her gaze moved to her daughter.

"Unreasonable? Again? Not your father, Annie. Such an idea shocks me." And she sounded shocked too, Zoey thought as she ducked her head and moved behind the counter to join Kelly.

"It isn't funny, Momma." Annette was obviously within seconds of stomping her delicate little foot if her expression was anything to go by.

"Of course it's funny." Her father stepped out of the office, his expression mocking as his daughter turned to him with a look of such teenage disgust he stopped and narrowed his eyes on her. "The very fact that you actually believed I'd give you permission to go is the funniest part. I'm still laughing."

Zoey smothered a smile as Kelly gave a little sign while throwing her husband a chiding look.

"You are just like Uncle Natches," Annette cried out furiously, her face flushing in anger. "You would just lock me up until I'm fifty if you could."

Rowdy seemed to consider the accusation. Bracing his hands on his hips he stared down at his delicate teenage daughter, the look on his face thoughtful.

"Fifty's going a little far," he finally retorted. "I'd settle for thirty. Maybe by then I'll be so senile that the shenanigans you and your cousins get into won't bother me near so . . ."

He stopped.

Zoey watched curiously as his head jerked up, his eyes meeting his wife's as she seemed to choke before turning her back on him.

In Kelly's eyes was such a wealth of laughter that Zoey was suddenly dying to know the private thought they'd obviously shared.

"Aren't you supposed to be helping your cousins outside?" Rowdy gave his daughter a "daddy" glare, arms going across his chest in a display of pure male command. "Get to it now, before I start checking out those convents your uncle Natches keeps finding."

"You are ruining my life," Annette cried, the tone of pure teenage drama causing her mother to choke on her laughter again.

Tossing her thick black hair Miss Annette Theadora Mackay lifted her determined little chin and stalked out the door, pausing outside only long enough to slip her feet into colorful sandals before stalking along the side of the building.

"God." Rowdy plowed his fingers through his hair in disgust. "I'm starting to repeat the same crap Dad used to yell when he was arguing with me, Dawg, and Natches."

Kelly turned to him with a laugh. "Better lock the windows tonight. She was more determined to attend this party than the last few she's demanded to go to."

Rowdy's look was filled with disgust. "She thinks she wants to go dance with that little brat that's been hanging around the marina the last few weeks." He turned his head to glare at the door before stepping closer and peeking out to check to be sure the brat in question wasn't there. "He's going to keep it up I'm going to call Natches."

Zoey's eyes widened at the threat.

"Rowdy Mackay, you will not," Kelly exclaimed. "He's a kid. Natches would traumatize him."

Rowdy snorted. "So? He traumatizes me and Dawg on a daily basis; let him spread it around a little."

"Not to mention his wife and daughter," Zoey pointed out. "And me and Doogan."

Rowdy turned back to her, his expression curious. "What did Doogan do?"

Zoey rolled her eyes as she turned to Kelly. "Notice he doesn't ask what his cousin has done, it's what has Doogan done. That is just wrong."

Kelly laughed at the comment, her brown eyes warm and filled with laughter.

A high-pitched scream cut the laughter off.

Before Zoey could think she and Kelly were racing behind Rowdy as he all but tore the door off the front of the store to get to the parking lot.

The scene that met Zoey's eyes was horrifying.

Terror dragged a weak cry, filled with complete blood-freezing horror, from her as she watched the overly large male trying to drag Natches's daughter, Bliss, into a van as her cousins, Laken, Annette, and Erin screamed and attacked the heavily muscled assailant. Annette was holding on to Bliss's arm for dear life, screaming for her dad, her voice filled with such overwhelming fury Zoey knew she'd never forget the sound of it.

At the sight of Rowdy bearing down on him, the dark-clothed, masked assailant pushed Bliss into her cousin and jumped into the van as it tore away, tires screaming.

Annette wrapped her arms around her cousin as the other girls surrounded her just as Rowdy, Kelly, and Zoey reach them.

"There were no plates, Dad, but he smelled like fish and smoke." Annette was flushed, her green eyes darker, the anger in them a sight to see.

"Get inside." Rowdy didn't pause to get details.

Pushing the girls from the marina, he was on his cell phone.

"Get to the dock," he yelled into the phone, and Rowdy never yelled. "Now, goddamn it. Get here now."

He'd called either Dawg or Natches, who would call the other. Soon, the marina would be swarming with reinforcements. Grabbing the cell phone from her back pocket, Zoey hit the first number programmed in.

"Babe?" Doogan answered immediately.

"Get to the marina."

The line disconnected. Doogan didn't waste time with words; he was a man of action. He'd be there within minutes.

Pushing the girls into the store wasn't enough. Rowdy didn't stop until they were safely behind the reinforced steel-and-wood barrier of the walls that surrounded it, his wife and Zoey dragged in behind them.

Kelly rushed to the girls, her hands catching Bliss's shoulders as her gaze went over the girl. "Are you okay, baby?"

Her voice was trembling, adrenaline and fear crashing through her as Zoey watched Rowdy move to the safe.

The guns were there.

Zoey rushed to him, catching his arm as his gaze snapped to her.

"No," she whispered. "Not while they're here."

She glanced at the girls, especially his daughter as she watched him.

"Let him get his gun, Zoey." Fury still raged in Annette's voice. "Uncle Natches will have his. Bet me."

Zoey felt like knocking her and her father's heads together.

"Stop being so bloodthirsty Annette," she ordered the girl. It was an order she heard often. "Your father isn't getting a gun. . . ."

Tires were screaming outside, and the rev of an engine accelerating from the marina entrance and more rubber howling in protest as the vehicle was forced to a stop had them all pausing.

"Bliss!" Natches's voice thundered through the store.

"Dad. Dad." Tears choked the teenager's voice as she tore away from Kelly and met her father at the doorway of the office. Instantly, she was pulled into his arms, lifted from her feet as Natches sheltered her against his chest, one hand at the back of her head as he held her with his other arm, his eyes closing as Bliss wrapped her arms tightly around his neck, the fear finally hitting her.

She was sobbing against her father's shoulder as such agony creased Natches's face that it clenched Zoey's chest.

"Where's Chaya, Natches?" Rowdy questioned him, his tone icy as Natches opened his emerald-green eyes, and focused on his cousin.

"Dawg . . ." He cleared his throat as his hold tightened on his daughter.

Moving to the chair next to him Natches sat down as though afraid his legs wouldn't hold him much longer. He cradled his daughter in his arms, her head still buried in his shoulder, her arms locked around his neck. "She was with Dawg and Christa."

At the same time the sound of tires screaming again just outside the marina had Zoey jumping in fear and moving quickly to look outside the large glass window where Dawg's truck nearly touched the glass.

Moving aside as Chaya raced inside, tears streaming down her face, Christa and Dawg moving behind her.

"Bliss. Bliss." Chaya nearly fell as she tried to get to the door, caught herself, then went to her knees in front of her husband and daughter.

"Mom. I'm okay, Mom." But she was still crying.

Bliss's looks were nearly identical to Zoey's but for the emerald eyes and Zoey's celadon green ones. They were often mistaken as twins to those who didn't know them.

Behind Dawg, Doogan pushed into the office, his features hard, his brown eyes ice until they found hers. Warmth blazed in them, then relief and love filling them as he moved to her, his arm sliding around her to pull her to his chest.

Still holding her hand over her lips Zoey realized Bliss wasn't the only one crying. Tears dampened her own cheeks, and as Christa ran to her daughter, the other woman was crying as well.

"Someone tried to abduct Bliss," she whispered, lifting her gaze to him, the horror of it still resounding through her. "They almost took her, Doogan. Someone nearly took her."

"And now they'll die." He shrugged, that ice lingering in his gaze, his voice. "Soon."

Angel packed slowly, not that she had much to pack. The saddlebags that secured to the back of the motorcycle didn't hold a lot. The rest of their gear, supplies, and various weapons had shipped out that morning with Tracker's 'vette and the black Range Rover that traveled from job to job with them.

She wasn't ready to leave Somerset yet. She wasn't ready to turn her back on the last dream that had survived her childhood. The dream already slowly dying in her soul.

After securing the pack and setting it next to the door, her gaze was caught by her reflection in the full-length mirror there. Shattered sapphire eyes. Once, when she was a child, her eyes had been a soft gray, her hair dark blonde rather than the sunlit color she kept on it.

She'd resembled her father then, but once she'd hit her teens, Tracker, the man who had saved her, said she began looking like her mother. She could see her mother in her features now. The shape of her eyes, the curve of her brow. The set of her chin.

She was shorter than her mother though, her frame more delicate than the former Homeland Security agent's. She had her mother's smile, Tracker would tell her sometimes, when she allowed herself to smile.

Pulling back from the mirror and blinking, not to hold back tears—Angel never cried—but to fight back the hurt, the pain that leaving brought.

Tracker was right; they had no reason to stay. They'd been away when Zoey had needed them, arriving back in town only days after Jack Clay had been killed. Two months was too long to stay in one place without a job. The Mackays were going to start asking questions, and Angel didn't want questions. She had wanted recognition. A recognition that hadn't come. All she saw was suspicion, and Tracker was right, it was killing her.

Picking up the pack and opening the door she stepped into the small living room of the cabin they'd taken after returning, her gaze narrowing on the three men standing tensely by the door.

"Eli?" Her gaze flicked to Tracker and their partner, Grog. Both men were tall, imposing, not so much handsome as roughened.

And she knew both of them. Something was wrong.

"Angel." Eli nodded his dark blond head before turning back to Tracker. "I have to go. I just thought I'd stop on my way."

He was in a hurry. Moving quickly from the cabin he left Angel with the two men who had rescued her when they were little more than boys themselves. They'd sheltered her, protected her, trained her to fight with them.

"Tracker?" She could feel the tension growing in the room, the knowledge that neither man was explaining Eli's visit.

"Gear up." He sighed heavily. "I'm sure you'll want to stop at the marina before we ride out of town."

"The marina?" she asked carefully. "What's happened?"

"Someone tried to kidnap one of the Mackay girls just minutes ago . . ."

She didn't wait to hear the rest.

She didn't have to gear up. Her weapons and thigh holsters were in the customized, hidden carriers built into the chest rest of her motorcycle, extra ammo stored with them. She raced outside, Tracker and Grog close on her heels.

Jerking the leather jacket and protective helmet on she was racing from the gravel drive in seconds, fear racing through her system with a shock of adrenaline pouring into her bloodstream.

This couldn't be happening. It couldn't be . . .

"Angel, get control of yourself," Tracker advised smoothly into the radio link built into the helmets. "Let's see what's going on before we do anything."

See what was going on? They knew what was going on. She should have expected this. She should have known it would happen.

"I'm cool, Track," she promised, her voice even, without the panic she could feel rushing through her. "I have to be sure, though. I can't leave without being sure they're okay. You know that."

"We're just making sure everything's okay then," Tracker repeated. "Friends checking on friends, Angel. Remember that."

Her heart was in her throat, fear pulsing through her and threatening to steal the small shred of control she possessed.

"Friends checking on friends," she promised. "That's all. Nothing more."

The chief of police, Alex Jansen, and his wife, Natches's sister Janey, were rushing inside to their daughter Erin. Behind them more than a dozen police cars were pulling in, their sirens thankfully silent.

"Zoey." Mercedes Mackay, Zoey's mother, followed minutes later with her lover, Timothy Cranston, and Rowdy's father, Ray, with Christa's mother, Maria.

The office was packed and still more cars were arriving. Her three sisters and their husbands, hard-eyed, dangerous Homeland Security agents moved in behind their mother. As Zoey's sisters rushed to check on Bliss, their husbands moved with predatory danger to the doorway, their gazes meeting Rowdy's before they turned and walked outside.

Rowdy, Dawg, and Natches, along with Alex and Janey were still holding on to their teenage daughters, their embraces tight, protective.

"What happened?" Dawg was the first to ask that question as he tucked his daughter close between his and his wife's sides.

"We saw the van coming and tried to hurry and get across the parking lot," Annette assured her father. "Just like you taught us, Dad. As soon as it turned toward us we were moving. The guy jumped out and grabbed Bliss, though, and I think we just went kind of crazy." She shook her head before giving her father a fierce look. "We weren't letting anyone take Bliss."

Bliss mumbled something at her father's shoulder.

"What, baby?" Natches's voice was thick, a hoarse growl as Bliss lifted her face from her mother's shoulder.

"I lost my knife, Dad." She pouted. "I did what you taught me to do, but he moved too fast and pulled it from my hand." She lifted her hand. "And he got his nasty blood on me."

She had her fingers fisted as though to hold the blood in her palm, and it wasn't just a smear.

"God love your little Mackay hearts." Tim sounded like the evil leprechaun her brother and cousins called him, Zoey thought. "Alex, get me an evidence kit."

"I have it, sir." The officer standing guard at the door stepped into the room, the evidence kit with its vials and cotton swabs, plastic bags and plastic tweezers was pushed into Tim's hand.

Tim turned to Bliss, pure pride beaming in his expression as he tore the pack open.

Joining him, Alex Jansen, the chief of police, helped the former DHS agent collect the blood from Bliss's hand as the adults stared among the teenagers in shock.

"When did you give her a knife, Natches?" Rowdy asked faintly.

"When she asked me to teach her to shoot a gun." Natches grimaced.

"She was ten," Dawg drawled, amused as he glanced at Rowdy.

"And she knows how to use it." Chaya touched her daughter's cheek gently, her voice trembling nearly as hard as her fingers were. "I taught her how to use it."

"I'm okay, Momma," her daughter promised, her expression solemn. "See? I told you teaching me to use the knife was a good idea."

She was damned proud of herself, Zoey thought, trying to dry her own tears. And she should be. All of them should be.

"Dad, the guy driving was yelling at the guy that tried to take Bliss," Erin Jansen spoke up. "He said, 'That damned Mackay is here. He's not supposed to be here.'"

Rowdy turned from his wife and daughter slowly. "What did he say, Erin?" he asked carefully.

"For the other guy to hurry because you were here and you weren't supposed to be. Uncle Rowdy, weren't you leaving when we got here with Aunt Kelly?" Erin asked, her gray eyes narrowed speculatively. "Someone knew you weren't supposed to be here."

"I was going to Dawg's," Rowdy said softly, suspiciously, as Tim finished collecting the blood Bliss had protected in her closed fist for DNA. "But Natches was running late to watch the marina."

The marina, Kelly, Zoey, and the girls, Zoey knew. They were never, at any time left to work at the marina without one of the men close by. Today, Natches and Chaya were scheduled.

Zoey saw the look the men shared and she knew, she absolutely knew in that second that no one should have known that Rowdy wasn't going to be here, but they'd known Natches and Chaya were running late.

Tim finished sealing the evidence bag, then handed it over to Alex.

"I'll contact Mark and Tyrell and we'll have a team in place by morning," Alex stated, the ice in his voice as scary as it was in Rowdy's.

Mark and Tyrell owned a private security firm out of Virginia staffed with all former military and Special Forces personnel.

"I want to know why." Rowdy's tone was graveled, a certain indication of his level of fury.

"There's been no chatter where Somerset's concerned," Timothy informed them. "I would have known immediately if there were."

"Tracker's here." Alex turned to the group as they all glanced to the office window where three black, powerful motorcycles were easing through the police cruisers still parked outside. "Looks like he has Grog and Angel with him."

Tracker.

Rowdy watched as the other man secured his cycle, then straightened and pulled the full face helmet from his head and stared around with narrowed eyes.

Six-four, black hair, and intense blue eyes, the mercenary had seemed to take an interest in staying in the county lately. Dressed in jeans, T-shirt, and heavy black motorcycle boots, he looked like a fight waiting to happen. Unfortunately, he was far more dangerous than he appeared as well.

Grog, Tracker's suspected brother, was just as tall, his eyes a startling shade of vibrant green, propped one foot at the side of his cycle before setting his helmet on the chest rest in front of him.

Between them, Tracker's second in command, Angel, drew every male gaze in the parking lot as she pulled her helmet from her head and released the long, sun-kissed blond strands of hair held captive beneath it.

Silken waves fell to just below her shoulders, giving her face a softer, sensual appearance. Until Rowdy glanced at her eyes. An intense violet blue, like a sapphire starburst she often had to use contacts to disguise, the color distracting from the fact that a complete lack of mercy gleamed in their depths.

That was, if a man got around to looking in her eyes.

Today she was dressed in figure-hugging jeans with leather chaps strapped to shapely legs, boots similar to Tracker's, and beneath the leather riding jacket she slid from her shoulders and threw over the seat of the cycle, she wore a tank top that did nothing to hide her feminine curves.

Angel was an enigma within a group he and his cousins had found impossible to pull any concrete information in on. Even Timothy, if he could be believed, knew very little about the group. He trusted them though, and that always managed to rouse Rowdy's suspicions.

"What the hell are they doing here?" Rowdy growled as the three moved past the officers positioned outside and entered the convenience store.

Seconds later Angel stepped into the office, her gaze going immediately to the girls who stared at her with some kind of damned hero-worship. Somehow, Angel had managed to "run into" the girls and their mothers enough times that Rowdy had begun to see a pattern.

"Angel." Annette's face lit up with pleasure. The girls moved to the other woman, delight filling their expressions as she was pulled into one of the group hugs the Mackay daughters were prone to bestow. "I thought you left."

For a moment, Angel's face softened and Rowdy swore he glimpsed relief on her face.

"We were on our way." Her voice was so damned gentle Rowdy was taken aback. "When I heard the report the four of you might have some trouble I thought I'd come back and check on you."

She touched Annette's hair so softly Rowdy doubted his daughter felt it, then touched each girl in the same manner. The action appeared completely subconscious, as though to assure herself they were all safe.

Rowdy lifted his gaze to Tracker. The other man was hiding it well, but he was furious, no doubt with Angel's determination to be there.

"How can we help?" The chill in his voice nearly had Rowdy smiling.

"I don't know if I can afford you and your group, Tracker," he began wryly.

"There's no charge, Mr. Mackay." That comment brought Angel's attention to him immediately.

Rowdy saw the roll of Grog's eyes as he leaned against the doorframe and the look of suffering patience on Tracker's face as he slid a glance to Angel.

"Tell him, Tracker." Not once did Angel glance back at him nor did her expression change.

Tracker turned his gaze to Rowdy and nodded firmly. "No charge. She won't leave until she's certain the girls are safe. We may as well have something to do while we're here."

Oh, they were going to have a talk soon, Rowdy decided. Angel wasn't known for her soft heart or compassion toward little children. She wasn't known for her compassion or mercy to anyone or anything.

"I assume you'll be keeping the girls together?" Angel spoke softly, but it was the girls' mothers whose gazes she sought. "If you do, I would like to spend some time with them."

She wanted to protect them.

"Angel." Tracker's muttered warning was quiet enough Rowdy didn't hear it; he only saw the other man's lips moving.

"Zoey, why don't you and your sisters take the girls to the other room, get them some drinks or something," Rowdy suggested. "Give us a few minutes here."

The four sisters were moving instantly and pulling the girls from the office. As though sensing their wives were leaving the protection of their brothers and cousins, Eve's, Piper's, and Lyrica's husbands along with Doogan, stepped into the store with them, placing themselves in defensive positions.

As soon as the girls were herded from the room, regret flickered in Angel's gaze for a moment before her shoulders straightened and she was staring back at them with cool unconcern.

"Why are you so concerned about our children?" Chaya, always suspicious, but no doubt in full paranoid mode now where her daughter was concerned, voiced the question.

"I apologize." Ice dripped from Angel's voice now but Rowdy caught the look of regret, of pain, that haunted her gaze for just a moment. "On second thought, I'm certain you have this covered . . ."

"You have insisted on placing yourself in a position to gain our daughters' trust and affection," Chaya continued, furiously, and Rowdy doubted she caught Angel's subtle flinch. "And I want to know why. Because I know women like you and I know it's not for the sake of those kids out there."

Rowdy watched Angel's face and for the briefest moment, he saw the soul-deep hurt flash in her eyes. Chaya had just wounded the younger woman far deeper than she would have believed.

"Chaya, that's a little harsh . . ." Christa objected.

"Women like me." Angel seemed to muse on the comment, her voice soft, without ice, without emotion, as she faced Chaya. "What kind of woman do you assume I am, Mrs. Mackay?"

"My damned name is Chaya," she was informed, a snap in Chaya's normally pleasant tone. "You've been here for a year, and I see you at least once a week. You're no child nor an employee so you cut the Mrs. crap right now."

Rowdy hadn't heard that tone since she'd first come to Somerset over a decade before.

As Chaya spoke, Angel stared back at her, unblinking, her expression even more emotionless, if possible. The starburst blue of her eyes went from sapphire to chipped ice, though.

"What kind of woman do you think I am?" Angel asked again.

"Chaya." Rowdy stepped forward, laying his hand on her shoulder easily. "We're all upset . . ."

"Someone just attempted to abduct my daughter." Her voice broke causing her to swallow tightly before going on. "To know why a grown woman is trying to ingratiate herself into four teenagers' lives. A mercenary, she sells herself to the highest bidder, along with those two." She flipped her hand to Tracker and Grog. "A killer. What makes you think my daughter is any of your concern?"

"Fuck. Let's go . . ." Grog hissed behind Tracker. "Now."

"As I said, I obviously stepped out of line, and in my concern didn't consider my words . . ."

"And what is your concern?" Chaya cried out, the sound of her voice causing Natches to wrap his arms tighter around her.

"Easy, Chay," he whispered gently, but his eyes were on Angel, just as Rowdy's were.

Rowdy wondered if his cousin saw that flash of complete devastation in those odd eyes as she glanced away for a second before meeting Chaya's gaze again. She was just standing there, taking Chaya's fury on her slender, young shoulders as though she deserved it for some reason.

"Don't any of you pretend you haven't asked yourself why she's so interested in our children." Chaya's gaze went around the room, fierce and demanding.

"Rowdy, Natches." Tracker stepped forward, easing himself in front of Angel as Grog stepped closer as well. "We'll be going now. If you need our assistance, please don't hesitate to call the service. They'll get a message to us."

"This is the wrong time to leave, Tracker." Rowdy sighed, pushing his fingers restlessly through his hair. "The question is easy enough."

"The question shouldn't have been asked." Grog's gravelled voice, rarely heard whenever Tracker was around, came with the broad soldier's step to the other man's side. "We were here when your family needed us, without charge or question. We could have refused that contract on Lyrica instead of trying to find out what the hell was going on and gone on with our lives. No one the wiser."

"I want to know why?" Chaya demanded, her voice rising as Natches stared back at Tracker and Grog coolly. "Tell me, Grog. Tracker." She faced them with a strength and confidence that came from years as a DHS agent working with Timothy's maniacal temperament.

"Rowdy," Tracker stated softly. "We're walking out of here. We came to help, and it was obviously a mistake . . ."

"She has a point, Tracker." He breathed out roughly. "We've all been asking ourselves why since you showed up last year. If you walk out of here without answering that question it's just going to make all of us real nosy. You know what happens when Mackays get nosy."

"Don't turn this into a war," Tracker warned for his ears alone. "Wrong move."

"If it becomes a war, then you'll start it. I'd hate it, we all would. But if Mackays were suddenly in your business without so much as an introduction, you'd be asking the same questions." Rowdy had his suspicions, they all did, but they'd pushed them back, ignored them, hoping Tracker would explain his actions before their patience was worn too thin. The attempted abduction had placed their security in the forefront of all their minds, though, and the question of friendly or unknown enemy was now imperative.

The knowledge of that was in Tracker's eyes. He was a smart

man, a damned intuitive man; he had to have known this was coming, and still, he'd remained in the area.

"I don't need your protection, Tracker." Angel pushed herself between the other two men, her expression still, her eyes like fractured sapphires frozen forever in whatever catalyst had shattered them to begin with.

"I wasn't trying to protect you," Tracker assured her. "I merely wanted to get back on the road."

And he was lying. Rowdy saw it in his eyes. And she knew he was lying. Lowering his gaze to stare into hers Rowdy saw her knowledge as well. She knew the man she followed had placed himself between her and the Mackays as though concerned for her welfare.

"Why do you think I give a damn about your kid?" Angel faced Chaya without so much as a hint of anger, reserve, or concern. "You're not a stupid woman, Chaya." Pure confidence cloaked her, the appearance unmarred by so much as a hint of doubt.

Chaya's nostrils flared as suspicion narrowed her eyes.

"Come on kids, let's play nice on the playground." Dawg stepped forward as though anything could break the tension at this point.

"Stop." Natches's gaze went to Dawg instantly.

He knew what his cousin was doing. Dawg would always stand before Natches and the world if his cousin would allow him to do so. What Dawg didn't want was the truth . . . Not right now.

"You're not answering me, Mrs. Makay," she said softly, a shadow of bleak, hollow pain turning her voice from ice to a whisper of beauty.

"Girl, you're testing my patience," Chaya informed her disdainfully. "And you don't want to do that."

"Bliss is my sister . . ." Angel stated. "I care, because she's my sister."

"Whoa. Fuck me . . ." Dawg stepped back, his eyes huge, going from Angel to Natches with the same shock reflected in his voice.

Natches laughed. Genuine amusement. It was frightening for the very fact that nothing said was the least bit funny.

"Good try, sweetheart," he drawled. "I was a bastard, but I was a careful one."

"You are not my father." Her eyes flickered over him with something approaching humor. "I would have had to kill myself."

"Then how is Bliss your sister?" Natches growled. "Kid, you need to take this act somewhere else, fast."

Angel didn't answer, but Tracker and Grog both moved closer to her as she stared back at Chaya, eye-to-eye. The silence was deafening now.

The same arch of brow, the same curve of lips. Darken her hair, or was hers lightened? Son of a bitch. Rowdy almost stepped back as his eyes narrowed at the roots of the blond strands. Just the smallest hint that the blond wasn't entirely natural.

There had been something familiar about her. Something that didn't make sense. But this was unbelievable.

"That's not possible," Natches stated in that voice that made Rowdy worry that Trudy was going to come out and play. "Chaya has no other children. Just Bliss."

But Chaya wasn't speaking. She was barely breathing. Her gaze was going over the other woman's face and if Rowdy wasn't mistaken, she was trembling.

"Is Bliss your only child, Mrs. Mackay?" Angel asked and for a moment Rowdy glimpsed fear in the woman. Angel was re-nowned for her lack of fear. She would, and had more than once, charged through flames, a flood, and it was rumored, a category five hurricane to follow Tracker and Grog.

Chaya still hadn't spoken. Her gaze kept going over Angel's face as though searching, desperation and agony reflecting in her eyes.

"Stop this," Natches snarled. "Get her the fuck out of here, Tracker."

Angel swallowed tightly and Rowdy realized the girl was holding on to the icy façade she placed between her and the world with the thinnest thread.

"Angel." Tracker said her name softly, gently, his hand tightening on her upper arm. "Let's go darlin'."

Angel stared into Chaya's eyes, the fractured blue of her own eyes appearing more like a shattered sapphire than before.

"Is he your lover?" Chaya's voice caused Rowdy to flinch. Hoarse, filled with such pain that for a moment Rowdy's gaze flashed murderously as it caught and held Tracker's.

"No, ma'am," Angel answered, that unfailing politeness never cracking.

"Angel . . ."

The younger woman's breath seemed to hitch, and if Rowdy wasn't mistaken, her lips nearly trembled. "I'm so sorry I've upset you and your family," she said then, her tone so unfailingly polite and sincere Rowdy felt his throat tighten. "I promise, I won't bother you anymore. I'm ready." Reaching around with her other hand she patted Tracker's fingers gently as they lay on her upper arm. "I guess we're heading out after all."

No one stopped her.

Rowdy watched Chaya, the paleness of her skin, the agony in her brown eyes as she watched the young woman leave. In Natches's eyes there was pure, demonic wrath. If Rowdy didn't stop him, he'd go after the girl. What really scared Rowdy was the fear he'd find that damned gun he'd named Trudy.

Outside, the sound of the powerful motorcycles revving caused a brutal flinch to jerk Chaya against her husband. Tearing out of his arms she raced from the office, a harsh sound of pain escaping her throat as the sound of a cycle racing through the parking lot to the exit echoed through the room.

Chaya stopped at the door, her fingers tight on the wood, her breathing rough, loud.

"She's lying," Chaya whispered, tears roughening her voice as Natches pulled her into his arms again, holding her to his heart as her fingers clenched in the material of his shirt. "She's lying . . ." she whispered again.

Rowdy met Natches's tormented gaze and in them he saw the suspicion that Angel wasn't lying.

"She's lying . . . That's not my baby. Oh God, that's not my Beth . . ."

If Rowdy wasn't mistaken, even Chaya wasn't convinced.